Timber Hills

Timber Hills

by
Vicki Baker

Sterling House

Pittsburgh, PA

Sterling House
PUBLISHER INC.

ISBN 1-56315-165-0

Paperback Fiction
© Copyright 1999 Vicki Baker
All rights reserved
First Printing—1999
Library of Congress #98-87017

Request for information should be addressed to:

SterlingHouse Publisher, Inc.
The Sterling Building
440 Friday Road
Department T-101
Pittsburgh, PA 15209

Cover design: Michelle Vennare - SterlingHouse
Typesetting: Drawing Board Studios

Printed in Canada

I gratefully dedicate this book to my daughter, Deanna, for her daily dose of love and faith in me, to my two Cocker Spaniels who rested patiently at my feet while I wrote, and to my son, Jon, who promised me he'd read my book.

Acknowledgments

To the kindhearted people who helped give *Timber Hills* its human warmth I thank you with all my heart. I hold a special gratitude to Glenn and Doris Baker, to my mother, Virginia Griffith, and to friends, Sherry Jackson and especially Jeanelle Reed, (your bits of knowledge were priceless). Thank you for lending your time and wisdom. To those who felt ignored by short answers, quick meals, my makeupless face, and undone supper dishes, I'm sorry and I'll make it up to you. To every one of you who helped make *Timber Hills* possible, I'll never forget your kindness.

PART ONE

A small part of his consciousness told him he was alone at the sawmill, that the sun had slid behind the hills. In a far corner of Gus's mind he remembered men picking up their lunch pails and going home for the night. It took the swooping motion and harsh scream of a hawk to make him glance up from the screeching circular saw. Gus blinked several times to force himself back to the present moment, peering toward the chicken coop then back up at the prowling hawk. He realized that most of the hens had gone to roost, then briefly wondered if Sara Jane had gathered the eggs. Gus sighed. Of course she had. It was his sister's favorite chore. He pictured her with her little blue apron, a basket swinging at her side and long silky banana curls swaying back and forth across her back.

His gaze wandered slowly toward the hills where smoky twilight was masking the multicolored trees. He hadn't noticed autumn's chill in the air until now, and when he shivered he felt goose bumps rise on his forearms. Gus had hoped the anniversary of this infamous day would be easier on him than it had been a year ago, but nothing had changed. The sadness was still there. Gil's absence was always with him.

Gus Wheeler delayed shutting down the mill until the evening's purple shadows were too thick for him to work safely. Disheartening memories gripped his insides as he pulled the lever that shut down the machinery. As the gears decelerated and stilled, the silence in the air was almost as loud as the buzzing of the saws had been.

Gus went through the motions of brushing sawdust from his overalls, then trudged toward the house through a sawdust haze that scented the air around Timber Hills Sawmill. He could still hear the resounding whir in his ears as he neared the sloping porch and sat heavily on the second step from the top, remembering the tragic day like it was yesterday. "One year," he whispered, staring at his dusty worn-out shoes. He felt a lump in his throat and swallowed back tears as he inescapably recalled the happenings on the nineteenth of October 1954. Sometimes I don't think I can hold up, Gus thought. I really truly don't.

He stood, straightened his long, lean body and paced back and forth trying to ease the memory. "Men don't cry," he mumbled, fighting to keep control of himself yet the sense of loss was like flood waters threatening a dam. Gus sat again, this time on the porch swing, but instead of pushing off gently with his feet, he sat rigidly staring ahead, at everything, at nothing. Memory and senses in harmony, Gus could feel Gil's breath on him, smell his skin, his slightly oily hair. Gilbert clung to his consciousness, an awareness as real as if they were sitting side by side. A brother he had taken first steps with, grown up with, lain beside in their mother's womb, the twin he'd loved more than life itself was now lying in the shadows of the town's only cemetery. He took off his cap, laid it aside and roughed up his hair. "Eighteen's too young to die," he moaned. Then Gus thought of Garrett, another brother only two years old when laid in his grave. Losing Garrett had hurt, a little-boy-not-grasping-what-was-happening kind of hurt, but nothing had ever been as painful as losing Gilbert.

Gus bowed his head and waited for the mirror in his mind to clear. Even after all these months, it took time for the oppressive spirit to relent and Gil's image to fade. "You may be gone, brother, but I see you plainly in memory," he whispered. Gus sat stiff and perfectly still, afraid to move, afraid that another tiny splash of memory would trigger the drowning flood waters. He heard the screen door slowly creak open, but still he didn't move.

"Gus?"

The word was a feminine, quiet breath. Gus slowly raised his head, opened his eyes. Katherine stood just inside the screen door wiping her hands on her apron. He could smell supper's warm, inviting aroma drifting around her silhouette as he gazed at her, not speaking.

"I miss him too," she whispered.

Gus tilted back his head and tasted the saltiness of sadness in his mouth. "I miss him so much, Mama."

He sat there letting autumn's cool breeze wash over him, thinking, remembering, watching scarlet leaves drift down from the twin dogwoods his folks had planted when he and Gilbert were born. A warm spicy scent was coming from the house and Gus knew Gil's favorite sweet-potato pie was in the oven. It was the first time she'd baked one since his death.

The night was quiet, even the ringing in his ears had stilled. Gus rose from the swing, stuck his hands in his pockets and strolled to the edge of the porch. He gazed across the yard, past chicken coops, the old outhouse, the barn, beyond the nearby trees to the peaceful Smoky Mountains. Crisp nights had turned the hills a maple red and poplar yellow, and with each gentle breeze, Gus heard an acorn or two clinking on the barn's tin roof.

His gaze drifted toward the empty vegetable garden and he sniffed the last of its dying vegetation, summer's labor of love all gathered and stored on shelves in the cellar. "Y'all eat supper without me," he said. When Katherine didn't answer, Gus turned his face toward the house and saw through the window that his mother was back inside tending to something simmering on the stove. He squatted and leaned his back against the cord of firewood that lined the porch near the back door. He could hear Arthur Godfrey on the family's black and white television set and knew his father was in his easychair, sound asleep in front of the new TV, Sara Jane sitting on his lap resting her head against his chest. The evening shadows that swept over the small, family-owned sawmill hummed a sad, yet sweet song. Gus sniffed the cool darkness and smelled wood smoke hanging in the air. "Winter's comin' on," he said. "It's time to rest the grief and get on with life." Gus rose, stomped dust from his boots. "Yeah," he said, his voice scratchy. "Gilbert would want that."

• CHAPTER 1 •

"Know what happened to Darius when his ma caught him playin' mumbly-peg?"

"I reckon he got a lickin'."

"Yup. Darius's ma don't cotton much to knife throwin' since he harpooned all their hens. She wagged him to the woodshed an' laid on at least a hundred licks."

"Who told you that?" Gilbert asked.

Gus Wheeler beamed an I-know-something-you-don't grin, and rested his forearm over his twin brother's shoulder. "Billy Ray Mudd was playin' hoops down by Possum Creek and could hear Darius bellerin' like a stuck hog. Heard him moanin' an' groanin' clear through the woods." Gus's voice died away as he took a piece of chalk from his bib pocket and scratched a large wiggly circle on a lightning-charred oak tree. "Reckon he lost some meat on his behind," he said, leaning over to pick up the handmade knife.

"She had no call to give Darius that bad a whoopin'," Gilbert said.

Gus shrugged his shoulders. "Darius had his little sister tied to the tree he was throwin' the knife into. Reckon that ruffled his ma some."

"That girl's mean as a bear," Gilbert said. "I'd tie her up, too."

"Mothers get riled up for puny things," Gus said, chucking the knife haphazardly toward the tree's chalked circle. The sharp tip held briefly then fell to the ground near a patch of May apples. "Wouldn't want no hundred licks like poor ol' Darius got." Gus loped over to the knife, picked it up and handed it to Gilbert.

Gil studied the circle briefly then flung the knife. The blade barely touched the outside edge of the ring. "Goldangit," he swore, yanking the knife from the tree's bark.

Gus squinted one eye closed and trained the other one on the circle. Drawing back his right arm, he thrust the knife through the air. "Look at that!" Gus yelled, leaping toward the tree. "Bull's eye!"

Gilbert pounced up next to his brother and jerked the knife from the tree's blackened trunk. "I can do that," he said, walking back to the toe line. "I can do anything good as you."

"You'll never be able to run the sawmill as good as me," Gus said.

"I don't plan to."

Gus shook his head, grabbed a limb and pulled himself up. "Feel bad for Darius."

"You'll get over it," Gil said. "Glad we ain't unblessed like Darius or Billy Ray Mudd. Billy Ray told Harley he wished he was never born."

"Billy Ray said that?" Gus sprang out of the crook of the low-hanging limb and shaded his eyes with both hands. His face took on a serious look. "Looky out yonder next to that big, leaning barn. See that hickory nut tree?"

Gilbert leaned forward and fixed his curious blue eyes on the tree. "What about it?"

"If you look really hard," Gus said, squinting, "you can see an old colored man swingin'."

"What're you talkin' about?"

"The nigger Billy Ray's pa hung up."

"Where'd you hear that?" Gilbert asked his brother.

"In Sunday school last week. They said Billy Ray's pa strung him up 'cause he caught him drinkin' water from their well."

"I can see Oliver Mudd doin' somethin' like that," Gil mused. "The devil's gonna place a claim on ol' man Mudd. You wait an' see. Where is he now?"

"Who? Mudd?"

"No. The nigger."

Gus shrugged. "Takin' a dirt bath, I reckon." He stared blankly toward the Mudd's old, run-down farm house.

"Reckon Billy Ray Mudd was better off at the orphanage. I don't know what kind of folks he had to start with, but the ones he's got now ain't worth a boar's tit. Come on, Gus. Let's go deeper into the woods."

"Reckon we shouldn't fault Billy Ray over it, you know, him bein' an orphan," Gus said, then, "Hey! Wait up." He caught up with his brother and fell into perfect twin steps.

"Coon pie is made of rye," Gil crooned.

"The coon is the meat," Gus followed.

"It's tough enough and rough enough,

And more than we can eat!" they bellowed out together.

The tree-shaded path became darker and denser as the towheaded Wheeler twins trekked along the earthy-smelling trail. When they reached a sagging barbed-wire fence, Gilbert sprinted over and kept on going, but Gus straddled a crooked, worm-eaten post.

"What's holding you up?" Gilbert asked.

"Billy Ray's comin' over the hill," Gus answered, waving toward their best friend.

Billy Ray Mudd trudged up to the twins, looked aside to spit tobacco and said, "Wharton Jr. says his pa's in Union County sellin' shine. Wanna see what he's got stashed in the barn?"

Gus remembered his Sunday school teacher saying drinking was sinful, but Gilbert was already walking alongside Billy Ray toward Wharton Reimer's barn. Gus caught up with the other two and the three of them caught up on the latest rumors about Eula Mae.

Wharton Jr. was leaning on a hoe in the middle of their vegetable garden. He wore no shirt under his overalls and the hot sun had burned his back and shoulders a blistering red. A skeletal coonhound rested in the shade of a 1938 De Soto sitting up on blocks. Gus picked up what looked like a pork chop bone and tossed it toward the dog. "That dog dead?" he asked studying the motionless canine. Wharton Jr. glanced up, sluggishly walked over to the hound and poked him with the hoe. The dog thumped his tail.

"Come sit a spell in the shade," Wharton drawled, sweat dripping down his pudgy, flushed face. He took off his straw hat, raked back fiery red hair and hooked his thumbs on the straps of his overalls. "Reckon it's time for a nap, anyhow."

"You're the biggest loafer I know, Wart," Billy Ray said.

"The old man been doin' any stillin'?" Gilbert asked.

Wharton Jr. put on his hat and grinned ear to ear. "Draw nigh, my friends and foller me," he uttered pridefully, gesturing toward the barn. Swinging his arms pompously, the redheaded youth led the three callers as they plodded one behind the other. They zigzagged their way through tall weeds, a tangle of old car parts, broken appliances, and past a Beware of Dog sign.

"Seen Eula lately, Billy Ray?" Wharton Jr. asked.

Billy Ray raised his head and let out a sharp whistle. "And how!"

Wharton Jr. slowed his pace, turned around and started walking backwards. "Where'd she let you touch her this time?" he asked.

Billy Ray's face brightened. "You'd really like to know, wouldn't you?"

"Come on, tell us," Wharton Jr. prompted, stumbling over a rusty lard tin.

"She let me touch her in the tobacco field," Billy Ray drawled.

"That's not what he meant," Gilbert blurted out.

Billy Ray beamed. "Eula Mae said she'd make a deal with me. Said if I'd milk Bessie every night this week she'd show me one of her titties."

The three other boys, walking backwards and facing Billy Ray, stopped dead in their tracks. Wharton Jr.'s mouth was opened the size of a baseball.

Billy Ray smiled cockily. "I told her I'd take delight in doin' the milkin'."

"You lucky shit," Wharton Jr. said, turning round and moving on toward the barn.

"You only get to see *one* titty?" Gus asked.

"She said if I'd milk Bessie the next week she'd show me the other one."

When they got to the barn, Wharton Jr. reached out and dragged open the heavy wooden door. Gus whiffed a pleasant mixture of hay and sweet corn as the door groaned and creaked open. Wharton Jr. allowed his guests to pass through the shaft of dusty light then tugged the large door until it was nearly closed. Clowning and laughing, the boys gathered round in their usual places on the barn floor. They watched eagerly as their friend pushed a mound of straw aside and yanked up a loose floor board. Stretching his arm, Wharton Jr. grunted and reached down into the dark hole, pulled out the floor-buried jug, uncapped the prize and took a long swig. He braced the jug between his overalled knees and drew a slow, rotted-tooth grin. He didn't say anything, but the other boys watched his face turn a deep shade of red.

"What's wrong, Wart?" Billy Ray grilled. "Can't take a man's drink?"

Wharton Jr. glared at Billy Ray. "You don't know beans when the bag's open, Billy Ray. I do this all the time," he told them as he wheezed for breath and roughly swiped his mouth with his stubby fingers.

"Then why's your face red?" Billy Ray probed.

"My hair's red, too, but that don't note up for nothin'! Anyway, I was workin' in the sun," Wharton Jr. answered defensively, his face returning to its natural tanned color.

Billy Ray shook his head. "I don't believe you. It's 'bout to kill ya, ain't it?"

"Hell, no. I was born and raised with moonshine."

"Why do we always have to wait till your pa's gone?" Billy Ray said in a bully's voice.

Wharton Jr. leaned toward the tormentor and yelled, "'Cause when he's here he keeps me workin' at the still!"

"You can't get out of first gear, Wart. I ain't never seen you work," Billy Ray wisecracked.

"Hey, Billy Ray," Gus said, tired of Billy Ray's belittling words. "Heard you got caught stealin' milk bottles off Thelma Jean's front porch." He took a swig from the jug and passed it to Gilbert.

"Who told ya that?" Billy Ray asked arrogantly, scratching his back against the coarse bale of hay he was leaning on.

"Word gets 'round," Gus answered, stretching and yawning.

Wharton Jr. choked on too big a mouthful, then asked, "What happened to your real mom, Billy Ray?"

Billy Ray shifted his body and looked away from the other boys.

"Well?" Wharton probed. "Why ain't you with her?"

"She died on the day I was born," Billy Ray answered, turning his head back to his friends. "Not from borning me, but from a fall. She slipped on her way to the outhouse and bled to death." Billy Ray fidgeted and jerked his shoulders back and forth. "I'm warnin' you. Don't be pokin' no fun about it," he said.

"Where was your pa when that happened?" Gus asked.

Billy Ray leaned back on his arms and stared off into the rafters. "Pa was there. He just didn't know what to do. Two days later he took me to the orphanage. Best thing that could've happened to me."

Gilbert took another gulp of the corn liquor before passing it back to Gus. Gus tilted back his head and pressed the rim of the jug against his lips. He'd had enough drink, but for appearance's sake, it was too soon to stop. He was no sissy. Gus placed the container between his legs, made a manly face and wiped his chin with the back of his hand. After another stately gulp, Gus passed the jug to Wharton Jr.

"You know, Billy Ray," Gilbert said, slightly slurred, "Ain't nothing secret around this damn place. You piss in the bushes and folks'll know about it." He leaned back on the straw and rested his forearms over his eyes. "I hate it here. I'm sick to death of it."

Billy Ray laughed a honking laugh. "I'd invite 'em to watch me pee in the bushes. I'd be proud for folks to see *this* log," he boasted, his hand grasping the crotch of his pants.

Gus glanced over at his brother, ignoring Billy Ray's charade. "I'm proud to live in Tennessee. Anyhow, we were born here an' whether you like it or not we're here for a right smart spell."

"Don't *have* to be," Gilbert mumbled, his arms still over his face. "Not by a darn sight." He made a grunting noise. "You're just like Pa."

Gus thought briefly about Gil's comment. "I guess I am like Pa," he said. "I like where I'm from."

"What'cha gonna do, Gil? Hightail it out of the hills?" Billy Ray asked.

"Yep," Gil answered, turning his head away from the others. "Soon as I'm able," he said, gazing up into the loft. "This place is like a pool of stagnant water."

Gus glanced at Gilbert. He'd never heard his brother talk that way. "What's eatin' you?" he asked, but Gilbert didn't answer. Gus thought briefly about Gilbert's remark. Yeah, he was a lot like his father. His mother told him that all the time and he liked hearing it, too. Gus was proud of being Norman Wheeler's son.

Billy Ray got up, sauntered to the far side of the barn and peed. "Don't the revenuers come out here?" he asked, buttoning his pants.

Wharton Jr.'s sheer, green eyes followed Billy Ray back to the circle. "They stop by to refill their jug now and then."

Billy Ray laughed and slapped his thigh. "You're full of manure."

"You think you know it all, farthog," Wharton Jr. said, swinging his freckled arm out in a hell-with-you gesture. "Pa's been in the jailhouse twice this year. He comes back in better shape than when he goes in."

"How's that?" Gus asked.

"He comes back with his rotten teeth pulled and mended, and he's fatter, not so pale. He can outwit the law if he wants, when his teeth ain't hurtin'. It's a good life, a full-time stiller."

Gus started feeling dizzy and off-balance. "This stuff ever make you sick, Wharton Jr.?" His face wrinkled with his distress.

"The last time I drank it I painted the porch with puke. Ma thought I was comin' down with somethin' and gave me a dose of cod liver oil to flush me out."

The boys busted up laughing, smacking their knees, rolling over, kicking up their legs. Billy Ray shrieked when he rolled onto a pitchfork. "Holy Cow! I nearly poked another hole in my butt."

Inside the dark, earthy-smelling barn, the boys took turns tipping the jug. With a manly belch and a queasy stomach, Gus had finally had enough. "I need some air," he slurred, getting up shaky-legged. He staggered toward the narrowly-opened door but just before he reached the opening, he arched over and retched into a tubful of field corn.

Gilbert and Billy Ray dashed over and stood one on each side of the wooden barrel. "He's sicker'n a dog!" Billy Ray teased, laughing. "Drunker'n a coon on stump likker."

Gilbert moved to within inches of Billy Ray's face. "Leave him be," he threatened, spraying Billy Ray with spittle as he spoke.

"Get the cod liver oil," Billy Ray heckled, ignoring Gil's warning.

Gilbert lifted his arm and shoved Billy Ray against the door. It banged shut, leaving only pinhole shafts of light in the barn. "I told you to stop pestering him!"

Billy Ray regained his balance, stepped back and monkey-pounded his chest dramatically. "What if I don't?"

"I'll smack a skillet full of crap out of you!" Gilbert said in defense of his brother who was wiping his mouth on the bib of his overalls. He took hold of Gus's arm with one hand and pulled the door open with the other. "Let's light out of here," Gilbert said, steering Gus away from the barn.

"I need to lie down," Gus moaned just outside the barn door. He slithered from his brother's grip.

Gilbert yanked him up. "Don't let them see you do that!" he told Gus. "They'll tag you milksop."

Gus cocked his head in the direction of the barn. "Thanks Wart," he mumbled.

"Wart can't hear you," Billy Ray yelled back at him. "He's pig-eyed and out cold." He laughed. "Wait till the old man gets home. Oohwee!" Billy Ray chuckled again and took off running across the hollow.

Gilbert glanced at Gus zigzagging on ahead of him. He caught up and grabbed his brother's arm. "I'm throwing you in the creek. That'll undrunk you."

Gus heedfully staggered along with Gilbert steering him. "Hey, Gil," he said, wrinkling his face with the bad taste in his mouth. "Remember our Sunday school lesson yesterday, about Noah?"

Gilbert straight-faced Gus. "You think I got holes in my brain? I was born first, you know," Gil bragged, then said, "and don't forget who got the A in arithmetic."

"You came first by a whoppin' ten minutes, Gilbert, and that don't make you smarter. And I'll always believe the A mark was a mistake," Gus admitted.

Gil laughed. "I know how much you wish it was. What about Noah?"

"Somethin's botherin' me about the lesson, Gil," Gus said.

"Yeah. What?"

"You know how Ma says drinkin's evil?"

"She'd pitch a fit if she knew we swigged Wharton Reimer's bootleg," Gilbert said, reaching into his pocket for the jawbreaker he'd saved from Sunday school. "If I can get this thing bit in two, I'll give you half." He scratched at a chigger bite on his arm then asked, "What's drinkin' corn liquor got to do with Sunday school?"

"Not exactly corn liquor," Gus said, bracing himself against a crooked-trunked oak tree. "Russ Whaley says when Noah landed on the mountain he found some grape vines, and made some wine."

"Well glory be!" Gilbert said. "I reckon he deserved a little whoopee grape after being closed in that boat for . . . how long was it?" He let out a burst of laughter and said, "Wonder if they had revenuers back then?"

The corners of Gus's mouth turned up. "Noah got swacked!" Gus's knees buckled and he slid down the trunk of the tree as he let Noah slide out of his mind. "Do you like goin' to church?" he asked, lying flat on the warm ground.

Gilbert shook his head. "Nope. All that old man talks about is how damnation and hellfire are waitin' for us. Ain't much to look forward to."

"I git the feelin' Reverend Reed knows what he's talkin' about," Gus admitted.

"If I have to memorize another shitty Bible verse I'll puke."

Gus studied his brother somberly. "Back there in the barn, what did you mean when you said you were leaving?"

"I meant what I said. I'd rather drag a board than work at the mill for the rest of my life. This life's too dull for me. I'm sick of gettin' up every mornin' knowin' exactly what's gonna happen. Don't you ever want somethin' more?"

Gus raised one eyebrow. "Like what?" he asked, stunned by Gil's question.

Gilbert looked away, then kicked the dirt with his bare toe. "I don't know. Forget it."

Gus shrugged then sang out, "We ain't lyin', Cause lyin's a sin,"

"When we go to Heaven, They won't let us in," Gilbert finished.

Gus stooped to pluck a twig from between his toes. "Hey, Gil."

"Um?"

"Don't tell Mom."

"About what?"

"You know. Church."

Gil tossed a handful of pine needles in Gus's face. "Naw." He shaded his blue eyes with a sun-brown hand and peered upward between the trees.

"What'cha see up there?" Gus asked, following his brother's gaze.

"California," Gilbert said dreamily. "Some day I'm goin' there. It's a paradise, you know. Ain't nothin' like this mosquito cursed Tennessee holler."

Gilbert's words added to Gus's dismay. He wanted to respond, but didn't know how. He rolled over on his side and propped his head up with his elbow and let Gil talk on.

"Like Uncle Worth just up an' left. He just done it, Gus, and didn't even ask anyone if he could."

"Yeah, an' the day after that," Gus said, "Aunt Mamie got caught up under a sickle bar while cuttin' their hay, cause *someone* had to stay behind and take care of things. Uncle Worth didn't even know about it until he called home, long distance, and Thelma Jean told him."

"Thelma Jean's always the first to know everything."

"Telephone operators always are. They know it all," Gilbert commented. He leaned over and brushed leaves and needles from his tangled blond hair. "Yup, she knows everybody's business."

"It's a fact about Thelma Jean," Gus said. "Ma says she's the town's busybody and would be a nobody without the telephone. She says Thelma Jean spreads gossip faster than the cold germ," Gus added, then frowning, faced his brother. His shoulders slumped. "You ain't goin' to California, Gil."

"Am so. An' when I *do* go, it'll be just after the first frost so I won't have to club them walnut and hickory trees."

Gus noticed Gilbert's trance-like expression and stared into his twin brother's pale-blue eyes. He could read that face like his fifth-grade reader. Gus had never seen Gilbert with this air of complete seriousness until now and the look bewildered him. He swatted at a gnat whirring around his eyes, rubbed his face and left a smear of dirt on his left cheek. "You'd leave me to haul the nuts home all by myself?"

Gilbert faced Gus squarely. A frolicsome smile animated his expression. "In less than no time."

"You ain't goin' to California," Gus said. "Maybe in a thousand years from now, or in 1980 or 85."

Gil laughed. "Nineteen *eighty*? We'll be dead by then!" His face became serious and he peered straight ahead. "I think about Euell and Flossie Hamelin, how they up and sold their farm, tractors, livestock, the whole kit and caboodle, and moved to Arkansas. I fancy their gumption, Gus," Gil said. "I'll prove I have the same courage. Pa thinks I'm sissy 'cause I don't take an interest in the mill, but I don't want to live my life camouflaged in the Appalachian mountains. I know I feel different about leaving home than you do."

"I just don't get it, Gil. It ain't fittin' you leavin'. What about the sawmill?"

Gilbert pushed his hair back out of his face. "I don't have the makeup for that. At first I couldn't understand my own feelings."

"You do, now?" Gus asked.

"Don't you believe in followin' your dreams?"

"I don't have any dreams that I know of, Gilbert. I'm comfortable here."

"I want to fly airplanes, Gus. They've got airplane factories in California. First I'll learn how they go together, then I'll fly one, you wait and see!"

Gus waited for Gilbert to say more and when he didn't, said, "I always thought twins shared the same thoughts and inclinations. That's what make us twins. I'd never leave home."

"That's because you're rooted here in the holler. I couldn't imagine you living anywhere else, Gus."

Gus cocked his hands on his hips. "Why would you want to leave here?" Gus felt a trace of betrayal.

Gilbert leaned back his head and looked straight into the hard sun. "You've always been Pa's favorite. You're the one who takes an interest in the mill. Ever notice Pa talks to you about the business and to me about the weather?"

"They love you the same as me. There ain't no difference."

"Pa's never told me he loved me," Gilbert said, "and I want to live somewhere that's fun, like California. It's a wild and secret joy, well, it *was* a secret until now. I feel a pull from this whole other world. A hungering for excitement, an ache for something I can't explain."

"You're doin' a pretty good job of it," Gus said quietly, his face turned from his brother. "You ain't just tryin' to take leave of the chores, are you?" He felt scared now. He'd never heard Gilbert talk so grown up. It's true Pa talks more about the mill with me, Gus thought. That's only because I ask all the questions, he told himself, then remembered Norman swearing one day that Gilbert was too damn lazy to make a red cent in sawmilling.

"I remember Uncle Worth saying he had journey-itching feet," Gilbert said, shaking Gus from his own thoughts. Looking down at his bare feet, Gil wiggled his toes and said, "Mine sort of feel the same way. Sometimes I can't stand the heavy feeling of wanting to get away. When I think of it, butterflies swarm in my stomach and give me this rightful, earth-shaking feeling."

"I wish you wouldn't talk like that," Gus said. "Hopes and dreams should involve home, the family, land."

"When I think about moving away, I can squeeze my eyes closed and see opportunity in this far away shiny city with gleaming streets and polished buildings."

"Do you see it now?" Gus asked, studying his brother's closed eyes.

"Just like in the *National Geographic* magazines I keep in the barn beneath an old grain barrel." After a steep, dreamy silence, Gilbert stood corn stalk straight and said, "Gonna find me a good woman, Gus. A woman like our ma. Ever since we hid behind Elmer Cotton's corn crib and watched Elsie wash her hair in the rain barrel with nothing on but her panties and undershirt, I've wanted to be like Billy Ray Mudd. He's self-reliant, daring, willing to take chances."

Gus started laughing fit to die. He slapped his thigh then slapped it again. "You've gone 'round the bend, Gilbert Norman Wheeler!" Gus shook his head like he was shaking straw from his hair. "You don't want no woman! You'd get yourself into a sight o' trouble."

"You're probably right," Gil rationalized. "I remember the thrashing Darius got when his ma found him kissing on Eula Mae." He folded his arms easily across his chest. "Maybe I'll just get a dog."

"One's good as the other," Gus said. He made a hacking sound. "I'd gag if I tongue-wagged with Eula."

"I'd kind of like to," Gilbert said.

Gus half-closed his eyes and watched Gil's face become sober. "Gotta get out of here, Gus. I got Uncle Worth's feet. Besides, I plan on seeing the Turncoat of Roses parade from the front row."

Gus nodded. "Turncoat of Roses," he repeated. Gus tried to smile, but his annoyance prevented it. Instead he shrugged and let out an exasperated sigh. "Californy's a fur piece from here," he said. "Fur as heaven." He looked away. "I'd hate like sin to see you go." He felt angry with his brother. "Kinfolk don't leave home."

Gilbert rubbed his chin like his pa did when he needed a shave. "I ain't workin' at the sawmill like Pa. He's killin' himself. Goes to work before sun up, don't come in until after the sun sets. Blows those big sawdust boogers out of his nose. That ain't for me, Gus." Gilbert dug his toe into the warm dirt then mopped sweat dripples from his head with his forearm. "Soggy summers' heat. This life ain't for me. Look what's happening to Corky McCall. Vern caught him turning over outhouses day 'fore yesterday. Plumb boredom is what it is. I got journey-itching feet. Have had, ever since I saw that first picture in *National Geographic*. You know, folks in California don't have shacks like they do here. People live in fancy houses with indoor toilets and big swimming pools in their back yards."

"You're crazy as a shit-house rat, Gilbert. That ain't California you're thinkin' of, that's heaven. You better get shet of that idea. Keep thinkin' like that and you'll end up like Uncle Worth with a grave-rock over your head."

Since Gilbert had no comment, Gus used the silence to wrap himself in thought. He wrinkled his forehead wondering what it would be like without Gilbert around. Being together was as natural as breathing. Being a twin gave him self-confidence. He knew Gil was always by his side. Even at night when they slept, Gil was snuggled down in the same bed. It'd always been that way. He couldn't image sleeping in a bed all alone. How could Gil feel differently from him? Didn't his brother have the same mind? The same inner voice? It seemed Gilbert had always protected him. Gil seemed bigger, stronger, smarter, the leader of the two, the one with fresh ideas. Gus didn't like the stir of gloom he felt just above his bellybutton. It frightened him. Not only for the sudden loneliness he felt, but scared for Gilbert. He'd heard his pa say that talkers most times ain't doers. The thought gave Gus some comfort. Maybe Gil was just talking. To his surprise, he could hear himself swallow. It sounded kind of like a turd dropping in a toilet bowl, he thought. Gus rolled his eyes at his brother's foolishness and shoved his hands deep into his pockets. His mind couldn't untangle the sense of it. "I feel good here," Gus said as they walked along. "The long walk home from church, the quiet winter nights, lightnin' bugs, Mason jars filled with sweet tea in the summer, the crunching leaves underfoot in the fall. It's all a part of my life." Gus looked sidelong at Gilbert who was traipsing along with sunny, full-of-promise steps and realized Gilbert wasn't paying any attention. He thought and tried to figure out his brother's logic as he trailed behind. I love the idea of working alongside Pa at the mill, Gus thought. The notion of doing anything different had never crossed his mind. He reckoned there wasn't a lot to do in the hills, Gil was right about that. The Reimer's made and sold moonshine, Jed and Ethel McCall lived off their bootlegging, and their son, Corky, spent the summers pitching hay and milking cows. That didn't seem so bad. The McCalls seemed to welcome each morning. They'd just got new linoleum in their kitchen. Corky was always cheerful. Why, just yesterday he said Eula had let him lip-kiss her again. Eula was twelve and a half and had those round titties. Life here's not so bad, Gus thought. He inhaled deeply and heard Gil's words in his head. Gil going away? It was beyond his imagination. Beyond his acceptance.

Gilbert looked sidewise at his brother. "Don't you got any dreams, Gus?"

Poking a finger through a hole in his shirt sleeve, Gus sighed theatrically. Even at his young age Gus knew his life was going in a different direction from his twin brother. It saddened him, yet he loved his brother and wanted him to be happy. I won't be passin' no judgment, he thought. "Dreams? Don't rightly know." He straightened his shoulders. "Help Pa run the mill. Raise me a pig. Maybe two."

"See what I mean? That's nothin' to dream about," Gilbert said. "If you could have anything you wanted, what would it be?"

Gus felt his dismay retreating. He smiled, looked up in thought. "Ma an' Pa couldn't afford it, but I've always wanted a catalog-ordered soap box. Not one like you and I make out of scraps, but a real one with a motor on the back, one that don't wobble because of different size tires. I want one like in Sears and Roebuck catalog."

Gilbert nodded and smiled. "One you can win the Soap Box Derby race with."

"Yep. The big race up in Akron."

"If I get rich workin' on them airplanes, I'll buy you one," Gilbert promised.

The boys remembered aloud some of their homemade carts, the one that lost a wheel and didn't even make it to the bottom of the hill, the one the steering rope broke on going full-speed downhill. "You always wanted to put a motor on one of them," Gilbert said and Gus nodded, recalling their previous efforts.

Gus thought that Gilbert was like a cow inclined to jump the fence and was worried almost to the point of throwing up again. Then he doubted himself, wondering if he was being a baby not wanting to leave the hills. Still, Gus cottoned to the feeling of being safe and secure. He swallowed again, trying not to think. "Gotta cool off," Gus said, as they neared the crooked part of the creek. He unbuttoned and took off his shirt, held it in his hands and fingered the frayed collar. God, he thought, I feel like crying. Gus tossed the shirt over a jutting tree branch, stepped out of his overalls, picked up a stone and skipped it across the water. He counted three bounces. "You coming?" Gus asked, kicking his overalls aside and grabbing hold of a lofty, twisted root-rope that dangled over the water. His toes pitted the spongy embankment as he propelled himself from the bank. He swung out twice, let go and splashed into the cool water.

"I ain't gettin' in," Gilbert said, swatting a bug on his arm. "Come on, Gus. Let's lickety-whoop out of here."

"You're a fathead baby," Gus said, grabbing the root and swinging out again. He stayed under the water to the brink of his lung's capacity, then popped up his head and thrashed about until he got his bearings. After shaking the water from his hair and ears, Gus swam several feet, turned shoreward and tromped out of the rain-swollen creek. Even the dark, liquid coolness couldn't quench his displeasure.

"I'm not a baby, Gus! I feel like I'm growing up too fast and I don't like it. Why are you all out of sorts?" Gil asked.

"Why do you think, pinhead?"

"Life."

"What's Life?"

"Magazine."

"Where ya git it?"

"Drugstore."

"How much?"

"Ten cents."

"Ain't got it."

"That's tough."

"What's tough?"

"Life."

"What's life?"

"Magazine."

"Let's do the monkey rhyme," Gus urged then rattled on with it, "I had a little monkey, his name was Tiny Tim. I put him in the bathtub to teach him how to swim." He glanced at Gilbert, waiting for him to join in, but his brother was silent. Gus shouted more of the lyrics, "He drank all the water, he ate all the soap. He died that night with a bubble in this throat." Still, no sound from Gilbert. "In came the doctor. In came the nurse. In came the lady with the alligator purse."

Gus stopped before going into the next verse. "Come on, Gilbert, say it with me, like we used to do."

"That's kid's stuff."

"We *are* kids!" Gus snapped.

In sequence, they turned round and headed for home because it felt like dinner time and because the hour was spoiled. Gilbert was silent, and Gus worried about California.

"Come on, Gil, follow me," Gus said, trying to save the day. "I heard Luther Hamby was putting his bull in the cow's pasture. It's piggyback time."

"That's no big deal anymore."

The words fell on Gus like a load of manure. Finally the truth was sinking in. Gil was really going to California. He was a changed person. There was a time not long ago Gilbert had camped out near Hamby's pasture just to see the mating. A premonitory anxiety was building in Gus's heart, no longer a blurry feeling, but sharp feelings of being ripped in two.

• CHAPTER 2 •

As the warm spring rain rapped against the window pane, Norman Wheeler sat straight-backed, his dark eyes fixed on the black, bell-shaped receiver he held in his hand. "Fifty-two acres," he mumbled. "I'd be a full-grown fool not to accept," he said to himself. "If the stand's as good as he described. . . ."

Gus looked up from his marble game and saw Katherine staring at Norman, a glass of water in one hand, a packet of Goody's headache powder in her other. Gus looked over at his father and sensed this wasn't a normal business call. Was it a creditor bothering them again? Norman's features were that of a man deep in thought.

"Come on, Gus," Gilbert burst out. "It's your turn."

Gus jumped at his brother's words, then made his play. He glanced back to his parents. Katherine started to tear open the medicine packet, then set the glass and package on the counter top. Perplexed about the telephone call, Gus watched Norman study the telephone's receiver, then watched his arm slowly move forward while his fingers groped for the hook to replace the receiver in its cradle.

"Who were you talking to, Norman?" Katherine asked.

"Do you want to play or not?" Gilbert yelled at Gus.

"My turn?" Gus asked, shifting his eyes back to the game. When Norman spoke, Gus's head lifted again in the direction of his father.

"It was a man by the name of Arnold Delvine," Norman finally said. "He's coming out to show me some wooded acreage. He wants to sell it fast and cheap."

Katherine turned back to the sink to rinse the breakfast plates. "We can't afford to buy any more land, Norman."

Gus waited for a harsh response from his father, but none came. "I've never heard of this man called Delvine," he heard his mother say.

"He's not from around here," Norman answered, settling into his chair. "Lives down in Atlanta." He leaned back his head. "This man's made me a good deal, Katy."

"Norman, we can't afford more timber." She reached across the sink and pushed up the window. A damp spring breeze drifted in and ruffled wisps of hair around her face. "Besides that, we have two or three other stands of timber waiting to be cut."

Gus sat up, told Gilbert he was tired of marbles and pushed himself off the floor. He could see his father's point. If this new timber was a sure-enough bargain, it would always be there to cash in on later. Gus ignored Gilbert's grumbling about him taking leave of the marble game and plodded to the cookie jar.

"Just one," Katherine said.

Gus took the oatmeal cookie and sank into a kitchen chair. He glanced down at his brother who was pouring himself over a circle of marbles, his long limbs spread out behind him. Gus stretched his neck to peer out the window and noticed that the rain had stopped. His gaze traveled along the honeysuckled fence that led to the sawmill. He watched hired men, wet from the quick-moving shower, ready logs, lift them onto the carriage, guide them through the various saws. He closed his eyes and let the smell of springtime and sawdust fill his head.

Gus opened his eyes when he heard Norman shuffle in his seat. There's nothing Pa could say that would make Mom feel differently, he thought. She's always been worried about the bills.

"I know we don't have the money, but this hardwood property is too good a prize to ignore," Norman told her. When he rose from his chair and walked up behind her she didn't turn around. "I'm going to look at it," Norman told her. "If it's as good as he says, I'm buying it."

Gus saw Katherine clenching her jaw and fixing her gaze on the sink's red water pump. She blinked several times, dried her hands on her apron, and turned to face Norman. Gus knew that getting deeper in debt worried her. She raised her hands and rubbed her temples. He watched Katherine pick up the headache powder then toss it back down. Gus knew she seldom took medicine now that there was a youngin' growing in her belly. He peered down at the cookie. He really hadn't wanted it.

Gus didn't have to be an adult to know they couldn't afford to buy more timber land. He glanced up at Katherine when he heard her sigh. Resignedly she asked, "and when's he comin', this man named Arnold Delvine?"

"Tomorrow. Calvin and I'll go look at it. I may even take Gus along. What do you say, kiddo?"

Gus opened his mouth then closed it. Maybe I should stay out of this, he thought. Katherine grabbed the dish towel off the rack. In the end, it was his father who decided what was to be. That's the way it was supposed to be, his mother always told him. It was taught in the Bible. Katherine lived her days by the Word.

She began drying the dishes and putting them away. "Calvin Hawkins *is* the logging operation's supervisor," she said. "If a deal's to be made, Calvin should be involved in it, but why drag Gus along?"

"Because he's taken an interest in the business. Unlike Gilbert."

Gus cringed at the words, his eyes glancing in Gilbert's direction. No wonder Gil wanted to leave here, he thought. Katherine paced back and forth over a large faded, flowered rug, then looked at Norman and said, "Are you sure this is something . . . ?"

Norman held his hands up for silence, walked up to her, cradled her face with his hands and said, "Katy, if it's anything close to what the man described, we can't afford *not* to."

Gus stared at the floor between his parents, observing the frayed edges of the rug. He hated it when his folks disagreed on things. He looked up and saw Katherine's shoulders slump. "The boys need things with the little money we do have," she said.

"This is Gus and Gilbert's future, Katy."

Katherine's voice remained calm. "For crying out loud. The boys are young. How can they possibly understand?"

"They don't go without," Norman said defensively. "They'll understand."

Gus felt knots tightening in his stomach. Why do they have to bring us into all their arguments, he wondered, and then heard his mother's words, "You've got foolish notions, Norm." Gus started to get up, but the sawdusty air suddenly nauseated him. He inhaled deeply and sat back down. It always made him feel like throwing up when his folks fussed.

"Norman," Katherine said quietly. "How can they grasp the logic when the finest toy they own is the erector set from my father?" Her words were slow. "When the only Christmas gift we can afford for them is a feedbag-covered box with an orange and a Moon Pie inside?"

Norman seemed not to be listening to her. "Mr. Delvine told me there was someone else interested in this property."

Gus looked quickly at Katherine and saw her anger building. He knew she felt like cussing and stomping away. Instead, she busied herself with the dishes and said, "That's every salesman's line."

"He sounded trustworthy," Norman said.

Katherine shook her head with a look of resignation. "Who else is interested in this golden-tree acreage? Someone from around here?"

"I didn't ask. My first thought was Ira Irving. He may be thirty miles away, but he's our nearest competitor."

"Norman, we haven't had many contract offers this past year. It's not a wise decision. Our borrowing power at the bank is nearly gone and it's not fair for Daddy to keep shoveling us out of our messes."

Norman raised his arm and pointed his index finger at her. Gus knew she'd overstepped her bounds. "There's no call for that!" Norman yelled at her. His eyes were cold and dark like rocks in a river.

Katherine closed her eyes and said, "Norman, I shouldn't have said that and I'm sorry." She swung her hands out as if surrendering. "Someone at church said Irving has hired fifty more men. He's doubling his operation."

"He's cutting twice as much timber as we are, too. I heard he's selling to some big companies up north."

"Buying this land will be a mistake. Had I known ten years ago what a rough time we'd be having right now, I doubt that I would have persuaded you to take father's offered money for the logging business. I love you beyond imagination Norman, but your stubbornness drives me crazy."

Katherine turned, her blue eyes glistening. Gus knew she was looking for something to fix her eyes on until the swelling signal of impending tears passed. Her gaze settled on the hands of the smooth-finished, wooden clock on the kitchen wall. "It's half past ten and I haven't even started dinner. You'll be starved by noon."

Even before the rooster crowed the next morning, Gus sat at the kitchen table watching Norman pull on his work boots. His stomach was full of excitement with the chance of being a part of a business deal. "Where is this place?" he asked.

Norman finished lacing up his boots and took a sip of coffee. "North of here about twenty miles," he answered.

"Close to Ira Irving's sawmill?"

"Up that way," Norman answered while stirring another spoonful of sugar into his coffee. "Go wake your brother," he said, setting his spoon next to the cup.

"He said he didn't want to go," Gus said, dropping his gaze, disappointed that his brother didn't show more interest in the family's work.

Norman snapped up his head. "Get him up! He's going."

"Gilbert isn't feeling well this morning, Norman," Katherine said, walking out of the bedroom. "He threw up last night."

"Twice," Gus added. "He nearly soused my boots."

Norman shook his head. "He doesn't have a shred of respect for this business. How is he ever going to learn the trade with his offhand attitude?"

Gus didn't want to hear this kind of talk so early in the morning. They had already said everything there was to say about Gilbert's indolent demeanor. He watched Katherine pat Norman on the shoulder and join them at the table. Her colorless face had lines of strain and Gus longed for the days when his mother laughed at the breakfast table.

"Maybe Gilbert wants to do something else with his life," Katherine said half-heartedly. "Perhaps he'll be a doctor or a lawyer like his grandfather and great-grandfather."

Norman humphed. "His great-grandfather was a no-good manipulator!"

"Pa," Gus said, losing interest in spending the day with Norman. "William Ashford is history. It's Gilbert we're talking about."

"He darn tootin' don't care a straw about the mill."

Katherine sipped her hot coffee and looked at Norman. "Did you sleep well?" Gus knew all she'd get for an answer would be a grunt. She cradled the cup of coffee in her hands and asked if either wanted sausage and eggs. "Gus and I are eating at Melva's," Norman told her.

As Norman rose and stomped his pant legs down over his boots, Gus finished drinking his milk then gazed through the screen door toward the woods where a patchy low morning mist was twining through the trees. The sun was rising now, sketching slanted bars of light.

"Did you both get a clean handkerchief?" Katherine asked, but Gus saw that her gaze strayed past them and through the dusty window where the rooster was now sitting on a fence post.

"We did, Mom," Gus answered for them.

"Norman, I wish you'd talk to me!" she said harshly.

Norman arranged his shirt, took his cup to the sink and reached for his hat.

Katherine stood up. "Sometimes I just feel like running 'round yelling with my apron over my head!"

Gus looked at her, brushed her arm with his fingertips and told her he was sorry with his eyes.

"Too bad Gilbert's feeling poorly this morning," Norman said. "He should be riding along with us, but then you know darn well he'd find the trip boring."

"Lord, thy will be done," Katherine murmured, reaching for the dish pan that hung on a peg next to the sink. Another day had begun.

Norman turned to Gus. "Ready?"

Gus nodded and Norman touched Katherine's cheek and traipsed out with Gus on his heels. Katherine shuffled over to the screen door and watched them get into the car. Gus cranked the window down, waved goodbye. Norman looked at Katherine for a long moment, gestured limply and drove away.

Calvin was waiting when Norman's green Buick rumbled up and topped the hill at the camp's post. He nodded, tossed out the coffee grounds from his tin cup and walked toward the car. "Mornin'," he greeted, his voice early-morning deep. He put the empty cup on a tree stump. "I see you brought your sidekick."

"He's chomping at the bit," Norman answered. Gus sniffed the smell of bacon frying on an open fire and wished he'd ate some breakfast. "We're meeting . . . " Norman drew a piece of paper from his shirt pocket. "A Mr. Arnold H. Delvine at Melva's Diner. He's buying our breakfast."

"I could eat two breakfasts," Calvin said.

Norman laughed and patted Calvin's big belly. "Looks like you double-up on all your meals," he said.

With a coffee pot in one hand and a bowl of gravy in the other, Melva greeted Norman, Calvin and Gus with a "Hello, honeys," shout.

Norman lifted his arm. "Mornin', Melva." Gus did and said the same. A pleasant mixture of chitchat, breakfast scents and tobacco smoke filled the room. Calvin nodded to friends as they passed by the busy tables. "Howdy, Tyler, George. Mornin', Smitty." The smoky, small room was filled with Melva's regular customers. Gus listened to lively unwelcome comments about how much he'd grown, like always, when he came to town. "He's nearly grown now," he heard Norman answer for him.

"Your table needs wiped off, honey. I'll be right there," Melva said, setting hot buttermilk biscuits and gravy in front of Sam Weston. "I'll be right back with your grits."

Norman pulled out a chair and sat at his table, the others followed. The three men chatted and waited for their coffee. Gus pulled the white cafe curtains aside and saw through the hand-smeared window, a black, 1931 Model A Ford roll by. The driver double-parked next to a light-colored Studebaker.

"There's Ella Rose," Norman commented, glancing out the window.

Calvin grunted. "Hasn't that woman learned to park that car, yet?"

"Apparently not," Norman answered.

Smitty turned his head and said, "Law, that woman can't drive down a straight road, let alone *park*."

"She knows who to block in, though," Tyler said. "That's Sam's Studebaker," he said, pointing to a skinny man with faded overalls. After an eruption of laughter, Tyler continued, "He ain't goin' nowheres. Sam sits here till noon swappin' yarns about the good-ole-days."

Sam Weston looked up and said, "Just takes Ella Rose a few minutes to scoot in here to fetch Riley's hank o' ham and red-eyed gravy each morning. She ain't hamperin' my parking none."

"Poor ol' Riley," someone said. "Never has been the same since his stroke."

Melva glanced over her shoulder when she heard the bell above the door jingle. "Mornin', honey," Melva said to Ella Rose. "There's Riley's ham an' gravy next to the register."

"I'll leave the quarter right here with yesterday's plate," Ella Rose said quietly, reaching for the covered dish.

"You tell Riley hello for us, honey."

"I'll tell him."

A smart-fashioned man with appraising eyes held the door open for Ella Rose. She nodded, then looked quizzically over her shoulder several times before getting into her Model A. All of the diner's customers looked up as the self-assured gentleman with a ruddy, broad face walked through the doorway.

"That must be Arnold Delvine," Norman said. "He looks like a foreigner."

Calvin, with his back to the door, cranked his body around to look. "Uh huh," he mumbled. Norman set down his coffee cup and raised his arm to the man.

Delvine nodded, took off his navy blue sport coat, hat, and hung them neatly on the coat tree. He wore a light blue, short sleeve shirt with a wide, navy tie. His well-creased pants matched his shirt. The man carried his short, stocky frame regally. He strode to their table with an air of pompousness, faced Norman, and outstretched his arm. Norman shook the stranger's offered hand. Calvin held out his hand, but Delvine ignored it. Calvin pulled back his dark-skinned arm, picked up his cup and sipped his coffee. Norman introduced Calvin Hawkins and Gus, but Delvine still disregarded the Negro man.

Calvin scooted his chair over. "Have a seat, Mr. Delvine."

Delvine dragged the chair from its position aside Hawkins and placed it at the end of the table. He leaned in toward Norman. "Your laborer is welcome to stay, however it's you I'm doing business with, Mr. Wheeler."

Calvin airily turned his chair and propped it against the wall. The chair balanced precariously on two legs. "Reckon the nigger situation down in Georgia is worse than it is here," he said matter-of-factly, a toothpick dangling from the corner of his mouth.

"It gets nasty," Delvine said, his wide-set, dark eyes intense. "They don't serve them in places like this. Wouldn't even dare come in."

"That right?" Calvin grunted.

"A couple of them tried it one day last week," Delvine continued. "They were dragged out and beaten raw. The waitress smeared them with ketchup and mustard. You should've seen the look in them niggers' eyes." Delvine glanced at Norman and then to Calvin. "No offense."

Calvin picked at his teeth and said through a smirky grin, "You must-a bent over laughin'." He nudged off the wall with his shoulder and the two front legs of his chair crashed to the floor. Melva's customers were silent, their ears cocked. Norman raised his eyebrows and Delvine's eyes popped wide open. Calvin smacked his large black hand onto the table top and said, "Yes sir, us'n niggers is gittin' bolder ever' day. Come a time we's gonna git brave 'nough to run fer Pres'dent."

Norman and Calvin glanced at each other, then Norman said to Delvine, "Mr. Hawkins is in charge of the logging end of the business so I believe he has a right to be here. He's the camp foreman out at Timber Hills."

"No harm," Delvine said, still not looking at Calvin.

"Well," Norman said, pushing back his chair from the table. "The day's had a sour start, Mr. Delvine. I'm really not very hungry, so let's go see this timberland."

"I'm ready, if you are. We'll ride in my car," Delvine said.

"I'm prepared to sell fast and make you a steal of a deal," Delvine told them as they stood before the wooded acreage. "I want fifteen hundred and twenty dollars for the property."

"What's the catch?" Calvin asked.

Delvine glanced at Calvin, then faced Norman. "I want five hundred-twenty dollars down, today, and the balance in thirty days." His voice was straightforward, but impatient. "I'm showing the acreage to someone else not far from here. You're lucky. You've seen it first." Delvine pulled back his coat sleeve and glanced at his gold-banded Hamilton wristwatch. "So," he asked, "What do you think?"

Norman held out his hand. "Sir, I want this property. Don't show it to anyone else."

Delvine appeared to relax. "Sold," he said. "I'll have the contract drawn-up immediately." They clasped hands firmly then patted each other on the back. Delvine walked over to his car, opened the door and leafed through some paperwork then drew out a receipt book.

With a happy grin on his face, Norman said to Calvin, "I can't believe my luck. This fifty-two-acre parcel of woodland has some finest virgin hardwood around." He play-punched the somber-faced logging supervisor between the shoulder blades. "Come on, put a smile on your kisser," Norman urged. "This is job security for you!"

Gus watched Calvin shake his head as Norman and Arnold H. Delvine concluded the verbal agreement. As they traveled back to the diner, Norman and Delvine chatted and guffawed in the front seat while Calvin and Gus sat silently in the back. Gus nudged Calvin's arm and whispered, "that man's a donkey's ass."

Calvin grunted and Gus studied his face. Although he didn't like this Mr. Delvine, the timberland was impressive. Gus knew they wouldn't be cutting soon, but it would be there when they needed it. He tended to side with Norman on this one.

Arnold H. Delvine tipped his hat and waved farewell. Norman grinned wide and nodded. "It's been a lucky day, so far," he commented. Gus watched Calvin suck audibly on a broken tooth as the Cadillac headed west, in the direction of Irving's Logging and Sawmill.

"If he's goin' back to Atlanta his car's pointed in the wrong direction," Calvin said.

"Ah," Norman said, "He's likely going down to the filling station to gas up before heading out of town."

Arnold H. Delvine sauntered into his office before seven the next morning. He had trouble keeping the smile off his face as he opened his file cabinet and took two blank contracts from the file folder. He laid the papers on his desk, walked over to the corner of his office and placed a record on the spindle of his High Fidelity console. After adjusting the volume, he sat, propped up his feet on his cherrywood desk and thought of the wording to use on the contracts. Delvine's self-assured gaze traveled through the opened window and into the rising Atlanta sun. The toes of his Connolly kangaroo oxfords bounced with the music from the console. He smiled, finger-combed his thick, white hair then gazed at the new, forty-nine dollar Bell and Howell movie camera still in its box ready to put into his suitcase. It was hard to think with a head full of happiness.

When the record ended, Delvine leaned back in the chair, took off his reading glasses and set them on the desk. Drawing his stocky frame from the chair, Arnold loosened his yellow-dotted tie and sauntered to the record player. His red-veined eyes squinted through the swirl of cigar smoke. Carefully Arnold picked up another record, took it out of its cover and centered it onto the spindle. Swaying along with the voice of Perry Como, Delvine put his glasses back on and studied the colorful travel brochure from Sunlane Cruises. His large head rocked back and forth on its squat neck like he was already on the ship. He reached down, slid the desk drawer open and raised the lid on a velvet-lined walnut box. Inside was his cash receipt for the cruise, precisely five hundred and twenty dollars. Norman Wheeler's down-payment had bought him the ticket for a cruise of a lifetime, and Ira Irving's money had bought the new wardrobe. Smiling with self-satisfaction, he fitted a blank contract between the Remington Super-riter rollers.

"Why you got that shitty grin linin' your puffy face?" the Negro janitor asked as he swept around Delvine's desk.

"What if I told you I just sold two parcels of prime woodland property?"

"I'd say you was either a liar or a cheat," the old man said.

"It's true, Oscar," Delvine said as his sausage fingers begin hunting and pecking the typewriter's keys.

The janitor snorted and shook his head. "If I hadn't known you since you was scootin' 'round in diapers, I'd prob'ly not like you."

Delvine ignored the Negro's comments. "Legal as shit," he muttered, grinning. He opened his desk drawer and took out correction tape. "Fools never read the fine print."

"You's up to no good, Arnie, I feels it in my bones," Oscar said as he pushed his broom around Delvine's small but wide size 7 ½ feet. "You's been givin' folks raw deals for a coon's age now. You's gonna git caught sum day, Arnie, an' it won't be no purdy picture."

"Shut up, nigger," Delvine said, smirking out of the side of his mouth, smoke billowing out with the words. "It's legal! Legal as shit. Looky, damnit! I got Wheeler's autograph right here," he quickly shuffled his paperwork, "and Ira Irving's great big John Hancock on this here itsy bitsy line. Legal as a load of shit," he repeated, obnoxiously tossing down his Sheaffer's White Dot pen on the top of his desk. Oscar caught it just as it rolled over the edge of the desk.

"You's gonna be swimmin' in dat shit," the Negro said, standing the pen in Delvine's pencil holder. He swept the pile of dirt out into the hallway and closed the door behind him.

Delvine laughed, lifted one cheek off his chair and let out a resounding fart. "If I hadn't known you since I was doing all that scooting, I'd not like you, either, cause I hate niggers," he said to the closed door, then got up and cranked out his window a few more inches.

Delvine raised his left arm over his head and sniffed his arm pit. He crumpled up his face, then massaged his forehead. "Been working so damn many hours I don't even have time to go home and take a bath," he said to himself as he looked over the documents. He scratched the top of his head then smoothed his hair back down. "Rest and relaxation's just a couple waves away."

Arnold Delvine rested his white-stubbled chin on a fleshy palm and thought about the cruise and the lonely single women that would be on the ship. He pushed back his chair and stretched out his short, stocky legs. When the door eased open, Delvine jerked up his head.

"How the devil did you do it, anyway?" the janitor asked.

"You son of a bitch," Delvine said. "When are you going to start knocking?"

"I stopped rappin' on your door nigh thirty years ago, Arnie. So how'd you do it?"

"Easy," Delvine said. "I sold the acreage to one party and the timber rights to the other. Of course, the hicks up in the Tennessee hills don't read the fine print." He laughed. "Those people are ignorant as hell, just like you."

Obviously ignoring the insult, the janitor said, "And you'll be on a year-long vacation by the time they guess they were gazoozled. You's a lousy egg-suckin' hound!" he said, laughing. "Why's you so evil?"

Delvine chuckled and looked down his nose at the loose ash bouncing on the end of the cigar. Still laughing, he took the cigar from his mouth and stubbed it into a large ashtray. "Go put your teeth in, Oscar."

"They don't fit so good no more, Arnie."

Delvine exhaled the last puff of tobacco smoke and studied the papers in front of him. "Not many folks on the ball up there. Appallingly illiterate, as a matter of fact." Delvine spit a speck of tobacco toward the wastebasket. It dotted the I on his wood-carved *A. H. Delvine* name plate.

"Go on, Oscar. I've got work to do," he said, as one finger at a time typed out the contract. "Why am I so evil?" he asked himself, repeating Oscar's question. For the first time in a long while Arnold Delvine felt a tinge of guilt. He wasn't raised that way. He thought of the fire that took the life of his mother, father, wife and little girl while they slept at his home on that Christmas morning and how he'd been the only one to make it out alive. It shouldn't have been that way. The Lord should have spared the others and taken him. But no, God was greedy. He had to have them all. Delvine slammed his fist on the desk. Well now I'm the greedy one, he said harshly to himself, then chortled as he gently tugged the paper from the Super-riter roller. "This stinks like dirty laundry," he roared, lifting his right shoulder and sniffing under his shirt sleeve again.

• CHAPTER 3 •

Gus tossed and turned, slept lightly, and rose at 5:30 in the morning. It had been more than a month since Gilbert had mentioned California, but Gilbert had planted a germinating seed of anxiety in Gus's chest. As he pulled on his pants, Gus glanced at Gil, still sleeping. He'd kept waking up in the night propping himself on his elbow to stare at his twin brother sleep. A sliver of moonlight through the curtains was all he needed to watch Gilbert dream of going away. Even a quick-moving thunderstorm during the night hadn't wakened him. Gus had wanted to cry, and would have if he hadn't been so peeved about his brother's intent.

On the top floor of the barn, Gus jabbed the pitchfork into a stack of hay and heaved it through the chute. His heart felt pierced with each poke of the fork. The more he thought about losing his brother the harder he worked. Before he knew it, he had dumped more hay than the animals below could eat. Gus leaned the pitchfork against the wall and slumped against the opening frame. Looking out, he could see the bedroom side of their weathered frame house. Through their window he could see his brother moving like a zombie, sitting on the edge of the bed bending over slowly, putting on one sock then the other like a slow-motion picture show. Gus shook his head and figured he would rather have Gilbert around, lazy as he was, than not have him here at all. He looked beyond the yard toward the timbered hills and watched dawn's misty light creep across the ridges, touch them, then steal softly into the coves and hollows. He closed his eyes and wondered what dawn looked like in California. When he opened his eyes, he glanced toward the house again and saw the morning's light, now stronger, touching the porch. Gilbert had pulled back the curtain and was looking out. Gus breathed in deeply, let it out noisily, then scrambled down the ladder to get on with his chores. Methodically, he strolled to the side of the barn to a grain barrel, stuck a bucket into the shelled corn, scooped some up, then measured out linseed meal from a burlap sack. Pouring the meal on top of the corn, Gus quietly cussed his brother because he never helped with the chores. Gus neither liked nor disliked it, not thinking about it either way, however this morning it bothered him. Gus clenched his jaw. "California," he said aloud. "He may as well go to Africa!"

Gus patted the shoulder of a Hereford and dumped the bucket of corn mixture into the feeding box. Walking out of the barn, Gus saw that Norman was already working at the mill. He glanced up at the early sun and figured it couldn't be much later than half past six. He'll still be there past six tonight, Gus thought. He pulled the barn door closed, and spotted Gilbert sitting on the top porch step pulling on his boots. "Aren't you going to help with the chores?" he asked, as he headed for the chicken yard to feed the hens.

"The sun's barely topped the hills," Gilbert said in a groggy, early morning voice.

"There's chores to be done." Gus said sharply. "Pitching hay to the animals is part of living on a farm, part of our everyday life, part of being a Wheeler."

"I'll feed the damn chickens," Gilbert said, grabbing the feed bucket from Gus's hand. Gus stood there and let him take it. It won't hurt him to finish, Gus told himself.

"I'll race you to the creek," Gilbert challenged after breakfast.

"Last one there's a rotten egg!" Gus answered, trying not to let his angry-morning thoughts ruin the day, hoping maybe Gilbert had changed his mind about leaving.

Gilbert lurched forward and bolted toward the woods. Gus trailed behind. "I'm Hop-a-long! Giddy-up, giddy-up," Gil chanted out, the freshness of the morning bringing out the little boy in both them. "Giddy-up all the way to Cal-iforny."

Gus stopped stone still and stared at his brother who was hippety-hopping ahead of him. "Haven't you forgotten that?"

"Not yet," Gilbert answered, gyrating round.

"Are you really goin'?" Gus asked, knowing his brother's stubbornness wouldn't let him change his mind.

"I done told you that thirty-eleven times. Can't you remember nothin'?"

Gus poked Gil in the ribs with a hickory stick he'd twisted off a tree. "I ain't no dummy," Gus said, staring up at the tree tops.

"Yeah," Gilbert replied, rubbing his side where the point of the stick had scraped his skin. "I figure if I start working soon I'll have the money I need to get there by the time I'm sixteen years old."

"That's only five years from now, Gil!" Gus said, hopping over a fence row and scrambling through tall, thirsty weeds.

"Nineteen fifty-one," Gilbert said. "June third, nineteen fifty-one, Gus, that's my goal. On my birthday, five years from now."

"That's my birthday, too," Gus said. "You wouldn't leave home on our birthday, would you? I'd never forgive you for doing that, Gilbert."

"I don't reckon I'll leave on that day, Gus, but I'll have the money saved by then."

"Maybe you'll change your mind," Gus said, staring straight into Gilbert's eyes.

The twins circled a scattering of sassafras trees then lumbered up a hill thick with scratchy, sprouting blackberry vines. By the time they reached the top, the sun was warm enough to bring out the boy-sweat.

"Here comes a cloud shadow," Gil said, pointing. "Run! Don't let it gobble you!" he yelled, but it was a small cloud and swept away from them. Below, they could see eight-year-old Eunice Hammer towing in a huge catfish from the creek. "Ain't she got the luck," Gil remarked.

Gilbert took their knife from a secret pouch he'd pinned into his overalls and with a quick snap of the wrist, sliced it through the air into a shagbark. It dangled pendulously for a moment before it fell from the tree, and when it did, it alighted directly into a mess of poison ivy. "Your turn," he said, grinning.

Hastily, Gus seized the knife. Gilbert held back a snicker. "Poison ivy, poison ivy," Gil sang out, pointing to the shiny-leaved vine.

"Told Darius we'd help with the mud chinkin' tomorrow," Gus said, not worrying about a forthcoming itch. He'd seen where the knife had landed and was careful not to touch the leaves. "Bet that cabin of theirs won't stay standin' much longer. Lots of cracks between the logs," Gus added.

"They're on their way to the poorhouse," Gus said.

Gilbert started the riddle:

"I had a little monkey. His name was Tiny Tim.

I put him in the bathtub to teach him how to swim.

He drank all the water. He ate all the soap.

He died that night with a bubble in his throat."

Gus smiled and joined in:

"In came the doctor. In came the nurse,

In came the lady with the alligator purse . . ."

"June third, nineteen fifty-one, huh?" Gus asked.

"That's my goal."

"How're you gonna make it on your own in a foreign land when you're only sixteen?"

"Hey, Gus," Gilbert laughed, obviously ignoring the question. "Don't get into any poison ivy. You'll keep me awake with your itchin' like last time." He opened his mouth to say something else, then closed it because something had caught his eye.

Gus followed Gilbert's gaze and saw Eunice Hammer's spaniel splash into the creek water below. They heard Eunice scold the canine and watched her jerk up her pole.

"Dog's scarin' away the fish," Gus said.

Gilbert looked over the hill, but it wasn't the girl or the dog he had his eyes on.

"What are you gawkin' at down there?" Gus asked when he saw Gilbert staring at Mitch and Elsie's barn.

"Who's that prowlin' around Mitch Wampler's tractor? They aren't back from Middlesboro yet, are they?" Gilbert asked.

"Couldn't be. Elsie's brother's funeral ain't until tomorrow."

"They told Pa they'd be gone for two weeks," Gilbert said, squinting against the sun's reflection on the tin roof.

The boys flattened down on their stomachs between two name-worn grave rocks and curiously watched the stranger. Gilbert riveted his attention to the Blue Tick hound lying contentedly at the end of his chain. The dog's tail slowly thumped the ground as he watched the man.

"Why's he there? What's he doin'?" Gus mumbled against his brother's cheek. He stuck a blade of grass in his mouth.

"Let's get closer," Gilbert said. "He looks familiar."

Gus whacked at a fly on his arm and missed. "Who do you think it is?"

Gilbert lifted his shoulders ear-high. "Don't know for sure, but . . . wait! Is it . . . it looks sort of like Billy Ray Mudd."

"Billy Ray don't have no business bein' there."

"Yeah. I know."

Gus covered his mouth with a dirt-caked hand. "Should we go down?"

Gilbert propped his hands under his chin and nodded slowly. "I think we should confront him, Gus. Scare the boogers out of him."

With squint-wrinkled eyes, Gus and Gilbert stared at the going-ons below.

"Can you tell? Is it Billy Ray?"

"If it is, Oliver's gonna whack him good. Maybe hang him like he did that nigger."

"Oliver Mudd run off with Beulah Maples."

"Who?" Gus asked. "Who'd Billy Ray's dad run off with?"

"You know. That old hag from Ohio. Oliver left Martha Jean. Billy Ray don't have a dad again."

"Beulah? Who'd want Beulah Maples? She'd make a train take a dirt road."

"Ugly as shit on a barn door as Uncle Worth would say."

Gus's eyes widened. "How do you know he run off with Beulah?"

"Had my ear to the door when Ma told Pa. She said Oliver and Billy Ray's ma got in a cuss-fight and he got unfaithful."

"Did he stop goin' to church?"

"No, dizzybrain. Oliver mustered up another woman to take care of him. You know, to fix his grits, rub his feet and stuff."

"Why'd they get in a cuss-fight?" Gus asked.

Gilbert had his solemn "born-first" look. "Cause Martha Jean Mudd sold the John-Deere and Oliver still owed money on it."

"Well, where'd *that* tractor come from?" Gus asked, pointing toward Mitch's barn.

"Martha Jean sold their Oldsmobile for the money to buy that one."

"Look!" Gus said, gesturing. "What's he doin' now?"

Gilbert squinted even harder. "Damn," he said quietly. "Damn if he ain't stealin' the tractor."

"Damn," Gus mocked. His blue-eyed stare fastened on the theft. "Boy oh boy. Billy Ray's in a heap of trouble now."

"Only if we tell on him."

Gus rolled over onto his back, sat up, and brushed off the dirt and leaves from his bibs. "Geez. What should we do?" His eyes still had a look of shock, but his voice was steady.

Gilbert took the knife out of the pocket and stared at it. "Make him put it back?"

"Not me, Gil. He's thirteen years old!"

"Chicken," Gilbert said, sliding the knife back into its pocket.

They moved heavily away from the ledge, downcast because of their friend's behavior. Wordlessly they ambled down one grassy hill and over another, away from Wampler's farm.

"Billy Ray's our friend. We can't double-cross him. We won't ever mention it. Deal?"

"Deal."

"I can't stop thinking about it."

"Me neither."

They sat silently on the warm grass with their legs spread out before them. Gus leaned back on his elbows and listened to the wood's chipperness. Bird twill surrounded them, insects chirped and in the distance he could hear Eunice Hammer's dog barking. They stared off in separate directions.

Gus turned his head slowly and looked at Gil lying back on the grass. He could only stare, mute and sick with shame for what they'd witnessed. He opened his mouth, closed it, then said, "I want him to feel like hell about what he's done."

"We have to talk about something else to get our minds off it," Gilbert said, covering his eyes with his forearm.

"Then it has to be now, before I think about it too much. Say something," Gus said, looking out over the sloping fields where tiny new tobacco leaves flashed now and then in the sun.

Gilbert sat up, scratched a mosquito bite on his arm until it bled, then asked, "Um . . . do you ever think about what's under a girl's dress?"

Gus looked at his brother. "I think about it a lot." Gus leaned back his head. "Once, when Miss Guffey was writing at the top of the blackboard, everyone could see the back of her knees. Do *you* know what's under there?"

"I've heard."

"Well, what'd you hear?"

"That they're all the same under their skirts. They just got different faces to tell them apart."

"But what's underneath?"

"Boy, would I like to know," Gilbert drawled.

"Billy Ray Mudd probably knows."

They stared into each other's eyes, silent again.

"Yeah, he'd know." Gilbert murmured.

The boys were quiet in thought until Gus said, "Betty Sue told me she woke up in the middle of the night once and saw her dead granny walk in the room with nothin' on but a lace shawl."

"Nothin' underneath?"

"Not a stitch. It likely wasn't nothin' we'd want to see. You know, her bein' dead an' all. It's not nice to talk about a woman's . . . you know, her parts."

Gilbert sucked in his stomach, reached down the side of his overalls and touched himself. "Probably not, but talkin' about it makes my pecker tingle."

Gus tilted his head, wrinkled his forehead and put his hand inside of his own pants. "Mine still feels the same," he said.

Gilbert pulled his hand out, scooted closer to his brother, and said, "Here, feel mine."

"Yeah," Gus agreed, examining his brother's penis, although he really couldn't tell the difference. "It feels funny," he said, dragging his hand back out.

"Here," Gilbert said, reaching into his secret pocket and drawing out the knife. He held out the cork end for Gus to take.

"You go first," Gus said in a faint voice. He cranked his head to look back over his shoulder, but the woods concealed what was taking place below. Gus had a crawly feeling about what was happening at the Wamplers'.

Gilbert aimed the knife, flicked his wrist and watched the knife's sharp blade fasten to the rough bark of a sugar maple. Smiling, he sang out:

"Ain't I glad I ain't a girl,
Clothes to wash and hair to curl,
Skirts a-flappin' in the breeze,
Ain't I glad that that ain't me."

Gus pulled the knife from the tree, scuttled back to the toe line they'd drawn in the dirt, turned, aimed, and tossed the knife toward the chalk-drawn circle on the tree.

"Now he's married and got to be good
And help his woman split the wood.
Chop it thin, sip some gin
And kiss her over and over again."

"We better get home," Gilbert said after a few more tosses. "It gives Mom fits when we're late."

"Yeah," Gus agreed. "She'll have a conniption fit."

Tromping through brush and tangled undergrowth, Gus and Gilbert Wheeler headed down the narrow, forest-shaded path toward home.

"We're not tellin' on Billy Ray, right?"

"Right."

"Pa," Gus shouted, as he galloped into the house. "Why ain't you at the mill?"

Norman looked up from a stack of bills with "PAST DUE" stamped across the front. "Had to make a phone call, son."

"Thelma Jean'll pass it on to everyone," Gus joked. "Pa?" Gus questioned, when he saw his father wasn't laughing. "Somethin' wrong?" Gus studied the blank face, turned down lips, dark hollow eyes. "Pa?"

Norman rose quickly from the kitchen chair and squatted in front of the radio. "Shh. Hush a moment, Son. Listen," he said, turning up the radio's volume. It popped and crackled, but Gus heard the report.

Gus watched his father's brown eyes open wide. It seemed to Gus that an enormous weight of blackness was enveloping his daddy as he listened to the radio. The announcer's words sawed through the house:

Yesterday, April 12, 1945, the President of the United States, Franklin Delano Roosevelt, died of a massive intracerebral hemorrhage. Death came. . . .

The president was dead? FDR had been the only president Gus could remember. A sudden welling of tears blurred the room, not from grief, but from dread of what was going to happen to the United States now that it had no president in charge. Gus watched his father remove his glasses, lay them next to Katherine's green pocketbook, and crumple heavily into his easychair. Gus didn't know what to say. He wondered what it all meant.

After a moment of motionless quiet, Norman listlessly put on his glasses, turned off the Victor, and trudged through the opened doorway. Gus followed as far as the porch and watched his father make his way past the chicken yard and down a daisy-covered hill toward the sawmill. Gus knew that Norman was upset and that worried him. His father seemed to be shambling through a gauzy haze. Gus turned slowly, walked into his small bedroom, and spread out across the featherbed. "That's just hunkydory," he said quietly. "Now what's the world gonna do? Reckon Billy Ray Mudd wouldn't even know."

Gus sprung out of bed and ran out the door. He caught up with his father and asked if he could come along. Norman nodded and Gus walked alongside, taking heavy, tired steps just like his dad. He stopped when Norman did.

Katherine was stacking short lengths of lumber. The whir of mill sounds filled the air.

"She shouldn't be lifting those boards," Norman said, and Gus nodded, yet not quite sure why.

"Norman, you look pale. What's wrong? It's something more than me stacking this wood, isn't it?" Katherine brushed long, blond, sweat-wet hair from her forehead and tucked it beneath her bonnet. Squinting into the sun, she stepped slowly toward him. "Norman, what's . . . . " Katherine's voice died away when Norman touched her arm and told her the news.

Gus looked from his mother's face to his fathers and saw uneasiness in both. Gosh, Gus thought. This is worse than I thought. To Gus, his father's words sounded as though they were caught thick in his head like flies in a web.

Wide-eyed with shock from the news, Katherine reached out and steadied herself on a stack of cordwood. Gus watched her stare in disbelief at the somber face of the man before her. His eyes were without energy and animation. "Has Truman been sworn in?"

Gus watched Norman's lips move slowly as he said, "I don't know. Probably. I don't think Truman ever wanted to be placed in this position."

"Do you think he's capable?" Katherine asked, and Gus watched the question bring a quick smile to Norman's lips.

"You're not kicking his work, are you?" Norman's frown lightened.

Arms hanging limp at his sides, Gus watched Norman turn and amble away, his feet moving slowly, one in front of the other, not going in any particular direction.

"Norman, wait," Katherine called after him.

Hesitating, Norman turned back toward his wife. Still not speaking, Gus stood there, unable to move. This news was bigger than all of them. He looked at his mother. The sun was full on her face but she wasn't squinting. Norman clicked his tongue and gestured toward the stack of wood. A wild turkey darted behind the shed, but Norman's dark eyes didn't follow its path.

Well, here it comes, Gus thought. He's going to lay it on her for lifting that lumber.

"What do you think you're doing, Katy?" Norman slow-kicked a rusty lard bucket. "Don't you care about yourself or the baby?" His excited voice climbed, then faltered. "You need to be resting."

Gus's gaze dropped to Katherine's large stomach. That's why Pa's so upset, Gus thought to himself. She might hurt that baby she has inside there.

"You're mad at me," Katherine pouted, removing her bonnet. Her damp hair framed her round face. Gus hated it when Norman hollered at Katherine, but knew his temper was always short-lived.

"Darn straight I'm mad. I should wallop you good." His tone wasn't threatening but it carried a thin impatience.

Katherine stepped forward and touched his arm. Their gaze held mutely. He sounded mean, but Norman was exactly the opposite, and Gus knew that, and loved him for it. Her mouth lifted in a faint grin as she turned to stack the last piece of lumber. "Just one more," Gus heard his mother say, yet his head was swimming with the words he'd heard on the radio. Standing tall, Katherine faced her husband.

A moist, sweet smell of weeds and mud mixed with drifting sawdust. Katherine's sap-stained hands folded over her extended belly. Gus looked over at Norman standing there with bent shoulders and a drapey face, like he'd lost his pet dog. He wanted to say something that would help, but he knew the shock of President Roosevelt's death bore deeply and no words would ease his discomfort. A breeze ruffled Norman's curly soft hair as he lowered his head. Katherine stepped forward and gave him a sympathetic pat on the shoulder. "How 'bout we walk to the crick and rest a spell?" she suggested soothingly. She held out her thin, sun-browned arm and Norman clutched her hand. Work-worn fingers connected and Gus watched his parents saunter off along the cool, oak-shaded path toward the woods.

Gus folded his legs under him and sat on the ground. Nothing this serious had ever happened that he could remember. He wanted to know more and wondered if he would get into trouble if he followed. Gus craned his neck. They were out of sight. He got up, looked over his shoulder in the direction of the house, then back at the path his folks had taken. Gus decided to follow them because he wanted to learn more about the dead President of the United States.

Gus crouched behind a tree and felt sneaky as he watched Norman sit on a fallen log. Norman lifted his leg and put one knee under his dark-stubbled chin, removed his dark-framed glasses and unbuttoned the top two buttons of the blue cotton work-shirt Katherine had made from an old tablecloth. Gus listened to their quiet words.

"He would've wanted to see the end of the war," Norman said, staring across the sunlight-spotted water. "It's so close, now." He hooked his thumbs into his suspenders.

Katherine sat side-saddle next to him. She patted his drawn-up knee then squeezed his callused hand and massaged his neck.

Gus was afraid to breathe, afraid they'd hear him. He stood frozen in the dogwood blossoms sprinkled beneath his feet and felt like a cauliflower-eared dog.

"The honeysuckle smell's strong," Norman whispered. Gus sniffed automatically allowing the sweet fragrance to fill his nostrils. When he saw Katherine lean closer into Norman, Gus began looking for a way to escape. This was obviously a personal moment for his parents.

Katherine stared into the water. "We should come here more often."

"How many times have I asked you to come down here with me?" Norman asked. He put his hand on her chin and turned her face to his. "You say you're too busy or too tired or . . . or anything else to put me off. I miss the happy times, the gratifying quiet times, Katherine. I miss *us*."

"I know," she said, turning her face away. "The mill takes all our time and lately I've not had enough time for you. The guilt I feel burdens me so much that at times I feel like jumping from a mountaintop. I haven't felt like talking or laughing or even living." Katherine looked into Norman's eyes. "It's because I'm so worried about this baby."

Gus felt awkward and knew he couldn't move a muscle or they may hear him. He silently prayed they wouldn't kiss. He knew that grownups did that sometimes.

Katherine went on, "I'm sorry for all of this, but right now I don't want to fuss about it. I want to feel good inside." She raised her arm and her fingers brushed sawdust from Norman's tousled hair. She turned her head and looked into the cool, deep creek. "I'll try to be more thoughtful to your needs." The curve of her belly pressed against her dress. She looked down lovingly at the arch and stroked it.

Norman smiled, and with a gentle gesture, rested his hands on top of hers. He lifted his gaze from Katherine's midriff and stared at the rippling water. "I wouldn't trade this for all the sophistication in the world," Norman said, rising off the log. He walked to the water's edge and crouched down.

"Nor would I," she said in a whispery, small voice. Norman turned to face her. Their eyes met in a way that Gus felt was perfect understanding between his folks. His eyes scanned the surroundings looking for a way to steal away. Instead of talking about the president, they're talking private stuff, he thought. I shouldn't be here, but I can't move! He peeked around the tree again.

Katherine leaned forward and picked up a small rock, then tossed it into the water. They stood closely and stared down as the circle smoothed. As the water calmed Gus could see their reflection as they stood there, arms around each others' waists and for a long moment he felt happy to be there, just to feel this moment with his folks. The comfortable feeling ended though when Norman brushed Katherine's hair back and kissed her on her ear.

"You're so beautiful right now. Can you see yourself . . . your glow, in the water? I love you Katy," Norman said, not looking at her, but staring into the water.

Katherine answered with her smile. "We haven't had a quiet, private time together for such a long time. I feel warm and for the first time in months I feel a desire stirring inside me. A need to be with you." She snuggled closer to him and he held her.

Gus silently prayed this moment between his parents would quickly pass and thanked God when he heard the clanging and squeaking of an old motortruck chugging down the rutty road. Gus looked in the direction of the noise and then back at his folks.

"Sounds like we're about to be blessed with another load of hardwood," Norman said, his tone becoming businesslike. As he let his arms fall from Katherine's waist, Norman turned and faced the rumble, then looked at his wife, down at the glasses he held in his hands, up into her face. He put on his glasses. "I'd better get back to the mill." He kicked at the dirt halfheartedly.

"Please don't go away. Stay with me. Stay because I need you, Norman."

"Katy," Norman said, looking toward the mill, "the truck needs to be unloaded."

"Norm," Katherine said, grasping her husband. "Do you remember when we rushed down here to make love after we were married? When you used to kiss me half to death and hug the devil out of me?"

"How could I forget?" he said, pressing closer against her, stroking her hair, her shoulders.

Gus closed his eyes and wished he was back at the house. He knew the right thing to do now was to try to escape, but when he turned to dart away, a branch snapped, and to Gus, it seemed to echo through the entire forest. He froze, looked up. His folks hadn't heard, thank God.

Calvin's truck horn blared again. "I need to be up there, Katy."

Katherine flung her arms against her side. "Of course you do!" she said and shook her head.

"Katy. . . . "

"Timber Hills is overshadowing our personal needs," she cried out then threw her hands out in front of her. She opened her mouth and then closed it again. "Just never mind," she said despondently and headed toward the house. Gus heard Norman start to say something about putting meat on the table, but Katherine stopped him and said over her shoulder, "Norman, this business is getting your thinking all out of focus."

"Timber Hills is our continuance, Katy," he blurted out. "It will never come before you or the children, but it keeps us from sinking into poverty."

Gus felt sorry for his mother, but Norman was right. The sawmill was their sole support, and Norman had worked hard to get the business off the ground.

Gus jumped when Katherine hollered and pointed, "Norman, look! Cattywampus 'cross the holler." Darting forward, Katherine stumbled over a tree root and almost fell.

Frowning, Norman reached out to steady her. His voice was patient, steady, "Whatever you see, it isn't worth falling and hurting yourself over."

"Norman?" she said, clutching his arm. "Mitch and Elsie aren't back from the funeral yet are they?"

"They won't be back till Thursday."

"But, honey! Isn't that Mitch Wampler's tractor . . . darn, I lost sight of it." Her head bobbed as she strained to look. "It just went over the hill."

"I was over there earlier today to feed the livestock and the tractor was there. More than one farmer owns a red tractor, Katy."

"But theirs was almost new," she said.

"Okay," Norman said. "I'll stop by the Wampler's farm after Cal and I get the truck unloaded."

Gus held his breath. Billy Ray wouldn't be stupid enough to ride around on that tractor he stole! Suddenly Gus was hoping that Billy Ray would get himself hidden in the trees before his folks figured out who it was. Why was he siding with a thief? Gus felt ashamed, but that didn't stop the feeling.

At last Katherine and Norman were out of voice range and Gus breathed a sigh of relief. "I won't do that again," he said aloud, shaking his head. "They act funny. I don't want to grow up," he said.

Gus trudged home trying to erase his parents mushy words from his head. He had wanted to hear about FDR. He closed his eyes, sighed, and when he opened them, Norman and Katherine were out of sight. I think I'll help unload that truck, Gus thought, and hurried home.

• CHAPTER 4 •

Gus could have taken his ease against a tree or run off to play the child he was, but instead he analyzed, dissected and sifted through every move the men made getting the timber off the truck.

"That's fine cargo," Norman said, eyeing the flatbed. "Shouldn't take more than an hour to off-load. What is it, 'bout a thousand board feet of black walnut?"

"The best the hills have to offer," Hawkins answered. "Ready to tackle down?"

"With might and mane," Norman hollered out, boosting himself onto the trailer. "Bring the crane over, boys."

Gus perched near the truck and felt an admiration wash over him as he watched his dutiful father rack and strain, taxing all his energies to make a better life for his family.

"Hey," Calvin said, pointing to Gus, "There's your next boss."

Norman grinned and said, "He's headed that way, Cal."

"Can I help, Pa?"

"Not this time, son, but stick around and watch how it's done."

"Fine boy you got there, Norm," Calvin said.

"The best the hills have to offer," Norman said, smiling. He pulled off his hat with one hand and wiped his forehead with the other. "Too bad about FDR," he stated flatly.

Calvin stood wordless, nodding his head. "Heard yesterday."

"Shorty Peeler had to drive into town yesterday for some shoe laces. Hard to climb a tree with unfastened boots, you know. He heard about it there."

Norman shook his head, then asked, "How's the crew doing, Cal? Any complaints?"

Calvin raised his arm and swore while digging for a wood tick imbedded in the center of his armpit.

"When was the last time you took a bath? A year ago last Christmas?" Norman asked.

Calvin lowered his arm and grinned playfully, the broad smile widening his homely face. "I belly-flop into the creek now and then," he said, laughing, then said more seriously, "Hank Kendall says the tar paper roof leaks when it rains. He's awfully ill tempered these days. Sure has a nasty constitution. Gives Elmer a hard time, too, and we couldn't ask for a better chokerman. Would get rid of ol' Hank, by golly, but he's the best lead notcher I've ever seen, especially in the heavy-topped and leaning timber."

"Intuition tells me you're making a mistake by not firing Hank," Norman stated. "The man spells trouble. I should keep the thought unvoiced. You know what you're doing out there. That's what I pay you for."

"I try to do right, Norm," Calvin said. "You're like family to me. If you want the man discharged, just give me the word."

"Let's see what happens," Norman told him. "He's got a whole slew of kids down in Mississippi. See if you can get the roof fixed, Cal. Tarwater has a four-cylinder motor and generator for sale. It would give you a refrigerator and electric lights out there. Those men work hard. They deserve a few extras." Norman pulled a tick from his ankle. "Damn! You're breeding the little bastards. They're thick as flies on cow pie this year." He pulled his socks up over his pant cuffs. "We need a good crew to get that woodlot felled and bucked." He took off his glasses, pulled his hanky from a back pocket and cleaned the lenses. "We need Hank right now. I signed a contract stating we'd have it done by the eighteenth of July. Can't afford anyone to get peeved and run off. Unless something else comes in pretty quick, this is the last job we have lined up. Things aren't looking too good for us, Calvin. Katy's not been herself," he finally admitted. "She's been mighty foul-natured lately."

"Sorry to hear, Norm. We're doin' the best we can, you know that."

"No doubt about it. You always have."

Calvin offered a comradely smile then hopped off the truck. "Well, that's done," he said.

"Irving got the fencepost contract last month," Norman said. "Ira's a gambler. Ain't afraid to take chances. His logging company took a turn for the worse last year when George Clinch started that fire. Destroyed a lot of their machinery. I reckon he's hurting like everyone else in the business, but the scoop is he's fanning out."

Calvin faced his employer squarely. "You've got a long face today, Norm. You're beginnin' to look old and worn. Can I do anything to help?" When Norman didn't look up, Calvin went on, "I know you're not one to ask for financial help, Norm, but I'd do anything in the world for you."

"You know me pretty well, don't you, Cal?"

"I know your pride was damaged when your father-in-law . . . "

"Ah yes. The prominent attorney, Henry Ashford," Norman said sharply. "Yes, he gave me the money for the sawmill. Katherine begged me to accept the money, not because she was in favor of clear-cutting—in fact, it saddened her to see the big trees cut—but because she wanted me and her father to have a common interest."

"And you agreed, only on the condition that the loan would be paid off, with interest, in two years," Calvin said. "You even insisted on throwing in the title to your old Buick until the loan was paid back. You should let folks help you when they want to, Norman."

"It gets me sore when Katy's father keeps providing for us. He spoils the boys with ice cream and candy . . . "

"Hey, Pa," Gus said. "That ain't so bad."

Norman looked quickly at Gus. "Run on, Son. We're finished here."

Gus bowed his head and reluctantly started to leave. When Norman leaned over to inspect the wood, Gus moved in a little closer to have a look, too. He was glad that Norman didn't yell at him for disobeying. He wasn't eavesdropping, Gus was only interested in learning all he could about the timber business.

"Like I was saying," Norman continued, "Ashford's always giving us his hand-me-downs."

"Well," Calvin said, "He's only trying to help."

Norman shrugged. "After Hannah died Henry nearly cleaned out the house of all their furniture. He said he couldn't bear looking at it. To be honest, Cal, Henry Ashford makes me feel second-rate. Katy just don't understand." Norman shook his head and grinned. "Calvin, you son-of-a-gun, when you gonna start minding your own damn business?"

Lifting his cap, Calvin scratched his head and cleared his throat. Birds fluttered in the honeysuckle bushes. "Had to repair the skidway this mornin'," he said. His size-thirteen-boot scuffed through the dirt. "Won't have to use it much longer, now. Was hopin' it'd hold out." His big black eyes stretched toward the woods' deep shadows.

"You got those trees off the slope, already?" Norman asked.

"Most of 'em." Calvin cleared his throat again.

"Well, looks like I need to shut up and let you run your crew just the way you're doing." Norman shoved his drooping glasses back up on his nose. "I meant to tell you a few days ago, Calvin. You're doing a good job."

Calvin smiled with his eyes. "I feel like I should be doin' more. You and Katherine have always been good to me. I owe you a lot, you puttin' up with me an' all."

Norman frowned. "What do you mean by that?"

"Me being a Negro. You heard the way Arnold Delvine talked. Others feel the same."

Norman gasped. "You're a Negro? Holy Cow, I hadn't even noticed. Damn! You *are* black as night, aren't you?" Their laughter rang through the woods and both men glanced up when Gus joined in. "Reckon I couldn't do it without you, Cal," Norman said.

Leaning his back against a tree, Gus lifted one foot and rested it on his other knee. He faulted himself at times, listening to the adults talk, soaking in what he could, hoping for more knowledge about mill operations. He felt good being a part of it.

Calvin leaned against the truck's cab door. "Don't really know what to do about Hank Kendall. We be hurtin' without him and he knows it. He's liked about as much as a weed in a flower patch, but dang, he works like a horse."

"Seems like it's always the weeds that grow the best. I'd like to quit holdin' sore feelings over him, but a dead skunk still stinks. Know what I mean?"

Calvin took off his cap again and swiped his forehead. "Man, I get hot under the collar just thinking about his wickedness. He's stupid as shit, but strong as an ox. The others step out of his way when he walks through. There's a peckin' order in camp, and six-foot-six Hank Kendall is chief rooster."

"Don't know how he can stand up straight and face people." Norman agreed.

"It's hard for an empty bag to stand upright," Calvin grumbled.

"Them union boys been prowlin' around lately, Cal?" Norman asked.

Calvin leaned over, picked up a sliver of wood and excavated an obviously annoying bit of meat caught between his teeth. "Ain't seen 'em since last month. Don't want no unionism." He twitched his jaw and spit. "Hank got into a vulgar jawin' with 'em. Stuck his gun right up the nostril of the headman. Worries me, too. Ol' Rooster—that's what the boys call him—keeps that pistol cocked."

"Well, we don't want them union boys telling us what time to get up, go to bed or how much wood to cut. I don't condone the gun, Calvin, but maybe Rooster scared 'em away for awhile."

Calvin paced back and forth obviously in thought, then slouched against a tree, his hands latched behind his head. "Hope so," he stated flatly.

"Where we cutting after this job, Cal?"

"The timberland over near Harper Cove. There's at least nine thousand board feet per acre on that land. Mostly yellow poplar, some basswood, a little maple. Timewise it'll work out fine with the completion of this job." He bent forward and beat dirt from the knee of his well-worn overalls.

"Well, guess you know your business, Cal. Just hope something else comes in soon. Arnold Delvine was a Godsend. Will be glad to get that property deed in my hands."

Calvin coughed. "Don't trust the man."

"I sort of felt you and Delvine hadn't hit it off well," Norman joked.

"I'm serious, Norm. Somethin' sneaky about him, like a chicken thief," Calvin said.

Norman shrugged. "Just the salesman in him. Anyway, he'll be sending the rest of the paperwork on that fifty-two-acre parcel we looked at south of here. It was tough coughing up the five-hundred-twenty-dollars down payment. Just don't know how we're gonna keep goin', Cal. Katy and I applied for another five-hundred dollar loan at the bank day 'fore yesterday." He scratched his head. "Proud to have that Delvine property. It's a fine piece of land. I got big plans for the profits I'll make on that one."

"You didn't really take the time to think about it, Norm. Shucks, you hardly even read the contract. You could have been signing a death certificate."

"I know when I see a lucky deal."

"Could mean it's too good to be true."

"You were with me, Cal, and saw for yourself. The price is well under what we paid for the Harper Cove property."

"You're the one who signs the contracts. I hope you're right."

"It's bound to work out. The good Lord watches after folks like us. We'll get plenty of board feet from that parcel. I did it for Katy and the boys, Cal."

"Pert near too good to be true," Calvin repeated.

"I almost have to agree. Two hundred less than Harper Cove, and more timber." Norman braced his back against the tree, dragged a hanky from his pocket and blew sawdust from his nose. "What supplies are you needing at camp, Cal?"

With his large, square hand, Calvin reached deep into his left pocket and drew out a rumpled sheet of paper. "We be needin' a couple boxes of thirty percent stumpin' powder, big rolls of black fuse, and a tin box of percussion caps."

"Well, take the vehicle with the best springs to haul it," Norman cautioned, "and," he glanced over at Gus, "take the kid. He'd likely want to ride along."

"You bet!" Gus shouted.

Lifting her arm in greeting, Katherine wibble-wobbled over to the men. A colorful sunbonnet was tied loosely under her neck.

"Well if it ain't Paul Bunyon, himself," she said. "How you doin' Cal? Sakes alive! You look all beat out."

Calvin's mouth formed a spacious grin. "I'm fine as frog's hair, Katy." Calvin gave her a friendly pat on the arm then quickly drew his hand away, looked at it and apologized for the dirt.

"How's Abby? I haven't seen her in a coon's age," Katherine asked.

"Abby's prettier than ever, Katy, too pretty for me."

"You got that right," Norman teased. "When you gonna ask that little woman to marry you?"

Calvin grinned and wiped sweat from his forehead. "It's gonna be a long, hot summer," he said, then, "And that reminds me. I heard Henry tellin' someone in town that he intends to put air conditionin' in."

"Hey, I heard about that," Norman said. "One of those new Fedders. It's an electrically refrigerated system that sits on your window sill and plugs in like a radio."

"Mama would have loved it," Katherine said.

Calvin smiled at her. "Missy, I wish your mama could be here to enjoy it." He looked at Norman and said, "They say you don't need no building alterations or water connections for them new air-coolin' machines."

Norman huffed. "It'd be nice to have one, but darn, they cost nearly two-hundred dollars from what I hear."

Calvin answered, "Yeah, that's why Humphrey Bogart advertises them. Takes someone with money to be able to afford one."

"Daddy works hard for his money. He started out with nothing, paid his own way through college. Now he's a hardworking attorney."

"And the best there is, Missy."

"Thank you, Calvin, and Abby is more like family than Daddy's maid. Mama loved her."

Calvin nodded. "Well, I best get back to work," he said.

Katherine started back to the house then turned to face them. "I overheard you talking about your next cutting," she said. "We need to get started on that just as soon as possible, Norm. Our mill payment to daddy was late last month and it's not looking good this month, either, with the compensation insurance due. That's a hundred seventy-two dollars, you know."

"We'll discuss your father's loan later."

"You still get all riled up about the debt. Sometimes I wish I'd never talked you into accepting father's money for the mill!" she snapped, and headed toward the house.

"Thought you were nappin'," Norman called after her.

"Too hot," Katherine yelled over her shoulder. "Air's so thick you can see it. I kept gettin' twitches in my stomach." She faced them and laced her fingers over her belly. "Baby don't like the heat."

Norman pushed his glasses up and a shining grin flashed across his face. "Can't be too soon for me," he beamed.

Gus's gaze slid over his mother's bulging body, then, embarrassed, he quickly looked the other way. When he turned back he saw Katherine staggering like a drunkard toward her tree nursery.

"She okay?" Calvin asked Norm.

"She's on pins and needles fretting about the baby. She feels something's wrong with it."

"I'd say all mothers-to-be have the same concerns," Calvin reassured.

Norman gave him a quick glance. "How would you know?"

"Yeah, that's right. I don't have myself a mammy and nine little niggers, yet."

"Let's ride up to the camp, Cal. I want to see how the crew keeps busy when their boss ain't around."

"I'd like that. You can see some of the changes we've made. Come on, Gus," Norman said.

After they'd packed themselves into Calvin's old truck, Norman said, "I need a break from the mill, Calvin. Little things are getting to me that shouldn't."

"I reckon you ain't 100 percent lately."

"That obvious?"

"Yup."

Calvin Hawkins walked Norman and Gus around the camp and showed them modifications his men had made. "We're proud of it," he said.

"Got to keep them smiling," Norman said. "They're the ones who keep me in business."

"Look at 'em all behavin'. They didn't even know I was gone," Calvin said.

"Tim . . . ber!" someone shouted, and the men popped their heads up to make sure they weren't in a precarious spot.

"Who's that?" Norm asked, gesturing toward a young man who was approaching them. "He's just a kid. I don't recognize him."

"Don't know," Calvin answered. "He's got a lean and hungry look. I'll bet you he's hunting for work."

"I don't bet when I know I'll lose," Norman said.

The boy trekked up to the men and stretched out his long-fingered hand. "The name's Spelling. Harvey Spelling. I'm in need of a job. I'm dependable and a hard worker." He must have seen Norman and Calvin looking at the shoulders of his shirt. He brushed at the black and white spots. "Looks like bird shit, doesn't it?" The boy said, still wiping at the splotches.

"You've been splattered good," Norman said. "Your face is a little dirt-smudged too."

The boy swiped haphazardly at his face. "And my ratty clothes smell bad, but that doesn't mean I'm not a good worker."

"Just means you need to jump into the creek," Gus said, and they all laughed, plainly easing the boy's discomfort.

"I am a little grubby," the young man said, humbly, more relaxed.

Gus looked at Spelling's canvas knapsack, probably full of necessities, slung over his bony shoulder. Chin-length sandy hair looked unkempt, but his eyes were honest.

"You been sleeping in a bird cage, boy?" Calvin asked.

"I must have nodded off under a nest last night." The boy propped his foot on a tree stump and tied his sole-worn boot.

Gus laughed, his eyes unable to ignore the white and black shower of bird dung covering the boy's shoulders and hair. Harvey Spelling smiled at Gus.

"The logging continues year round," Calvin said. "Ten hours per day, two hundred seventy-five to three hundred days a year. The balance is accounted for by Sundays, holidays, shutdowns for repairs, bad weather, inventories or other unfortunate delays."

Gus watched Harvey Spelling's unwavering gray eyes as he listened to Calvin give the young man a pre-hire lecture. He noticed Norman was studying the boy's face, also.

"The wages are two dollars and fifty cents a day plus meals, which don't amount to more than a mess of beans sometimes. It ain't fun. There's no electricity and the camp is crude. Work strenuous and harsh. We start cutting at the top of the slope and gradually work downhill so the skidding is done through the standing timber. It requires building a skidway. You'll learn to set up a new camp in twenty to forty minutes. I'm the boss here, and don't tolerate no horsing around. One crew is expected to fell and buck three to five thousand board feet a day. You're a little young, ain't'cha, boy?"

"No, Sir, I just *look* young. I turned fifteen yesterday."

The boy dug at his ear, then laid the knapsack on the ground between his long legs. "I'd appreciate the opportunity to prove myself."

"Whether you go to work or not, you're welcome to clean up here," Norman offered.

Calvin pinched the boy's upper arm. "I'm not sure you can handle it, son. You're kind of puny-like. Takes muscle. Most of my jacks are husky and swing a double-bitted ax as though it were a ping-pong paddle."

Calvin looked at Norman. "What do you think, Norm?"

"You want my approval? I leave the ball in the supervisor's hands," Norman mumbled.

Calvin looked at the boy who was looking back at him. "Excuse us for a moment, son. The owner of the company and me . . . we need to talk in private." He peered down at Gus. "Show the man around."

"If I asked you what you thought, what would you say?" Calvin asked Norman while Gus and the young man wandered around the well-organized camp.

Norman shrugged. "I'd probably be a little reluctant to hire someone this young, but I guess I'd say give him a chance to show his capacity."

"Sir," the boy yelled in a treble voice. "I can drive that tractor!" He pointed to the Allis Chalmers.

Calvin's dark eyes looked from Norman to the kid. Calvin raised his arm and rubbed the back of his neck. "The plain truth is," he said, ambling back over to the boy, "I *do* need more beefy men for the strenuous work. No use in wasting a burly, able-bodied man behind a tractor's steering wheel. We've got two tractors. A fifteen-horsepower Caterpillar and a forty-thousand pound HD-19 Allis-Chalmers. It has a hydraulic torque converter and hydraulic steering, but the steering's been foozlin' out a lot, lately. That's why it's parked. Which one do you want to drive?"

"I'll take the Chalmers. I'm pretty good at mechanics. I'll take a look at that steering."

"Where ya from?" Norman asked, after Calvin had made his decision to hire the boy.

"Chicago."

"You look German," Norman commented, "with your fair complexion."

"Scandinavian ancestry, Sir."

Calvin reached behind the boy and grabbed an ax-like tool. He held it up between him and the kid. "You know what this thing is?"

"It's a pike pole, Sir."

Calvin leaned over and picked up another tool. "And this?"

"That there's a grapple hook," the boy answered correctly.

"Up at five," Calvin directed. "Breakfast five-fifteen and work starts at six promptly. You can sleep in there," Calvin instructed, pointing to the smallest of five tar-papered, rough lumbered structures. "Them the only pants you own?"

"These are lasty britches, sir."

"Well, what're ya waitin' for? Your funeral? Git your gear put away. And remember. *You're* the *boy*, not me."

"Thank you, sir. I'm grateful." The three men shook hands.

"What did you say your name was?" Calvin asked.

"Spelling. Harvey Spelling." He turned and zealously walked toward his sleeping quarters, looked over his shoulder and said, "By the way, Mr. Hawkins, I never was prejudiced about the coloreds, sir, and I won't dissatisfy you."

"I liked his honesty and enthusiasm," Norman said on the way back to the mill site.

"You know," Calvin said, "I don't think that boy will disappoint us."

Gus walked into the greenhouse and saw his mother watering the seedlings. "The little plants are nearly ready to be set into the ground," he said.

Katherine smiled. "I feel good about replanting the forest. The National Recovery act says cleared land has to be replanted, but even if a law didn't exist, we'd do it anyway." She sighed heavily and turned to Gus. "Sometimes my head feels like it's being pulled apart, one side arguing with the other," she said. "I just wonder if we'll ever get ahead."

"Don't we make any money from the sawmill?" Gus asked.

"At times the mill work brings in profits, but usually more goes out than comes in. Now there's the loan at the bank for the land your father just bought from Delvine."

"I know, Mama. I'm sorry it's not better for you." Gus didn't know what else to say. He just wished she didn't feel so blue. He lifted his head and gazed toward the woods. It rang with the clear resonant notes of biting axes.

Katherine clicked her tongue. "Lordy, Lordy," she mumbled, lifting the bonnet from her damp hair and placing it on the work bench beside her. "Sometimes I hate the timbering business." With the back of her hand she wiped trickles of sweat from beneath her chin.

Gus silently watched as she watered and gently tended the tiny branches of the new, green life and listened as she told him stories of how the folks in the area once hated the logging business. "The loggers went into town and started fights, getting drunk, sinning like crazy." She gazed languidly through the opened doorway. "It's an indecency to steal away what God grew," she said, "but then I think of Crawford Wheeler, your father's grandfather who was in the sawmill business and come through just fine."

"Pa knows his way around a mill and loves the business," Gus told her.

"I believed it could work for us and wanted your father to be happy continuing his family's business." She turned to face Gus, cocked her hip and rested her hand on it. "And now you're showing an interest in the work and frankly, Gus, that tickles your daddy to death."

"What about you?" Gus asked.

Katherine turned back to the plant life and held up a small oak seedling. "This one's for me," she vowed, not answering. She removed a yellow ribbon from her almost-as-yellow hair and knotted it around the little tree. Her loosened tresses fell freely around her face. The corners of her mouth drooped. "We won't cut this one down. I promise."

With a sigh Gus stared out into the vacant space where recent logging had taken its toll. His eyelids lowered, shutting out the hole. His mother's view of logging gave him a different perspective. He was torn between the two views.

Katherine looked into her son's eyes. "I don't like looking at the death of a forest," she said tearfully. "To be honest, I wish neither of you boys had an interest in the mill."

Gus felt helpless and disappointed that his mother saw their business in that perspective. He wondered if it was because of the baby. She'd mentioned several times that she was worried about the baby's health. How can a mother know if a baby inside her stomach is sick? Woman talk was something he couldn't understand. When he looked up, he saw Norman stepping through a flock of dust-bathing chickens. A large speckled hen fluffed up her feathers and hissed at him. Norman ruffled Gus's hair then straggled up behind Katherine and put his work-calloused hands on her shoulders.

Without turning she pressed her cheek against the coolness. "Mmm. Your hand feels good." Gus quickly turned to leave but Katherine asked him to roll up the watering hose and gather up some of the replanting tools. He hurried along as fast as he could. He didn't want to get stuck listening to grown-up talk again.

"I wish you could look at the tree's beauty instead of imagining it bucked and in a millpond," Katherine said to Norman, fondling the small oak tree.

"We've had this conversation hundreds of times, Katy. There's always been two angles in the logging business. One commercial, the other personal appeal. This is our life. We have to merge our two different views."

Gus glanced up at his mother and wished she could do just that. He stepped outside the greenhouse and watched the men busy at work, hoisting logs onto the carriage, examining randomly that they made their way to the band saw, the edger, trimmer, dip tank. God, he loved sawmilling as much as his father did. Gus rubbed his eyes leaving dirt smudges across the bridge of his nose. He turned back to his folks and saw Norman drop his hands from Katherine's shoulders.

"I'm tired of the unending bickering, Katy," Norman said, and tucked his thumbs into his suspenders. "Why don't we . . . " He leaned in close to Katherine's ear and whispered, "Let's go down to the creek."

Katherine cast a glance in Gus's direction, then back at Norman. She placed her palms flat on the workbench and turned her face from him, but Gus knew she wasn't through. He hated it when she kicked up a shindy. Norman had offered a truce. Why couldn't she cast it aside? He'd heard it all so many times.

Gus rolled up the hose while Norman shuffled his feet around and listened to Katherine's grievances. Gus saw Norman pull out his handkerchief, clean his glasses, put them back on, take them off and clean them again.

"Now we're in debt up to our chins because you wanted to be as big as Weyerhaeuser!" Katherine went on. "You know, Norm, sometimes I wonder if . . . "

"That's enough," Norman interrupted sharply, putting his glasses back on for the third time. "There's just no call to go on with this."

Not looking up, Katherine nodded. "I have dish towels to hem." She smiled and gently touched Gus's arm as she brushed past him but Gus knew the business gnawed on her and he prayed she'd have the strength to carry on.

Dusk was on the road when Calvin Hawkins drove off, honking and waving his sweat-shiny muscle-bulging arm out the truck window.

Katherine shouted, "Come to supper tomorrow evenin'."

"What'cha havin'?" Calvin asked.

"Gizzards and grubs!"

"I think I'll pass on the offer. Buster's cookin' ham hocks and beans."

"Count your blessings!" Katherine yelled.

"That won't take long!" Calvin hollered back, and honked the truck's horn again.

Norman hooked her elbow. "Gizzards and grubs? That's not what that spacious HOLE out there's all about!" He gestured sharply toward the clear-cut with his other hand.

Gus knew his mother's remark was unfit, but didn't like it when he saw Norman gripping her arm. She jerked her arm from his hold. "Yes, Norman, I know. We rape the forest so we have the extra money to put *steak* on the table. It takes five minutes to eat a steak but forty years for a tree to grow back. It just doesn't seem right, does it?"

"Kath . . . "

She took a quick step away from him and reached for a fresh bucket of milk.

"I'll get that," Gus said. He felt his stomach knot up as he watched Katherine plod on into the house. "When are we cutting the woodland Delvine sold us?" Gus asked, wishing to soften Norman's temper. He surprised himself with the question, but understood that it *was* their livelihood, and he was a big part of it.

"That timber is still a few years away from being cut, Gus. We've got Harper Cove yet. In this business you have to plan way ahead, and I have a feeling this Delvine timber will be our deliverance." Norman opened the creaky screen door for Gus and asked, "Doesn't Gilbert have the milking chores this week?"

Gus poured the milk into the electric cream separator. "Suppose to," he answered as he watched his mother slip off her house slippers and peer down at her swollen ankles.

"I never puffed up like this when I was expectin' the twins," she muttered.

Norman started to console her, then picked up a paper bag on the floor next to the knitting basket. "What's in the sack?"

Gus cringed. He knew Norman would be upset when he learned the gift was from his grandfather. Before Katherine answered, Gus said, "Swimming' trunks. Grandpa bought them for us. We cleaned his yard."

Norman raised his eyebrows and looked at Gus.

"For the yard work we did over there," Gus said quickly, knowing Norman's discomfort when Henry bought them things. Gus couldn't understand why Norman felt second-rate to Henry Ashford. Not many men in town owned a lumber mill.

"It was an agreement between Daddy and the boys," Katherine added in the boy's defense. "Don't you remember?"

"Billy Ray skinny dips," Gus said, "but Gilbert and I don't," he lied.

Katherine grinned and blushed. "Billy Ray's the type that would," she whispered.

Norman smiled too, and whispered something into Katherine's ear.

Gus saw his mother's face turn dark red. "No we didn't!" she loud-whispered.

Norman took off his glasses, held them in his hand. "Yes, we did," he said, then peered down at the trunks. "I thought they wanted the shirts with Coca-Cola bottles on them."

"The Coca-Cola shirts were $1.89 each. That would make pretty high wages," Katherine answered. "Daddy offered to buy the shirts for their birthday."

"We can buy our childrens' clothes!"

Gus felt his head throbbing as he faded into his room and closed the door. He wanted to cry, yell, run away from all the family pressures. Gus flopped down on the feather bed feeling like his head would explode. He clenched his jaw and covered his head with the pillow. Where was Gilbert, he wondered, then remembered he'd gone to town to look for a job. Gus could hear his folks arguing and covered his ears. It was always about not having enough money, the new loans at the bank, all the bills. Gus sat up, threw his pillow and opened his bedroom door. Norman was stomping angrily from the kitchen and Katherine had her hand over her mouth.

"You okay, Mom?" Gus muttered, while Norman doubled his fist and shoved the screen door open. The door flew open and Gus ran to catch the door so it wouldn't slam shut. Norman stormed toward the mill and Gus sat on the top porch step.

Slowly, visibly weary from the heat, Katherine reached her hands behind her and untied her apron strings. She held the apron in her hands, rubbing the fabric between her thumb and index finger. Gus gazed briefly at the red dust that swirled behind Norman's boots, then stood up, faced his mother and said, "Too much is getting to all of us."

CHAPTER 5

Gus finished picking up the monopoly pieces and Gilbert stacked them into the box. "How long we been playing?" Gus asked.

"Forever!" Gilbert said, stretching out the word. He laid back on his elbows and looked at the grandfather clock in the corner of the room. "How long has Mama been there?" he asked.

Henry Ashford rested his head back on the chaise lounge, pulled out his pocket watch. "Nearly six hours," he answered. "We should hear some news soon," he told the twins.

"How long does it take to have a baby?" Gus asked.

"Sometimes a long time," Henry answered.

Despite a distant rumble of thunder, it was sunny and hot. Gus yawned, rose from his chair and sauntered to the window. The afternoon sun was stretching over the veranda and would soon be pouring into the living room. Gus pulled the drapery cord and the heavy burgundy fabric drew together and shut out the light.

"She had a stomachache this morning," Gilbert said, "but Pa said it wasn't time."

"The cat's had another litter of kittens," Henry said. "Why don't you go check on them? They're in the old tobacco barn."

"Who cares about a bunch of cats?" Gilbert said, leafing through some comic books.

"It'll give you something to do," Henry said, thumping the News-Sentinel with his hand and tossing the newspaper aside. "It's high-time the yellow devils surrendered! A lot of good men have been killed in this God-forsaken war."

"It was a long, hard war," Abby said, refilling their lemonade glasses.

Henry squatted in front of the large walnut radio and began tinkering with the knobs. "Reckon the air waves are in our favor today?"

Gus sat on the edge of the sofa. "No one really knew much about that bomb, did they, Grandpa?" he asked, leaning forward slightly to listen to the broadcast. "I've never heard of nuclear energy."

"Few people have. A new era's commenced," Henry remarked, then stood and said, "We'll see a lot of changes coming." He sat again, this time in an arm-chair across from his colored maid.

"Are you nervous for Mama?" Gilbert asked Henry.

"It's hot in here. Let's all go out onto the porch," Henry said. "It won't be any cooler, but there may be a breeze out there. Come on, Gilbert. You can bring the comic books."

"I'll bring some ice and napkins," Abby said, and moments later when she opened the screen door, she had a full ice bucket in one hand and the porch broom in the other.

"For Pete's sake, Abby. Rest a spell." Henry gestured toward the basket chair. "Sit there."

"Oh, Mr. Ashford, I couldn't do that. That chair was Hannah's favorite."

"She won't care," Gus told her. "Mama sits in it."

Henry gestured again. "Go on, Abby. Hannah would want you to enjoy it as much as she did."

"Thank you, Mr. Ashford," she said, sitting easily in the chair. "This is nice. I know now why Hannah loved it."

Gus watched her appraisingly for a few seconds then turned his head when Henry spoke somberly, "I don't know what I'd do without you, Abby, now that Hannah's gone." He peered out over his land.

Gus felt a wave of sadness wash over him. He hated listening to Henry mourn Hannah. "She was my whole life, Abby." Gus looked at Abby who was nodding mutely.

"Henry, Hannah's been gone nearly ten years now. It's high time you stop grieving."

Henry strolled down the steps and stood under the shady, wisteria-covered archway leading to the courtyard. "Are those rain clouds popping up?" he mumbled, gesturing skyward. He lifted the cold, beaded glass and held it against his forehead.

"I'll bet you'll be glad to get the air conditioner," Gus said. "Pa says it should arrive soon."

"It's been on order for three months. On order like everything else since the war began."

Abby fanned her face with the August issue of *Every Woman's* magazine. "You've also been on the new car list for a couple years, haven't you, Mr. Ashford?"

Tall, still handsome for his years, Henry Ashford nodded and smiled at the maid. Slowly he ambled back up to the edge of the porch. "Hannah would have enjoyed so many new things now that the war's over," he said, resting his arms over the banister. "She used to stand here with me and chitchat about how much she loved this summer-green view with the mauve-blue color of the Smokies beyond." He laughed quietly. "*Mauve-blue*," he said. "She'd say the mountains were *mauve-blue*." He turned sharply toward Abby. "Is that really a color?"

Abby smiled. "I know how much you still miss her, Mr. Ashford. I loved Hannah, too," she said in her quiet voice. "She was my best friend." Abby bowed her head then went on, "Hannah said that next to lookin' into your clear blue eyes, what she loved most was sitting out here in the early mornings looking out over the gentle valleys and little rounded hills. Yes, mauve-blue would be the color of the Smoky Mountains."

Gilbert coughed and rubbed his head. "I'm a little bored with this talk."

Gus glanced up and watched feathery clouds glide above the trees, dragging and creeping along as if tangled in the tops. He took a long drink of the lemonade then pointed and said, "Look at the Holstein cattle down there. They look busy doing nothing."

"Them cows are havin' a picnic in that flower-sprinkled meadow," Abby said.

"Who cares about the cows?" Gilbert said. "Look! There's an airplane. I'm going to be flying one of them some day!" He ran down the steps and out into the yard squinting and peering into the sunny sky. "Hey, Mr. Pilot," he yelled, waving his arms. "Come down here and get me!"

Gus sniffed the air. "Is that stewed rabbit I smell?"

Abby nodded. "You hungry?"

"Yeah, I could eat a bite," Gus said.

"I hate rabbit stew," Gilbert said. "The tomatoes in it make me puke."

"What's eatin' you, boy?" Henry asked.

Gilbert shuffled down the steps and off the porch toward the old tobacco barn.

"Ah," Gus said. "I think he's just worried about Ma." He jiggled the ice in the bottom of his glass, leaned back his head and savored the aroma coming from the kitchen.

The ringing of the telephone stirred the quietness. Abby ran inside to answer and when she came back out she had a big grin on her face. "That was Norman. Katy just gave birth to a little boy."

Gus jumped up and down. "Yippee! I prayed it wasn't no girl!"

Abby wiped her hands on her apron. "The nurses told Norman that Katy needs to rest. He's on his way over here."

"What about the baby?" Henry asked. "Is he okay?"

Gus saw Abby's expression change. "He's small," she said, and nothing more.

Henry sighed, rested his back against a porch column and glanced out over the land. "Norman wanted another boy." He smiled. "It's hard to believe that Katy is grown and has children of her own."

"Is the little baby all right?" Gus asked, gazing into Abby's eyes.

"We don't know yet," she answered and smoothed Gus's blond hair with her fingers. Abby set her lemonade glass on the hand-woven coaster and said, "I know your mama's glad it's all over." She glanced at Gus, then down at the newspaper. "Things will be changing now that the war's over."

"You don't have to change the subject because of me," Gus said. "Mama talked to us about having babies. She told us she felt like the baby in her belly was sick."

Henry cleared his throat. "The U.S. should be lifting its wartime ban on television sets. Won't be needing the electronic factories for war arms now."

"You buyin' a television set, Grandpa?" Gus asked excitedly.

"Mercy! I'd never get rid of you, then," Henry teased, then glanced up when a car caught their eyes. The roof of the green Buick shimmered like water in the sun as it rumbled up the long driveway.

"There he is," Gus said, rising from the step.

"Hi, Papa!" Henry greeted, holding out his hand in congratulations.

Norman removed his jockey cap that Calvin had given him for Christmas, and sat on the warm step near Henry. "Did they tell you?" Norman asked. "The baby isn't doing very well. They want to do some tests." He glanced at Gus then back at Henry. "Hope we aren't hindering your supper none," Norman said.

"Heavens, no," Abby told him, pouring another glass of lemonade. "You'll be stayin', won't you?"

"No," Norman said. "Can't be gone from the mill that long. It's smelling mighty good though," he added, his face turning toward the kitchen door.

"Lordy be, young man," Abby said. "This is a special occasion!"

"I *am* mighty hungry," Norman decided.

Abby picked up the current issue of *Reader's Digest* and began to fan herself. "Can't bear the hot spell much longer. Needin' rain so badly." She glanced upward. "The clouds have gone to tease someone else."

Henry fanned the front of his shirt. "Too hot to wear clothes." He wiped his face with his hanky.

"Watch what you say around the children," Abby said. "There's a platter of cookies in the kitchen," she told Gus. "I just took them from the oven."

Moments later, Gus pushed the screen door open with his foot. He held a white china plate full of warm oatmeal cookies. Abby got up and took the plate from Gus. "I'll set them here, next to the lemonade pitcher," she said. Gus's blue eyes sparkled with enthusiasm as he politely took a cookie.

"Do you want milk with that?" Abby asked, and Gus followed her into the kitchen. Abby opened the turquoise-colored refrigerator, took out the frosty bottle of milk, then took the aluminum ice cube tray from the freezer. Gus could hear Henry asking Norman how the lumbering business was going. Gus peeked out through the screen door and watched Norman twitch his shoulders and shift his weight. Abby glanced at Gus. "Got to defrost this thing," she mumbled, closing the door. "I'll take these outside then we can find a shade tree and talk."

Gus looked out through the door. "Slow, but it'll pick up come cooler weather," Gus heard Norman answer. "The loan payment won't be late this month."

Gus squeezed his eyes shut. "I hope they don't start fussing again," he mumbled between his teeth. "Pa always gets so defensive." He opened his eyes and shook his head. "Why can't they get along, Abby? He gets in a pucker whenever money's mentioned." Gus looked up at Abby. "Does it have something to do with the Ashford wealth?"

"It might," Abby said, "however Hannah and your mother never considered Henry rich, any more than she had considered herself poor when she was growing up in the hollow. They were still the same people. What did money have to do with it? I just can't understand your daddy's insecurity. I remember how pretty Hannah was with her long red hair and green eyes. Henry gave her so much happiness, yet sadness, too. Their eleven short years of marriage were blissful before she found out about the cancer poisoning her body."

"What was she like, my grandma Hannah?"

Abby leaned back her head and closed her eyes. "Well, Hannah Elder and her mother made all their own clothes, grew their own food, and had no reason to leave the hollow. I recall Hannah telling me one day about falling in love with a rich boy named Henry. He lived in a mansion, she said."

Gus's eyes skimmed the surroundings. This *is* a mansion, he thought.

"Hannah told her mother that although she was dirt poor and lived in a tiny two-room log cabin, it didn't stop Henry from loving her. 'I didn't know you were rich,' she told Henry when she learned he lived in a palace. 'I didn't know you were poor,' he answered. Poverty made your grandma strong, gave her far more appreciation of life than any amount of money could bring. Maybe it's strange to be grateful for growing up poor, but that's how both Hannah and I felt. The love that radiated from Hannah Elder and your mama Katy's log cabin bound life together and made love as complete and warm as maple syrup over hot cakes."

Abby reached over and touched Gus's arm. "You okay, honey? You look peaked."

"I just wish I'd known her," he said, then turned back to the door when he heard his father hollering something at Henry.

Abby groaned. "Honey, I don't know why your daddy gets so put out. There's no call for his fumin'. Henry never did nothin' wrong and Hannah loved Norman like her own son. He gets his dander up for nothin'."

Gus looked again and saw Henry quickly rise from his lax position. Gus went to the door and peeked out. Henry's penetrating blue-eyed gaze burned into his son-in-law as he placed his face very near to Normans'.

"You listen to me," Henry said to Norman. "I loaned you that money only because you wouldn't let me *give* it to you! If it still gets your bristles up, consider it a loan to my *daughter*." Henry's voice quieted. "I owe her much more than that stupid sawmill business. I deprived her of sixteen years without a father. My conscience won't let me forget those lost years."

Gus turned his eyes away from them and skirted the yard beyond. The breeze was gone and the heavy, still air shimmered with heat waves. His head snapped back to Henry when his grandfather began to speak.

"I have no doubt that the loan will be paid," Henry said to Norman. "Can we be of the same mind in the meantime? For Katy's sake, and the boys?"

Gus quietly opened the door and walked to the far end of the porch. He peered out over the vast land his grandfather owned and wished his dad and

Henry could understand each another. Gilbert walked around the corner of the house and Gus slid off the porch and sat under a tree with his brother. They looked up and saw Henry lean closer to Norman and say, "The naked truth is, if it was only you, I wouldn't give a shit."

Norman tensed, then faced Henry squarely. "I resent pity," he said. "I'm not an ill-bred hillbilly. I just don't want your charity. Buying that Delvine property will eventually take us from this beggarly financial condition we're living in. If I'd bought it ten years ago, we wouldn't have had to borrow the money from you." Norman loosened his shirt collar and looked away.

"For christsake!" Henry yelled, then apologized to the twins who were now staring at him. With a quieter voice he continued. "You just don't get it, do you? Life should be an effortless give and take. Maybe your grandfather started *his* business from scratch and built it up to a profitable livelihood, but not everyone has the means to do that. Accept the help you're offered, boy. You're part of the family, now." Henry reached out and put his hand on Norman's stiffened shoulder. "You have been for more than ten years. Families work together and help each another. It's not called *charity*." Henry jiggled the unmelted ice in the bottom of his glass, then clunked it down on the banister. "It's called love. L O V E," he spelled.

Norman was silent, his head tilted downward. "I don't know what to say. Maybe I *have* been a lowbrow."

Henry clicked his tongue on the roof of his mouth and squatted next to his son-in-law. "Son, you blink and a lifetime's gone by. Let me be your kin. We'll work out our differences."

Gus sat quietly and drew up one knee and clasped his hands around it. Gilbert put an arm around Gus's neck and pulled him near to whisper in his ear. "Geez. They sure got their vowels in an uproar."

Gus squished spit between his front teeth. "It's *bowels*, not vowels." He looked back up at the men.

Henry looked directly at Norman's profile. "I don't know if you're aware of this, but my mother's folks owned a lumber mill in North Carolina." He glanced away. "Now, let's go pop the hood on that Buick. I heard a rattle when you pulled in."

Norman got up and began walking toward the car. Henry caught up to him. "I'm not good at walking on eggs, Norm," Henry said. "Why can't we feel comfortable with each other? Why do I feel that everything I say to you is a potential stick of dynamite ready to explode?"

"I don't like it any better than you do, Henry."

Without speaking, Gus and Gilbert fanned themselves, drank their lemonade and looked at the men's rear ends poking out over the car engine. "They look like two gophers trying to get into the same hole," Gus said. "Want to play hoop war?"

"Naw," Gilbert said. "I'm goin' down to the creek."

Abby walked to the edge of the porch. "Your grandfather's going to the cold-storage locker tomorrow to get a side of bacon. Does your mama need anything?"

"Could use some sausage," Gus said.

"I remember when we made it ourselves," Abby said. "I always dreaded hog-killing time. Lots of work."

Gus briskly rubbed a leg that had fallen asleep. "Tell me about it." He walked up and sat next to Abby who rested in Hannah's basket chair.

"Law," she said. "I remember it clear as day. The cabin stunk like raw meat for a week after we ground all that pork. My job was ripping cotton rags and wrapping the meat. My mama wouldn't let me dip them in the hot wax because she worried I'd burn myself. Some folks used the intestines for the casing."

"Chitlins," Gus said. "Mama cooks them sometimes." He lifted his hand and brushed hair off his forehead then looked at his father and Henry. "Wish they could get on better."

Abby leaned her head against the back of the chair and closed her eyes. "Your daddy needs to get off his high-horse."

Gus's eyes became distant and he glanced away with a pained expression.

"Gus?" Abby asked. "Is something riling you?"

Gus crossed his arms across his chest. He took a deep breath. "It's our new baby. Mama felt it would come out ailing."

"Mercy! All mothers worry about that, Dear. It'll be a perfect baby and happy as a fly in a pie."

Gus shifted his weight, flailed a hand in the air and pushed himself up out of the deep cushioned chair. "I'm glad it wasn't no girl."

Abby leaned over and touched Gus's arm, her eyes intent on Gus's. "Honey, we're all God's children."

Gus exhaled and shook his head. "I know, Abby. Mama says that, too."

Abby turned her head toward the door when the grandfather clock in the parlor chimed. "Gonna have to wind the clock this evenin'," she said, fanning herself briskly. "Weather's energy-sapping, ain't it?"

• CHAPTER 6 •

It didn't take long for the news of the Wheeler's new son to spread throughout the camp.

"Have you heard?"

"About the Wheeler's new boy? Yeah, we heard awhile ago. They named him Garrett. Too bad there's a hitch in his health."

"He was three weeks premature."

"They say he's the spit and image of Norm. Wheeler wanted another boy. He's got to have the sons to keep the mill running. I'd say we got good reason to uncork the moonshine."

"Just don't forget to get up in the morning," Calvin told them, then took a swig, himself.

Thirty-seven year old Hank Kendall sat and listened quietly as the men prattled on about the new kid. He flipped up the gold-plated lid of his watch and said quietly to himself, "Nine thirty-five. Squaw should be separating the last of the wood."

"Reckon it's pretty quiet around the mill tonight," Calvin stated, "with Norman likely at the hospital, and the end-of-the-war celebration still going on in town."

"No one will be near Timber Hills Sawmill, tonight," Hank Kendall said. He smiled, removed the snuff tin from his pocket and stuck a wad between his gum and cheek. Another grin parted his lips as he twisted his bandana tightly and tied it around his forehead.

The atmosphere was nearly tangible with the smell of body odor and cut plug tobacco as Kendall sprung from the top bunk, his heavy calked boots hitting the ground like a felled oak. The flame from the lamp flickered with the swift air movement when he ducked under a rope strung between two bunks draped with stained socks and shirts.

"Gonna take a walk, boys."

"We ain't stoppin' ya," someone said. "Ain't gonna mess with the Rooster."

The poker game continued in the dim light of the kerosene lamp. Hank Kendall ambled to the corner of the bunkhouse, picked up the canthook and walked out into the resin-smelling, cicada-throbbing woods. The air was thick with humidity and a chirping of night insects as Hank Kendall silently stole through the dry thicket. Just outside of camp, Kendall led one of the mules through the opening of a fenced enclosure and continued toward the sawmill.

"Look at that," he said as he neared the sawmill. "The unmarked lumber's stacked just where Lenny Squaw said it would be," Hank Kendall said as he hooked the mule to the wagon.

"Squaw," he called out quietly. "You here?"

"Over here, cousin."

"Anyone around?" Kendall asked.

"Dead as a door nail," Lenny Squaw answered.

Kendall spit a wad of plug and wiped his mouth with the thumb side of his hand. He watched Squaw lead the donkey to the stack of lumber. "Some of the best red oak God made," Kendall said quietly. "I should know. My sweat scents it." With stout, well-formed arms, the men loaded the timber onto the small wagon.

"Homer know we're comin'?" Kendall asked.

"Meetin' us at the county line," Squaw confirmed.

Good humor abounded at Timber Hills the next morning as workers clustered to offer their congratulations. Echos of celebration infused the air until Norman discovered the missing lumber. He summoned the men to gather round him.

"Did any of you see anything suspicious last night?" he asked.

Lenny Squaw spoke first, "Not me, boss."

"No one was here, Norm," Yates said.

"Maybe we should put a guard out here at night, Norman," another worker said.

Norman shook his head and shrugged his shoulders. He marched over to Squaw and faced him directly. "This is exactly why it's so goddamned important to mark our lumber! Putting the Timber Hills name on this lumber is your job!"

"Yes, sir," Squaw said. "I'll do better, sir."

"Okay, men, get back to work."

PART TWO

The dog days of summer passed with the heat wave giving way to fair weather. With a pencil and tablet at his side, Gilbert took his ease against a cool, mossy tree trunk. Across the top of the first page he'd written, *ELIZABETH TAYLOR*. Below that, he wrote: *I can feel her thirteen-year-old breasts pressed against my chest.*

Gus sat close by and watched his brother roll a pinch of Bull Durham in paper and light it. "Ahh," Gilbert said, after inhaling. "This beats coffee grounds, any day."

"Makes me puke," Gus said. He closed his eyes for a moment and let the warmth of the late afternoon sun wash over him. "What are you writing'?"

"The words I read in *National Geographic*. The piece about the ocean." Gilbert read aloud what he'd written. "I'm on a California beach listening to white-capped waves push onto the shore leaving little shells and seaweed behind. Sea gulls are squealing above the breakers as I pillow Liz's head on my thick, curly chest hair." Gilbert looked up at Gus who was now laughing and slapping the ground with his hands.

"Stop poking fun at me," Gil said and laid the pencil down. "I can dream, can't I?" He glanced back down at the paper. "It could only be better by being real," he said, then yelped when Billy Ray Mudd lunged out from behind them.

"You scared the poop out of me!" Gilbert shouted, springing to his feet. "Next time, give me some warning."

"It's more fun scarin' the shit out of you. You were moanin' an' groanin'. Let me see what you wrote." Billy Ray's quick hand grabbed for the writing tablet and missed.

"Leave him be, Billy Ray," Gus defended.

"Yeah!" Gilbert hollered. "It's none of your business."

"It is if I say," Billy Ray mocked, reaching again for the tablet.

Gilbert tossed the notebook behind him and shoved Billy Ray backwards with both arms. Billy Ray grabbed a tree branch for support then charged forward and knocked Gil from his feet.

"I said to let me see," the older boy said, his weight on top of Gilbert.

"You're a bully," Gus said, not really offering his brother any help. The writing about California had got him into a bum mood.

Billy Ray reached out for the tablet, his fingers barely touching the edge. He stretched enough to grasp it, then hopped off Gilbert and ran.

"Give me that!" Gilbert yelled, charging after the boy.

"Make me!" Billy Ray shouted back. He read aloud as he ran. "I pillow Liz's head on my thick . . . " Billy Ray let out a loud honking laugh.

"I hope you smack into a tree!" Gilbert roared.

Billy Ray slowed to a stop. "You only *dream* about girls. I right-down kiss, *and* touch 'em, too."

"Oh, yeah? Like who?" Gus asked.

"Like Eula Mae," Billy Ray bragged.

"That's no booty," Gilbert said. "Eula lives across the tracks where the coloreds live, and I hear she gives little nigger boys a penny to lip-kiss her," he jeered.

"I think I'll show this to *every*one," Billy Ray bullied, juggling Gilbert's writing tablet.

Gilbert sprinted forward and shoved Billy Ray, causing the older boy to lose his footing. The notebook flew from his hand as he tumbled over backwards. Gus jumped on top of Billy Ray and snatched the tablet. "You better be mindful," he said, "cause I know something that could get you into a heap of trouble." Gus lifted himself off of Billy Ray and started to walk away.

"Yeah, well what? What do you know?"

"Do something like this again and you'll find out," Gus threatened, then doubted that he'd ever really tell anyone that Billy Ray had stolen Mitch Wampler's tractor.

"You're just sayin' that. Hey. You guys mad?"

"Nupe. We won," Gilbert said.

"Like hell," Billy Ray said, loping up to Gil. "I'm goin' to the crick. Wanna go?"

"Last one there sucks cow snot through a straw," Gilbert yelled as they took off running.

"Comin', Gus?" Billy Ray asked, looking over his shoulder.

"I got something I need to do," Gus told them, and headed off in the opposite direction.

The hot smell of the iron told Gus that his mother had taken the bed sheets from the line. He took off his shoes and padded into his room, easing the door shut with his foot. With eyes intent on the door, Gus reached under the mattress for his G.I. Joe billfold and slid it into the rear pocket of his overalls. He stood dead-still, listening, before slithering back out the door, then peeked back in to see if his mother had heard him. This was *his* secret, something he had that his brother didn't share. Katherine continued humming a lively tune as the crisp cotton fabric gathered round her stocking feet.

Gus ran all the way to the post office. He stood in line until Maude Applebee was finished, then moved up to the counter, counted out eight pennies and handed them to Mr. Koontz.

"Howdy, Hopalong! How the folks farin'?" The mail clerk then commented on the nice looking two-tone western style shirt and red felt cowboy hat.

Gus nodded. "It's Roy Rogers," he corrected. "Not Hopalong. I'd like an airmail stamp please."

"So you sat down and wrote a letter, huh, Gus? That's admirable in a young man your age. William Boyd would be proud."

"No, sir. I've been savin' my money so I could join the Superman Fan Club."
His grin went from one wall to the other. "Cost me ten cents to join and eight
cents for the stamp. Been savin' for two months."

"I can understand why you'd be all hopped up over it." He handed Gus the
stamp and watched as Gus dropped his dime and application form into his already addressed envelope.

"No, Mr. Koontz. You see, it ain't enthusiasm. It's necessity because Gilbert
thinks he's top dog. This'll show him. He'll be beggin' me for my secret code."

Mr. Koontz nodded then said, "That's a nice Trigger pistol and holster set
you got riding on your hip."

"Thanks," Gus said as he pranced out of the post office.

Gus walked home ponderously, thinking about the secret he was keeping
from Gilbert. They had never had secrets from each other. It was a weighty decision he'd made, but he felt it was time to differentiate the two of them. It was
always "the twins". He was a little embarrassed over his desire to have the silly
button. Boyhood confronted manhood and the boy in him seemed to be fighting
harder. He could have saved his money for the hog he was buying, and most likely his dad would be disappointed in him, but belonging to the Superman Fan
Club was every boy's dream. He might not *wear* the button, but he'd sure-as-
hell's-fire pull it out in a snap if someone wanted to see it.

"Pa," Gus said, as he perched himself on the edge of the log carrier.

"Get off there, Son. It's not safe!"

Gus pounced down and stood watching the saws spinning. "Can we talk?"

"What is it, Gus," Norman said, a little too loudly, yet his tone was unthreat-
ening. "You see I'm busy here."

"I really need to know something. It's been bothering me."

Norman stuck his pencil behind his ear. "What's that?" he asked.

"Why wasn't Superman allowed to go to war?"

"Hold on a minute, Son. I need to finish guiding this log through the saw."

Gus watched curiously as the carriage returned to its starting position and the
log turned. His eyes glazed in concentration until Norman pushed the kill button and propped up his foot on the platform.

He lowered his gaze to his son, then drew near and repeated, "Why couldn't
Superman get into the service? Now that's a question worth shutting down the
sawmill for."

Hearing the question repeated made Gus feel childish. He scratched his head
and started to walk away, but Norman followed, caught up, and laid his hand on
the boy's shoulder.

Gus turned to face Norman. "Was that a stupid question, Pa?" he asked with
unblinking blue eyes.

Norman smiled. "There is no foolish question."

Gus tilted his head and questioned, "Why're you grinnin' like that?"

"Because it's amazing how much you look like your mother," Norman answered. His gaze lifted momentarily then returned to his son. "Even with all the financial suffering from the stolen timber," Norman said, "I know these are going to be the best years of my life." He dropped his foot, swiped his forehead with his handkerchief, then wiped a smudge of dirt from Gus's face with the hanky. "Superman was ruled four-F."

Gus cocked his head. "Ruled what?"

"A four-F status means he wasn't acceptable for military duty because he flunked the army physical. You see, he had X-ray vision. He looked right through the eye chart and read another chart in the next room."

"Well, I'll be a monkey's uncle!" Gus blurted out. He took in a long, thoughtful breath, let it out quickly in an airy puff, then tossed his hands in the air. "Right through the wall!" Gus's feelings of being trapped between being a boy and a man gnawed on him. "Do you think I'm too old for a Superman button?" he asked his father.

"No, not yet. I think next year you will be. Where's Gilbert?" Norman asked.

"Probably somewhere in the woods dreaming of California," Gus said. "He says he wants to work in one of the aircraft plants out there because he wants to learn how to fly a plane someday."

"His mind's already flying in the wrong direction. He needs to lay aside that harebrained notion," Norman said.

"He has his mind set, but I sure do wish he'd lose sight of California, Pa."

Norman sniffed in disgust. "That boy's sleeping on a volcano."

"Gil's a daredevil."

"With a devil-may-care attitude."

"Can we talk about something else, Pa?"

"Yeah, you're right, son. It only gets me riled." He glanced over Gus's shoulder then said, "Your ma feels uneasy about you boys going off into the woods. There's been some going-ons, you know."

Gus looked out into the shadowed green woods, thought of Billy Ray, then turned back to Norman and said, "With the help of Thelma Jean, the news about Mitchell Wampler's tractor spread like fire on a windy day, didn't it? Tell Ma she has no need to worry, Pa."

Norman smiled and shook his head. "I hope not," he said, patting Gus on the back.

"I'd really like to help today," Gus hinted, his eyes intent on the milling operations.

"I knew you were going to ask," Norman said, glancing into the sun-mirrored band saw blade. He blinked a couple times then said, "Maybe tomorrow." He grinned at Gus then turned and walked to the side of the tool shed. When he turned back, Gus was still standing there, his concentration unwavering. Norman snatched a straw hat off the peg, smacked it a couple times against the building to oust likely insects and resumed his work, hurrying faster, now, because he'd wasted too much time. "Okay, men, set it in motion."

Movement caught Gus's eyes as Katherine lumbered toward the mill. "Here comes Ma," he said and watched Norman raise his arm and smile. "Come on over here," Gus kidded. "Pa could use another hand."

"It's past noon and your dinner's ready."

"I'm afraid we're too busy to eat, Katy." Norman answered. "Save it for supper."

Katherine stood before Norman and said above the noise, "You need to take a rest. You've been making small mistakes lately, sometimes in figuring profit, sometimes in carelessness with the machinery. I worry about you. It's not like you, Norman, a man who's always had all his wits about him."

"Ah, Katy, I'm just extra busy these days. You know that."

Katherine stood there, sharp eyes cast directly on her husband. "Norman," she yelled above the saw's whine, "Take a break. You'll feel better." Gus saw her smile, though there was a stiffness on her face that suggested otherwise.

Norman shook his head. "It's close to contract deadline. My stomach's all gnarled and I couldn't eat."

"You work past sunset each night and watch the sun climb over the hills every morning. You can only do so much."

"Tell that to the creditors. We're going to be late on the note again this month, the insurance is due, we . . . " He lifted his arms into the air. "What's a man to do?"

Katherine rolled her eyes. "Father has offered more help."

"I won't listen to any more of that!" Norman's voice was hard and dry as he curtly tramped away.

Gus glanced uncomprehending at his father and suddenly thought of the Delvine timberland waiting to bring them their relief. "That land is a means to your mother's heart's ease," Norman would tell him each time Gus asked when they were cutting the timber. "I'm holding on to the best until last." Gus couldn't really understand Norman's reasoning. Garrett was sick, they needed money for doctor bills. Why not cut now? Norman wouldn't even go look at it, and Gus reckoned it was for fear of the temptation to cut. Gus turned toward his mother and said, "Dad may need my help, Mama. Save me some dinner."

"Hey, Squaw!" Norman hollered. "Over here!" Norman pointed to a stack of hardwood that was missing the TIMBER HILLS stamp. "Why aren't these stamped?"

"Just been too busy," Lenny said.

Norman turned around and whistled to Gus who was standing nearby. "How would you like to start working at the mill?"

"Really?" Gus asked.

"This man is fired," Norman said, touching Squaw's chest with his pointing index finger. "Do you want his job? You can start out by stamping our lumber."

"Yes!" Gus said avoiding Squaw's dark eyes. "I'll take it."

"Get out of here," Norman said to Squaw.

Gus watched Lenny snatch up his lunch bucket, glance back at Norman, then without a word, get into his dark-blue Chevy pickup and speed away. Before the dust had cleared Gus turned to Norman. "What do I do first?" he asked, smiling inwardly with his happiness. "I want to learn it all."

"The time will come," Norman answered. "Right now all you do is stamp the wood."

Norman took off his hat, banged it against his knee a couple times, smoothed back his damp hair and put the hat back on. "Something about Squaw always carped me," Norman told Gus. "Kind of like the itch of a chigger." Disgruntled and tired-looking, he trudged back to the dip tank and watched the big wheels push the boards into the dark, stain-preventing chemical liquid. "If I sat down, I'd fall asleep," Norman told Gus.

Gus stood for a moment to watch the chains carry the wood to the grader. Giving free reins to his imagination, he visioned the day he'd be able to run the mill himself. With lively interest, he moved closer to Norman. "I could never fall asleep out here, Pa. It's all too interesting. I want to know the business well enough to run it by myself. Can I help run the saws, now, Pa?"

"You ask me that every day. Someday I'll surprise you and say yes."

They stared in silence at the men's rhythm and efficiency. "Tell me about your grandpa's mill," Gus asked. "You said that sometimes being out here brought back memories." Gus looked straight into Norman's eyes. "Maybe I could see those memories, too," he said.

Norman looked down and with his arm around Gus's shoulder, he pulled the boy closer. "I think about my grandfather and how he persevered, even under the grimmest adversity. I recall how my grandad, Crawford Wheeler, kept adding improvements to increase the output of his mill. Sometimes I wonder if *I* could do it under the same circumstances."

"What do you mean by that?" Gus asked.

Norman smiled at the boy. "For one thing, he had a crude water-wheel that provided power for his mill." He raised his arm and with his finger, drew a wide, slow circle in the air. "Lazily turning; round and round and round," Norman droned. "Right now, I can almost hear the forceful ssshwish of the water pushing against the blade of the big wheel." He glanced down at Gus. "Can you feel the cool spray?" Norman hiked his heavy-booted leg onto the sideboard and rested his sawdusty arms across his knee.

"Did he like milling?" Gus asked.

"Crawford was addicted to the whistle-scream of the saws."

Gus closed his eyes and visions of a great wooden wheel emerged. "I want you to see and feel more," he said.

"Well . . . ," Norman said, and closed his eyes, too. "I see a proud, red-necked man, and hear his sawdust-choked voice say, 'Water power's dependable, Son. Safe, controllable, and most importantly, cheap!' He was always searching for ways to save money and get more production."

Gus opened his eyes and saw Norman smile at the recollection. "He built the mill from hewn timber," Norman said, "the gears shaped and whittled from oak. The mill put out five thousand board foot a day on the average. When the water was abundant, it could be as high as nine thousand feet. I helped him put in the water turbine to supplement power. Gran'daddy gave me two dimes for helping."

"Two dimes? You must have been happy as a king to fare so well."

Norman grinned. "After that, I made a man-to-man agreement with him to work for seven pennies a day. I told him I preferred to be paid daily. I remember Grandad taking a five-dollar bill to the bank. He brought home five hundred pennies. He dumped them all in a whiskey barrel and left them just inside the back door. Every night after we shut down, we'd walk side-by-side into the house and I'd count out my own seven pennies. That's how I bought my first car."

"What else, Pa? Tell me more."

Norman laughed, a sound Gus hadn't heard from his father for a long time. He patted his son on the back and looked into Gus's attentive eyes. "You do me proud, son. Just wish Gilbert felt the same way. That boy goes round in a dream-created world." He patted Gus on the back again. "I'm glad you don't go building castles in the air."

Gus was annoyed that his dad would talk that way about Gilbert. "Tell me more about your grandpa's mill," Gus said, wondering if he should say something in Gil's defense.

"The mill soon went through transformation again because Grandad heard that steam power could produce ten to twenty times the footage he was getting. Crawford put in a new circular saw at the same time. That's when he lost the thumb and first two fingers on his right hand, but that didn't stop him. With steadfast faith and iron will, he kept the mill operating."

Norman's foot slipped off the board and he lost his balance. Gus watched his father's quick hand shoot out and grab hold of the emergency stop-lever to regain his balance. The entire operation cut to a slow whine the second he grabbed the control.

"Everything okay over there, Boss?" Cletus Yates yelled.

"Yeah, just slipped." Norman's mouth formed a foolish-looking grin. "Wasn't too smart."

Yates came to Norman's side. "Looked like you was hundreds of miles away."

"Just remembering the way my grandfather ran *his* mill, and what brought it all to an end."

"And how was that, Norm?"

"Yeah, Dad, how was that?" Gus asked, truly wanting to hear more.

"It's a long story. I'll tell you about it someday." Norman adjusted his glasses and cleared his throat. "It's a mistake to let sentiment interfere with my work. Could be dangerous."

Suddenly a fierce blatant outcry rumbled from the upper lot. Gus's head bolted up. "There, Pa!" Gus hollered, pointing to Calvin's bear-like body thundering down the hillside. Norman pivoted and rushed toward the logging supervisor. In the shadows of the mountain Gus saw two men lugging a man down the hill. The lifeless body looked like a hammock swinging from a tree, with one man holding the arms and the other clasping onto the limp legs.

"Lord have mercy," Norman said. "My God, what happened, Cal?"

"It's Harvey!" Calvin hollered breathlessly. "The hydraulic steering went out of the tractor and crashed down the slope! It crushed him, Norman! Harvey Spelling's dead."

Norman's face went slack. He pivoted toward the shock-struck workers. "Shut down the mill!" he directed.

The screams of the saws faltered and silenced once again.

That night slow, steady rain fell. Gus laid in his bed staring at the ceiling, thinking of the loose, lifeless body Calvin and his men had brought down the hill. He had only seen Spelling a few times but the young man always had a friendly smile. Gus could hear tossing and turning from his folk's room. He pushed off the covers, sat on the edge of the bed, then looked over his shoulder to see if he'd woken Gilbert. Gus yawned, stood up, wandered over to the window and watched the light rain trickle off the tin roof. He wondered about Spelling's family, if he had brothers or sisters. Slowly Gus walked into the kitchen and poured a glass of milk. Carrying the glass he shuffled to his parents unclosed bedroom door and tapped on the wall. "Come in," Norman said, and Gus did. There was no need for words. They understood each other. Norman got out of bed and moved restlessly around the room while Gus settled into an overstuffed chair. Katherine mumbled, pulled the quilt around her neck while Norman gazed through the window toward the dark woods. A white full moon appeared from behind a dark cloud and poured an eerie, shimmering light over the cold wet ground.

Katherine murmured something again and turned over. "Honey, please try to get some sleep," she said more clearly.

The clouds once again hid the moon and Norman stood in darkness. He shook his head slowly and pressed it against the cold window. "I was at the camp the day Harvey Spelling showed up," he said quietly. "I can't stop thinking about that day. The boy said he could fix the steering on the tractor."

"I was there, too, remember?" Gus said, swallowing a swig of milk.

Katherine sat up in bed. "Please, Norm. Come to bed."

"It's my fault, Gus," Norman said.

"You didn't kill him, Pa," Gus answered.

Katherine reached up and turned on the lamp next to their bed. "Honey," she said to Norman, "God sets the life-clock. He saw fit to take Harvey home."

Norman, still facing the window, spoke to Katherine's reflection. "Don't you see? I should have told him to come back in a couple years. He was too young to be out there."

"It wasn't you, Norm. It was the Lord's wish."

Norman laid down on top of the covers, but didn't close his eyes. Katherine put her arm over his chest and snuggled close. "You're not going to be able to sleep tonight, are you?"

"I don't think so," Norman said. "It seems Gus is having the same problem."

Katherine sighed and rested her head on Norman's chest. "I'm going back to sleep. There's a piece of pecan pie on the stove, Gus."

He didn't answer, there was no call to. It was his mother's way of saying 'I love you'. He drank the rest of his milk, leaned back his head and stared at the lemon-yellow curtains neatly framing the window, clean, starched, ironed. She ironed everything, even the pajamas he was wearing. Tuesday. She ironed on Tuesday. Mondays she washed, dipped some of it in starch, then hung it all on the line. Then she'd sprinkle, roll everything into tight little cylinders. Gus let out a long breath while he thought about how hard a woman's life must be. He looked at the curtains, the matching bedspread, the yellow rug, a little darker than the curtains, then at the shimmering blackness outside the window. Gus looked at his mother lying there with soft blond hair like a halo framing her face. He felt sad for her. "I'd like to go with you to the depot tomorrow, Pa," he said.

Gus watched Norman nod, then rest his forearm over his head. "It's your choice."

In the dark of the early morning, Calvin, Norman and Gus stood at the railroad station in the cold rain as Harvey Spelling's simple pine coffin was lifted onto a Chicago-bound train.

Even after the train rolled away, the three stood solemnly, staring in the direction the train had gone. A gray, wet dawn poured over them as they stared.

Norman sniffed and cleared his throat. "I keep . . . " he cleared his throat again and continued, "I keep imagining the boy's parents standing and shivering, waiting for the train to bring home the body of their son. I should have said no," he said. "I should have said no, Cal, when you asked what I thought about him working for us."

"Don't blame yourself, Norm," Calvin said. "It was just as much my fault."

Norman shook his head. "My bones of guilt are picked clean. The whole thing seems shadowy and unreal. Unreal, because Harvey Spelling was only a child, and children aren't supposed to die."

Gus stared at the ground, watching the toe of Norman's polished church shoes plough a small furrow in the shiny, light-reflected mud. He pulled a freshly ironed white handkerchief from the pocket of his topcoat and blew his nose. The three of them stood there on the station's platform, sometimes swaying, sometimes shivering in the cold dampness, unaware of pungent smelling wetness wrapping around them.

Norman flung up his hands. "I want to push it all away. Harvey's death, the problems at the mill, Katy's misery because of Garrett's illness, Gilbert not giving a shit about anything." He took off his glasses, rubbed his eyes to clear his vision then began walking up and down the soggy walkway that ran along the tracks. Gus counted eight paces forward, eight paces back. His footsteps splashed on the wooden planks as his church shoes filled with water.

Gus didn't know what to say or do. He stood perfectly still, looking away from his father. Norman stopped at the concrete-mounted PLEASE STAND BEHIND ROPE sign. His gloved hands griped the upright poles, and Gus stepped back a few inches when Norman shook the hell out of the bars. He pulled against the sign with a visibly futile gesture of anger. "Life's gone to hell!"

"There's another train coming in," Gus said, seeing the dim outline through the fog. He still did not look at his father.

Norman disengaged his fingers and stared down at the sign. "I'm exhausted, Calvin. And prayered out." He placed his hand between Gus's shoulders.

"There's nothing more we can do here," Pa.

"You're right, son. My car's around the corner. Come on, Cal, let's go home."

In a thin, quavery voice, unlike the thunderous voice that came roaring down the hillside the day before, Calvin declined. "Think I'll walk. You two go on."

"Take off work the rest of the day. All of you. It don't seem fitting for a fellow to be working when there's been a death," Norman said.

The following month brought colder and wetter weather. It was the sound of rain pelting the windows that woke Gus. He hated dark winter mornings. Gus couldn't read the clock but knew it was time to get up and start morning chores. He laid still and stared at the pine ceiling waiting for Gilbert to stir. Finally he pushed off the covers and stretched one leg over the side of the bed. When his foot touched the cold hardwood floor, he pulled it back onto the bed.

"You're pulling my covers off!" Gilbert mumbled harshly.

Gus sat up, considered lying back down, then raised himself off the bed, taking all the covers with him.

Gilbert bounded off the bed and wrestled Gus to the floor, seized the quilt and nestled back into their featherbed.

As Gus shuffled across the floor, he heard the familiar sound of the floorboards creaking underfoot and hoped the noise wouldn't wake Garrett or Katherine. Gus knew she'd been up all night with Garrett. He hated seeing his mother so depressed and resented his baby brother for making her that way. Gripping the bedpost for balance, he slid his cold feet into red plaid house slippers and pulled on his flannel robe. He walked past Katherine's door and when his sleepy eyes caught the brief reflection of a tired old lady in the mirror, he wanted to cry. Gus stood and watched Katherine rocking her tiny son, holding on tightly as if to keep him from slipping away from her. She'd known right from the beginning this child wouldn't be wholesome.

Gus heard Norman shuffling around in his slippers, pouring coffee beans into the grinder, slowly turning the handle. He could smell the fresh-ground beans and although he'd never tasted coffee, the smell of it revived him.

Katherine shuffled slowly into the kitchen and took the coffee basket from Norman's hand. "Let me," she whispered, setting the filter basket into the blue metal pot. She took a wire basket of eggs and some sausage from the refrigerator.

Katherine made patties from the ground sausage and placed them in a cold iron skillet. As she reached into the cupboard for the covered butter dish, Garrett started to whimper. Norman walked to the doorway of their room. Katherine turned down the fire under the skillet and said, "I'll get him."

Gloom permeated the house. Gus opened a jar of Katherine's preserves without even looking to see what kind it was. He reached into the cupboard and brought out four plates, then opened the refrigerator for the milk bottle. Norman pulled open the drawer and took out silverware. Sugar, salt and molasses were already on the table. Gus slid the chair out from under the table and sat heavily.

"He's burnin' up, Norman," Katherine whispered, shuffling into the kitchen, clutching her robe around her. Gus saw a look of tenderness on his father's face when he said, "You look done in, Katy."

"Plumb tuckered out, but no more than you. I see you've already got the table laid."

"How is he, Mom?" Gus asked.

"Doin' poorly," Katherine answered numbly, almost as if she were talking to herself. She reached into the cupboard and handed Norman a bottle of Creomulsion.

"Did my cough wake you?" he asked, taking the glass bottle of medicine from her.

Katherine nodded, reached for the fresh cream from the refrigerator then set it onto the table. She stood staring out the kitchen window. "This chilling winter's freezin' everything to death," she mumbled. She poured two cups of coffee and shivered visibly.

"I'll take some," Gus said, and Katherine poured a third cup without questioning him.

Norman set the medicine aside, cradled the cup of hot coffee in his hands, took too-big a gulp and set the cup down quickly. Frowning, he stretched his arms across the table top and pillowed his head on top of them.

"You can't work today, feeling this way."

"I've got to."

Katherine shuffled to the bedroom door and leaned against its frame. Garrett began to cry again. "I'll call Dr. West today."

"I don't know where the money for doctor bills will come from," Norman said, shaking his head, then took off his glasses and rubbed his forehead with the palm of his hand. "Take the money from the cookie jar," he said.

"No, Norman. That's for your new glasses."

"I said, take the cookie jar money." Norman fingered his glasses, picked them up, laid them next to the coffee cup. "These'll last another few months."

Katherine picked up the glasses. The left lens was cracked and loose in the frame. Norman had taped it in. She hugged his neck and pressed her face into his uncombed hair. "I love you," she muffled.

"When Gilbert or Gus got sick, they mended quickly," Katherine told Norman at the breakfast table. "Garrett never seems to recover."

"Dad," Gus said quietly. "If we need the money to fix Garrett, why not cut the Delvine timber?"

Norman slowly shook his head, got up, moved to the stove and turned over the sausage patties. "These are done," he said. "What do I do now?"

"Turn off the fire and put them on a platter," Katherine answered.

Norman set the plate of meat on the table, looked at Gus and said, "Son, the price of that timber is growing. When we do cut, it'll be worth twice what we paid for it. We'll not have any money problems then, but for now we have to let it build in value."

"Today's your day to wash dishes," Gus told Gilbert when his brother shuffled into the kitchen and dropped into his chair.

"I'll do them!" Gilbert blurted.

Katherine cradled Garrett, tried to nurse him, and struggled with her composure. Her ailing son came first in her life now, Gus knew, and as the dark cold days slowly passed, he watched her became more lethargic, moving zombie-like about the house.

After breakfast Norman went outside to stack firewood on the back porch. Gus heard him coughing and blowing his nose. The night had been fitful for all three of them.

From the table Gus could see into his mother's room as she shuffled to her dressing table, sat, picked up her hairbrush. With her cold fingers gripping the hairbrush, she stared past her own image in the mirror and focused on her baby son. "You're already a year old, she thought. It seems only yesterday we brought you home and introduced you to your brothers," she whispered. Katherine didn't smile, only stared at the infant lying motionless in his crib. She looked down at the brush in her hand, mechanically lifted her arm and rested the soft bristles against her head. Her hand moved slowly, one stroke and then another. Katherine laid the hairbrush aside and rose from the vanity bench. Silently she kissed her fingertips then lightly touched Gus's cheek as she padded back into the kitchen.

Gus thought of how Garrett had whimpered all night, his deep-set brown eyes afraid to surrender to sleep. Now Garrett was resting peacefully and Gus thanked the Lord for giving him this respite. Gus got up from the table, tiptoed to the baby's crib, leaned over and kissed Garrett's wet eyelashes. His gaze swept over to the basket full of diapers stained with deep-yellow urine. It shouldn't be like this, he thought.

• CHAPTER 7 •

December brought sharp, frosty winds, but that didn't stop the logging. Keen, crisp air kept the men alert and active. Icy hands set the chokers, operated bulky chain saws and moved the timber to the mill. At the mill, the circular saw developed a wobble and Gus helped the men struggle to lay it flat on the frozen ground and beat it flat. While down, several steel teeth were replaced. When the heavy blade was back in operation, it was as good as new.

The next day it started raining again and soon turned to sleet. "We're havin' a log-roller 'n toad-choker," Willie Gibbons joked, a cigarette dangling from his mouth. "Hate to miss work because of this damn weather," he said.

"Just remember how dry and hot it was back in August," another man said, trying to be cheerful.

"Yeah, dry as a goat's butt." They looked at each other and each gave a helpless shrug.

Since the men couldn't run the saws, they pulled up their collars and stacked wet lumber. After working three hours in the freezing wet weather, Norman told the men—as uncomfortable as mortals could be—to take the rest of the day off.

"We all need the money, Wheeler. We're willin' to work in the weather."

"Inside I'm as cold, miserable and broke as you are," Norman answered. "I'm sorry, but what can I do?"

Norman shuffled into the kitchen warming his cupped hands with his breath. Looking toil-weary and footsore, he pulled off his wet overcoat, tugged off his boots, poured out the water and said "shit" as he wrung his socks. Freezing drizzle spattered the window as he removed his spectacles and rubbed his eyes. Katherine kneeled down and rubbed his cold feet with her warm hands, then lit the fire under the coffee pot. In front of the fireplace, Norman turned all sides to the flames like a pig on a spit, then hugged himself for warmth.

"Best linger up by the fire. The air's stirrin' cool, even in the house."

Norman mumbled something about the wind blowing cold, settled in his easychair and leaned his head against its back. Moments later he was asleep.

The boys came in soon after, grumbling because of the wet weather. "My hands are freezing," Gilbert said, blowing on them.

Katherine fried pork chops, breaded tomatoes, and baked a green-apple pie for dinner. She spread a red gingham cloth over the pine table and set a basket of hot buttered biscuits in the middle. When she reached into the pantry for the honey, a little box labeled "zinnia seeds" fell off a shelf. Biting her lip, Katherine's eyes fixed on the floor.

"I'll pick 'em up, Mom," Gus said.

Katherine and Gus squatted down above the scattered seeds. "I remember when I collected these seeds from the shriveled blooms around the windmill," Katherine said. "It was the day I went to see Dr. West. 'Mrs. Wheeler, there's going to be another baby on the knee come early summer,' he told me."

"Were you happy?" Gus asked.

Katherine's voice was awkward and strained. "I told him that I was worried that something would be wrong with the baby."

"What did he say to you?"

Katherine smiled at Gus. "He told me I couldn't unscramble an egg."

Gus wrinkled his face. "I don't get it."

Katherine roughed his hair and rose. "I know."

Norman began to cough and Katherine rubbed her hand over his forehead. "You've got a fever." She walked to the sink and pumped water into a kettle.

"Your cold's getting worse," Gilbert said to Norman, and Katherine rested a protective hand on his shoulder.

"Just a little cough," Norman told them.

Gus gathered the rest of the seeds and put them back into the small box. He shook his head. "Scrambled eggs?" he questioned softly. "Why can't they just say what it's meant to be?"

After changing into woolen trousers and high-top shoes, Norman smoothed back his half-dry hair and sat to eat. "Calvin says another barrel of gasoline's missing," he said, cutting into the meat, but not taking a bite. "Last week it was a hind quarter of beef."

Gus waited for Norman to say more. When he didn't, he asked, "Do you think it's the same person who's stealing the lumber?"

"I don't know, son, but I wouldn't put it past Lenny Squaw. He was really mad about me firing him."

"It started long before that, Norm." Katherine said, wiping her hands on the sides of her checked apron.

Norman set his fork next to the plate and looked at Katherine, "How's Garrett today?"

"Not good." Her shoulders drooped. She laid an embroidered tea towel down and took her seat at the table. Gus noticed the little teddy bears she'd cross-stitched across the top of her apron.

Katherine cleared her throat and said, "I sat him in the rocker. He sat there, still as death. When I lifted him, he just stared with those dark empty eyes."

"Isn't it time he came out of this?" Norman spat. "Damn! His liver trouble's getting worse, not better."

Gus was shocked with the violent burst and looked over at his mother. "I feel as helpless as you do," Katherine said. "Norman, I don't even know what hepatitis is or what causes it. Doctor West says he's worried about . . . wait. I wrote it down." Katherine got up, walked into their dim lit bedroom and dug into her pocketbook. Paper in hand, Katherine slowly walked back into the kitchen. She sat and read from a piece of paper. "He's worried about cryp . . . crypto . . . cryptogenic cirrhosis."

Katherine placed the biscuits in front of Norman's plate and took off her apron. "Gilbert, would you ask the blessing?"

Gilbert put down his fork, bowed his head and said, "The pork chops look good, and so do the greens. Thank you, God, for hogs and gardens."

Gus closed his eyes for a second to acknowledge the prayer, then opened them and said, "Is it curable what Garrett has?"

"Cirrhosis is irreversible," Norman said, his voice angry.

Katherine reached over and touched his hand. "Eat your supper," she said.

"Is he going die?" Gilbert asked.

Norman took a few bites of his breaded tomatoes then said, "Vern Peele's calling another meeting tonight about Mitchell's tractor. He's offering a reward for any leads. Hopefully. . . ." He took another bite then dropped his fork on the half-eaten meal.

Katherine arranged her starched and ironed apron across her knees. "Truth's been slow to unfold. It's been nearly a year since that happened. Mitch's wife has cried a million tears. That tractor was their only means of getting their tobacco harvested in time. Poor Elsie. It brings sickness to my stomach to think about that man still being out there to break down other families." Her hand gripped the edge of her plate. "We were so close to seeing whom it was. I know that was Mitch's tractor going over the hill that day."

"There's something else, now," Norman said. He looked into Katherine's eyes. "Another tractor's been stolen."

Gus's stomach lurched and he looked at Gilbert who was staring at him.

Katherine shook her head. "What's become of this once respected town?"

The door suddenly burst open from a gust of wind and they all jumped. Gilbert scooted his chair back, got up at closed it. The room was so quiet they could hear the latch catch.

"That cyclone came thundering in like a herd of buffalo," Gilbert said as he sat.

"I'm hungry enough to eat coon bait, Ma!" Gus said loudly, hoping to change the subject from the second tractor Billy Ray had probably stolen.

"Well, I'm hungry enough to eat a stink bug off a dead skunk," Gilbert blared.

Norman leaned back in his chair. The two front legs lifted off the floor. "Feeding you boys puts me in mind of Ofis Tarwater slopping his hogs."

After several minutes of school news, Norman turned to Katherine and asked, "We still having the old buzzard for dinner on Sunday?"

Katherine cleared her throat, her fiery glare going from Norman to the children. "Yes, Norman," she whispered harshly. "Reverend Reed is still coming to eat with us on Sunday."

Katherine rose to clear the dishes and Gilbert slid off his chair laughing. "What's so funny, Gilbert?" she asked, only making Gilbert laugh louder.

"You've gone round the bend, Gil," Gus said, shaking his head. He would have laughed, too, but when he saw his mother's weary features a flash of sadness swept over him. As Gilbert joked about Reverend Reed, Katherine smoothed the faded, lavender-printed dress and buttoned the top button of the old gray sweater she wore over it.

"Buzzard? We eat buzzards?" Gilbert giggled and held his hand over his mouth.

"Gilbert, dear, your father should not have referred to Reverend Reed that way."

"But, Mama, buzzard?"

Katherine clunked a coffee cup on the table and scolded her son.

"Okay! Okay!" Gilbert said, setting his plate down into the sink. "We've got to act proper when Reverend Reed comes callin'."

"We're proper already," Gus corrected as he pumped water over the dirty dishes. His words were fitting, but his blue eyes sparkled with amusement. It *was* sort of funny.

Gilbert punched Gus in the arm and they joked and laughed with each other.

Katherine glared at Norman. "Now look what you've started," she reprimanded as she cleared the table. "Thelma Jean said Vern Peele's asking for help to try to find the tractor thief. That's what the reward is all about."

"It'll be in the paper tomorrow about the latest theft. Thelma Jean woke up this morning and found a Ferguson in her flower bed."

Gus nearly choked holding back a laugh, then covered his mouth with his hand.

"I know Vern's putting up posters asking anyone with knowledge to come forward. He's hoping there was a witness," Norman said.

Katherine added more dishes to the sink then plunged her hands into the hot water and lye soap suds. "If only we'd got into the truck and tried to follow the tractor that day."

"We didn't know what was happening that day, Katy."

Katherine squeezed the sudsy water from the cloth, wiped the table then pulled the cotton fibers up on the Wizard Green Wick bottle. "Posters may help more than the weekly prayer meetings," she said. Refreshing pine scent drifted from the green glass bottle. She inhaled and exhaled loudly, then set the deodorant bottle on the window sill.

Norman's forehead wrinkled. "You've never doubted your faith."

"I know, Norm. Lately I've been making excuses not to go to the prayer meetings."

"Because of Garrett doing so poorly?"

Katherine wrung her hands on her apron. "I don't know," she said, shaking her head. She pulled a chair from the table and sat down. Katherine looked out the window. "I *am* doubting my faith," she said, passing round clean plates. "Come get some pie, boys," she said loudly.

The sky was blue with brittle brightness as Reverend Reed sprightly marched to the Wheeler's after services on Sunday. His thin red hair was artfully combed sideways to cover a bald spot, a-little-dab'll-do-ya holding it together.

Billy Ray, Wharton Jr. and the twins squatted behind a fallen log.

"Where is it?" Billy Ray asked impatiently.

Wharton Jr. patted the front of his jacket. "In here."

"Well? Get it out!" Gilbert told him.

"It'll cost you each a penny," Wart told them.

"You didn't charge us to look at it last time," Gus said.

"That was just to wet your appetite," Wharton Jr. told them. "Pay up or you don't see it," he said defiantly.

Billy Ray shoved Wharton Jr. sideways. "Come on, Wart. It didn't cost you anything. You stole it from under your pa's mattress."

Wharton pulled out the magazine. "Okay, okay."

"Ahh, look at that," Billy Ray whispered, pointing to the picture of a woman in a black slip. They jumped and slammed the pages closed when the reverend jaunted by. The boys darted behind trees out of sight.

"Boy that was close!" Billy Ray said, the magazine tucked under his coat. "Wonder where he's goin' in such a happy hurry?"

Wharton Jr. raised his face upward and sniffed the air. "A slap of Old Spice must-a give him that goin' callin' feelin'."

Gus covered his mouth, snickered, then said, "It's our turn to have him for dinner." He turned to Gilbert. "We need to get home. I think he's early."

"No," Gilbert said. "We're late."

The joyful preacher's reversible, all weather topcoat and a bright red scarf billowed out behind as his short legs sped along. Dry leaves crunched under his shoes like potato chips as Gus and Gilbert skirted around him just out of sight.

Squirrels darted from the minister's path. Deeply inhaling and exhaling the crispness, his breath billowed around his face. "Praise the Lord for this beautiful weather," the preacher said aloud. His cheeks puffed out like plump red apples as he whistled a made-up tune. As he approached the Wheelers, he raised his head and sniffed the scentful smell of lumber. "I love the smell of this mountain hollow," he said, and did a little kick dance before walking into their yard.

Gus and Gilbert both laughed into their hands. They ran into the house and into their room where identical clothes were laid out.

"Thank Jesus Mom didn't make us wear our knicker suits," Gilbert said, picking up the dark brown Sears and Roebuck longies.

"I like this fly front," Gus said.

"It's imitation," Gilbert corrected. "Try peeing out of it," he said, and they both doubled over laughing. "I like this leather belt," Gil said.

"It's artificial leather," Gus said. "You know, I used to like people looking at us and ohhing and ahhing, but now, well, we're just too old for it." Gus finished buttoning the tan, broadcloth button-on shirt. "Whoopdeedoo," he sang out.

"Don't forget your tie," Katherine said, barging into their room, ignoring the Please Knock sign.

"You know we hate wearing a tie, Mom. We're not going to church!" Gilbert sassed.

"The church is coming here," Katherine said, "and I hope you'll behave."

"Can we wear our Roy Rogers saddle boots?"

"I don't think it would be proper, son."

"If we can, we'll be extra good," Gilbert vowed.

Katherine clicked her tongue. "Okay, but ONLY with your faithful promise to behave and not talk unless spoken to. If I let you wear your cowboy boots, you have to promise with all your heart to mind your manners. Say it. Say you will."

"Promise," Gil said.

"Gus," Katherine said, touching his arm. "And do you promise to behave?" Gus rolled his eyes. "Yes, I promise."

The Wheeler family and their guest sat at the perfectly arranged table just as the grandfather clock bonged twelve times. "Right on time," Norman said.

The preacher cleared his throat and tucked his napkin into his collar. "I'm . . ." Norman started speaking at the same time. "We're . . ."

Everyone laughed.

"Please speak first, Reverend," Norman said, gesturing with his hand.

The preacher nodded. "I was just going to say I'm delighted to be here with such a fine family. And, please, I'd feel privileged if you'd call me Aaron."

"Iron?" Gus said, twisting his face. "I didn't know that was your name."

"Gus," Katherine said, "his name is Aaron, not Iron." She stretched her leg and tapped his Roy Roger boots. It reminding him of his promise to behave.

"Well, Aaron," Norman said, "we're happy to have you here with us."

Whoopdeedoo, Gus thought.

The preacher glanced around at the family and said, "I'll say the blessing."

All heads bowed, but Gus and Gilbert had their heads tilted toward one another with their eyes open. Gus crossed his eyes, then Gil did the same. They swallowed back a laugh.

Reverend Reed went on and on.

Gus's hands fumbled in his lap and when he peeked up, he saw Norman's head bobbing. Was he dozing? He tried to stretch his leg to kick him, but it wouldn't reach.

Gus needed to go to the bathroom and couldn't sit still. He leaned over to Gilbert and whispered, "I can't believe there's so many things that need to be blessed."

"Excuse me, Aaron, but the taters are gettin' cold," Gilbert quietly interrupted.

Katherine kicked the top of Gilbert's boot, hard.

"Amen," said the preacher obviously not annoyed by the boys' intrusion.

Garrett's illness was discussed first, church going-ons next, then silence fell except for the clicking of silverware and the clock's rhythmic pendulum swing.

Reverend Reed swallowed and put his fork to the side. Gus almost wet his pants when the preacher said, "Gus. . . ."

The preacher looked him straight in the eyes. The boy's hand pressed up against his crotch to hold the pee in. Katherine reached over and removed his hand from between his legs.

"Young man, were you in church this morning? I didn't see you."

Gus tried to swallow the load in his throat but it wouldn't go down. "I was there."

"Gus had diarrhea this morning, Reverend," Katherine said.

Gus had a gut-sinking feeling in his stomach and thought he'd choke. He hadn't had the squirts since he lost the bet with Billy Ray and had to eat a prune sandwich. Did the Reverend know he'd sneaked out and ice skated at the creek? His Sunday shoes *were* scuffed up. And now his mother had made it *worse* by saying he had the Hershey squirts!

"Oh, mom!" Gus mumbled loudly trying to whisper. He kept his head bent over his plate.

"I was there," Gilbert announced, sitting up proudly. "I was in church."

"And what did I preach from, this morning, Gilbert?"

"The platform, sir."

The preacher fingered the napkin tucked into his collar and cleared his throat.

"These children are well brought up, Reverend Reed," Norman pardoned. "Really they are." Norman glared at the boys.

The reverend wouldn't let Gus go. "What did I talk about, Gus?"

Gus felt a numbing sensation all over his body. "Sin, sir."

"What about sin?"

"Uh . . . you don't approve of it."

Katherine rolled back her eyes.

Gus wanted to say something about God. He wanted to say God's name. He wanted to show the preacher that he always had God in his thoughts. After a moment of contemplation, he said, "This is a GODdamn good dinner."

"This certainly is mouthwateringly delicious, Mrs. Wheeler," the preacher commented, plainly ignoring the boy's remark and the parents' deep and obvious embarrassment. "You sure do set a fine table, Mrs. Wheeler," the preacher

complimented. "Beulah and Silas Beeler put on an out-and-outer last Sunday."
He took a bite and said, "umm," and rolled back his eyes as he swallowed. "May
I ask what this is?"

"Buzzard," Gilbert blurted out.

Katherine turned crimson. Norman glared at the boy.

"Buzzard?" the reverend asked. He took a big bite and said, "Well bless my
soul."

"Yeah," Gilbert declared. "Pa asked if we was having the old buzzard for
dinner on Sunday. Ma said we was."

Gus bit his lip then coughed a bite of meat right out of his throat and into his
napkin. He glanced at his mother who was red-faced and visibly one step ahead
of a fit. She seemed to be sinking deeper into her chair.

"I'm afraid there's a misunderstanding, Reverend Reed," Katherine offered.
Slowly she stood and faced the boys. "GIT ON IN THERE AN' TAKE THEM
BOOTS OFF!" she shouted, then turned abruptly to the window. "It's stifling in
here." She sprang the window wide open.

Gus knew the cold blast that blew over her face wasn't enough to mend her
embarrassment. There's going to be the agony of hell's fire around here tonight,
he thought.

Confused, but hungry, Reverend Reed brazenly said, "Well, by God, pass
another hunk o' that buzzard. It's the best darn bird I ever ate!"

• CHAPTER 8 •

"Well I'll be jiggered," Mr. Koontz said as he stared down at the torn and crinkled envelope. "It got here even with part of your address torn off," he said.

Gus shook his head. "This is fit for the dust hole!" he said, searching inside what was left of the envelope. "The button and secret code's missing."

"Sorry it's all buggered up, Gus, but sometimes the machine catches it wrong." He picked up the morning paper and stepped away from the counter.

Gus fingered the torn envelope. In the upper left-hand corner he could barely read *Superman Fan Club*. The rest was smeared like it had been left out in the rain. He pressed against the counter edge. His voice was small, but strong. "I think I should have my money back, Mr. Koontz. Ten cents to join the club and eight cents for the stamp."

Koontz laid the morning newspaper aside and glared down at him. "I'm afraid it wasn't insured."

Gus stepped back, fixed accusing eyes on the postman, then in a flash of temper, yelled, "You didn't tell me about insurance!"

Mr. Koontz let out a long, slow breath. "I can't help you, Gus. Things like this happen." When the bell on the door jingled and Opal May Hubbard strolled in, Mr. Koontz sprang to his place at the counter and smiled broadly at her. "You're lookin' mighty spiffy today, Opal May."

Gus cleared his throat and scowled at the postmaster. He noticed Koontz's brown wool sweater had a moth hole in the elbow and he was glad about it. "But what about. . . . ?"

"Step aside, please," Mr. Koontz commanded, his large hand pushing gently on Gus's shoulder. Koontz checked his watch. "You're early today, Opal May. Is your mother still ailin'?"

"Maw's fit as a fiddle but Pa took sick last night." The woman glanced down at Gus then back up at Mr. Koontz. "Guess you heard about Luther Hamby's boy. Come down with polio."

Gus's face flamed with anger as he flashed past Opal May and out the door. It wasn't so much the fact that he didn't get the Superman button, but the way Mr. Koontz treated him. Just because Koontz is sweet on Opal May didn't give him the right to push me aside, Gus thought. At the fork in the road Gus paused, then took the path that was the long way home.

The cold blue sky was smudged with snowy-gray clouds. Before he reached home, the biting gusts of wind had brought stinging showers of sleet. He'd never felt so cheated. The wind howled and Gus walked bent over against the gusts, protecting his eyes and face from the cold. He was halfway up the hill next to the old tobacco barn when he heard the blades at the sawmill whirr to a sluggish stop. Gus peered up at the steely, gray clouds darkening the day and knew the weather had shut the mill down early, again. He thought of his dad working extra hours so he could buy Katherine a new Lewyt vacuum cleaner for Christmas. "She'll never get it," Gus said, shaking his head. He knew they needed to keep the mill running. Money was scarce and he could see the worry in his folks' eyes. He felt exasperated and angry at Mr. Koontz, angry at Garrett. He was angry with himself for still being little-boy enough to want to be in the stupid Superman Fan Club, and especially he was mad at Gilbert for wanting to go off to California and leave all the work to him and Pa. Gilbert said he wanted to go to California to escape the hardship. Inside Gus's heart, he knew his brother was ashamed of their way of life. He hadn't actually said it, but the comment about the high paying jobs tipped it off. Timber Hills wasn't good enough for him. Gilbert wouldn't leave his family if he was proud of them. That's what hurt the most, Gus thought, the way his brother had selfishly turned his back on family loyalty. "Gosh, I'm mad about everything," he said aloud and stamped his feet.

The sleet changed to spitting snow. Gus watched the last of the men leave the mill and head for the logging camp, all except Squaw, who squatted on a small hill behind a holly bush peering down at the lumber. Squinting against the stinging arrows of snow, Gus watched Squaw stand, pull his knit cap down over his ears and walk away toward a stand of trees nearby. He's not supposed to be there, Gus thought. Pa fired him. Why is he there? Did Pa hire him back?

Gus still felt angry inside because Mr. Koontz should have told him about postal insurance. Then I'd be an official member of the fan club, he thought. He stomped his feet. There I go again, being a kid! He gripped his coat collar, drew it up around his neck and pushed his cold hands into his pockets. He squatted down and sniffed the brisk piney-smelling air. Gus knew his inescapable destiny was Timber Hills.

Someday I'll be running that mill, he thought and I'm old enough to start learning. At least Norman allowed him to stamp the lumber, do odds and ends like clean up small pieces of wood, and sometimes help at the pond. I'm old enough to start running those saws!

Gus squatted next to an old minnow bucket and watched Squaw take another good look at the stacks of lumber, then hurry off through the snow-dusted, hibernal woods. Gus squeezed shut his eyes and could see his Superman button. Darn! He screamed inside his head as he got up and sauntered on, listlessly making footprints in the snow, one foot this way, the other one that way. He leaned back his head, opened his mouth and let large cottony snowflakes melt on his tongue until he tumbled over an old kerosene generator. Raking the air to catch his balance, Gus stomped and cursed. His gaze wandered toward the woodshed attached to the back of the chicken coops. He entered the chicken yard, sat on the chopping block and spotted the axe lying next to the stump. He leaned over, picked it up and ran his fingers along the cold, smooth wooden handle. With both hands, he gripped the axe with all his might, heaved it above his head, then hurled it into the side of the weathered woodshed. The frequently-sharpened head attached briefly, wobbled, fell. When Gus looked up his eyes focused on their tractor parked next to the barn. It was old and rusty but never failed to run. Mitch Wampler's was almost new, and one of his best friends had stolen it. The worst part of it was, he knew he could never snitch on Billy Ray. He and Gil had made a promise not to. It wasn't right, and that gnawed on him, but a pact was a pact. As wrong as it was, Billy Ray's secret would be guarded.

Gus trudged over to the sawmill, snapped off a couple icicles then turned a few cold-stiff knobs. He'd practice right now, with no one to boss him around. He thought of Mr. Koontz bossing him and decided when he got his hog in the spring, he'd name it Koontz. Heck, he'd name them all Koontz. Koontz one, Koontz two. . . .

Gus's heart started racing as he fingered the instruments on the machines. He imagined hearing the whirl of the blades and it was like a song to him. With Gilbert going to California, it would be up to him to help his pa, and he was going to be good at it. When no one was around, he'd learn the controls. He'd pretend, and in no time at all he'd be running the mill himself. He couldn't figure out why Gilbert didn't want to be a part of it. Gus hated this breeding ire he felt toward his brother. The Wheeler's ran a sawmill. It was who they were and everyone knew it. Operating the Timber Hills Sawmill was Wheeler continuity.

When Gus tired of self-instruction, he trekked toward the barn. A rusted Coca-Cola sign hung next to the wide double doors. Gus looked at the thermometer in the center of the sign. It read 36 degrees, but the damp chilly wind made it seem colder. Gus blew out a spirited breath just to watch the fog come out of his mouth, lifted the wooden lever out of its rusty bracket and pulled open the heavy barn door. It moaned and groaned like an old cow in labor. Pale winter light fell through the open door. Gus smelled a potpourri of odors, damp hay, grain, tobacco, the tractor's oil, gasoline. It was a good, satisfying smell. He walked into the barn's fertile crispness, and, like so many times before, climbed the rickety wooden ladder that led to the loft. At the top he turned around, sat and placed his feet on the top rung. In the quiet of the semi-darkness, he thought about Garrett's sickness, Gil's crazy desire to leave Tennessee, his mother's sadness. Then Gus thought of all the money they'd make on the Delvine timber, and suddenly it didn't mean a thing. Could all that wealth make Garrett well, keep Gilbert home, make his family happy again? Belonging to the Superman fan club seemed insignificant now. Maybe Mr. Koontz did him a favor.

Gus stared down at the narrow beam of sunless light flooding in from the half-closed door. His eyes scanned the unobstructed neatness of the barn. Everything in its place. His gaze settled on a small white object sticking out from under one of the grain barrels. Unable to make it out, he climbed down the ladder and walked to the barrel. Gus tilted back the barrel, leaned it against a feed grinder and pulled out a *National Geographic*. Gus fingered through the pages. Pictures of Santa Barbara, San Francisco, San Diego. Pretty girls in fancy dresses and houses with swimming pools. How many times had Gilbert come into this barn, squatted behind the hay and dreamed of California? Gus turned the pages and saw that Gilbert had underlined city names, checkmarked articles about the climate, employment, history. Aircraft plants seemed to be Gil's major interest with entire columns on Douglas, Lockheed and Vega boldly marked with black ink. Gus looked off, then back at the magazine. He leafed through the pages. "The Tournament of Roses Parade," Gus read aloud. He thought Gil had said *Turncoat,* and that's exactly what Gus thought Gilbert would be if he went to California. He tried to see Gil's thoughts through his own eyes—eyes beginning to well with tears, but all he could see was a double-crosser. He shoved the magazine back under the grain barrel, rubbed his eyes to clear his vision and walked to the hook on the wall where his bow and arrow hung. He slung it over his arm, kicked a lard tin, and clomped out of the barn. Bracing the bow and arrow between his legs, Gus fastened the door, then darted into the woods. Faster and faster his legs scissored through the dried leaves and brush. "You're makin' a big mistake, Gilbert!" he yelled.

Like a rugged backwoodsman, Gus hunched down silently behind a tree waiting for his prey. His gaze scanned the dreary-shadowed woods then rested on an old branch-covered pickup truck several feet away. He zigzagged his way to the truck. It had been there for as long as he could remember. Rust had nearly eaten the fenders away. He'd never wondered who the old truck had belonged to. It didn't matter. It was part of the woods, part of their lives and belonged there, like he and Gilbert belonged there. Gus lifted his foot and kicked at the rusted fender. Brittle bits of metal blanketed his pant leg, his shoe and dusted the light snow. He kicked again. "Damn you, Gil." He squished spit through his teeth then swabbed his chin. "Things will get better here!" His sharp, angry voice cut through the cold woodsy air.

Gus leaned against the old pickup and thought of Mitch's tractor and the day they watched Billy Ray jump up onto the seat and drive it away. Someday it'd show up, rusted and buried forever in kudzu, another mark of the countryside. No, he thought, Billy Ray was smart. He'd somehow get that tractor sold to an unknowing individual in another county. Puffs of breath billowed around Gus's face. He shivered and pulled his collar tighter around his neck then duck-walked around to the rear of the truck.

When Gus spotted the buck's silhouette, he stopped breathing. Slowly he pulled his bow around before him, drew an arrow from the pouch and fitted it to the gut. Gus, still holding his breath, raised the bow, drew the arrow back and pointed it toward the unsuspecting deer. It was the largest buck he had ever seen. Gus brought the bow down and heard the *thwang* as he let go. "Bull's eye!" he yelled, as the arrow quivered in the center the full-color picture of a deer he'd torn from a hunting magazine. With a Comanche-like cry, Gus ran to the bale of straw where the magazine page was attached. He started to retrieve his arrow, then decided to leave it there to prove to Gilbert that he'd struck the buck in the heart. The page from the magazine fluttered in the chilly breeze. Gus briskly rubbed his hands together to warm them. It was the first he realized he was hungry and hoped he hadn't missed dinner. Gus glanced again at the arrow's tip interred in the center of the deer's chest. "Gilbert won't believe it," he said, suddenly feeling happy and mighty darn important.

Gus ate slowly that night, detached from the family chitchat. He wondered if it was the right time to ask about the hog. This is as good a time as any, he thought, setting his fork down next to his empty plate. Gus waited until Gilbert had excused himself from the table, then said, "Mother, Father."

Geez, I never call them that, Gus thought. He glanced quickly at both of them. No turning back now. He had their full attention. "There's something I want to talk to you about." Gus picked up his fork then set it down again. "I've been thinking about raising some hogs. We've always got our pork from Ofis Tarwater. Why is that, Pa?"

"Sometimes habits are hard to break," Norman answered. "He's got the hog farm. Folks 'round here just leave the slaughtering to him. He sells the meat cheap. I don't see anything wrong with you raising a couple of hogs. It's not a far-fetched idea. Try it for a year or two."

"Do you think you have enough time, with your chores and school?" Katherine asked.

"I've done a lot of thinking about it. I'll make the time," Gus promised. "It makes sense to me. I think it'd be a good investment."

Norman nodded slowly, regarding his son.

"It's actually a short term commitment. A calf for beef takes at least ten months. A hog only takes six."

"You've been doing some planning," Norman complimented. "Even hens tie you up for a year or more."

"Pigs are sexually mature at six to seven months," Gus added. "And it only takes three months, three weeks, and three days for a litter to be born."

Until Gus said that, Katherine had been sitting relaxed with one leg tucked up under her. Quickly she shifted her weight, put both feet on the floor and looked wide-eyed at Norman who was looking straight into Gus's eyes. Katherine dropped her gaze and stared into her lap.

"Uh huh," Norman said, nodding in agreement, then asked, "Three months, three weeks, and three days from what point?"

Gus felt his face turn red. That never should have happened. He thought he was prepared for this conversation. He swallowed hard, then answered, "From the point of conception."

Gus couldn't look at his mother. He felt her embarrassment.

"Do you know the process of killing and preparing hog meat?" Norman asked.

"I've been studyin' up on it." Gus went on to detail what he'd heard. "You have to shoot it in the head, stick him in the throat and bleed him, and when the blood stops running, you put him in a big pot of water, almost, but not quite boiling."

"Norman, do we have to talk about this at the table?" Katherine asked.

"Let him finish," Norman said. "It's all part of living on a farm."

"Where was I?" Gus asked, then remembering, said, "You keep him in the hot water for a minute or two so that his hair can be scraped off easily. Then tie his hind legs together and hang him from a cross pole and wash him really well." Gus paused, thinking, shifted his weight, then continued, "After that you cut off the head and cut him up in pieces." Gus went on talking, "We'll use the manure as fertilizer, they'll eat the garbage, they eat snakes," Gus added.

"So do opossums," Katherine said, still not looking up.

"Get yourself some housing made for them and I'll ask Tarwater if he'll have piglets for sale this spring. Do you have any idea what a thirty-pound piglet goes for?" Norman asked.

"It's a small investment," Gus said. "I'll have the money by then. Oh, and I already know what I'm naming them," he joked.

"And what's that?" Norman asked, smiling. "I've never heard of naming meat."

Katherine quickly began stacking dishes, leaned over and whispered in Norman's ear, "He's way too young to be saying, S E X," she spelled.

Gus grinned. "I heard that, Ma. I know about those things, now. Me and Gil learned by watching Luther Hamby's bull. It didn't take us long to figure it all out."

Katherine sighed.

"These boys are cutting their wisdom teeth, Katy."

Gus thought it was sort of cute how his mother seemed embarrassed about the sex thing.

"Are you going to the town hall meeting tomorrow night?" she asked.

"I need to," Norman answered. "We're discussing the thievery going on in town. The tractors, farm machinery, supplies, our own timber." He glanced at Gus. "Would you like to go with me? I think you're getting old enough for town meetings."

Gus wanted to go, wanted to be conversant in community affairs, yet the core of the discussion would likely trouble him. "I'd like that, Pa."

"Good," Norman said, pushing his chair from the table. "Good."

"I'm naming each hog I get Koontz," Gus said. "In honor of our big cheese postmaster." Gus got up from the table feeling good. He smiled as he opened the door and strode out, down the porch steps and into the barn yard. "Soo-ey!" he hollered. "Soo-ey!"

Gus and Norman knew who was already at the meeting by their automobiles. Gus saw right away that Mitch had the best parking spot suggesting the Wamplers had gotten there first. Norman rolled into an empty parking space on the east side of the building. Gus hadn't expected such a large crowd and felt nervous.

"Ready to whistle down the wind?" Norman asked.

Gus nodded, unsure. They got out of the car and walked into the fire station for the seven p.m. meeting. "I think every man in the county's here," Gus remarked.

"I expected it," Norman said, "with the recent thefts going on in the county." They said their hellos, shook a few hands, then took off their coats and hung them on pegs near the door. Gus followed Norman and felt uneasy when they sat near Mitch Wampler. Gus avoided eye contact and turned his face to the door just as Sheriff Peele walked in and sat in the front row.

Voices echoed off the metal walls and ceiling, undecipherable words blending in a high-pitched roar. It was the men's night out, their night to vent frustrations. Tobacco smoke filled the large room like a heavy fog. Norman leaned back into the chair and stretched an arm across the back of Gus's chair.

"If the meeting will come to order!" came a directive voice from the front, and it only took a minute to get to the night's agenda. No one wanted to listen to the minutes from the previous gathering, so they were excluded by vote.

"We 'outta git our pistol-guns and go huntin' for the bastard!" Billy "the Bear" Burchfield shouted. "Take Wheeler, there. He's been havin' timber planks stolen from right under his nose, an' out at the camp things turn up missin' all the time. There's an out-of-control thief in this here county. Next thing you know they'll be stealin' our wives!"

Taylor Tipton sprang up, knocking his rifle aslant. "What I can't understand is why Mitch's tractor hasn't turned up somewhere. If'n we don't get this cur soon, we ain't gonna see hide ner hair of him nowheres." Tipton grunted, then added, "Gonna be an early winter. Caterpillars are coated heavy. Better git him now 'fore the snows set in."

"If I find out who it was stole Mitch's tractor I'll blow his head off!" someone shouted.

When Norman sprang up Gus jumped. He was already thinking of ways to hide Billy Ray. He watched his father's lips move as his words said, "Don't get pushed out of shape. We aren't a bunch of uncivilized hicks. Maybe that's how things were done in the old days, but this is 1950."

"Stealin' is an offense against society, Wheeler!"

Gus saw that the men were hot and there was no stopping them now. He wished Gilbert was there. Billy Ray was in a heap of danger and was going to be needing help.

"That's why we got criminal laws," came a voice from the rear.

"Society's taken over the function of revenge on the individuals who break the laws," said another voice.

Norman spoke up again. "Society should protect itself against criminals rather than revenge itself on them."

"And how is that supposed to be done?" the voice from the rear asked.

"Either by reforming the criminal and teaching him to become a useful citizen or by removing him from society. That's what the prisons are for."

"I vote we REMOVE HIM!"

Loud cheers and applause told Gus that the townspeople weren't listening to reason.

Moses Cobb raised his hand and said, "Let Mitch have his say about this. It was his tractor that got stolen. How do you feel about this, Mitch?"

Mitchell Wampler took the pipe stem from his mouth and cleared his throat. "It's a cryin' shame a man cain't even go to a funeral without comin' home an' findin' his belongin's gone."

Mrs. Wampler patted the knees of her husband's overalls and Mitch added, "Stealin' farm equipment is a serious crime. Farmin' is a man's livelihood. What's been done about it, Vern?"

Gus looked down at his knees. He couldn't help the wave of sympathy he had for Mitch.

Vernon Peele stood and paced to the front of the room. "There's not much we can do except keep a look out for the tractor, Mitchell. I put up the posters asking for witnesses. This ain't a murder, you know." He half-laughed. "It would probably be easier if it was. We'd call in a crime expert from Knoxville."

"Maybe that's where we should start. Get an ace on this," Clem Guffey said sarcastically. "What would he do?"

"Depends on the case," Vern answered. "If there were tracks, he'd probably make a plastic cast of the shoe print."

"What would that prove? That the killer wore shoes?"

The sheriff cleared his throat. "It can determine the height, and weight of the individual. They'd send it to the crime lab of the FBI in Washington, D.C., but why are we talking about something that hasn't happened? We're jumping off the track. We'll get him and he'll receive the maximum penalty."

"I say we hunt him down like the animal he is!" Jethro Depew blurted. "Tree 'im like a possum and shoot 'im!" He waved a 12-gauge shotgun above his head.

Norman pushed himself up. "Let's be reasonable. Although this thievery is serious, you men are acting like there's a murderer in town. No one's been killed. Maybe this man's been in trouble before. Vern, have you checked past records?"

Gus listened shockingly as his friend, Billy Ray, was being portrayed as a murderer. Gilbert was right, they should have tried to stop him! Gus bowed his head, then slowly rose. Words from behind whispered, "The boy's got something to say." When the room quieted, Gus said shyly, "This is the first time that I know of that a man's tractor's been stolen in our area. We know that because there ain't nothing in this town that escapes us."

"Hogwash!" someone yelled, and Gus jumped. "Who knows how many reports get lost."

"Let him finish, Ray Bob," Norman said calmly.

"When is someone gonna show an interest in MY opinion?" Ray Bob grumbled, striking a match to a Herbert Tareyton cigarette.

"Maybe we don't respect your opinion." Moses said.

Norman spoke up again. "Gentlemen, could my son have your attention?"

Gus stared at smoke curling around the bare light bulb that hung above Sheriff Peele's head. Several moths were being lured to the glow. His eyes scanned the crowd. They were all staring up at him waiting for him to continue. Gus straightened his posture and said, "A lot of time has passed since the theft. There's a possibility this person won't be found."

Taylor Tipton boo-hooed. "This ain't a dispute over cowpeas!"

"What you need are some paid deputies, Vern," Norman said when Gus took his seat. "One man can't run the law business by himself."

A couple of "Amens" came from the group.

Vern stubbed a cork-tipped cigarette out. Sweat circled the underarms of his tan, long sleeved work shirt. "You know as well as anyone, Norm, the county has no money for public services."

"The Sheriff's Department should have a full-time staff capable of handling trouble quickly without hours of telephone calls to round up part-time deputies," Rye Mirts submitted.

"Darn right," Burchfield agreed. "Right now we have to depend on untrained farmers, loggers, businessmen, or whoever else is available at the time."

Tipton stood. "We do need more help. More power would deter crime. Remember back in 1933 when Prohibition was lifted? Alcohol dropped from forty dollars a gallon to five dollars. Criminal activity would drop, too, if some changes were made around here."

Vern nodded with understanding. "I agree the county court should find funds to hire at least one full-time deputy. With more folks takin' a likin' to the area, we'll need to do something soon."

Gus stood slowly once again. "Gus?" Vern said.

"Why can't the county raise their own funds to pay for elective public services? Organize bake sales, pancake breakfasts, catfish suppers. The church could have rummage sales . . . " Gus heard a low mumble of agreement.

"I say we go home and think about tonight's meeting and gather back here a week from Tuesday," the sheriff said. He pulled a pack of cigarettes from his shirt pocket. "Meeting adjourned."

Before opening the door, Norman faced Gus and said, "You did good tonight.

I'm glad you went with me. I'm sorry Gilbert didn't want to go."

Tiptoeing across the kitchen toward his bedroom, Gus stopped in front of the sideboard and stuck a finger into the frosting of a cake. He could faintly smell his mother's lilac talcum that she powdered herself with after a bath. It was a nice smell, and he was glad to be home.

Sitting on the edge of his bed, he silently worried about Billy Ray. The town was angry and they had a right to be. He undressed, laid down and stared silently at the cowboy papered walls in the room. The door was slightly ajar and the dim light from the front room streamed in. He could hear his folks talking quietly.

Katherine was wrapped in her old flannel robe and her hair was wound in little pin-curls. Her face was scrubbed and shiny.

"How did the meeting go?" she asked.

"The meeting has drifted from my mind."

Gus glanced out and saw Norman coax her closer.

Gus heard Katherine sigh. "Let's talk, Norman," she said. "I'm worried about something and we need to discuss it. That's why I waited up."

"What's bothering you, Katy?"

"I'm worried we won't be able to pay next month's bills. I figured and re-figured our budget tonight. Norman, I don't know how we'll manage. I thought the mill would help us get ahead, but after all these years, we're just getting farther and farther behind."

"I know that, but what am I suppose to do? Sell out? Then what?" Norman scratched his head. "Maybe it's time we cut the Delvine timber," he said. "I was hoping we could hold on to it for our retirement."

"For now we can borrow more money from Daddy."

"No. I won't do it," Norman said firmly. He stretched out his hand toward her. "Come here," he said. "I don't want to argue about this. You know how I feel about borrowing."

She shrugged his hands away. "I thought you and Daddy had an understanding, Norm. It seemed that you two were getting on really well, lately."

"We do get on well, just as long as I don't feel indebted to him. Katy, damn it, I want to be able to take care of you and our children myself. Don't you understand that?"

"I only understand one end isn't meeting the other. We've got to do something soon. Talk to Daddy, Norm."

"Give me some time with this, Katy."

"We've got to do something, now," she said, rubbing both hands nervously over her abdomen. "I'm worried, can't you see? You know I'm not one to borrow trouble, Norm. I've been over the books several times tonight."

Norman sat up stiffly looking away from her. "Things will have to get a lot rougher before I ask Henry Ashord for more money."

"I know you feel guilty for not being able to provide for our family. It's naked in your eyes, Norman, but it isn't your fault. We took on too much right from the beginning. It was just as much my fault as yours."

Gus got up and stared through the night-time window. The barn's rusty tin roof reflected a jagged edged moon. He could feel Norman's reluctance to borrow more money and his mother's urgency to do so. Why did his father have to be so stubborn? Gus pressed his forehead against the cool glass and closed his eyes but his mind could still see the wooded slopes and hollows receding toward a wide, winding creek. Gooseflesh pebbled his arms. I wish I could help, Gus thought. I hadn't realized they were in such a financial bind. He felt saddened because his mother fretted about their monetary needs. Damn him! he thought. Damn his stubbornness. Gus turned around and glanced again into the front room. He saw Norman put his arms around her. He's doing something right, Gus thought. Mama needs held.

"Norman, I'm sorry I brought this up tonight but there's something else," Katherine said in a low voice. "We're having another baby."

Gus felt angry. Another baby? Gus thought. With Garrett so sick why would they want another one?

Katherine was mixing up honey dew biscuits when Gus plodded into the toasty oven-warmed kitchen several weeks later. She was wearing the rose printed, smocked, maternity dress that she wore when she was heavy with Garrett.

"You nearly missed supper," she said as she kneaded the dough. She turned to look at Gus standing in the doorway. "Close the door. You're letting cold air in," she reprimanded, then rolled the dough to just-right thickness.

Gus looked at the dress and thought about the conversation he'd overheard the night of the town hall meeting. So it was true. The baby-having dress proved it. His chipperness faded. Wasn't Garrett's illness giving her enough heartache without having another baby to worry about? Gus swished past her, rolled his eyes and headed for his room. "You plan on having forty-'leven kids?" he yelled. He didn't understand his own temper. He'd never talked that way to his mother before. It's because I care, gosh darn it! Gus chucked his coat on the bed.

"Landsake!" she called after him, reaching for a towel to wipe her hands. Her tin measuring cup and the biscuit cutter flew to the floor and bounced with a showering puff of flour.

The old springs grated and squeaked as Gus pounced down on the double-sized featherbed. Katherine craned her head into his room. "Gus. . . ." But before she could say more, Garrett began to gasp and choke.

In the draw of a breath Katherine was at the baby's side, cradling him and patting his back. His blood-gorged face had a frightened expression as his thin arms flailed through the air. The wheezing gasps were thick with mucus.

"Garrett!" she screamed.

The child was silent. Gus watched the baby's hands shake and his tiny body go rigid. Afraid with a feeling of helplessness, Gus realized he was holding his breath.

"GO GET YOUR FATHER!" Katherine screamed, breaking the terrible silence.

Gus drew back, startled from the strength of her strange, thick, gravelly voice. He raced around the corner, through the kitchen, and out the door. "Pa!" he yelled. "Come quick!"

Under the beam of the barn light, Gus found Norman re-bolting a toolbox bracket onto the frame of the tractor. Gus yelled again and Norman stood up as if in slow motion. Gus was sure by the sober look on his father's face that he knew something was wrong with Garrett.

Norman wiped his hands on a shop rag and pushed up his glasses. "It's Garrett isn't it?"

Garrett didn't make it to Christmas. He died on that cold December night, his tiny, weak and withered body giving way to death's lure. Gus knew his little brother was dead when Katherine and Norman tenderly laid him on the adult-sized gurney in the cold, white sanitized emergency room.

Gus and Gilbert stood paralyzed as they watched Katherine scoop her child into her arms and shake him, his loose, white body like a sheet flapping in the wind. Katherine held Garrett against her chest and rocked back and forth, crying silently. Norman reached for her but the doctor shook his head and whispered, "Let her grieve."

Unemotional robot-looking men and women staggered by, shaking their heads like they were programed to do so. Several of them stopped and patted Gus or Gilbert on the head. On each side of the room were metal, upright chairs. Gus and Gilbert shared a chair and sat grief-strickened as their mother clung to her dead child. The stinging smell of disinfectant nauseated Gus as his disbelieving eyes stared at the tiny bundle she cradled. He dropped his gaze and stared at his and Gilbert's clamped-together hands. "He's dead," Gus whispered and Gilbert clenched his hand harder.

The room was a blur of antiseptic white when Gus raised his head. He saw Norman pry Katherine's fingers from Garrett's miniature shoulders and lead her to an orange, coffee-stained sofa. He watched Norman lift Garrett from her arms, take him to the gurney and lay him down. Gus cringed as Norman pulled a white sheet up over the baby's body, stare briefly into Garrett's face, then cover the child's head. Gus felt as though there was a brick in his throat and he wanted to vomit it up and strike Norman with it. How dare he cover Garrett's head, declare him dead? That one move denoted the truth, the finale. Their baby brother was dead.

Katherine rose from the stained sofa, her shiny green pocketbook falling from her lap. She stepped over her purse, wandered down the dim-lit hallway and stood before a decorated Christmas tree. Gus got up, positioned himself next to his mother and clasped her icy-cold hand. Without words, they bowed their heads and saw the tree's blue lights flickering on a miniature baby Jesus, his tiny body draped with a white sheet.

The next morning, as Katherine rested with sedatives, Norman painstakingly chose the best timber planks he could find and made a tiny casket. When the box was finished, he went to the bank and borrowed a hundred dollars for a burial plot and a marker.

On the morning of the funeral Gus woke early, stretched, yawned. In the middle of his stomach he felt an empty sadness. He pushed the covers aside, got up, and pulled back his curtains. With his hand he wiped the condensation from the window. The morning was cold and gray. He turned back to the bed, shook Gilbert to rouse him awake then looked at his dark suit hanging on the door. His clean underwear had been laid out on the foot of the bed, his Sunday shoes polished and placed against the bed stand. Just like a church day.

Rolling hills framed the small cemetery and a white picket fence marked its borders. Gus heard Christmas music, *Silent night Holy night* . . . Pain clutched his heart as he watched Norman help his mother to a chair in the front row. A thin film of morning frost was still white on the ground. Small dark twigs stuck out like porcupine quills. A few curious passers-by came down the side street and stood motionless at the white wooden fence. They were dressed in bright colors of Christmas. *Away in a manger* . . . The sharp wind chilled Gus even through his heavy coat and he shivered. He looked up at his mother. She pulled her black scarf tightly around her neck. He hated seeing her so sad. Darn you, Garrett, it wasn't right for you to do this to our mom. Gus looked at the tiny casket and thought of Garrett's tin soldier still wrapped beneath their Christmas tree. Why hadn't they laid it in the death box with him? He turned and looked up at Norman. When he saw the tears in his father's eyes, he felt even more embittered. Norman smiled down at Gus, but it was an odd smile, contorted and it appeared to be drawn-on. He held his coat closed with one hand and patted Gus's shoulder with the other. Katherine glanced down and took hold of Gus's hand. With her free one she reached for Gilbert. Gus watched him lean into her and rub his eyes.

Gus looked around at friends and family gathered, eyes downcast, puffs of clouds coming from each nostril and mouth. There was a rolling in the pit of his stomach as Reverend Reed said some weightless words that he didn't understand. *His will be done.* An empty ache gnawed at his soul. Gus reached into his pocket for his wadded up hanky, clamped his eyes shut and blew his nose. The music somewhere nearby continued. *Oh holy night* . . . His little brother was lying there in the box, all dressed up in his tiny suit and bow tie, but he no longer existed. Where was he right now? Where would he be tomorrow, next year? Where would he be when Gil was in California? Suddenly Gus felt lonesome, and scared. Scared to death. Is this all there is of Garrett? Is Garrett all over with forever, he wondered. Will he still be a part of the family? Gus's pale eyes searched the crowd. Across the way stood Park Hensley in his dark, worsted flannel suit. With ungloved, bluish and veined hands he held a black hat against his chest. He had to be close to seventy years old. His wife, Hazel, her back rounded into a C shape, looked even older.

Gus looked up at his mother again and wondered how she really felt inside. Would her grief feel the same if I died? he wondered. Gil? Was it the same for everyone? He leaned in closer to Katherine. She squeezed him and it felt good.

Gus half-listened to Reverend Reed's words, his mouth huffing out puffs of frost. His gaze rested on Seth Jones. He was old, too. He was with his wife Lou Anna, and Gus looked down at her legs. He remembered his mother saying the black seams in her hose were always crooked like a mountain road. Standing next to them was Ralph and Betty Jo, both with canes at their sides. They were almost prehistoric. "Why did God have to take our little baby?" he cried, burying his face in Katherine's shoulder. "Why not them?" Gus looked up into his mother's pale, watery eyes. She squeezed him again, but didn't answer.

Gus poked his head out and around Katherine to look at Gil. Gilbert looked away and shifted his weight from side to side. Katherine bent down and whispered something into his ear. Gus looked at Norman. His eyes looked quickly at Gus then away. Gus saw him press his glasses against his face, but it didn't hide the tears. And when Katherine started crying, too, their tears burned Gus's own eyes like salt in an open wound. Then Gilbert started crying and now Gus was infuriated with Garrett. He didn't even want to stay and watch him get put into the ground. He wanted to go home and turn on the saws and shove logs through, one after another until the whole damn woods was gone. How could Garrett go and die and make everyone so miserable?

As Gus stared at his infant brother's miniature burial box, he wondered why life was so unjust. His eyes scanned the small gathering. Why didn't God take one of these *old* geezers? he asked himself. Why this tiny bundle of new life? Garrett was just beginning. Gus closed his eyes and imagined angels with white, gauzy robes hovering over Garrett's cold body waiting patiently until the preacher said his final word. He imagined the cherub-like spirits reaching their arms under Garrett's tiny inert form and taking it away. Gus's merging feelings of sadness and anger tore at his heart. He tilted his head down. A damp chill bit through his body and he hugged himself for warmth. Katherine wrapped her arm tightly around him and pulled him nearer.

The distant Christmas music continued. *Oh little town of Bethlehem . . .* There wasn't a shop in the whole town that didn't display some jovial symbol of the season. Even all the grave markers wore green garlands and wreaths of holly. Christ was born and Garrett died.

When the funeral was over, Gilbert stood quietly next to Gus while Katherine and Norman hugged people and listened to quiet words of sympathy. Then the well-wishers left to share Christmas happiness with their own families.

Gus's attention was drawn to a bright red cardinal perched majestically on the white picket fence alongside Garrett's grave. Gus's eyes lingered on the bird's brilliance. Suddenly the bird resembled a buzzard and he thought about the day the preacher came for dinner. The thought made him smile. He jerked when the cardinal suddenly flew away. Away, like Garrett.

The cemetery emptied quickly and the Wheeler's stood staring at the little carved lamb on the baby's grave marker. Gus saw his folk's faces twisted in anguish. Norman's fingers inched under Katherine's coat sleeve and tightened around her wrist. He whispered to her soothingly. Their sad eyes met. Norman's face showed lines of strain. Katherine took his gloved hand and pressed it to her chest as the tiny casket was lowered.

Katherine's shoulders shook. "He never knew me," she wailed. "He never even had a chance to call me Mommy."

A painful, heavy silence was in the air that night. Katherine had asked Gus and Gilbert to come sit with them. Gilbert fidgeted with his bag of marbles and Gus stared at the rug-covered hardwood floor. Norman lay on the sofa and covered his tear-swollen face with his forearm. Gus knew Norman didn't want his family to see him cry. Dry-eyed, Katherine rocked in her rocking chair, the same chair she'd rocked Garrett in so many times. Gus looked sadly at his father. His chest and shoulders were bouncing like they were driving down a bumpy road.

Gus wanted to comfort him, but his arms felt frozen to his sides. He was angry. This awful thing never should have happened. Garrett should be here, his tiny body packed with life and hope. There would be an empty space now, not like the skyline when a tree was felled or a missing tooth, but like a heart plucked from its warm bosom.

Gus grimaced when he stared down at his mother's swollen belly and saw the baby moving inside her, a small, weak thumping against her robe. She flattened her palms over her stomach. What was she thinking? They say for every death there's a birth. Gus wondered if Katherine would think of this child as Garrett's replacement. She must resent it, he thought. Gus thought of how easy it was for one baby to die and another to replace it. Would this new child, curled in her belly, be crippled? Flawed? He looked into her pale, slack face and saw a can't-fix pain. Nothing he could say or do would help her.

The house was silent, eerie. Gus wanted to talk; about Garrett, the new baby, anything. His heavy lids closed against the harsh stream of moonlight piercing through the white, lacy curtains. Behind his still-dry lids he saw Garrett's pudgy little fingers with their small nails, always clean, never crusted with dirt or mud like his and Gilbert's fingernails always seemed to be. Gus looked away and spotted Garrett's booteed pajamas hanging limply over his tiny rocking horse.

Norman was still now. Could he have cried himself to sleep? Gus saw his mother touching her breast and guessed she was remembering Garrett nursing, silently, in slow rhythm, sweet, warm, private. Tonight the thought didn't embarrass him like always before. Tonight it seemed natural, maternal. Then Gus saw those tiny hands flailing the air just minutes before he died. He saw Garrett's terrified, helpless face and felt a sudden, stunning sense of loss. She must be feeling it, too, Gus thought and felt his heart ache. He looked at Katherine as she stared, unblinking at the ceiling until her lips started to move and she spoke in a low monotone.

"He'll never know poverty," she said. "I've been thinking of all the bad things in life Garrett won't have to go through." Katherine looked at Gilbert, over to Norman's still outline, and finally her eyes rested on Gus. "I knew the hardships of growing up," she said. "When poverty tried to defeat us and we refused to let it. I remember our loss when the cow smothered her calf. And I recall . . . " Her voice fell silent.

"I didn't realize growing up was so hard for you," Gus said.

Katherine smiled at Gus. "I didn't know it, either."

"I guess that's what family love is all about," Gus said, glad his mother was now talking, thinking of something other than Garrett. He had to keep her talking.

"What else do you remember, mama?"

Katherine was silent for a moment then said, "I remember when it rained too much and the potatoes rotted in the ground. When the crows stole the corn, when the deer stripped the gardens bare, the hens' infertile eggs, the storm that ravaged a crop that had been growing all summer. But the poverty my mama and I had back in those days contributed something indefinable, something that will be with me always."

Katherine rested her head against the back of the rocker and Gus noticed her white, slack skin. She'd aged so much in the past two years. Garrett had done it to her. Her chin moved and her lip parted. "I remember the nights I lay wondering who my daddy was and felt the pain my mother carried, loving and not having Henry with her. When I was old enough, I searched for my father, not knowing at the time, that he was in prison for a crime he didn't commit—the accident on Old Cemetery Road. I'll tell you about it some day." She covered her face with her hand and rubbed her eyes as tears trickled down her hollow cheeks. "Henry Ashford," Katherine said, wiping her eyes. "Right now, the person I need the most is my father. I want him to rock me in his arms."

"I can call him for you, Mama," Gilbert offered, looking up and putting his marble bag aside.

"No, honey. It's late. It's time we all went to bed."

Ache borrowed deep inside Gus's chest. He turned on his side facing the wall and ran his hand across the cool, ironed sheet. Garrett's image filled his head and broke his heart. Why did this happen? Was his mother being punished? Was it because she wore the lifelong stigma of illegitimacy? For some reason the Lord had seen fit to take away Katherine's mother and her son. Was the sentence fulfilled?

The questions battered his brain making his temples throb. Only God knew the answers. Gus closed his eyes and saw behind his lids a vivid, red bird above a dark hole in the ground. A weak glow of moonlight streaked through the curtains. Gus's dried, powdery tears made his cheeks itch and he rubbed his face with the sheet. He heard his father snoring lightly and sat up wondering if his mother was okay. He walked silently to his parent's bedroom doorway and peeked in. Katherine was sitting up in bed staring at Norman. She pulled the quilt up around his neck, then to Gus's surprise, struck out at him, beating Norman on the arms and shoulders. She pounded and pushed and screamed and poked and lifted her legs from under the covers and kicked at him. Shocked, Gus stepped away from the door, then peeked back in. Was his father going to wake up striking back? Gus held his breath and watched as Norman rose to a sitting position. He reached out for Katherine, held her tightly and rocked her gently and softly as a baby.

Norman brushed Katherine's disarrayed hair from her wet, contorted face. His voice was level and controlled. "We'll beat this pain down together."

"Oh, Norman, even with your arms around me, I feel this icy skin encasing me and wonder if I'll ever be able to feel warmth again. Please hold me and don't let go," she wailed.

Gus watched painfully as his mother's tears spilled over and she wiped them harshly away with the crisp cotton sheet. Her shoulders shook and her round stomach shook and she looked like a floppy rag doll in the warmth of his father's arms.

Gus tiptoed back to his room. His heart felt heavy and perplexed. When he thought everyone was asleep, Gus quietly got out of bed and crept outside. His footsteps made no sound as he tiptoed across the porch and down the path to the mill. He stood in front of the control panel pulling levers and pushing buttons. Gus felt powerful as he handled and touched the cool metal blades and jiggling the levers up and down. The band saw was his favorite. His pa told him it traveled a hundred miles an hour. He couldn't understand why he wasn't allowed to operate any of the saws. In another year he'd be a teenager! His father had taken him to a town hall meeting. Why wouldn't he permit him to run the machinery? Gus bounced up onto the carriage and imagined it moving back and forth pushing the dark, rough logs against the blade of the band mill. In his head he heard the whizzing sound. He jumped down and touched the controls of the edger saw and the trimmer saw and imagined the planks being cut into even lengths.

When Gus tired of piloting the sawmill, he jumped like a five-year-old, head first into a pile of finely ground sawdust. He rolled over onto his back, folded his arms under his head and watched long, eerie shadows unfold as ghostly clouds erased the moon. He opened his eyes wide to try to see through the deep, opaque darkness. The trees were like black cutouts against the mixed-up sky. Gus felt damp and cold as the plump, round moon reappeared. He sat up and gazed briefly at the lunar glow on the tin roof of their home then down at the gray, weathered boards that wrapped around the house. Silence. He strained his ears for a shred of sound but heard only stillness. Slowly his sleepy gaze moved through the frost-crystalled kitchen window. A night light in the room cast a homey warmth on the neatly arranged violets on the window sill. The tenderly-cared-for blooms warmed his soul and his lips formed a tiny smile. He felt safe, cared for. Gus looked over at the new cut, fresh-smelling lumber in neat stacks near the mill and felt a stirring challenge sweep over him. "I'll make my daddy proud," he said. When snowflakes began to drift down and dot his face, Gus pushed himself up, dusted the damp wood flour from his pajamas and slipped back into the house.

He moved silently past the platters of food the folks from the church had brought. Billy Ray Mudd and his mom had paid their respects. Gus didn't say anything when he saw Billy Ray stuffing his pockets with cookies and fried chicken. Later, Gus had wrapped a hank of ham and taken it to them. "We had too much," he told Martha Mudd. Gus moved on into the living room. He touched a branch of their decorated tree. They'd had a ball going into the woods and choosing just the right tree. The family's laughter had rippled through the house as they made the paper chains and popcorn strings. Even Garrett had laughed and gurgled. Who was to know their pleasure would soon turn to tears and the gay, holiday feeling erased. The five packages under the tree were un-opened. He knew what was in each one. After the funeral Katherine had told them they could open their presents. She told them it might make them feel bet-ter. He and Gilbert had peeked between the folds of the bright colored paper and seen their gift. Nevertheless, the mood was somber and opening them didn't seem fit. Gus looked sadly at the packages with the boxing gloves for him and Gilbert, the tin soldier for Garrett. He touched the handle of the awkwardly-wrapped vacuum cleaner, then glanced down at the neatly-wrapped pair of glass-es. He sighed. Why did you have to die? Why now? Why spoil our Christmas? Gus thrust aside the unanswerable questions and went to bed, yet as hard as he tried, he couldn't sleep.

Gus envisioned Garrett's casket and suddenly missed Garrett more than he thought his heart could stand. He padded to the window and his gaze fell upon the flat tree stump where Garrett had sat just a few days before he died and Gus wondered if maybe some element of Garrett was still there, still lingering on that stump; a scent of baby powder, a hair, a fingerprint? He felt cold and alone. Gus remembered the day Katherine told them that Garrett might die. It was on that night Gilbert had slid an ace of hearts under the baby's pillow for luck. Gus got mad at Garrett one day shortly after that, and replaced the ace of hearts with an ace of spades. Did that bad-luck card cause Garrett to die? It wasn't until the first frail, morning light, that Gus drifted off to sleep.

Gus had slept only a couple hours when a nightmarish, bloodcurdling yell woke him. He heard his mother scream and men hollering. Gus ran to the window and saw Gilbert jump into the Buick. The car lurched forward with a roar and a swirl of dust. Gus rubbed his blurry eyes and pushed up the window. "What's happened?" Gus yelled, then saw his father lying on the ground in a pool of blood. His heart knocked against his chest so hard Gus felt it would burst through. His eyes darted back to the car's tail lights. "The Buick's out of gas!" he shouted and ran to the telephone. "Thelma Jean!" Gus yelled into the dead receiver. He pushed the button on the side of the box and rang again for the operator. "Damn," he hollered and slammed the receiver down. "Where is Thelma Jean when you need her?"

Gus raced back to his room, yanked his pants off the floor, lifted one foot to put them on and nearly fell. He grabbed the bedpost for balance. With no shirt or shoes, he ran out of his bedroom and through the wide-opened kitchen door. "The car's out of gas!" he yelled.

Gus saw Cletus Yates, dash toward Norman and fall to his knees at his side. "We've got to stop the bleeding!" Yates shouted. He pointed to the severed limb. "Pack the arm in ice," he ordered, "and get some blankets!" Katherine ran to the house as instructed. Yates elevated Norman's right shoulder and applied pressure to the artery. The bleeding continued. He yanked a hanky from his back pocket and wrapped it tightly around the stub just above the elbow where Norman's arm had been severed. "Give me a screwdriver," he directed. Yates placed the tool on top of the knot and twisted to tighten the tourniquet.

Katherine rushed out of the house and down the steps with towels, dishpan and ice cubes. A red wool blanket was draped over her shoulder and flapping in the wind as she ran. Fear clouded her face. "What do I do now?" she asked, her voice high-pitched and trembling.

"Wrap the arm in towels and be careful the arm doesn't touch the ice directly," Yates commanded.

Gus looked at his mother's panic-struck face. "I'll do it, Mom," Gus said, squatting and lifting Norman's arm as gently as a newborn baby. He swaddled the still-warm arm and tucked it into the ice then sat back on the ground petting the arm as if it were a sick kitten.

"His pulse is weak," Yates said as Norman moaned incoherently. "He's probably in shock," he mumbled, resting the side of his head on Norman's chest. "His breath's short and weak."

Gus draped his father with the red blanket and kneeled beside him. "Please don't you die, too," he said, gripping Norman's good hand.

"Where are they?" Katherine cried. "Gilbert should be back with Dr. West by now."

"Let's pray Gilbert didn't run out of gas," Gus said. "He's got a sprained ankle and it'll be hard for him to walk." He stood up and peered down the path. "I'm going to go see, Ma," he said, darting down the dirt road barefooted.

Gilbert turned the key again and again, but the engine wouldn't turn over. "What's wrong with you, you damn bugger!" he cursed. "Damn!" Gilbert yelled, stomping his feet on the floorboard. "Just two more miles to town!"

"Gil," Gus shouted, reaching in through the opened window and grasping his brother's cold hand that gripped the steering wheel. "It's out of gas. I'll run on into town. You go back and help Mom."

Gilbert shoved the door open with his shoulder and lunged from the car's front seat. "I can't do anything right," he said.

"It's not your fault," Gus said. "Stop feeling sorry for yourself," he said, running in the direction of town. His bare feet moved as fast as his legs could carry him, over dried leaves, twigs, acorns. All the way to town he sped, past Ruth Ann's Guest House, the Rooms for Let sign, past Buford's Bait and Tackle Shop, and between the Ethel and Regular pumps at the Sinclair gas station. He paused only long enough to catch his breath before vaulting the steps to Sheriff Vernon Peele's office.

But the sheriff was out. Gus jiggled the knob; the door was locked. He pressed his nose against the cool glass window. A curling thread of smoke from the butt of a cigarette teetering on the edge of an empty tuna fish can. "Shoot!" he said.

"Vern's on a disturbing-the-peace call Gus," someone shouted from across the street.

Gus's eyes darted both ways. He sighed, grabbed up his loose pants and ran down the steps. He stopped briefly and looked both ways before he headed west on Main Street. Breathlessly, he rushed through Dr. West's double doors.

"Come quick! Pa's lost an arm."

Calvin Hawkins and several men from the camp were lifting Norman's limp body into the truck when Gus and Dr. West sped into the yard.

"Looks like you did everything right," the doctor said, scanning the situation. "Now let's get him to the hospital. Help me, Gilbert," Dr. West said.

Katherine quickly dabbed at her bloodied skirt with a clean towel. "I'm going with you," she said.

"What happened?" Norman asked groggily, after surgery. Katherine held his other hand.

"The main lever was turned to full power. When you pushed the start button, the saws started at maximum speed. Your arm was across one of them."

"But . . . I never leave the main lever up!" Norman said, then grimaced with pain. "I always double check the power switch before I leave. It was off, I tell you."

"The men say someone tampered with the machinery last night," Katherine said.

"Squaw," Norman said. "Was it Lenny Squaw?"

"We don't know, Norm."

He nodded toward the bandages. "Is it gone?" Norman asked weakly.

"Oh, Norman," Katherine cried, dabbing her eyes. She smoothed back Norman's damp hair and kissed his forehead.

Norman closed his eyes. "I feel wuzzy," he said, then asked, "Was Lenny Squaw around the mill last night, Katy?"

"I don't know," Katherine said.

But Gus knew. He had played with the machinery the night before. He knew he was responsible for his father's arm. Yes, Lenny had been near there, but he hadn't touched the controls. Tears scalded Gus's eyes and his legs felt weak. He touched Norman's pale forehead with a damp cloth. "I'm sorry, Pa," he cried.

Norman half-opened his eyes. "We'll manage all right." Closing his eyes again, he said, "I'll learn to work with one arm."

"But you don't understand," Gus said hastily, wiping away tears. "It was me. I messed around at the mill last night," he cried, squeezing Norman's hand. "Because of me, you lost an arm."

Norman turned his head away and Gus turned slowly to leave. He couldn't blame his father for turning away. He'll never speak to me again, Gus said to himself, but Norman turned back to his son. He held out his good arm and pointed to Gus. "Guess I'm gonna have to teach you to do it right," he said drowsily.

For Gus, the next few days passed slowly and were full of remorse. He didn't try to fight off the feeling because he knew it was his due. Gus knew his parents were going to have a hard time coming up with the money for the doctor and hospital bills. He was in the barn reaching for the hay fork when he remembered the notice asking for information about Mitchell's stolen tractor. Gus hung the fork back on the wall and headed for Vern's office.

Billy Ray had been a friend ever since Gus could remember and he wondered if Billy Ray would snitch on him. Something told him no. When Gus passed the post office, he saw that Vern had taped the reward sign there, too. Vern had hung copies everywhere. Gus knew Billy Ray had been wrong. I *have* to come up with some money. It's my fault father lost an arm, Gus argued with himself. If there's a reward, I need to tell what I know. I have to help with Pa's medical expenses. He felt like the double-crosser he knew he was.

"Yes, Gus, there's thirty-some dollars in a fund for a reward. Tell me what you know," Vern Peele said, dropping his cigarette on the wood floor and crushing it with his shoe. Gus watched the smoke curl around his face as he exhaled.

Gus took a deep breath and swallowed cigarette smoke. "Gil and I were on the hill behind Mitch's barn," he started, feeling like a no-good traitor. "We saw someone take the tractor," Gus said. Gus felt like Judas at the last supper, but his family needed the reward to pay for doctor bills. This was an emergency and he had no choice but to tell.

"And?" the Sheriff asked, jutting his head forward and raising his eyebrows.

Gus shifted his feet around and looked up into the long, chin-stubbled face. He noticed Vern's receding hairline for the first time. "And, . . . ahm. . . ." Would Billy Ray do the same thing to me? Gus painfully asked himself.

"Well?" the Sheriff asked. "Who did you see take the tractor?" Vern waited briefly for an answer and when it didn't come immediately, stepped behind his metal desk and sat in his small wooden chair with wheels on it. He shuffled some papers on the desk in front of him, looked up, cleared his throat, waited.

Gus's downward gaze studied a hole in his pants, then went to Vern's cigarette butt on the dark unclean floor. No, Billy Ray would never betray a friend, Gus thought. Not in a million years. He drew his head slowly upward. "We were too far away to see anything," he said.

PART THREE

• CHAPTER 9 •

Gus sat on the porch step watching dawn's light gather strength for a new day. He thought of how easily night slid into day, months into years. Seasons melded one into another, springs full of tender, rejuvenating expectancy, summers with verdant lushness and thunderstorms. Through the years he'd sat on these same steps and saw hillsides sheathed with autumn colors and feathery snows drift silently into winter's rest. The pulse of time ticked on, opening room for more of life's heartaches, joy, and love. He took a sip of coffee and finger-combed his hair. His long-stretched gaze swept slowly, contentedly over Wheeler land, home, where even the life-draining, kudzu-smothered thickets seemed right with it's almost human-like need for closeness. Gus stretched out his legs before him, leaned back on his elbows and sucked in a fresh woodsy breath. When he looked up again, he saw a fawn appear over the rim of the hill. Gus was shaken all at once with a dizzying gladness as he watched the still-spotted deer nibble on tender grass. He was happy to be sitting here on the porch steps listening to birdsong fill the air, content to be a part of the Wheeler family, living in a place where hard work could be rewarded at the end of the day with a fishing pole or a refreshing dunk in the creek.

In the peace of the early morning, Gus thought about the day's work ahead, and realized how lucky he was to be working alongside his father. Norman had learned to operate the mill with one arm as easy as he had with two. Even after four years, Gus felt remorseful for causing his father to lose an arm, yet Norman had never let the loss of a limb slow him down. Six days a week Gus and Norman worked from dark to dark to keep the sawmill going. Gus smiled and said aloud, "Some days I feel like I'm throwing a ball at one end and running to catch it at the other, yet I feel it's all worth it." He never tired of the work, yet, looked forward to the Lord's day when the family walked to church, ate a large dinner then called on neighbors.

At sixteen years old, Gus knew nearly as much about operating a sawmill as Norman and regretted as much as his father that Gilbert chose to detach himself from the family business. Gus couldn't understand his brother's crazy, intense ambition to achieve independence. Gil's taking the job at Buster Foch's Meat Market, working long, double shifts, was beyond reason.

The sun was peeping over the horizon now and Gilbert had already left for work. Norman finished his breakfast, patted Gus on the shoulder and headed on down to the mill. Gus poured out the last few swallows of cold coffee, got up, stretched, and walked back into the house. He smiled when Sara Jane padded out of her bedroom. "Good mornin' little one," Gus said, messing up her already disarrayed hair. Sara Jane giggled in her usual early-morning chipperness. Gus gazed down at his young sister with Norman's dark wavy hair and Katherine's fair eyes and porcelain skin. He recalled how he had resented it when he learned his mother was pregnant at a time when Garrett was so gravely ill. And now, he wouldn't give her up for all the money in the world. "Hold up your foot and let me tie your shoe," Gus said, leaning over and placing his sister's small foot on his knee. She reached out for the table to balance herself. "There now," he said, smiling and putting on his hat. "See ya soon," he said.

Winding his way down the path to the mill, Gus thought about how proud he was of Sara Jane. Smart as a tack, she was. At almost five years old she was singing nursery rhymes and church hymns in the choir. Sara Jane never knew her brother who died before she was born, but no one let her forget that Garrett was still a part of the family. Gus remembered the day him and Sara Jane had sat near Garrett's headstone and Gus told her lovingly that Garrett had been someone special who came briefly into the Wheelers' hearts, leaving behind quiet memories that would never perish. He thought of the Sundays when the family walked through the graveyard and laid flowers of the season on Garrett's tiny, lamb-carved stone. Sara Jane's tiny hand would touch the cold marker and she'd say, "I love you, little brother". Even though Garrett had been older, he would always be, to Sara Jane, her "little brother".

"Mornin'," Gus said, as he raised his arm to greet the men at the mill. He nodded at Norman, straightened his hat and began his day of hard work. "It's gonna be a steamer," Gus said, already beginning to sweat.

By midday, the heat was heavy and the sun granted no mercy. The dominant smell of sawdust intensified the summer's heat. Gus looked up from a set of circular saws and wiped sweat from his forehead. The wet leaves he'd tucked inside his hat had long dried. "Must be nigh dinner time," he said as he turned off the saw and headed for the well. Norman caught up to him and walked alongside. "Look at that heat dancing over the hills," Gus said, pointing.

On the clothesline, near the house, blue-white sheets hung heavy and unmoving in the hot sun. Gus looked toward the house. Katherine was sitting in a straight-back chair on the porch, her shoulders stooped over a pan of scalding water. "Damn," Norman said. "That woman deserves more. I think it's time for Calvin to prepare the Delvine timberland for cutting."

Katherine saw them looking and lifted her shoulders. Gus could see her smile. Sara Jane was on her tippy toes at the well, slowly pumping the big, red handle. She held her dress above her knees while cold water gushed over her thin tanned legs. Under the spout was a silver milk bucket overflowing with sun-reflected ice-cold water.

"For you, Daddy," she yelled, with all her childhood exuberance. Sara Jane took the dipper off the hook and filled the tin cup with the drawn, crystal clear liquid.

"Just what I needed!" Norman thanked, glancing down at his wet-with-sweat navy work-shirt. "Pour some in here, first," he said, holding his hat out. "Pour it over the leaves."

"That keeps your head cool, huh, Daddy?" she said.

With one arm doing the work of two, Norman hoisted her into the air and onto his shoulders. He smiled with her peal of laughter.

"You're all wet, Daddy! It's wet on my legs and feels like I peepeed in my pants."

Katherine sprinkled Super Suds into the new electric washer. She used the cut off end of a broom handle to push the dripping clothes through the big double rolls of the wringer. "Don't smash your fingers again, Mama," Sara Jane hollered.

"Scrubbing clothes on a washboard is safer," Katherine answered. "I know for a fact the washboard got the clothes cleaner."

"You use a washboard if you got hillbilly jeans," Sara Jane said.

Norman took off his hat and scratched his head. "Do you mean *genes*?"

"That's what I said!" Sara Jane said sarcastically.

"Where'd you hear that?" Katherine asked her and Gus cocked an ear to hear her answer.

"Beulah Maples says people who still use washboards have hillbilly jeans," she said.

"That explains it," Katherine said. "That sounds like something Beulah would say, her and that prissy sister of hers. Beulah and Trula are foreigners to these parts, Sara Jane. They should have stayed up in Toledo." Katherine leaned forward and stared into her daughter's clear blue eyes. "Now don't you go and tell her I said that!"

Gus laughed. "I'll tell her," he said.

A grin spread across Norman's weather-tanned face. He held out his hand. "What's that I feel? A breeze?"

Sara Jane grinned and held out her arms, too. "It feels good on my sweating skin," she said, lifting her dress to her waist. "But it swirls sawdust into my nose."

Norman pressed his glasses against his face then reached into his pocket and pulled out a handkerchief. "Here. Blow."

Sara Jane made a sniffing noise into the hanky then handed it back to Norman. She glanced around behind him and said, "I have to help Mommy pin clothes on the line, but first we'll cool off in the water."

Gus watched as Norman pumped the handle and Sara Jane danced around waiting for the water to begin gushing out, and when it did she stretched her legs into the cold liquid rush. Her pealing laughter made Gus laugh as her and Norman hopped and bounced around splashing each other like two jumping beans.

"Okay now, go help your mama," Norman said, and Gus watched her turn perkily and run to the clothes line. The child's long, shiny dark hair bounced at her waist and her yellow dress puffed up behind her like a little parachute as Gus and Norman hurried to the house to eat their dinner. "Looks like it might rain 'fore the day's over," Norman said, looking up.

"Air's coolin' some," Gus said, "but still hot and sticky."

"Better eat quickly and get back to work before it starts," Norman said.

"Over here, Gus. Help with this," Cletus Yates shouted as they walked back to the mill.

The two of them lifted boards that had slid off the sloping ramp on the way to the grader.

Norman took his glasses off and mopped his forehead again. "Wish Gilbert had taken an interest in the mill," he said, cleaning his glasses with his handkerchief. He put them back on and looked up at the threatening sky as thunder clapped above them.

"Me too, Pa. He still says he's going to California when he gets enough money saved."

"I'm afraid he'll be in for a rude awakening. It's a whole different world out there," Norman said, the words sounding sad to Gus.

"I don't think he likes working at Foch's meat locker. He's putting in double shifts, though, determined to make big money," Gus said.

"He could make money working right along with family," Norman huffed. "A person should bloom where they're planted. He comes home late, goes into his room and turns on the Philco until he falls asleep. He doesn't take part in any of the family's activities."

"His mind's on California, Pa. Has been ever since I can remember."

"Lord, help him," Norman said. "He'll end up filled with bitterness and failure."

Gus wiped his sweaty neck with his hanky. "Maybe not. He might get lucky."

"Lucky once a month when he walks to the mailbox in shoes made from old tires to get his relief check," Norman smirked.

"Like half the folks in this here holler!"

Norman snapped his head around. "Whoa now, just a minute. Let me tell you something. You've been siding with that wayward brother of yours all your life. Him going off to California is wrong, son, and you know it as well as I do," he said, raising his voice above another thunder boom.

"Oh-h now, I wouldn't say that," Gus said, weighting down some paperwork that had blown from the work bench. "He's not interested in Timber Hills Logging and Sawmill. If you forced him to work it, he wouldn't do a good job. Gil would never be productive if he hates what he's doing," Gus said and quickly reached up to hold down his cap.

"He'd learn to like it," Norman said, turning back to work.

"That's almost laughable. After sixteen years he hasn't learned. He never will, so stop expecting him to change. I wish he'd taken an interest in this work as much as you do!"

"Yeah," Norman grumbled, his chest rising in a long sigh. "You're probably right."

"I heard you tellin' Mom there was another stack of lumber missing this morning. How long is this going to go on before someone sees something?"

"I can't figure it out, son. I wake up sometimes during the night and look out the window. I've never seen anyone near the mill at night."

"I do the same, Pa. We need a big guard dog," Gus said.

"I think you're right. Why don't you look into that for me? I heard Tarwater's hound had pups again."

"I'll get us a watchdog, Pa. We still cuttin' the Delvine timber next week?"

"Calvin says they're ready and I say it's high time our family got out of debt. Your mama deserves more. It's the most beautiful piece of virgin woodland I've ever seen. They'll be setting up camp sometime next week. It's been a long time since I've been up there. Would've had it cut and sold a couple years ago if it hadn't been for the new housing contract up yonder."

Gus smiled. "Sure can't complain about that. It was a good contract and kept us busy for a year." Gus stuck his hanky back into his hip pocket. "I would have thought we'd have cut and replanted the Delvine timber by now," Gus said. "You bought that years ago?"

Norman smiled and nodded, "Fortunately we got that government contract just after Garrett died and then Calvin decided to cut those other two lots of ours north of here." He looked Gus straight in the eyes. "You've done me proud, son. Your enthusiasm, your interest in the business, it's more than I could have hoped for, Gus."

Gus shrugged it off. "I'm just doing what I always wanted." He glanced up and noticed heavy black clouds forming above the hills. "Wind's picking up," he commented.

Norman nodded and went back to work. "One good thing about owning timber property is, it never spoils, only gets better with time."

Wind began to blow in gusts and the sky turned nightfall-dark. The men at the mill were hurrying round gathering hats and paperwork. "Better shut it down," Gus yelled over the roaring wind. "You men go on home before the storm hits."

"We'll call it quits for the day," Norman said as the strong wind whipped and tormented them. "It's nearly quitting time anyhow," he said.

Norman and Gus hustled down the path. When they got nearer the house, they saw Katherine and Sara Jane scrambling to get the clothes off the line. The heavy hot air felt gelatinous with moisture.

"Look at them dark clouds churning," Katherine said to Sara Jane as they hurried to collect the clothes from the line. "Storm's a-comin' fast," she said, wiping the sweat pouring down her face.

"Better get the windows closed," Gus said, rushing into the house.

"Every one of 'em's opened," Katherine answered, pinning her hair back with one hand and pushing sheets into the basket with the other.

Inside, Katherine poured vinegar and sprinkled allspice into the pot of simmering tomato catsup. A homey, comfortable smell drifted through the house. "Sara Jane, you get the jars ready to pour this catsup into," she said, turning out the flame from under the pot of bubbling tomato puree. "It's thick enough, now."

"It's too stuffy in here," Norman said, raising a kitchen window part way. The wind caught the screen door and slammed it open with a bang. Katherine pulled it shut and hooked it.

"Mama, the curtains are blowing straight out!" Sara Jane yelled, just as a vase full of cut straw flowers clattered to the floor.

"Oh, for Pete's sake, Norman. Now close that window," Katherine said, tightening the canning jar lids. "Sara Jane, stay away from there with your bare feet!"

"I'm going to check on things outside," Gus said, walking out of the kitchen and onto the porch. Shielding his eyes, he headed for the barn, then turned toward the mill to recheck that everything was shut off. When he was satisfied, he dashed over to secure the crashing barn doors. The strong wind beat against his body as he ran to the hog lot to check on Koontz One, Two, and Three. "You in there?" he asked, leaning over the opening. "I hope you're hangin' on!" he told the three hogs he'd named after the stingy postmaster. When Gus was satisfied that all was secure, he pushed against the wind toward the house.

Scrambling into the house, he placed his hat on the peg and walked up behind his mother as she stood against the kitchen sink peeling potatoes. "You look sad, Mama."

"Gilbert telephoned," she said, not looking up.

"And?" Gus asked, watching her pump cold water over the potatoes. She picked up the chicken and plucked a few missed feathers.

"Working overtime again tonight."

"Well, he usually does," Norman said, moving the bucket of mop water onto the porch.

"And," Katherine quietly added, "he says he has enough money to get to California." She didn't look up, just plucked more vigorously.

Gus felt a rolling in the pit of his stomach, a feeling of abandonment.

"He's not old enough to leave home!" Norman raged.

"You were seventeen when you left home," Katherine said, blankly.

Norman scratched his head and unbuttoned his shirt. "I was more mature!"

"I think the storm's nearly over," Gus said, not wanting to talk about Gilbert leaving home. He opened the windows and stood at the kitchen door peering into the steaming wet yard.

"He's got a brain the size of a cowpea," Norman said. "Gilbert has a lot of growing up to do."

"He's saved every penny he's earned," Gus said, trying not to let his feelings show. "He won't even spend five cents for a bottle of Coca-Cola." He pushed open the screen door and walked out onto the damp porch. "It's cooler out here," he said, plopping down next to a basket of shelled butter beans. Pulling his legs up, Gus inhaled the rain-clean freshness and leaned back his head against a butter churner. "The rain cooled things off," he said, brushing sawdust from the knees of his overalls.

Katherine walked out and sat on the porch in her rocker. A large bowl was balanced on her knees as she shelled more peas. To Gus she looked like an old worn out dishrag sitting there bent over that big porcelain bowl. His heart felt sad knowing how hard she tried to conceal her feelings about Gilbert leaving. "Phew," he said, wiping his glistening forehead. "It didn't stay cool long. I feel like I'm in a steam bath," he said and got up and walked to the water pump. Under the wide-mouthed spout, Gus leaned over and doused his head with icy water.

Katherine got up, set the bowl aside and dumped the mop bucket out over the far edge of the porch. Gus heard her say something about Gil's desire to see a bigger part of the world than East Tennessee, and Norman grumbled, "It's a fool's desire, Katy." Then Katherine said, "Chicken needs to be fried," as she reached out and pulled open the squeaky screen door. It dragged on the porch's floorboards. Then Gus heard his mother say something about "a sense of things unseen" and Norman threw up his hand and protested "Gawdamighty, California won't enlighten him any. It'll only rape him of his values."

"What's cookin'?" Gus asked, stamping into the pink kitchen, longing desperately to end the constant subject of Gilbert's abandonment.

"Fried chicken, creamed potatoes, black-eyed peas and cornbread," Katherine answered, taking off her wet apron and putting on a clean, starched one over her faded house dress.

Norman glanced at the bushel of beans she'd put up that morning. "The perfect all-American woman," he bragged, looking at her over the rim of his glasses.

"Yeah," Katherine answered, whisking a strand of hair from her eyes, "just like Doris Day." She lowered the fresh-plucked chicken pieces into an iron skillet bubbling with hot lard.

"Looks more like she's a chore-burdened housewife," Gus said, taking in her hueless dress, limp, tied-back hair and tired eyes.

"Ain't that the gospel truth," she murmured, adding two tablespoons of vinegar to ingredients simmering in a double boiler on the back burner.

"We've got a little extra money now for nicer clothes and household goods," Norman said, steepling his fingers and resting his chin on them. "You should get yourself a new dress. That Delvine property will set us up real good."

"Honey, the imprint of being thrifty lingers from the Depression days," Katherine said. "I could never justify buying a new dress unless it was absolutely necessary."

"You making vinegar pie?" Gus asked, when Katherine added butter and lemon extract to the hot, thickening concoction in the double boiler.

"Yes I am," she answered, smiling. "Just for you." She reached up and smoothed down Gus's wet hair then looked into his eyes and said, "Tillie Mudd phoned this morning and said Billy Ray got called up for service. He's headed for Korea. Tillie's just one step ahead of a fit. Cried all morning."

"I've heard the news, Mama. Thelma Jean has probably let everyone know by now," Gus stated.

Norman sighed. "Billy Ray's still wet behind the ears."

"He's two years older than Gil and me."

"He ain't done much except dig ginseng ever since he got that sanging hoe," Katherine said, shaking her head.

"There's money in sang root," Norman said, and Gus saw a disapproving look cross his mother's face since Billy Ray had already been hauled down to Vern's office twice for digging the herb.

"He's been doing some poultry raisin'," Gus told them, in his friend's defense.

"Looks like the Korean War has put a halt to his farming," Norman said.

"He should've cleaned their yard 'fore he went off. It's given over to weeds," Katherine sighed. "How's Tillie going to keep up with it?"

"As a matter of fact," Gus said, "I talked to Billy Ray a few days ago. He was expecting to be called up and he said he'd be tending to the yard before he left. I told him I'd help whenever I could," and then Gus wondered when he'd ever get time away from the mill to do it.

Buster Foch hung the CLOSED sign on the window and handed Gilbert thirty-four dollars and seventy-five cents. "Gonna hate to see you go, Gilbert. Don't seem fittin' you runnin' off to Californy. Family's here. A man should stay with his kin."

Gilbert smiled. "Got goals, Mr. Foch."

"Keep 'em in reach, son."

"I'm going to work in an aircraft plant. After I learn how they go together I'm going to fly one. You'll hear that roar in the sky, look up and it'll be me, Mr. Foch."

Mr. Foch shook his head. "I hear a doctor makes ten-thousand dollars a year out there in California."

"It's the land of opportunity, Mr. Foch. I know the family's against it, but I can make ten times more money there. The folks need it. I'll be sendin' them what I don't need. I used to think I was doin' it for myself, but really, it's them I'm doin' it for. Ain't no dreams to chase here in the hills."

Foch emptied the cash drawer. "What about Gus? He stayin' here?"

"Gus has hopes and ambitions different from mine. Always has. Gus is easy to please. He'll make do." Gilbert folded his dollar bills neatly and slid them into his pocket. He thanked Mr. Foch for the job, went to the door, stretched himself up tall and smacked the bell hanging above the screen. Gilbert sprightly walked out of the store, then glanced back over his shoulder. Mr. Foch was standing just outside the door watching him lift his bicycle from the curb.

"So long, Mr. Foch. Thank you again for the work. You take care now, hear?"

"You gonna be okay, boy?"

"Sure I am."

"Where you headed now?"

"Greyhound bus station to buy a ticket to California."

"Are you sure you're gonna be okay?"

"I'm sure, Mr. Foch."

"Sure?"

"Sure as a water-witch with a forked stick," Gilbert said as he peddled off into the dark night. When he'd turned the corner Gilbert lifted both arms high over his head and let out an Indian-screeching "Yeeoww!"

Twenty minutes later with a bus ticket in his pocket, Gilbert peddled the bike into the barn at Timber Hills and walked slowly toward the house. The Wheelers ate supper in silence, eyes lifting now and then to look sullenly at Gilbert. He knew Norman was giving him glowering looks of disgust, but continued eating like nothing was different. Gus leaned over and whispered as if in a hushed library, "Are you all right?"

Gilbert swallowed and answered just as quietly, "The knot in my belly keeps getting bigger and harder." He kept eating, and when he had soaked up the last of the chicken broth with cornbread he quietly excused himself. Closing the door softly, he headed for the outhouse. They had inside plumbing, now, but Gilbert's nerves were twisted to the point of nausea and he didn't want to give his father the satisfaction of hearing him be sick.

When he'd closed the kitchen door, he heard a scraping noise then a chair turn over backwards, then he heard his father's rough voice. "I knew you'd never amount to a hill of beans!" Gilbert heard glass break and knew Norman had thrown his empty tea glass against the door. "Do you know what you're doing, goddamnit? Are you willing to relinquish all title to Timber Hills?"

Katherine half-stood, her chair, also, nearly tipping backwards. "Gilbert, don't you want some vinegar pi. . . ." She stopped in mid sentence and Gilbert knew Norman had stopped her.

"You might as well be preaching about the birth of Jesus," Katherine said. "He ain't listenin' to you, Norman. He has his mind made up. You ain't doing a scrap of good by yellin'."

"He's making a mistake!" Norman hollered, slamming his fist onto the table. "Someday he'll know what a fool he was!"

Katherine jumped with Norman's outburst. "He's got to find out for himself."

Norman held his hand out, palm up. "You're his path, Katy. He listens to you. Tell him he's making a mistake."

This time Gus smacked his hand down on the table. "We've been telling him that all his life!" He gave Norman a foul look then stooped down to pick up the broken glass. "Gil's chosen his own path, Pa. He's worked his butt off for the money to go. He's not asking you for a penny and he's not taking off broke," Gus said.

Norman glared at Gus. "Does he think it's beneath his dignity to work at the mill?" He glanced out the opened window, then back at Katherine. "Why can't he be more like Gus instead of so absorbed in himself?"

"Maybe Gus *hates* the mill," Katherine answered. "Could it be he's just hanging on to please you? Gus may end up bored with it, but he'll be sawing logs for life 'cause he knows that's what *you* want him to do."

"Hello, Mom, Dad. I'm still sitting here with you. You're talking like I'm not even here," Gus said, waving his fork. He looked outside and saw Gil leaning against the outhouse door. "And Gilbert can hear every word you're saying in here." Gus let his fork drop from his fingers into his plate. "Gilbert don't need your scolding, your angry words. He needs your blessing." Gus pushed back his chair, excused himself and stomped outside to be with his brother.

Gus sat over one hole while his twin brother vomited into the other. "I know I'm a big disappointment to them," Gil said, wiping his mouth. "Pa's always made me feel like a square in a circle. I've got to find out if it's right for me to go away. I'm breaking away, wanting something more than just getting born and living for seventy or eighty years. I'd always wonder if it was meant to be, and resent it if I didn't give it a chance." He gripped his stomach and hung his head over the hole again. Afterward, he looked up at Gus and said, "We had a good childhood. I couldn't have asked for anything different, but I'm not a child anymore and I want more out of life." He sat over the hole and faced Gus. "I'm sorry," Gilbert said.

"You don't have to be," Gus told him.

"You don't have to stay in here with me, Gus," Gilbert said. "It stinks in here."

"I'm sitting here because you need me right now," Gus said, swatting at a couple insects. "It's not too late to turn back."

Gil laid his hand over Gus's knee. "I don't know much now, except a little about what goes on at a sawmill and what I learned at Foch's market, but I'll develop my skills. I may have to start out as an elevator boy, but I'll work my way up." He grinned at the unintended witticism. "I'll make a lot of money in California, Gus. I won't end up a no-good rolling stone and I know that Mom and Da . . . "

Gus stood up and held his hands out. "Gil, that's enough. You don't have to prove anything to me, and if we don't get out of this covered shit hole, *I'm* going to puke."

"Hey, Gus," Gil said as they stepped from the outhouse.

"Yeah, Gil?"

"Roses are red, cabbage is green. You have a head like a lima bean."

Gus shook his head and smiled. "Hey, Gil."

"Yeah?"

"Do you carrot all for me?"

"My heart beets for you," Gil answered, also grinning.

"If we cantaloupe, lettuce marry."

"We'd make a swell pear," Gil laughed.

The rhymes lacked the punch they had had in earlier times. Gilbert stopped walking and faced Gus. "Do you think I'm wrong to leave?"

"Dead wrong."

As hard as he tried, Gilbert couldn't sleep. Tense and wakeful, he tossed and turned and prayed about his journey, wondering if he was really being as selfish as Gus had told him years before. In a small way he knew he was. In another way he could never forgive himself if he didn't go. For years he'd known he couldn't adapt to the timber business. Lord knows his father had pounded it into his head often enough. Why can't I be more like my brother? he wondered. Maybe then Pa would love me like he loves Gus. Gilbert turned over and tried to sleep, but it was useless. He thought of his folks how they barely got by. Gus didn't see it. His brother was complacent, accepting life the way it fell. Gus wanted to carry on the business and he'd be good at it.

Gil's body turned this way and that, lying on his side, his back, his stomach. He tried to sleep but his enthusiasm wouldn't let him. Everything he'd read about California, every picture he'd seen promised wealth and happiness. His folks lived in poverty yet they seemed pacified. Not me, he thought. Not as long as there's a place called California. If this humdrum place is what makes them happy, so be it. I love them, he thought, but I won't stay in a dead-end place. A sudden sense of shame tugged his heart. His thoughts jumbled with ambivalence.

Enough moonlight streamed through the window for Gilbert to see Gus sleeping soundly next to him. The breeze rippling through the magnolia tree outside their window made flickering shadows across his face. He'd miss his brother. He remembered the day he'd told Gus about his California dream. Gus hadn't liked it then and he still didn't approve. How can identical twins be so different? He wondered. They were formed from one egg with identical genetic material. They had lain skin to skin inside their mother's womb, were best friends from the very beginning.

Gilbert laid back on his pillow and let his wide-awake eyes wander around the room. It was a rough and tough room with the Lone Ranger and Silver galloping all over the wallpaper. Boots in the corner, a holster over the bedpost, a dust-gathering wooden horse against the wall.

He was tired, yet restless, half thinking, half dreaming. Tears wet his cheeks and it angered him. Boys don't cry, their teacher at school had taught them. But more tears came and he sobbed silently, not a feel-sorry-for-myself cry; he cried with deep sorrow in his chest for Gus. He cried for his parents and their way of life. The tears were for everyone but himself.

Gus mumbled something in his sleep and turned over. He lifted his head slightly, laid back down and raised his arms above his head. Gilbert pulled the sheet up over his brother's bare chest then sank back down into the pillow. The bonds were strong, but not strong enough to keep him here in the poverty-stricken hills and hollows of Tennessee. Gus is so much like Pa, Gilbert thought. They'll always be one of a kind. Gilbert stared at the ceiling and secretly wished he was more like Gus.

He could smell a combination of sunshine and a hot iron on the pillowcase and knew he'd miss his mother's loving maternal care. His heart beat with a restless and unsatisfied longing for . . . freedom? Approval, applause? "No," he whispered. "I long for pure and uncomplicated love from my father." Gilbert tossed, turned and wanted to stop feeling guilty. His tears ceased and dried stiff on his face. He remembered the day he told Billy Ray Mudd he was really leaving. Billy Ray told him he didn't have the balls. Gilbert wondered why Billy Ray didn't just take off. Hell, he was an orphan. His substitute folks beat him to pulp. Talk about unloved. Why didn't Billy Ray just leave? Maybe Billy Ray wasn't as brave as he pretended to be. Or maybe Billy Ray truly liked Tennessee. Gilbert heaved the pillow onto the floor. It rested against the rocking horse.

The smell of sausage frying aroused Gilbert from his sleep. He sat up, listened, heard early morning conversation. Bleary-eyed he looked at the clock on his night stand. Six o'clock straight up. He slid his legs over the edge of the bed and looked at his Sunday clothes he'd set out for his trip. His mother had always laid out his clothes when they were going somewhere, but not this time. The thought gave him a slightly sad feeling that mixed with soon-to-be independence. He sprang up, put on the clean white shirt, tie, overalls and suit jacket.

Breakfast wasn't any easier than last night's supper had been. Katherine poured coffee, buttered biscuits, refilled the gravy bowl twice. "More sausage?" she asked, but no one answered. She turned out the flame from under the iron skillet and sat at the table, then got back up and spooned more grits onto Norman's plate.

"Don't be angry with me," Gilbert said to her bowed head.

"We aren't, son."

"The hell we aren't!" Norman shouted. He threw his fork across the table. It landed on Sara Jane's lap. Norman apologized to her then asked her to go check on the new calf.

"Norman," Katherine scolded. "I won't have this at my table."

Gilbert's appetite was ruined and he excused himself. He leaned over and kissed his mother on the forehead. Her lips were slightly parted and she started to say something, but she cried instead. She put a hand over her mouth. Gilbert put an awkward hand on her cheek then hugged her neck. He glanced up at the wooden clock on the wall and said, "It's time to go." He walked into his room, gave it one quick look, then picked up his suitcase and quickly walked back to the kitchen where the family sat, unspeaking. He hurried through the door and onto the front porch. No one spoke, only watched him through the screen door, walking, turning to wave, then he was gone.

Slowly, each member of the Wheeler family got up and walked outside. They stood just outside the door on the front porch, Katherine quietly sobbing, Norman with his jaw set hard. Streams of morning sun filtered through the bird-filled trees. A faint smell of sweet clover scented the midsummer air.

Gus looked up at the cloudless sky, inhaled the sunlit fresh of the morning. "Pretty day for a trip."

"He's hurting us badly," Katherine sobbed.

"This isn't like a hangover he can sleep off," Norman said.

"Yes it is," Gus said. "He'll be back."

At the bus station Gilbert pulled at the knot of his tie, twisting his neck this way and that. He glanced over his shoulder and saw Zebedee Booker setting up his watermelon stand. Next to the curb was Zeb's rusty old pickup truck leaking oil. Gilbert looked away and unbuttoned his stiff shirt collar. A small cluster of boys were squatted on their hunkers around a circle of marbles. They were snacking on boiled peanuts. When Gilbert looked up, a little colored girl was staring straight at him. She was slender and long-limbed. Her thin, dark arms were wrapped like honeysuckle vines around a white-faced doll.

"That your baby?" Gilbert asked the little girl.

Her face lit up like the sun. "Her name's Betsy."

"What's yours?" Gilbert asked her.

"Vicki Paige."

"That's a very pretty name," Gil complimented, patting her head.

"We're goin' on a trip. Goin' to see Grandma." She turned her head to look over her shoulder. "We gotta wait over there," she said, pointing to a sign that read: NEGRO WAITING AREA.

A heavyset colored woman with a small suitcase at her side called, "Vicki Paige, don't go pesterin' no white man."

With a mixture of feelings, Gilbert straightened his shoulders, bought a newspaper, and walked inside. The knots in his stomach were tightening, a mixture of sadness and excitement. He scanned the large, cold-designed bus terminal for the restrooms and headed that way.

The Greyhound station was buzzing with voices and loud speakers. Gilbert leaned against the cool, green-painted wall and closed his eyes. "Is this the fitting thing to do, Lord?" he whispered, then his eyes popped open when a tall Negro man bumped into him. "Pardon me," the man said, gesturing. Gilbert turned and realized he was leaning against the COLORED ONLY restroom door. "Sorry," he said.

Gilbert moved away from the privy door and sat on a gray wooden bench. A cloud of smoke enveloped his head. He fanned the suffocating smell away.

"Chesterfield?" a white-haired man offered. His eyes had a busy look to them.

"No sir, I don't smoke." Gilbert spoke sharply, abruptly, not meaning to. He folded the unread newspaper into a square and laid it aside.

"Smart kid. It's a damfool thing to do. At twenty-one cents a pack, folks can't afford to smoke." He rubbed his chin. "You chew?"

"Birch bark, now and then," Gilbert said, not liking the smell of the old man's breath.

Neither man offered more conversation.

After a few moments, Gilbert got up, walked outside. His gaze traveled across the street. He read a JOHNS-MANVILLE ASBESTOS BRAKE LINING sign over and over until a blue '47 pickup truck rolled between Gilbert and the sign. Gil glanced at the tool box bolted to the running board. A dirty glove was sticking out. He inhaled the warm air, pulled a watch from his pocket and noticed there was still a thirty minute wait before the bus left. He took off his jacket and tossed it over his shoulder. Not even the hustle-bustle could diminish his sense of expectation. Full of energy and high hopes, he took a few quick breaths. The morning sun was bringing sweat to Gilbert's forehead and under his arms. He wiped his head and rolled up the sleeves of his starched, white shirt, then stepped back into the shade of the building to wait for the bus to take him to California.

• CHAPTER 10 •

Thunder rumbled in the east as Gus and Norman passed by cloud-darkened, summer hillsides. Tall grass and black-eyed susan waved in the breezy, moist air. Gus raised his hand and pushed back his baseball cap. The dry, unpaved road twisted up, down around and over, leaving the feeling of getting nowhere. The old truck groaned going uphill and purred going down. Mismatched tires threw dust and rock behind as they bumped and chugged along. "This road ain't fit to drive a hog to market on," Norman grumbled. A red 4-wheel-drive Willys truck pounded up behind them. Gus quickly steered from the center of the road to the far right, his front tire coming within inches of the deep weed-lined ditch. "Who . . . ? Is that Web Taylor? When did he get that beauty?"

Taylor slowed as he evened alongside Gus's old truck. "Wheeler, is that you? I ain't seen you in a coon's age."

"Law," Gus yelled out his window, eyeing the Willys. "If that don't beat a hen a-peckin'! If I had your money, I'd throw mine away!"

Taylor laughed. "Acquirin' this belle took a lot o' hard work."

Norman leaned across the seat. "Takes effort for any reward, Web," he said as the new Willys sped off, shrouding their windshield with rock and dust. "Damn fool," Norman cursed.

Gus could smell and feel the hot floorboards through his thin soled shoes as his eyes scanned tobacco fields and thigh-high corn reaching for the sun. He slowed the truck before crossing a rickety wooden bridge and heard the rotted planks creak as the hot tires rolled across. Norman frowned and leaned forward, his head turning left then right. "That property wasn't this far past the colored schoolhouse."

"Can't be too much farther. Clem Guffey's place is just around the bend," Gus said, straining his eye's view through the dust. The bug-crusted, dusty windshield didn't help his view. He stopped the truck and cut the motor.

Norman let out a deep breath and wiped the sweat from his face. He looked around, opened the door and got out. "Something don't ring true," he said, moving around to the driver's side of the truck.

"It's been a right smart time since you've been here, Pa. I'll drive on down to Clem's."

"I *know* it ain't that far!"

Gus opened the truck's heavy, creaking door and stomped out. A moisture-laden breeze ruffled his hair and he pushed it back off his forehead. The yellow-tinted air smelled of rain and he watched the swelling breeze turn the tree leaves backwards. He glanced up into the sky and saw dark clouds gathering overhead. Gus's shoulders twitched and heat rose to his neck and face when he peered through the brush and small-trunked trees that grew along the road. There was no sign of the Delvine timber.

Following the rutted tire path, Norman walked a few steps, stopped, turned around. "It's all wrong, son. How could fifty-two acres just disappear? That was prime woodland." His voice trailed off as he gazed diagonally across a dry river bed and up a weedy, snaky knoll. "I'm going to walk up a-ways," he said. Gus followed.

At the top was a near-new fence, and beyond, the stumpy, sawdusty remains of a not-so-long-ago, choice woodlot. Gus's chest felt fiddle-string tight and he could feel his heart beating beneath his shirt. He looked over at Norman. Behind the eyeglasses, there was a fire in his father's eyes that even the approaching rain couldn't put out.

"That's it!" Norman yelled with a sharp pointing gesture. "Right there!" His anger seemed to grow claws, tearing, ripping out his insides. He yanked off his hat and threw it in the dirt. "Delvine, and I stood right here on this spot." His head moved side to side, his eyes looked up, down, sideways. "This can't . . . who would . . . ?" Norman pivoted round. "This is a goddamn crime." His voice tolled over the vacuous acreage. He shouted something else, but booming thunder washed it out.

"There's gotta be an explanation, Pa." Gus hurriedly backed away. "I'll drive up to Clem's place. Maybe he'll know something."

Norman's voice lowered and he mumbled, "Someone's cut our timber, Gus. Someone's come right in here and stole it right out from under us." His words sounded muddy. He winced toward the cloud-covered sun, his eyes, cold as ice blocks.

Gus shuffled dust under his feet. He worried his father was working himself into a heart attack. "Maybe this isn't the spot, Pa." But he knew it was, and fifty-two acres of Timber Hills lumber was gone. Just like that. "We'll replant. Start over," Gus tried to console. "The land's still here."

Norman stared at his son. "You're a heap like your mother." Norman picked up a small green branch and twisted it in his hand. "Calvin said he never trusted that Greek ass-hole. He said Delvine was like a sneaky snake."

Gus hunkered next to a fresh-cut stump. "You think Delvine was behind this?"

"I do, and you can bet he's long gone." Norman kicked the stump. "Just like our timber." He wiped his nose with his hand. "And our dreams of a better life."

"I'm sorry, Pa." His heart filled with disappointment.

Norman straightened his shoulders. "Well. Can't do anything about it here. Let's go home, son. We'll talk to Henry in the morning. I think we're going to need your granddad's services. He's the best lawyer I know."

"Damn straight," Gus agreed.

But neither man moved, not even when the clouds swept over and blotted out the hills around them. Not even when the sky opened and warm, sweet rain fell. The two of them stood deathly still and stared at the hundreds of sawed-off stumps around them. They heard the sound of a rattler, but never saw the snake, just saw the tall, wet grass parting as the snake crawled away.

Gus felt like a wrung-out mop. He sat on top of one of the stumps and Norman sank down heavily beside him. "We still got the land, Pa," Gus said. Rain drops clung to his long blond lashes and he blinked as rain rolled down his cheeks.

Gus jumped when Norman lurched forward and struck out wildly with his fist, pounding the wet air. "That Goddamngoodfornothingsonofabitch Arnold H. Delvine!"

Gus had never seen his father carry on like that. For a crazy moment he wanted to laugh. Norman was hopping around like a hurdle racer, punching at the air with his one arm, while the other shirt sleeve flapped loose like a sheet in a windstorm. Rain water slinging off Norman's face and neck reminded Gus of a dog shaking out after a dive in the pond. Gus turned away to hide the grin that he couldn't hold back.

"Calvin didn't trust the man right from the onset," Norman said, after he'd collected himself. "He has this way with people. I should have listened to him."

Gus looked at his father's dark, defeated eyes and the humor he'd felt a moment before diminished. "You couldn't have known."

"Whatever happened to the believable handshake? When a man's word sealed an unwritten agreement?" Norman asked. "I pumped that man's hand without the slightest dash of skepticism and gullibly assumed. . . ." He roughly combed his rain-drenched hair with his fingers. "Where's my goddamn hat?"

Gus could see that Norman's frustration was growing into anger and anger into hatred. "It wouldn't seem so bad if we didn't make our living with the lumber we cut," Gus said. "I'd like to tie Delvine to a long board and start up the circular saw."

"That wouldn't put the trees back into the ground," Norman said quietly, defeated.

"It'd make some pretty good fertilizer, with all his bullshit."

Sara Jane was the only one with words at the supper table, a rush of light-hearted sociable words. Her light jabbering floated in and out of Gus's head. It was times like this when Gus missed Gilbert the most. Although they hadn't spent much time together in the past few months, he wondered what Gilbert would have done or said about the lost timber. He fought an empty feeling inside his chest as his eyes saw the misery around the table. "Maybe we should think about something else," he said, hoping to change the mood. Katherine was the first to react to Gus's intent.

"I think we should get a television set. Would you like that, Sara Jane?" Katherine asked.

"Whew!" the little girl hollered, her face aglow. "Goodness gracious, yes!"

Gus wondered if Katherine should have put that hope into Sara Jane's heart. Yes, they would eventually get one, but it may be a while. He looked at Norman and saw a frown on his face. Yes, he told himself. Mama spoke too soon.

"Billy Ray says the Coopers got a television and they can't get no picture on it," Gus said.

Norman kept on eating, his eyes on his food. "Depends on your distance from the station," he said flatly. "Your location in respect to the hills, buildings and stuff. The Coopers are too far down in the holler," he answered, still not looking up.

"I heard the Silver-tone set gives good reception if you live within fifteen or twenty miles of the station," Katherine said, dribbling more vinegar on her greens.

When Katherine walked to the pantry Gus cringed because Norman followed. Gus heard his father ask in a stern voice, "Why, Katy? Why did you tell them that?"

"About what?"

Norman grabbed Katherine's arm roughly. "You know what I'm talking about! The television set. When will we be able to afford one, now that the Delvine timber is gone? For God's sake! You shouldn't get their hopes up. That was a stupid, stupid thing to do!"

Katherine shrugged his hand from her arm. "You're right, of course, but I feel things will get better for us."

Norman backed away. "They have to," he said, trailing her to the table.

When the wooden box on the wall rang with it's identifying two shorts and a long, everyone except Sara Jane jumped. Norman got up, lifted the bell-shaped receiver and said hello. "What's that, Thelma Jean?" Norman asked, pressing the receiver tighter to his ear. "You say there's a long distant call with reversed charges?" Norman hesitantly accepted the call and waited for Thelma Jean to unplug. She didn't, though. She never did. How else would she be able to pass on the tidings? "It's your son," Norman said, stretching the cord of the receiver for Katherine to take the call.

She gave him a dirty look and snatched the receiver from his hand. "You can't even talk to your own son," she mumbled, holding her hand over the mouthpiece. Katherine turned her back to Norman. "Gilbert, is that you?"

Gus and Sara Jane closed in around the telephone. Norman walked back to the table, sat, and started eating.

"I can barely hear you, Gilbert. Where are you?" Katherine shouted into the telephone, then held the receiver up to Gus's ear to see if he could decipher his brother's words over the crackly phone line.

Gus could barely make out the words. He shook his head no.

Katherine snatched the receiver from Gus, stuck it back into her ear and yelled, "Thelma Jean, Goddamn it! Unplug so I can hear my son!" It was the first time in Gus's life he'd ever heard his mother curse.

Norman snapped up his head and flashed a flabbergasted did-I-hear-right look. Gus shot a glance at Sara Jane who was covering her mouth to hold back a snicker. Katherine had the receiver wedged deeply into her ear and her lips pressed against the mouthpiece. "You heard me right, you nosey busybody," they heard Katherine say. "You rang up Ruby Mae just before you did us. We heard their three short rings! I'm sure she's talking to Marilyn about Walter's . . ." Katherine cupped her hand around her mouth . . . "affair," she whispered. "Listen in on them!"

The line suddenly became clear, and Katherine apologized to Gilbert. "Yes, I surprised myself," she said into the phone. "I reckon everyone in East Tennessee'll know about my cussing. I'll likely be hurled out the church window."

Katherine talked and the other Wheeler's listened intently to the one-ended conversation. "Yes, your father and Gus looked at the land. It wasn't quite what they expected but we'll write to you about it," she said. "I love you, too, baby. Yes, I'll tell them."

Katherine slowly hung up the phone. Before she turned around Gus saw her wipe a tear from her eye. "He's in Arkansas, and he loves you."

Norman was quiet for a few seconds then took a deep breath. "I should have spoken to him. I was wrong and should have told him to get his fill of wandering and stay away until he's convinced there's no place like home." He turned his head and looked through the opened door. "I should have told him he'd be welcomed back any time, that the door's never locked. And I should have told him that I loved him." Norman got up and walked from the room.

Katherine stood trembling for a moment, and then, with a movement of strong decision, she turned and walked back to the table.

When Sara Jane asked her mother what was wrong, Katherine said, "It's hard seeing your children grow up and leave home. It's hard to let go."

"I'm never gonna let my dolly go," the little girl said. She rushed over to Gilbert's chair where she'd placed her baby doll. "You can sit here until Gilbert comes home," she whispered, her fingers stroking the doll's cheek.

Gus reached across the table, broke off a chunk of cornbread, looked up and said, "Sometimes you have to set the practical side of life aside and live your dream." He put the cornbread into his mouth and shoved back his chair. "He'll be back."

"There's a storm in the air," Gus said the next morning after breakfast.

"Don't matter," Norman said, walking out onto the porch after Gus. He looked skyward. "So much time has passed, I don't know if an attorney can help now," he said, "but our appointment's at nine o'clock, and we're going to be there," he added, looking at Gus and then back up at the darkening sky. "It'll blow over," he said, stepping back into the house.

They parked the Buick along the curb in front of the red brick building, got out and walked up the steps to Henry Ashford's office. Gus reached out, opened the heavy wooden door then followed Norman in. The air-conditioner was on in the office and Gus smiled as he absorbed the cool air. He pulled his watch from his pocket, noted they were right on time, then sank into a maroon upholstered couch. Norman sat next to him and crossed his one arm over his chest.

"It was never recorded," Henry told Norman. "Fraud. Pure and simple fraud," he said.

Norman's dark eyes narrowed as he slammed the fake contract down on the table. "Takes a man's savings and is gone without a backward glance." He lowered his eyes and shook his head.

"Norman, I did some checking," Henry said. "I believe it was Irving who cut the timber. Some men saw his crew out there at the site."

"Ira?" Norman questioned, jerking his head back up. "He wouldn't do something this crooked. Ira and I have always been friends even though we compete for the work around these parts." He peered at Henry.

"Perhaps he was tricked, like you were."

Gus walked to the window and looked down. Sheriff Peele was changing a flat tire for a fat lady in a purple-flowered dress. She stood over him like she was telling him how to do it. Gus saw Vern nodding as the woman gestured with her hands. Gus smiled briefly then turned back to the other two men.

"I just don't understand. Things like this don't happen," Norman said.

"Ira might be a competitor, but he's always been a friend," Gus added.

Henry patted Norman on the shoulder. "I know you feel hurt and powerless, son. I'll do all I can to help you through this, but unfortunately the way the contract was written. . . ."

Norman and Gus stepped out onto the curb. "Weather looks bad," Gus said, checking out the night-dark sky. "There goes my hat!" he yelled as a strong gust of wind lashed against them.

"We'd better make a run for the car," Norman hollered above an ominous roar. Gus glanced up at the threatening sky, picked up his heels and darted toward the Buick, but before they reached the car, they saw Earl Mosley's parked Packard jerk forward and bounce against the curb. "Damn!" Norman gasped. "Run for cover!"

Suddenly huge drops of rain poured downward, then horizontally. The wind's howl became deafening and their ears popped from an air pressure change. Abruptly, the dark cloud layer gave birth to a tilted, dark funnel. The enormous pressure hurt Gus's ears as he shielded his eyes from flying debris. Hearing shattering glass, they ran chaotically for shelter, but not before a large piece flew by, only inches from their heads.

"God forbid!" Gus yelled as rocketing debris wailed past them and shards of glass whizzed by like ricocheting bullets. "Those cars are hopping like jumping jacks!"

The screaming wind blew ice balls and razor-sharp chunks of stone and metal into their path. Hunkered beside a concrete pillar, Gus and Norman held on for dear life. They saw the top floor of Henry's office building whirl upward, explode, and crash back down. Pistol cracks from bare wires hitting the pavement made fiery dances. The walls of buildings exploded outward and roofs collapsed into their own basements.

"Jesus!" Gus shrieked.

"Hold on, Gus! Ride it out."

"I feel like a cotton ball," Gus shouted, then saw the plate glass from Sonny's Sinclair blast away.

When the weather stabilized, they rose on shaky legs from squatting positions. Gas escaping from broken mains fouled the air. "Don't light that cigarette!" Gus screamed when a befuddle-eyed man lifted a pack of Chesterfields from his shirt pocket. The man jumped, obviously not seeing the two men standing near him. He slipped the cigarettes back into his pocket and stood staring at his dented automobile. "Holy willikers," the man sighed. "It used to be a Studebaker."

"Looks like a lot of things *used to be*," Norman said, gaping at the damage. He turned to Gus and said, "We'll wait until tomorrow to talk to Ira. We need to check on your mom and Sara Jane."

"I'd forgotten about Ira," Gus said, getting into the drivers seat of the car. Norman opened the passenger side door and dropped in. "I can't believe this damage," Gus mumbled, pulling out of the parking spot and onto the rubbled street. He shifted into second gear and slowly shook his head. "Trees are broken off like mowed grass. The Buick fared well, only that small dent on the hood."

The car's tires rolled slowly through the flooded, dismantled streets as Gus pulled the gearstick down into third gear. He carefully dodged rubble and belongings that were scattered about. He shook his head again at the devastation as he headed out of town and toward home, and prayed aloud that his family had survived the disastrous storm. When they rounded the final curve, they were comforted to see their house had endured the tornado. Katherine and Sara Jane were standing on the porch. "Thank God," he said.

"Daddy! Daddy!" Sara Jane shrieked, pulling on Norman's armless sleeve. "I saved my frogs an' Mommy saved the calf, but Koontz Two got crushed by the barn roof," she cried. "The roof was goin' this-a-way an' that-a-way, then crashed down on him."

Gus peered at the barn's mangled tin roof lying on the wet ground. "I'm just thankful you're all right," he said, lifting Sara Jane, and hugging his mother with his free arm.

"The sawmill's still standing," Norman said.

"Yeah, it's standing," Gus said, "standing in a foot of water."

"Sorry about Koontz Two, Gus," Katherine said, putting an arm around her son's waist.

"We'll just have bacon sooner than we planned," Gus said as they walked toward the barn dodging tree limbs and debris. "Better get him butchered and salted. This sure ain't hog-killin' weather," he said, wiping sweat and rain from his arms and face.

"I'll help fix the pickle," Sara Jane said.

"We may need more saltpeter," Katherine said as she kneeled next to the wounded calf. "We'll get you back out to your mama soon," she soothed.

"She's out there sinking in the mud," Gus said.

"The screen door's hangin' from only one pin," Sara Jane said, and Katherine added that there was no electricity. "The phone's out, too," the youngster said.

Norman struck a match on the sole of his shoe and lit a kerosene lamp. Sara Jane pointed toward the chicken coop. "It got so dark the chickens went to roost," she said. "When we saw that big black cloud comin', we ran to the storm cellar!" she screeched in her little-girl voice. "We were so scared we forgot about the snakes! My ears was ringin', too."

Gus swooped up his little sister again. "What'cha got there?" he asked. Sara Jane gripped a green Ball jar. "Tree frogs. I saved 'em from drownin'," she answered. "Wanna see?" she asked, as she twisted open the lid. "They jump when the light hits 'em."

"They jump when they're thrown in a hot iron skillet, too," Gus teased, pulling one of Sara Jane's corkscrew curls.

Sara Jane slapped his hand. "Why you do that?" she screamed.

"Just to see it bounce back," Gus said.

"Better get out to the camp," Norman called to Gus, looking toward the dark green wall of the woods. "See what kind of mess Calvin's got out there."

Gus and Norman jumped into Gus's truck, positioned their rumps around the springs sticking up through the seat, and started the truck. The lights in the house flickered and came back on, and a few seconds later the telephone rattled the familiar Wheeler's ring.

"Let's wait to see who that is. Possibly bad news," Gus said and Norman agreed. They got out of the truck and walked back into the house.

"We're fine, daddy," Katherine was saying into the receiver. "Gus lost a hog. One of the calves got cut up pretty badly. We can save her, though. I haven't seen a tornado this bad for a long time. Yes, Daddy. He's right here," Katherine said, and waved the receiver out. "He wants to speak to one of you."

"Go ahead, son," Norman gestured.

When Gus hung up the phone, he turned to Katherine and Norman and said, "Vern Peele just called and said the twister took Hammer's place. Homer was killed. An elm tree smashed through the front of his shop and crushed him."

"I'm sorry for his family," Katherine said. "I'll pay my respects to Mrs. Hammer. Peggy Lou hasn't been well. This must be very hard for her."

"I knew you'd be there for her," Norman said, hugging his wife.

Katherine shook her head. "I heard that their little boy has polio. It'll be up to Eunice to care for her mother and brother now. And she's only nine or ten."

Norman glanced at her. "Buford Paul come down with polio? Gosh, it's striking everywhere." Norman took a long breath and exhaled slowly.

"Pa," Gus said. "I wasn't aware you were selling Timber Hills lumber to Homer."

"We aren't," Norman and Katherine said at the same time. "Why would you think that?" Norman asked.

"Grandfather said they found a room full of it," Gus said. "All with the Timber Hills stamp. I thought it odd, since you've been shipping your lumber to Middlesboro for the past year."

"We've never sold to the Hammer's. You know we have to meet the contract's quota each month. We work six days a week to fulfill the demand. Is he sure it's our lumber?" Norman asked.

"Got our stamp on it. How much surer do you want?" Gus asked.

"We've had a lot of lumber stolen over time. You don't think. . . ."

"Hammer wouldn't knowingly buy pilfered lumber," Gus said. "Or steal it."

"Lord," Norman said, "if it's not one thing, it's another. Let's get out to camp."

The men spoke little as they drove the muddy, narrow path to the camp. Gus shook his head as he assessed the downed limbs.

Calvin and a worker were clearing a large tree branch from the roadway when Gus and Norman drove up. "A few trees have toppled around the camp," Calvin told them, "but the funnel lifted before it got to us. We were lucky," Calvin said, a hat in one hand, rubbing his head with the other. "Heard there was a terrible blow-down west of here."

"Folks in town got struck bad," Norman said, sighing. "Been in these parts all my life and never seen the likes."

Calvin put his hat back on. "Burrell Calder's dog went plumb crazy and shot off to beat the band. Burrell's been out hunting for him. He heard a loud yelp. Burrell thinks the dog may have been hit by lightning."

"That dog is Burrell's soul mate," Calvin said. "He loves that dog like a kid."

Gus pulled off his hat and rubbed his forehead. "Hoke and Edwina let their dog, Ogdin sleep between them so they won't have to get twin beds. That's what Ethan, their little boy, told Gil and me."

The men laughed, easing the plight of the storm damage around them. "Law, these kids are talking about mighty personal stuff these days," Calvin said. He stuck his work-worn hands into his pockets. "Sure hope Burrell finds his dog."

Norman bowed his head and laughed. Behind his glasses, his eyes crinkled.

"Never would have guessed Hoke Smith would allow a dog in his bed."

"Guess you ain't seen what Edwina looks like," Calvin said, grinning.

"Yeah I have," Gus said. "She's beefy and graceless like a bull."

Norman laughed again. "We better be getting on back. Got some cleaning up to do around the mill. Glad everyone here is okay, Cal."

Gus and Norman waited a week after Homer's funeral before calling on Peggy Lou Hammer.

"I never knew what was happening in the business," she said. "I stayed out of it best I could." Mrs. Hammer wrung her hands then tucked her floral house dress tightly around her swollen ankles. "I did think it a bit odd that Homer met your men out near the old slave graveyard to pick up the lumber. I never knew it was stolen from you, Mr. Wheeler, I swear. Homer wouldn't be involved in anything like that."

A hollow look of grief shadowed her eyes. "Not my Homer." She kept shaking her head.

"I know this is hard for you, Mrs. Hammer."

She nodded and mumbled "yes." Her voice was a whisper.

"We just want to ask you one more question, then we'll leave," Norman said kindly.

"What is it?" Peggy Lou sighed as she got up, pulled her dress down, and walked toward the kitchen. Her run-over house slippers padded silently on the hardwood flooring. "I should have offered you some tea," she said, not turning around.

"No thank you, Mrs. Hammer. Do you know who it was that Mr. Hammer was buying the Timber Hills lumber from?"

"Of course I do. It was Lenny Squaw and Hank Kendall. I wouldn't know them if I bumped into them on the street, but that's who it was."

Norman and Gus looked at each other. "Thank you, Mrs. Hammer," Norman said, turning back to the woman. "You've been a good help. Our sincere apology for bothering you in your time of sorrow. Do hope little Buford Paul gets better, soon."

"Oh, Mrs. Hammer," Gus said as they were walking back to the truck. "We nearly forgot. Mama baked you a Paw Paw Pie." He opened the truck door and lifted the pie from the torn seat cover.

Peggy Lou put her hands to her chest. "How thoughtful," she said, "and Katherine has wrapped it in a pretty cloth. It takes a lot of work to pick, peel and seed a peck of paw paws. Thank her for me, Mr. Wheeler."

Gus settled into the truck's seat, pulled the gearshift to neutral, pulled out the choke and pushed the start button. The motor turned sluggishly, caught, sputtered and died. He started over and the truck chugged away, leaving behind a cloud of smoke. The old Ford was filled with a mixed order of sweat, boot grease, moldering woods, and sawdusty heat. When they were out of Mrs. Hammer's view, Gus punched the steering wheel. "Ain't this hell?" His teeth clenched. "Those two'll be suckin' air through a gap where teeth used to be before I'm through with them!" The muscles in his face corded as he unbuttoned the frayed collar of his blue denim shirt.

"Hold your temper, Gus. My gut's knotted up, too, but we'll let the law handle it." He shook his head. "I hate a theif."

"Those kinds of men stink, Pa. The kind of smell that lingers like skunk spray on a pooch." Gus humphed and spit out the window. A steamy, airless heat rose off the floorboard as he stomped down on the accelerator. "Well, they got problems up to their eyeballs now." He raked his fingers through his hair. He still wasn't used to the short crew-cut his mother had given him. He felt a small lump and pulled a tick from his scalp. Gus stomped the accelerator. He felt numb with anger. "We'll have to fire Hank Kendall now," he said, "And Kendall's one of the best workers we've ever had." Damn! he thought, slamming the steering wheel with the palm of his hand.

"How many years has this been going on?" Gus wondered out loud. "Shoot, Pa, I remember years ago, seeing Squaw stack lumber in separate piles. It happened right under our noses."

"Same with the Delvine property," Norm remarked. "We just trust folks when we shouldn't," he added.

"What gets me is," Gus wondered, "why wasn't he more careful to get *all* unmarked lumber?"

"We watched him too well. He probably thought he was stealing the unmarked stuff," Norman reckoned. "If we hadn't been paying *some* attention to business, it would have *all* been unstamped."

"Hell, I stamped some of it myself!" Gus said. "I thought he'd just overlooked it."

"I stamped some of it, too," Norman said. "Guess if we hadn't. . . ."

Gus slammed his foot on the brake pedal and stopped the truck in the middle of the unpaved road. Dust rolled around the cab and through the windows. Norman fanned the dust and gave the boy a questioning look. "I have an idea," Gus said, punching the steering wheel again. "We'll set the bastards up. I'll peck shit with the chickens before I let them steal another inch of lumber."

Norman nodded contemplatingly. "What's your plan, other than kicking their rears so hard they'll wear their ass as a hat.?"

Gus told his father what he wanted to do and for the next several weeks they developed a plan they were almost certain would put an end to the pilfering.

The sun was bright as Katherine walked from the dark barn, set down the milk bucket and fastened the bonnet ribbons tighter around her neck. Gus's old

Ford rolled slowly past her and slowed to a stop near the hog lot. Gus waved and thought how pretty his mother looked standing there patting their heifer on the rump. She waved, smiled, laid a work-roughened hand to the small of her back, then leaned over and picked up the bucket of warm milk Betsy had just rendered. Gus watched her skirt flap gently around her legs, noted her long golden braids draped over her shoulders. He backed the truck until the tailgate aligned with the loading chute, got out and walked to the back of the pickup truck. Through the stock rails on the truck Koontz Four and Five steadied themselves.

"You're back from the auction sooner than I thought you'd be," Katherine called out.

Norman stepped from the outhouse and waved good-naturedly. Gus waved back. "Got yourself a couple of beauties," Norman said.

"There's a few yards of sausage here," Gus answered, releasing the hogs into their pen. The pigs answered with barking snorts and headed for the trough.

"Harff, yourself," Gus said to them.

"Supper's ready," Katherine called out, reaching for the white knob on the new screen door. Sweat dripped from her forehead, and the hem of her blouse had worked itself out of her skirt.

"You're lookin' pretty as a buttercup," Norman said as he walked up and took the milk bucket from her hand.

"You are pretty, Mama. You don't look at yourself in the mirror often enough."

Katherine giggled a little-girl's laugh. "You're both crazy as old June bugs."

"That fried chicken smells good, darlin'," Norman told her, "but Gus and I are going to the old slave cemetery shortly. Vern and two volunteer deputies are meeting us at Willow Creek."

Katherine stopped stirring the gravy, laid the spoon aside and turned to face them. "It's been over two months since you and Gus planned a way to trap Squaw and Kendall stealing our lumber," she said, and took a deep breath. "I hope it works." She walked up to Gus and hugged him. Her aqua-blue eyes said to be careful and his eyes reassured her they would. "My faith is strong and what Squaw and Kendall have done is wrong. It has to stop." She held Norman tightly and Gus knew she was worried. "Don't you have time to eat first?" she asked.

Gus grabbed a chicken leg from the platter. "We'll be home before you know it, Mama." He squeezed her hand and turned to Norman. "You ready, Pa?" he asked.

They took the county blacktop to Farley's tobacco field, made a sharp left on a narrow dirt road and went fifty feet to a one-lane wooden bridge. Dusty weeds curled over the feeble guard rail. Late afternoon sun laid dark shadows over the road. Just over the next hill on the right was a gray revival tent in the center of a grassy field. A big white sign out front read BROTHER ROSS AND THE LORD WELCOMES YOU. As the truck rolled by, they saw overalled men setting up folding chairs. Gus drove another quarter mile then turned the truck off the roadway. The tires slowed and stopped as dust clouded over the truck.

"Wheeler! Over here," the sheriff called from high, shadowed brush.

Gus and Norman opened their doors, stepped out of the old Ford and walked toward Vernon. "We're waiting for Riley," Sheriff Peele said. "Should be along soon."

"Well, this is it," Norman said, taking off his glasses and cleaning them with his shirt tail.

The sheriff nodded his head. "Peggy Lou Hammer has arranged for her brothers, Wilber and Webber to pick up the truck load of lumber." The low roar of a slow-moving vehicle made the men look up. George Riley pulled his blue Hudson next to them and stuck his head out the window. "We all here?" he asked.

As planned, the men drove to the tree-shaded, dirt intersection near the cemetery. Hunkered under cover, they waited anxiously for Lenny Squaw and Hank Kendall. Briars tugged at their clothing as Gus ate blackberries, George smoked a Lucky Strike cigarette, and Norman cracked his knuckles.

All was quiet until a dark-blue Chevrolet truck bounced over the rutted logging road just north of the slave cemetery. Gus glanced over at Norman, then back to the blue truck with Timber Hills lumber loaded top-heavy on the truck. He shuddered to think how much money Kendall and Squaw had made over the years from the piracy. He reckoned it was several thousand dollars.

The truck slowed to idle speed. From the east, a red Dodge flatbed truck was approaching. Wilber, Peggy Lou's brother, honked quickly three times as planned. Squaw and Kendall walked to the rear of their truck and waited. Squaw took off his baseball cap, shook it and put it on backwards. With very little conversation from the men, the Dodge backed to the load of lumber. The men nodded, exchanged cash, and began transferring the lumber.

Vern bounded from his cover. "You're under arrest!" he hollered, holding his .38 Colt Revolver straight out in front of him. The other men followed him out.

With lightning swiftness, Kendall dove into the cab of his truck. The sheriff fired with the bullet grazing Hank's left arm. "You bastard!" Kendall cursed, as he brought up a double-barrel shotgun and fired. The men leaped for cover. Squaw sprang into the cab of Wilber's borrowed flatbed and pushed the starter button. "Get in," he yelled to his cousin. Hank duck-trotted swiftly behind the truck and pushed himself up. "Damn, it hurts like a sonofabitch," Hank mumbled, twisting his bandana around the bleeding arm-wound.

Vern Peele rushed to the brush-hidden police car, jumped in, and reached for the key. It wasn't in the ignition. "Shit!" he said, as he ran back to where he'd been squatted.

One of the men hollered just as Lenny Squaw shook his fist in the air and stomped on the gas and sped away. The truck bounced and jerked as the two criminals fought to keep seated. "Hold on," Lenny shouted, "this wasn't supposed to happen!" Lenny snapped his head around to look over his shoulder.

"Look out!" Hank yelled, but Lenny's reaction was too slow. He hadn't seen the old, kudzu-covered hay wagon in front of him. The truck hit the wagon head-on. Lenny flew forward, his head busting through the windshield, hailing Hank with blood and glass.

"Get out of the truck!" the sheriff yelled.

Hank fired two more shots, one bullet striking Gus's knee.

"Gus's been hit!" Norman yelled.

"I'm okay," Gus answered, grimacing and covering the wound with his hand.

"Hel . . . help me." Lenny Squaw sputtered.

Hank quickly turned to his cousin. "God forbid! What'cha gone an' done to yourself?" When Hank turned his attention to Squaw, Gus, hobbling on one leg, bounded into the cab of the truck and grabbed the gun from Hank's lap. Vern and George Riley wrestled Kendall to the ground and held him as Norman, with just one hand, put the handcuffs around Hank Kendall's wrists. "Well, Rooster, you ain't King Cockodoodledoo no more," Norman said.

"Hold him while I radio for an ambulance for Gus. Don't think Squaw's gonna need one. He's gone."

"I don't need an ambulance, Vern," Gus said, pressing his hand against the bleeding wound. "Pa and I'll drive to the hospital ourselves. With his one arm and my one leg we can do it," Gus half-joked, yet the pain of the gunshot wound made him clench his jaw and grimace with pain.

As Norman and Gus drove away, Sheriff Peele shoved Hank Kendall into the back seat of the police car. He radioed Orsen's Mortuary and Delbert's Towing, and George Riley drove the load of lumber back to Timber Hills.

• CHAPTER 11 •

Gus drifted in and out of consciousness as the doctor removed the bullet from his left knee. "Did we get them?" he slurred, dopey from a calmative.

"We got 'em," Norman answered.

Katherine moved a bowl of green Jell-O from the night stand next to the bed and took hold of Gus's hand. "You did a good job, son." She squeezed his hand and sighed. Norman walked over to her and kissed her forehead. "He's strong. He'll be okay."

The doctor walked in behind them. "Gus will need to stay here for a couple of days. I've ordered a pair of crutches for him and he's just been given a strong sedative for the pain. He'll sleep for several hours."

"I'll stay with him," Katherine told Norman. "You go on back to the mill. I'll send someone out for you if there's a change," she told him.

Sheriff Peele grinned as he booked Kendall into jail. "You were finally out-smarted ol' boy. Those Wheeler's ain't as stupid as you think," the sheriff taunted, turning his back on Kendall to open the cell door. The Sheriff reached out, pulled the barred door open, then turned back to Kendall. The prisoner was gone. "Jesus Christ!" Peele yelled, rushing through the door and out into the street. "The jailbird's escaped," he hollered. He ran to the corner, looked both ways for the prisoner, then bolted back into the police station. "Talk about *stupid*!" he said, rebuking himself. Vern ran to his desk and grabbed his gun from the top drawer. "I've got to let Norman know," he said, talking to himself. He asked Thelma Jean to ring the Wheeler's residence and when there was no answer, he slammed the office door and darted to his car. With his siren sounding and bubble light flashing, Sheriff Vernon Peele headed toward Timber Hills.

Norman was getting out of his car when he heard the siren. Quickly he walked toward the approaching police car. Men at the mill stopped working and turned to see what the commotion was all about.

"He's escaped, Norm," Peele yelled. "He may be out for revenge."

Several workers had gathered round Norman and the sheriff. "Where's Gus?" one of them said.

"God," Norman said. "We've got to get to the hospital!"

Hank Kendall tipped his cap lower over his face and hid behind a tree until a woman pushing a boy in a wheelchair passed by him. When all was clear, he slipped up the hospital's wheelchair ramp and eased past the information desk. On a small table near the fire alarm box was an in-house telephone. Hugging the wall, to avoid as many people as possible, Kendall made his way to the phone, picked up the receiver and told the hospital operator he had flowers to deliver to Gus Wheeler. After he was given the room number, he darted in and out of door-ways until all was clear, then hurried toward Gus's room. When he got to Gus's half-closed door, he reached out and pushed it open. Noiselessly he slithered in and closed the door behind him.

Katherine lifted her head and glanced quickly toward the doorway. "What are *you* doing here?" she gasped, nearly knocking the straight-backed chair over backwards. She positioned herself in front of her son's bed as if to protect him. Her eyes were big and round with fear. "What are you going to do?" she asked.

"Kill the boy. Maybe you. Then go back to the sawmill and . . . "

Kendall dodged the bowl of Jell-O Katherine swooped up and hurled at him. It shattered against the wall as he rushed toward her but stopped when Gus stirred. "Well, now. Looky who's wakin' up."

"Guess I won't be workin' at the mill for a few days," Gus said drowsily, rubbing his eyes.

Without taking her eyes from Kendall, Katherine rested her hand on Gus's leg, just above the bandage. The coolness of her hand felt good on his warm skin.

"It's okay, Mom. It doesn't hurt . . . much." His eyes began to focus. "Ma?"

Katherine's eyes seemed to pierce Kendall's. "Please," she murmured.

Kendall grinned. "Got some business to handle here," he said to Gus, then with the loud sound of sirens, Kendall turned and fled through the door. Katherine ran after him and yelled at a nurse as she walked from another room. "That man's escaped the sheriff's custody!" she yelled, pointing. "Call some-one!" Katherine ran back to her son's room. He was sound asleep. Shaking, she sank to the chair. "Oh my God," she said.

The sheriff and Norman rushed into Gus's room. Katherine jumped up and pointed in the direction Hank had run. "Please get him," she said. "He's threat-ened us, Norman."

Norman reached out and held his wife. "It'll be okay, Katy. Vern'll get him." Norman patted her arms, glanced at Gus, then rushed out the door. "Norm, be careful," Katherine said as he fled through the doorway and down the dim cor-ridor. "Because I love you," she whispered. "And because we're having another baby," she added, barely audible.

The sheriff had handcuffs on Hank Kendall before Norman rounded the cor-ner. "Good work," he heard Vern say to a large-built man standing in front of the prisoner.

"Weren't no trouble," the man said, rubbing his arm where Kendall had scratched him trying to get away from his grip. "Weren't no trouble at all," he said bravely.

Norman walked back into Gus's room, leaned against the wall and let out a long breath. "Thank goodness," he said quietly. "Thank you, God," he said, looking up at the ceiling then back to the boy.

"You'll need to stay in bed for a while like the doctor says, Gus," Katherine said. "Your father and the men can manage without you until you heal."

Norman let out a short laugh. "Holy willikers, Katy. You know this isn't going to keep him from the mill." He strolled over to his son's side. "This boy eats, sleeps and breathes the sawmill. Timber Hills wouldn't be the same without him."

Katherine gave him a dirty look. "Well he'll just *have* to!"

Gus's anxious eyes looked at the doorway Kendall had darted from, then back at his folks. They were trying not to worry him. He grinned and picked up a fresh bowl of Jell-O the nurse had brought in. "Is this all I get? Where's the meat?" he asked.

Gus took two bites then laid aside the bowl. "Do you think they got him?" he asked.

"He didn't have a chance," Norman said. "There were at least a half dozen men after him."

"He came right into this room and threatened us."

"He wasn't too clever," Norman answered. "His luck's finally run out."

"His, *and* Lenny's," Gus said.

A few days later the Wheeler's called on Peggy Lou Hammer. The home was a modest wood-frame, painted white with green awnings. A hand printed Beware of Dog sign was nailed to the white picket fence in front. The screened-in front porch had a swing and potted geraniums all around, scenting the warm, humid air. Gus hesitated before knocking, then inhaled and tapped softly. A floppy, long tailed cocker spaniel bounced off the porch swing and greeted them. Maybelle Hawkins answered the door with a steaming, woolen hot pack in her hand.

"Come in if you're willin'," Maybelle said. "The local health department wants to mark the doors and windows with a quarantine notice. Just thought I'd warn you first."

Katherine smiled. "We're willin'," she said. Stepping through the opened doorway, Gus glanced around the dark room while Katherine put her pocketbook and a tinfoil-wrapped box on the table near the door. Norman held his hat in his hand.

"I've volunteered to help Peggy Lou and Eunice with Buford Paul," Maybelle told them and gestured for the three guests to sit.

"They call him Four Legs," Peggy Lou sobbed, and all heads turned to her as she strolled out into the living room. "They inspected the garbage, plumbing . . . Buford Paul feels so ashamed for getting sick. He thinks he did something wrong. He can't get used to the braces. They're so heavy and painful to use." She sat in a trance-like daze without bothering to wipe away her tears. Dots of perspiration dotted her forehead.

Gus felt uncomfortable in the stuffy, small room. He wanted to say something useful, but didn't know what to say or even how to say it. He shifted in his seat.

Katherine rested her hand on top of the grieving woman's. "I'm so sorry, Peggy Lou."

A faint smile softened Peggy Lou's expression. "He complained of a headache before he went to bed, then woke up unable to walk. He had a slight fever and was feeling poorly, but I didn't think much about it, you know, with kids, they're always sniflin' or sneezin'. Next morning I heard him scream that he couldn't lift his head. I ran in there and he said he couldn't move."

"It's such a dreaded disease, now-a-days," Katherine sympathized and Norman shook his head.

"Just strikes without a visible source or pattern," Maybelle said, shaking her head.

"You're fortunate to have Maybelle here with him," Katherine said to Peggy Lou.

"Yes we are, Katherine, and I've told her that a thousand times."

"Oh, heavens, Miz Peggy, what would I be doin' if I couldn't be here helpin' y'all? I wouldn't have it any other way."

"Well, you know, Maybelle, you've been farin' poorly, too, with your bad knees, an' all," Peggy Lou stated. "I worry about you, dear." Peggy Lou's voice sounded thin and fragile.

Gus watched Peggy Lou's small hands sweep back falling wisps of hair from her face. Her mousy-brown hair was piled high on the back of her head and held loosely by two tortoiseshell combs. "You have our sympathy for the loss of your husband and for the unfortunate illness of your son," Gus said.

Peggy Lou blew her nose on a thin lavender hanky. "Nothing's as solid as it seems."

"Fragile like a bubble," Maybelle whispered.

Katherine nodded. Gus glanced at Norman and he was nodding, too.

Peggy Lou looked at Gus. "How's your knee, honey?"

"It still hurts some, but not bad. We got 'em, though, didn't we?" Gus smiled then added, "That's why we're here, Mrs. Hammer. We come to thank you and your brothers, Wilber and Webber, for what you did to help us catch the thieves who were stealing our lumber. Without your family's help . . . well, we just come to thank you," Gus said.

Peggy Lou flicked her hand dismissively. "I heard your other son went to New York, Katherine. I'm sorry to hear it. So alone and far away."

"Actually he went to California, and, yes it is a long way, and I miss him deeply," Katherine answered, smoothing her dress down over her knees, then, "We brought you some meat stew and a sorghum molasses pie," she said, nodding toward the table near her pocketbook.

Peggy Lou nodded her thanks and fiddled with her damp handkerchief. "Maybelle has been a Godsend," she complimented, putting the soiled hanky on the floor. Katherine reached into her pocketbook and handed her a dry one. "Thank you," Peggy Lou said, drying her eyes. "Maybelle works double shifts lugging Buford Paul around, wheeling in respirators and huge vats of hot water.

Endlessly wringing out heavy wet towels . . . Oh, mercy," she said, wringing the hanky.

Maybelle held out her hand. "Children are so undeserving of this misery. I hear someday soon there will be a vaccine against polio. It should have come sooner."

Gus felt claustrophobic and shifted positions again. We've paid our respects, how much longer do we have to sit here with our hands courteously on our knees?

"We traded his bike for a wheelchair. He'll be doomed with a sickly life," Peggy Lou murmured. "And poor Eunice, bless her heart, we pray she's not strickened."

"We should go now," Katherine said, hugging Peggy Lou. "I'll be volunteering for the Mothers' March on Polio," she said as they were leaving. "I'll be going door-to-door collecting for the March of Dimes."

"You're a kind, good-hearted woman," Peggy Lou Hammer said as she waved goodbye and thanked Katherine for the stew and pie.

Gus took a big breath of fresh air and headed for the car. "It just ain't fittin'" he said to his folks. "All the sufferin' and pain."

"There's been a lot of it lately," Katherine answered just before she stepped into the car. "Garrett's illness and death, Norman's lost arm, Gilbert leaving home, you getting shot, Buford Paul. I just don't see a reason for it all," she said, looking up into the blue, cloud-flecked sky. "Lord, sometimes my faith is stilled."

Ira Irving and Norman Wheeler slouched over Henry's desk comparing contracts.

"They're identical!" Irving said.

"Not exactly," Norman corrected. "This one says, 'I do hereby sell all *land* . . . ,' and this one says, 'I do hereby sell all *timber*. . . .' "

Henry nodded. "Then look at each contract closely. Down here at the bottom in very small type. This one says, 'excluding land' and this one says 'excluding timber'."

Norman's hand shook as he laid the pen across the contract. "It's my own fault," he said, plainly inflamed by his own ignorance. "I should have read the contract thoroughly. It was too good to be true," he said quietly, "just like Katy said."

Ira's hands fumbled nervously in the pockets of his navy trousers. His voice was impatient. "Now what?" He paced the room nervously. "What do we do, Henry?"

Norman looked at Henry and shrugged. "Yeah. What do we do?"

"Well, Ira, your contract depicts *land only*. There are a couple options. The two of you can agree to *trade* contracts, now that you've already cut, giving

Norm the land portion, or you could give Norm a percentage of the profits from the timber. Or one of you could sell your contract to the other. Because you each signed, there is really nothing that Delvine can be prosecuted for. It's up to you and Norman to work out an agreement." The attorney propped his chair against the wall. "It wasn't ethical. I'd like to see the man punished, but unfortunately, the contracts are legal."

"It stinks," Norman said, his face glowering over the contracts.

CHAPTER 12

Gilbert jumped off the bus wearing the smile of a five-year-old boy on Christmas morning. He shoved back the bill of his OLIVER TRACTORS cap, lifted an arm over his head and whooped a greeting. "Hello, Paradise!" Heads turned to look and Gilbert nodded. He wanted to see it all at once. He turned his head left, right, tilted it back and peered into the sky. It wasn't exactly the glowing golden like he thought it would be, but it was early and there would be a sunset soon. Gilbert set his suitcase between his feet and stared at the group of people still clustered around the bus depot. He took a deep breath. The air was warm, but not sweet smelling like home. He inhaled deeply, then let it out slowly. He turned and faced the bustling multitude of people and realized he'd never seen so many different people gathered in one place. "Day one," he said aloud, then turned and bumped into a sun-glassed woman with shorts up to her crotch. Gilbert couldn't help but look. Before he could speak, she was gone and a man with a bottle half-hidden under a worn, pilly sweater was at his side. Gilbert nodded and the tallow-faced man slithered away like he was afraid someone was following him.

Gilbert slowly moved on, his blue eyes skimming the flock of people. "Howdy," he said, but no one took the time to stop and talk. Did he just imagine folks having dead eyes with no color? Gil's joy began to fade. He glanced around. Were people really detached and unapproachable? He wrestled with his thoughts and as he walked, feelings of dismay mingled with elation.

He glanced around, saw no grass or trees, no watermelon trucks, no hills with hay rolls. Before crossing the street, Gilbert bought a newspaper, folded it and shoved it into his back pocket. Cars swished by, and when the pedestrian light flashed the word WALK, Gilbert shook his head in wonder. He walked to a tree with a skinny trunk and a cluster of fanlike leaves on top, set his suitcase aside and hunkered down. "Not really the shade of an almighty oak," he mumbled, looking up, then began searching the newspaper for a job and a place to live.

A fancy-cut poodle trotted up to him and sniffed his foot. "Hey, boy," Gilbert said, reaching out to pat the dog's head. He nodded at the woman behind the leash. "Ma'am," Gilbert greeted in his southern way. He looked up into the woman's face. "Is it far to 7th Street?" He hoped his voice hadn't sounded nervous.

"Walk four blocks toward the ocean," the woman said, then pulled her dog from Gil's friendly hand and walked away. "Nice overalls," she said over her shoulder.

"Thank you," Gilbert said.

Gilbert looked from side to side. He didn't know which way the ocean was. A tanned man with a surfboard under his arm was at the curb waiting for the light to turn. "Excuse me," Gil said, "could you tell me how to get to 7th Street?"

"I'm going that way. I'll give you a lift."

"It's not in a very nice neighborhood," the man told Gilbert when he read aloud the ad for the apartment.

"Well, I've got to start somewhere," Gilbert said, then asked, "Say, do you know if any of the aircraft plants are hiring?"

The driver shrugged his shoulders. "Have an uncle who worked at Vultee in Downey. He died last year, though. There's Lockheed in Burbank."

The car slowed and pulled to the curb in front of a two-story apartment building. Gilbert opened the car's door and stepped out. He opened the back door, grabbed his bag, shut the door and watched the man drive off.

Standing in front of the door that said *Manager*, Gilbert inhaled deeply then raised his hand and knocked. When the door opened and a heavyset, stocking-footed man stepped onto the threshold, Gilbert nodded and smiled.

"I'm here to see the apartment you have advertised." Gilbert held up the paper but the man didn't look at the newspaper.

"I'll get my shoes on," the manager said, shutting the door behind him leaving Gilbert standing there with his suitcase in one hand and the newspaper in the other.

Gilbert stepped away from the door, his eyes scanning the cracked stucco siding on the building. Loud music caused his gaze to drift upward to an opened window. The manager came out and Gilbert followed him upstairs to the furnished apartment. Gilbert got a whiff of old cigarette smoke as he walked into the front room. There was a lived-in smell to the room, old grease, sweaty socks. He scanned the living room's dark brown carpet, wood-paneled walls, a gold-framed picture of a bridge. With the manager following, Gilbert peeked into the bedroom.

"The rent is seventy-five a month and five dollars deposit for the key."

Gilbert pulled a handful of crumbled bills from his pocket. He unwrinkled the money and handed the man four twenties. After the landlord had gone, Gilbert pulled back the lined drapes, saw half a dozen dead flies on the window sill then looked down at the busy city sidewalks. "This sure ain't Tennessee."

Gilbert sat at the table and braced his chin on his fist waiting for the light-hearted, optimistic feelings he'd had for so many years to return. Where were they? Buried under these new feelings of ambivalence? He laid his head on his arms and dozed off. When he woke, it was dark. Without turning on a light, he staggered to the bedroom and tumbled into bed. There were no sheets on the bare mattress. Right now he didn't care. He slept soundly, dreaming of him and Gus walking down a muddy twin-rutted path singing rhymes. *I had a little monkey, his name was Tiny Tim. I put him in the bathtub to teach him how to swim.* In his dream, he saw them with their rolled-up faded overalls and no shirts. They passed weatherboarded farmhouses with Model A Fords and white oak barrels bound with strips of hickory bark. Bed sheets waved from clotheslines in the fresh-scented breeze.

Gilbert turned over on his bare mattress, slowly awakened by the plink, plink of a leaking faucet. For the next few hours he lay awake listening and thinking. In his mind he could see bits and pieces of home; the quilt frame swaying from hooks in the pine ceiling, sawdusty eggs in a basket, Gus's hogs.

Gilbert got up and walked to the window. The empty street below looked cold, synthetic. There were no green hills, no crooked creeks, no night owls or lightning bugs. He shook his head and thought of all those pictures he'd idolized from *National Geographic*.

Gilbert laid back down, but didn't sleep. At the first sign of daylight, he got up, stepped to the door and opened it. He glanced down at pale morning light trickling through the doorway and sniffed the cool city air. Gilbert closed the door, showered and changed clothes. Before walking out the door, he turned around and glanced at his new home. "I can't believe this," he said, smiling. After a moment of silent thought, he walked out into his first whole day in California.

Gilbert walked to a busy restaurant and sat at a small round table. He picked up a menu, scanned it briefly, and decided on the #1 breakfast with a glass of buttermilk. It came with hash browns. The waitress said they didn't serve grits, and hash browns were potatoes grated up then pan fried. Gilbert glanced around, shifted his silverware from one side to the other, smiled at a couple with an olive-skinned child.

"Thank you," Gilbert said when the waitress brought the glass of buttermilk. "I need to call about some jobs," he told her, then asked if he could use their telephone after he finished eating. She pointed toward the public telephone in front of the beauty shop next door. Gilbert nodded his thanks and watched a man sitting in the corner bobbing up and down in his seat trying to catch the waitress's attention.

Gilbert opened the morning paper. Inside, his body shook, but outwardly he put on a strong pretense. "Okay," he said quietly, sagging over the newspaper and running his index finger down the Help Wanted section. "Which one will it be?" He scanned quickly for information on aircraft jobs.

The sound of a register ringing up sales and the buzzing sounds of voices kept Gilbert from concentrating, but by the time he'd finished with his breakfast, he had seven possible jobs circled. One of them would be his, Gilbert was sure of it. After breakfast, Gil walked to the phone box and arranged for an interview at Rohr Aircraft in Riverside.

"I've come for the interview," Gilbert heard his voice say to a brunette woman who was typing at her desk. The flat chested woman smiled brightly and extended her hand. Gilbert was shocked at how cold and hard it felt.

"I'm Florence Peabody. Fill this out," she said, handing Gilbert the application. When he was finished, she introduced him to a well-dressed man with a limp. Gilbert followed the man through the plant. "We've just begun, hopefully, a long-standing relationship with Douglas Aircraft making DC-7 airliner power packages," the man shouted above the noise of the shop. He continued as he described the work Gilbert would have to do, then led him back to the personnel office. "If you're interested in working, be here at 7:00 in the morning."

Gilbert said nothing for a moment, thinking about the job, the long bus ride to get there each day, the luck of finding what he had wanted so quickly. He sensed Florence's questioning eyes on him. He stared at her for a spell, then said, "I'll take it."

"Good," she said, then turned and walked from the room. Gilbert moved slowly about the office looking at pictures of airplanes on the walls. "Lord have mercy," he mumbled with a full grin on his face. His eyes scanned the orderly, brightly-lit room. "If Billy Ray could only see me now. And he always thought *he* was the chief."

Gilbert stepped onto the sidewalk, inhaled deeply and sat on the bus bench. Had he made the right decision? He wrestled with his feelings. Even if he hadn't found a job so quickly, he wasn't going home the fool, crawling back telling everyone he'd changed his mind. Gilbert couldn't imagine sawing logs for the rest of his life. He'd always said he envied Billy Ray Mudd for being unconstrained and wondered what his friend was doing now. Funny how he'd thought of Billy Ray Mudd. He could see Billy Ray standing tall and handsome in his neatly pressed military uniform. "Yes, Billy Ray," Gilbert said aloud, "I've always envied your way of life. Your freedom, your detachment, your lack of apprehension. If you could only see me now," he said, forgetting home and feeling self-satisfied. "I followed my dream." Gilbert remembered the tinge of jealousy he'd felt toward Billy Ray, yet there was a sense of kinship between them. Billy Ray was a teacher—no, he was a hero. Billy Ray did things boys always wanted to do but didn't dare try. Youth is gone so quickly. A few laughs, a couple of spankings and it's over. Gilbert thought of the fun the three of them had had in the creek. He laughed out loud remembering Billy Ray's bravery in the water. Gil would have bet his life on Billy Ray drowning before he reached manhood since he couldn't swim a lick. Gil thought of Billy Ray's reckless disobedience and shook his head. Ol' Sheriff Peele never found out it was Billy Ray who stole Mitch's tractor. Gilbert looked up at the sky, an expanse of hazy blue, unobstructed by trees or hills. The sun was climbing directly overhead. It was dinner time, but they didn't call it *dinner* here. The noon meal was called *lunch.* Supper was dinner. Law! He'd have to learn all the funny ways of saying things.

The first three months at Rohr sped by for Gilbert as he grasped his duties and learned the cruciality of perfection. The next few months gave Gilbert more free time to join with friends for a beer or a day at the beach. He felt content, yet never a day went by that he didn't think of home.

It had been a good week. Gilbert cashed his check, bought a few groceries and stuffed the rest of his pay into a box under his bed. He sat in his small apartment rubbing blisters and thinking about his work. Every part of his body ached and his shoes were worn through the sole, but it wasn't a bad job and the salary was good, and it was Friday night. Gilbert combed his hair, put on his shoes, walked out of his apartment and shut the door behind him. He'd walked two blocks before he realized he didn't have his billfold. He elected not to go back. The night was cool and foggy with an ocean smell in the air. As cars sped by, their lights shone coldly through the fog. Gilbert heard a noise and turned to see a man lifting the lid of a garbage can. He had long white hair, a beard to match and wore a coat with cavernous pockets. When the vagrant spotted Gilbert, he withdrew into the darkness. A girl with Capri pants and a sleeveless white blouse bounced by. Gilbert nodded, noticing a six-pack of beer in her hand. "She's a tramp," the man in the shadows grunted.

At a late-night grocery store, Gilbert filled a Styrofoam cup with coffee and picked up a *Life* Magazine. It made him smile as he recalled, *What's Life? Magazine. Where do you get it? Drug store. How Much? Ten cents. Ain't got it. That's tough. What's tough? Life. What's Life* . . . Oh how he wished Gus was here with him—or was it that he missed being home? Gilbert pulled some change from his pocket, paid twenty-five cents for the magazine and a nickel for the coffee.

"Hi, honey," the girl with the beer said to him as he walked out of the store. She fell in step and said, "Are you lonely?"

Gilbert thought it was nice of her to ask. Did he really look that desolate? "To be honest, yes I am," he said, liking her twinkly green eyes and fluffy hair. She even wore earbobs and Gilbert thought that was classy.

"Follow me," she said, taking his arm, then, "What's your name?"

"Gil. Gilbert Wheeler," he said, and felt she was only listening with mild interest. Gilbert thought of Billy Ray and wondered if his friend would have followed this female stranger. Yes, I think he would have, Gil said to himself as the girl led him to who-knew-where. She held the bottles up. "I'll share," she said and Gilbert answered with a smile and a shrug. A neon light illuminated the otherwise cellar-dark stairway to a basement dwelling. Gilbert could smell spilled beer as he followed the blond in Capri pants down the litter-sowed steps. Inside, there was a heavy musky scent, almost primal and the odor excited him. She handed him a cold bottle of beer and he thanked her with a weak toasting gesture. Gilbert couldn't read the name on the label because the only light was from a fish tank along the far wall. "I charge ten dollars," she told him, her voice quiet and tired.

Gilbert moistened his dry lips with his tongue, but couldn't speak. Her face was part in the tank light and part in the shadow and he could tell from the lit side that it was drawn, almost ghostly looking in the aquatic light. Strange he hadn't seen that look outside. He felt drawn to her and wondered why. *She's a tramp*, the stranger had said. His curious eyes scanned the small room. Even in the dark he could see her unmade bed partially hid behind a plastic accordion wall divider. With the lighted aquarium behind her, he admired her silhouette as she pulled her blouse from the Capri's and slowly took it off. Gilbert could see droplets of perspiration sliding between her apple-size breasts and he felt a rustling of excitement ripple through him. "Ten dollars," she repeated.

It was the first time Gilbert realized she was selling sex. She's an alley cat, he thought. He felt his body and his mind take different directions. She scared him, yet excited him. Gilbert jerked from his thoughts and reached into his pocket. It was then that he remembered that he'd walked out of his apartment without his wallet.

"Well," she said, noticeably impatient. "Do you want to or not?"

Gilbert's mouth felt like it was crammed full of cotton. "Um. . . . " He fumbled with the change in his pocket knowing he couldn't make it add up to ten dollars.

"Sometimes I charge five," she said, obviously misreading his hesitancy. "Tonight's a slow night and I've never had a chinwhisker hick from the backwoods of Kentucky."

"Thanks for the beer," Gilbert said, setting the bottle on a book shelf. He hurried out of the whores basement room with her cold-hearted words burning his back.

"What are you, some aftermath of inbreeding?" she called out after him. Gilbert reproved himself for following her, but then if he'd had the ten dollars. . . .

He felt it had all been a bad dream and quickened his step wondering if what he was feeling was from being ashamed or disappointed. Actually, he was furious with himself for forgetting his billfold!

Gilbert stopped in front of a department store window and peered through the glass at a television set. He read the sign next to it: CAPEHART BEDFORD. $229.95. CAPEHART POLAROID PICTURE FILTER SYSTEM WITH 21-INCH ALUMINIZED TUBE. Gilbert gazed open-mouthed with astonished admiration and wonder at the new television set.

At home, he took a lukewarm shower, tore some mold off a slice of hard bread and dropped it into the toaster. As he ate, Gilbert thought about how fast life moved in California, including the women, and how everyone was always in a hurry. He loved it. Gilbert was getting into the West Coast routine and was certain he'd done the right thing by coming here. Today the hills of Tennessee were far from his thoughts, until he got the letter from Gus.

Sitting here on the crick bed with a pole in the water. Rarely get time to fish anymore. Pa's so busy. Christmas wasn't the same without you. We could use your help, here, Gil. It's been nearly a year since you left. Has all the glitter rubbed off, yet? Your family misses you. Not only is your body there, but your heart seems to be far away, also. You never write.

Mom's expecting again. She had a miscarriage after you left. She was in the hospital for nine days. The doctor advised her not to have more children, but she said the Lord knows best. She's wearing the same two maternity dresses she wore when she was expecting Sara Jane. Thought you'd want to know you'd soon be a brother again. The baby's due in late spring.

Not quite smiling, Gilbert laid the letter across his knees and squinted into memory. He could picture in his mind Gus sitting there along the bank, holes in the knees of his overalls, his old fishing hat stuck full of flies, hooks, necessities. Gilbert squeezed his eyes closed and tightened in on the memory. He could feel the pure air, hear the cool, clear water swirling round his feet, smell the warm, piney scent of the hemlock. He laid back, opened his eyes, and stared at the straight-back chair in the corner covered with clothing, some dirty, some clean.

Gilbert got up, pulled back the curtains and looked at the hustle-bustle of Long Beach streets. Two different worlds, he thought. He rolled back his sleeves, picked up his brother's letter and started reading again.

You should see Ma right now. She's got flour dust all over her face. There's fried chicken bubbling in the iron skillet. She's getting ready to fry up a mess of okra and green tomatoes. There's hot biscuits rising in the oven. Can you smell supper cooking? Smoke from the hot grease scents our kitchen and there's a Sunday dinner feeling all around. God, I miss ya.

Gilbert walked over to his unmade bed, propped the pillows against the headboard and laid down.

When you coming home? Ma's not doing well since she's all blown up with a baby in her belly. She gets tired easily and her feet swell up like they're going to pop. She can't stand too long at one time because her feet bother her so much. Pa's the same, overworked, not sleeping well. He's getting all stoop-shouldered. Sara Jane's growing like a weed in the cow pasture. She looks a lot like Pa. She's a big help to Ma, does the dishes and some ironing. Sara Jane's the only light-heartedness we see around here.

Gilbert leaned back, soaking in the words. Life at home hadn't changed. He glanced down at the letter in his hand and read the rest of Gus's letter. Gilbert's composure changed from fair complacency to outrage as he read:

Gil, we never told you this because we didn't want to give you something to worry about, you getting settled into your new home and all, but Pa got cheated badly over the big boundary of Delvine timber. Turned out that just after you left Pa and I went out there and damn if it wasn't gone. All harvested.

Gilbert gripped the letter and sat upright as he continued reading about the Delvine timber loss:

I thought Pa would have a heart attack. I still believe he's on the verge of caving in. Delvine sold the same piece of land to both Pa and Ira Irving. Irving got to it first. Devil's own luck, huh? Delvine worded the contract so it was actually legal! Folks heard he'd taken our money and went on a cruise. Grandfather and Pa tried to contact Delvine at his office in Atlanta, but they said he'd moved. No one knows where he went, but I bet he's getting rich off unsuspecting decent folks. Arnold H. Delvine's become a dirty word around these parts.

Gilbert felt his face redden with anger. "The bastard!" he yelled, slapping the letter down on his knee. "You won't get away with this, Delvine. I'll get you if it's the last thing I do. I'll have you puking up that timber!" He laid Gus's letter aside. For the first time since he'd come, Gilbert wanted to go home. For the first time ever, he actually felt like he was needed there. Why had he thought otherwise? Was it because Gus was the one who showed an interest in the mill? Gus asked the questions, Gus begged to help Norman even before his head reached the conveyer belt that drew the logs through the saws. It was with Gus that Norman shared long tales about his grandfather's mill. It was Gus that absorbed every bit of it by listening intently, genuinely enthralled. "I wasn't interested in the lumbering trade," Gilbert said aloud. "And it still doesn't appeal to me, but that doesn't mean I'm not a part of the family."

Gilbert felt that a torch had just been lit in front of him, bright, like sun on a mirror, illuminating the truth. Yes, it was clear now. Naturally Norman would show more of an inclination toward the son that would carry on the family business. "And I was jealous!" Gilbert said loudly, almost ecstatic because he finally understood his own feelings.

Yes, he could smell his mother's golden fried chicken. He smiled at the thought, then laughed when he thought of the whore he'd met the night before. Gads! If folks back home knew about my close encounter with that woman, the Baptist Church would cave in. Gilbert looked back down at the letter in his hands. He frowned, then reread the part about Delvine. His hands shook and his blood boiled. "That no-good. . . . "

The day hurried on as usual, but Gilbert's anger grew over the lost timber. He was going to find out, one way or another where this Delvine bastard was. He owed it to his kin and for the first time since coming to California, Gilbert realized that his father might have been right about his leaving. Maybe I *was* a self-serving asshole.

Gilbert sat with his head in his hands for most of the evening, thinking, figuring, counting his money, planning. He was going home, but before he'd walk up those porch steps at Timber Hills, he had something to do. Something to take care of. Someone by the name of Arnold H. Delvine was going to pay for hurting his family. During the next few weeks, Gilbert ate little and put every extra penny into the box under his bed.

• CHAPTER 13 •

Gus wasn't prepared for two letters he received on Saturday afternoon just before he and his family sat down for dinner.

The mailman tapped on the screen door. "I have a Special Delivery letter for you," he said, reaching into his carrier bag. Gus noticed there was sadness on his face as the postman opened the door and walked into the Wheeler's kitchen.

Gilbert wrinkled his forehead. "Special Delivery?" He rose from the table, took the letter, nodded his thanks.

Katherine looked curiously at the letter in Gus's hand. "Is it from the Draft Board?" she asked.

"No, Mama, it's from The War Department." Gus recalled several months earlier when Jed and Ethel McCall received the letter from the War Department telling them that their son, Corky, had been seriously wounded in combat. "Excuse me, Mama, Pa," Gus said as he walked into his bedroom and closed the door.

Gus opened the envelope. Inside were two letters. He looked at the signature on the first letter. Billy Ray. He looked at the second letter. Tears formed in his eyes as he read the news.

On August 17, Billy Ray Mudd and 34 other Americans were captured by Communists. They were found lying face-down with their hands bound with shoelaces. Only five men escaped. We are sad to report that your friend, Billy Ray Mudd, was killed. . . .

The Red Cross has unsuccessfully been able to locate his parents. Your name and address were all that he had given us. We are forwarding a letter to you written by Billy Ray Mudd. It was found in his belongings.

Gus eased down on his bed. He closed his eyes, turned onto his side and drew his knees to his chest. "No, it couldn't have been Billy Ray. Not by a darn sight."

In his mind's eye Gus saw a circle of boys sitting Indian style in a damp-smelling barn. They passed around a jug of moonshine. He saw three boys splashing and dunking each other in the creek. Then Gus saw Billy Ray being dipped gently into a baptismal tub, the only time his friend was in a church. Gus felt a tear leak down his cheek.

Katherine tapped on his bedroom door then opened it slightly. "Are you okay?" she asked.

"Leave me alone for a while, Mama."

Gus leaned back his head and stared wide-eyed at the light bulb hanging above his head. How many other childhood buddies were destined to die? He lay there for over an hour, and in that time Gus relived years of blessed childhood.

Finally Gus found the courage to read Billy Ray's letter.

Dear Gus and Gil,

It feels like a lifetime since I've seen you. I miss our times together and home, although I didn't have much of one. When I was drafted, I had no idea this life would be worse than anything I've ever known. I don't know why I feel the need to write this letter to you. I've never written to anyone since the day I left home. We're squatted here waiting for a signal to lower ourselves down the sides of the ship and head for shore. Our nerves are fiddle-string tight, and . . . . There it is. The prompt. I'll finish this when I get off the boat.

Down, now. We had to hit the beach with full field packs and weapons. I can't remember being this scared, not even on the day Crum Harper dared me to steal Wampler's tractor. I was so nervous I pushed the gas pedal instead of the brakes going round a corner and rolled it over the side of a hill into the Tennessee River. It nearly killed me. I don't know why I did it, except that maybe it was to get back at my folks for putting me in an orphanage. I don't know. Life wasn't happy for me. I never told you that. I always pretended like I had it made. Hell, I was jealous of everyone, especially you two. You know, Crum said the dare was off since I hadn't delivered the tractor to Thelma Jean's front yard. Crum dared me again a few months later. That time it worked. I laugh when I think of it, Thelma Jean waking up and finding a tractor in her flower bed. I could just see that nosey old maid Hershey-squirting down the leg of her pajamas when she looked out the door and seen an International Harvester sitting at her front door.

The sergeant just told us we'd have to sustain ourselves until supplies can be brought ashore. Lord, I'm scared. Ready to shit my pants. We're assembling on the beach ready to move inland to take up our defensive positions. Truman's administration said it had no stake in the defense of the South Korean Republic. You can't trust government.

I never thought I'd be sitting here like this, my weapon across my knees. But here we are, the bunch of us, scared, hungry, weighted down with rifles and ammunition. I'm going to rest now and give this letter to the sergeant to mail. Somehow I feel I'll never see your ugly look-alike faces again. Always remember me. Your best friend, Billy Ray Mudd.

Gus felt a lump in his throat as he laid Billy Ray's letter aside. He remembered the three of them as kids, good-humored, hunkered down on the porch. Gus squeezed his eyes closed and could see Billy Ray with his back against the screen door, telling stories until the moon rose unnoticed high into the sky. He opened his eyes and Billy Ray was still there. His hands clenched with the vision. At last he sat up, addressed an envelope to Gilbert and put the two letters inside.

Two months later Gus received the letter he'd been expecting from the Draft Department. He tried to take the news casually, every young man had to do it. Gus thought of Billy Ray, then shrugged off the thought. Not every man ends up in a hole in the ground. Yet the truth was, Gus worried his father would push himself too hard without his help at the mill. Norman was a good candidate for a break down.

"At least it won't be Korea," Katherine said, not looking at him, and Gus knew by the unsteady sound of her voice she was going to cry. She stared out from her opened kitchen window letting the gauzy curtains billow out and brush her shoulders. Gus wondered if she was thinking of Billy Ray.

"I'll be fine, Mama."

"How's your father going to make it without you at the mill?" she asked, still not turning around. Her voice was shaky.

Gus walked up behind his mother and hugged her. He knew she wasn't feeling well, although she seldom complained. The baby was due in a few weeks and she'd had a rough time with this pregnancy. He knew she needed him here, not somewhere overseas. Norman worked so many hours a day that he barely had time to tell her hello. Sara Jane did the best her small hands and mind could do to help around the house.

Katherine slouched forward, resting her awkward body against the counter top for support. Gus patted her shoulders and backed away. He heard her inhale and sigh as he pulled out a chair from the table and sat. Gus looked at his mother's back, her blond hair rolled into a bun high on her head, perspiration-damp ringlets falling from the loose ring. He gazed at her stooped shoulders, the old and frayed, yet clean and freshly ironed maternity dress, now pulling tightly across her swollen stomach. His gaze dropped to her fallen arches and fuzzy, worn-out house slippers. Gus rose from the chair and walked up behind her. She turned around and, with her dishwater-wet hands, cupped his face and smiled.

"You've grown up so fast. It seems like just yesterday you were running around the house with your Roy Rogers shirt and hat."

Gus grinned. "Where *is* that shirt?"

He made her smile. "In a box in the attic."

"You kept it?" he asked, surprised.

She smiled and he gently embraced her again. Through her smocked, rose print dress Gus could feel her large abdomen, spongy, warm. It made him feel awkward, yet so much a part of her. For a moment there were no words, but the silence was full. He hoped his arms would give her comfort, reassurance that he'd always be there if he could and that his absolute devotion to home and kin would never cease.

Katherine laid her hands lightly over his. "I love you so much."

"I know, Mama."

Nine days later, on a busy Monday morning, Gus Crawford Wheeler was sitting in the third to the last seat on the bus headed west toward Nashville where he would be sworn in. He stared through the opened window and saw old white farmhouses with children and dogs at play, women hanging clothes on the lines, men in the fields with their tractors. The world from his window looked warm and peaceful in the late morning sun.

The low engine rumble and voices on the bus were steady, but Gus wasn't listening to the sounds that surrounded him. He was listening to the voice from within. He thought of Gilbert as the farmscape rolled by outside his small rounded window and struggled to make sense of his twin brother leaving home. Gus felt homesick already and they weren't even twenty-five miles out of Knoxville. Gilbert had always wanted to reach beyond his realm, Gus thought, just outside of his own touch. Gus wrinkled his forehead wondering if Gilbert felt like a nonessential factor to Timber Hills because of his lack of interest in the family's business. Did he consider himself an expendable appendage? Had they - including him - unwittingly made Gilbert feel that way because he didn't choose to be a mill worker? Gus played over and over in his mind Gil's leaving, his unpretentious hug, the airy lift of his arm after he'd turned to walk away. Should I have tried to convince him to stay? I felt the same way Pa did. Should I have tried to stop Gil from going? Is that what he wanted? Did Gilbert need confirmation? A display of proof? Gus felt conscience-stricken. I'm closer to him than any other individual, made from the same fertilized egg. We developed together, side by side, in our mother's womb. I should have known what he needed.

A Willys truck passed them on the left, and Gus saw that it was Web Taylor. It broke his thought pattern because the last time he'd seen Web was on the day he and Norman discovered the Delvine timber had been cut. Gus's eyelids lowered and he leaned back his head against the cool seat. The rough drone of the bus's engine vibrated through his bones.

Gus had been asleep when the bus pulled into Nashville's station. It appeared he'd been the only one to fall asleep. The others were standing in the aisle, pushing forward, waiting for the bus to come to a complete stop and the door to open. Gus rubbed the sleep from his eyes and gathered his belongings. Another chapter in his life had begun.

The physical Gus had to take was grueling, the doctors twisting and x-raying his bad knee. Two days later Gus and his mates boarded a train to South Carolina for basic training. He was proud to be serving his country, yet felt an unwieldy guilt for leaving his father with the mill. He smoothed the fold lines from his drab-green fatigues and rubbed his palm over his "white sidewall" hair cut. He wondered if Gilbert had received notice. He folded his arms behind his head to make a pillow then closed his eyes. He felt an all-encompassing fatigue.

The dream-shattering reveille at 5:30 in the morning jolted Gus, but he was used to getting up early. Even the inhuman drill instructor's growling didn't bother him. He knew this wasn't going to be forever. Ten hours later, and after a bone-tiring work out, Gus called home.

"It's Gus callin' long distance," Thelma Jean said brightly, when Sara Jane answered the phone. "He's reversin' the charges. Run an' git your mama!"

"She's at the camp with Daddy, Thelma Jean. Put my brother through."

Sara Jane talked proudly with her brother, then asked, "Do you have a gun?"

"Yeah, your big Marine brother is carrying guns. Two of them. One is an M-1 rifle and the other is a .45 caliber pistol, and you don't know one from the other, do you?"

"Shucks no! I'm a girl," Sara Jane shouted, then, "Are you eatin' good?" she asked him. "Mama keeps wonderin' that."

"The food's a far cry from home cookin'. Tell Mom and Pa I'll call back later if I can. I love you."

"I love you too. Will you be careful?"

"I promise," Gus told her.

"I can't believe this," Gus cried, two weeks later. His hands gripped the sides of the examining table. He wanted to sit up but the doctor shook his head no.

"Be still, Gus, until we look at your knee."

"You've already put me through these tests, Doc. The wound has healed," Gus said, remembering how they had captured Lenny Squaw and Hank Kendall. "I thought I'd passed my physical."

"It took some time to get all your medical reports completed," the doctor said.

Gus scanned the sterile-looking room with no windows. The blinding bright lights over his head made him squint. "It doesn't even bother me except when it rains," Gus told them. "My knee's fine. I don't belong in this base infirmary. Don't you have anything better to do?" Gus asked the doctor.

It didn't take long for a decision to be made. On the following Monday Gus sat on the edge of his bed staring at his medical discharge papers. He felt like a dimwit. A Negro man in uniform came in, told him he was sorry about the tough luck, and that he was assigned to take him to the Greyhound bus station. "Here." He held out his hand. "It's a homebound ticket."

Gus nodded but didn't say anything. He was angry and embarrassed that he'd be returning home so quickly.

"You packed?" the colored man asked.

"Yeah, I'm ready," Gus answered.

"Praise the Lord! Oh, my heavens, honey, praise the Lord," Gus heard Lilly Mae Beasly cry as he stepped off the bus and walked toward the telephone box. "Law, darlin', when we heard you was comin' home we thought you was shot. Our hearts are still broken over the Mudd boy being killed. Oh, my heavens, praise the Lord!"

"Mornin', Miss Beasly," Gus greeted. "I'm still in one piece."

"Praise the Lord!" Lilly Mae howled one more time. Gus grinned wide, happy to be home, but embarrassed to face folks with the truth of what had brought him back. He wasn't even whole enough to serve his country. He moved toward the telephone box.

"Come on in here and use my phone," Buster Foch said, peering from the doorway of the meat market.

Gus smiled. The whole town had stepped out to welcome him back. Gus walked across the store's dark, hardwood floor, lifted the phone's receiver, pushed the button and cranked the handle. When the operator came onto the line, Gus asked her to ring his home.

"I've been waiting all day for you to call. Are you okay?" Katherine asked.

"I'm fine, Mama," then Gus added, "Praise the Lord."

"I'll tell your father to come pick you up."

"No, don't do that. I want to walk home."

"You can't walk! Your leg's all shot up!"

"You know that wound healed long ago. They've made this into something it isn't. I want to walk home. I'll see you in about an hour . . . or two."

The welcome sun struck down with a fragrant, penetrating sweetness. Gus lifted his face to let the warmth of it wash over him. It felt good to do nothing, to be alive, to be home, yet he couldn't forget Billy Ray coming home in a box. Gus stopped and looked up at the tree tops. Bird song came from every direction. "Thank you, Jesus," he praised. "Thank you for all my blessings," he said, and welcomed the friendly breeze moving over his body. Gus rubbed his hand over the rough bark, then moved forward and hugged the tree. "I don't care if the whole world is watching," he yelled. "Hello tree, hello barns, hello bales of hay lying over there in your fresh-mown field." He rested his weight against the tree. "Hello, home."

For the life of him, he couldn't understand why he started to cry. He wailed like a baby, but felt no rightful sadness inside. Gus dried his tears with his shirt collar and inhaled as deeply as he could. The honeysuckle scent was almost melodic, gently veiling the countryside with harmony. Yes, he was home.

As he walked, Gus looked out over the sloping fields where tobacco and corn were coming up in perfect rows, and then to the green hills, leading to hazy blue ranges overlapping each another. A warm wave of comfort enveloped him. The warmth spread in his chest and through his body. Love. That's what it was. The greatest emotion in the whole world.

Gus stopped at the cemetery gate, peered in the direction of Garrett's grave. Genuine sadness surfaced now because his infant brother had died before he had a chance to discover this wonderful life. Gus thought about the many times he looked into Garrett's sad little eyes, slightly slanted up, and thought he saw something angelic. When he mentioned this to his mother, she had told him it was his love for Garrett. But Gus knew there was something special there. Something he's giving to the other angels in heaven. "Lord, I didn't want Garrett to die," Gus said out loud. "You never gave him a chance to smell the sunshine or

the rain or new-mown grass. He will never graduate, never marry, never love."
Gus sadly realized that for some, time just doesn't permit for all life's blessings.

Gus jumped when he heard a voice call his name, then saw Eula Mae lope
up to him.

"I heard you were coming home! It's swell to see you." She leaned forward
and touched his knee lightly. "Sakes alive. Does it hurt?" Eula asked.

Gus was amazed at how grown-up Eula looked and realized she was actually very pretty with her noticeable green eyes and long auburn hair falling in
waves over one shoulder. He smiled, opened his mouth slightly, but the cat had
got his tongue. He looked at her neat white blouse, full red skirt with big dots
on it, penny loafers, bobby socks. This wasn't the Eula Mae Pearson that he remembered, the girl everyone made fun of because of her looseness.

"You farin' okay?" Eula asked and to Gus it sounded like genuine concern.
He held out his bad leg. "Except for this."

She tilted her head to one side and made a sad face. "I got a ribbon at the fair
for my rhubarb pie." Her eyes twinkled again.

"I didn't know you could cook," Gus said stupidly, regretting it.

"I made two. There's some left." Eula smiled shyly. "I can save you a piece."
She said it like a question.

"Yes, ma'am," Gus said, his gaze once again reviewing her shapely form.
"You're lookin' mighty pretty, Eula Mae." He saw her blush . . . Eula blushing?

"Why thank you, Gus." She dropped her gaze and twisted a lock of hair.

Now Gus knew that she was embarrassed, and sheerly on instinct, he said,
"See you later if you see fit." It came out half question, half statement.

Eula fingered the ivory snap-beads she wore around her neck and quietly
said, "Okay," then twirled and moseyed on her way. Gus watched the bottom of
her skirt move back and forth with the sway of her hips. Just before he moved
on, Eula looked back and waved over her shoulder. "I'd take kindly to seein' you
again."

It took awhile to get Eula from his mind. Gus kept seeing the flippant, pig-
tailed, girl Eula Mae Pearson used to be. A little-girl-lost, raised by an uncaring
uncle, seeking approval in the only way she knew. He remembered her lifting her
skirt above her knees, luring the boys to come near, and when they did she would
lean forward and let them kiss her, but as far as he knew, that was all, even though
Billy Ray said he got to touch her titties once because he milked her cow for her.
She had been the butt of every boys joke with her easy virtue, and no better than
she should be, just a young girl trying to find a warm place in her lonely world.
Yes, he'd see Eula again, he decided, as he carried on his task of getting home.

Before he knew it, Gus had reached the shade-dappled lane that would take
him to the front door of his home. He stopped, gazed toward the mill, and deeply inhaled the sweet smell and taste of the moment.

PART FOUR

• CHAPTER 14 •

Gilbert liked to walk the length of the pier near his apartment. Locals called it The Pike. Sailors in uniform were everywhere, and young girls with makeup and sprayed-stiff hair flocked around them like gulls over fish. A fine, soothing calm usually washed over him when he walked along the pier, but tonight he was thinking of stolen timber and a villain by the name of Delvine. A girl with maple-sugar colored hair bounced past him. She smiled as she passed and Gilbert turned around to get a look at her backside, but even a firmly rounded buttock couldn't alter his mind's focus. She turned her head over her shoulder and smiled again.

Gilbert looked up at all the flashing lights, a colossal roller coaster, then at a sea-diving capsule on display. Music blasted out of the small cafes and beer stands. He listened to the sound of the ocean's salty waves rushing to shore and slapping the sand. "Long Beach, California. Most folks back home don't even know a place like this exists," he thought aloud as two sailors with a young girl in the middle brushed past him.

The loud beat of Negro rhythm and blues blasted from an opened doorway. He could see the dark silhouettes of young men and women swaying with the music. Several doors up he heard Bill Haley and the Comets new song, *Rock Around the Clock.* He stopped in the doorway and rocked back and forth on his heels, swivelled his hips slightly and twitched his shoulders to the beat.

Gilbert liked the bubbling, spirited part of being in California. There was no slow pace. Everyone was on a fast track. He relished the tempo, the unlimited adventure. The hills of Tennessee paled to the vivacity here, yet a voice inside him said, *go home*.

With his hands buried in his pockets, Gilbert walked to the side of the pier and watched white waves churn succumbly over the sand. Easing himself over a concrete barrier, he jumped over. His shoes settled into the sand. He squatted down, scooped up a cool handful and watched it sift through his fingers. Gilbert turned his face toward the shoreline and let the salty breeze brush back his hair. He loved the ocean, big city ways, the pull of innovation. It was a world he had just begun to explore. Gilbert rose from his crouched position and walked toward the heaving, rumbling waves. Just before he reached the wet sand, he took off his shoes and socks and pitched them to the side. A small wave swished over his bare feet and he curled his toes into the coolness of the ocean's water. Gilbert stepped forward, stopped, rolled his trousers up to his knees, then slowly moved into the dark, salty water. The waves felt powerful and brisk as he shivered and pushed onward. The swell and rocking of the ocean made him sway from side to side and Gilbert felt like a kid with a new toy, splashing with his hands and arms. Before he knew it, he was to his waist in sea water. The moon glimmered on the whitecaps, illuminating the swells like silver treasure. His legs moved against the water's robust muscle, as icy fingers curled around his knees, thighs, chest, soaking his clothes and making him draw a sharp breath. He had never realized the power of the ocean.

When he got home, Gilbert peeled off his wet clothes and took a long hot shower. Afterward, with the damp towel tied round his waist, he sank onto the sofa and reread his brother's letter. Ambiguousness consumed him. He had to make some serious choices. Should he stay here, *be selfish*, as Gus had told him, or go home and assume the life of a southern mill worker? He couldn't deny that self-centeredness wasn't a part of his nature. *Don't let your temptable mind run down paths that aren't safe to travel,* he recalled Gus saying. He thought of his mother and imagined her as Gus had described, swollen ankles, stooped shoulders. He could see Gus sweating and working hard enough for the both of them, and knew his twin felt no malice for him. He saw his father, the strong fortitude, his grit. Gilbert clutched at his chest and could feel his father's anguish over losing the Delvine timber. It was a new, peculiar feeling.

Gilbert clenched his jaw and gritted his teeth together. He rolled back his head and squeezed shut his eyes hoping his eyelids would hide the pictured misery; the struggle for survival on a farm in a shaded hollow in Tennessee. Gilbert tried to shrink from the disquieting thought but his conscious awareness thrashed with anger. He let out a grumbling sigh and rubbed his aching head. "I can't stay here while my family is suffering!"

Gilbert opened his eyes and sat in the dim light, his eyes fixed on the brown-carpeted floor. He looked at the letters then sat hunched over them as his watery-blue eyes focused on the words. He skimmed the part about the stolen Delvine timberland repeatedly. Lumbering was his family's livelihood, Timber Hills their existence.

Gilbert's breath deepened as old feelings battled with new ones. Should he stay in California where he was happy, or go back home and help his family weather this setback? He tossed down the letter, opened the cigar box and counted his money. "Delvine," he said, "you can't hide. You'd better be watching your back!" Gilbert slammed the box shut and pulled out his suitcase from under the bed.

• CHAPTER 15 •

With his hillborn spirit and stamina, Gus heaved a large log onto the carriage and guided it through the various saws. Sweat gushed down his face and burned his eyes. "Slow down, son," Norman said. "Think safety," he added then hurried on with his own toil alongside Gus.

"There aren't enough hours in a day," Gus shouted above the noisy mill sounds. It had been a year to the day that Gilbert had walked from the kitchen of their humble home to the Greyhound bus depot, and if Gus felt indignance toward the fact, he didn't take time to think about it. Time was running out on the present contract, the men were working double shifts and the crew's nerves and muscles were being stretched like rubber bands. "One, two, heave!" the men shouted as they lifted the cumbrous logs. "One, two, heave!"

In the hot summer sun Katherine leaned over the laundry basket, lifted the last work shirt, then stretched herself to pin it onto the line to dry. "Ooh," she muttered, rubbing her abdomen. She lifted the large straw basket and started up the porch steps. Before she reached the top, she doubled over and dropped the clothes basket.

"Norman," she yelled, hoping someone would hear her over the grinding saws. "Norman, help me," she hollered.

Katherine struggled to her feet, picked up the basket and continued up the steps. Letting out a deep breath, she grasped the screen door's knob and pulled it open. Inside, she gripped the edge of the table.

"Katy," Norman blurted out, zipping into the kitchen. "Cletus said he thought he saw you fall. Are you all right?"

"Help me, Norman," Katherine groaned weakly. "The baby's comin'."

"You've got to be fooling! Where's Sara Jane?" Norman questioned.

Katherine grimaced and reached for the black kettle. "She's taking her piano lessons."

"I'll get Dr. West!" Norman said as he rushed toward the door.

"There's no time, Norm. Help me into the bedroom and put some water on to boil."

"Oh, Katy, don't do this!" His eyes focused on the telephone, but Katherine moaned and Norman helped her to the bed. "Should I call. . . . ?"

"It wouldn't do any good as fast as the contractions are coming," she said, raising her skirt and slipping out of her panties. "They'd never make it here on time." Her breath was coming in heavy gasps as Norman smoothed the sheet over her body.

Katherine pushed the cover from her. "You've got to help me now, Norman."

"But I . . . " His nervous-strained words came out whiny. "My God, Katy, the baby's comin' out!" Norman backed away and took huge noisy breaths, in, out, in, out, then knowing what he had to do, reluctantly moved to the bedside and helped his wife deliver their fifth child.

A few moments later, Sara Jane hopped up the porch steps and into the house.

"We're in here, Sara Jane."

"Why are you in bed, Mama?" she asked, tripping into her mother's bedroom where Katherine was lying in bed with a blanket-wrapped bundle in her arms.

"What's that?" she asked in a squeaky, frightened voice. "Is that our new baby?"

"A little boy. Come look," Katherine said, uncovering the infant's face.

Sara Jane walked cautiously to her mother's bedside and peeked at her new baby brother. "Can I play with him?"

"Not for a few months," Katherine said, smiling.

Sara Jane pouted, then asked, "Did that baby come with a name?"

Katherine smiled and nodded. "Jon Wesley."

Sara Jane craned her neck toward the slumbering child. "He's kind of ugly."

The Tourist Bureau told Gilbert there was a family with two young children heading to Atlanta, and if he was interested, it would cost him $10.50 for the ride. They were leaving at nine that morning.

"Tell them I'll accept," Gilbert said, not believing his luck. He showered quickly, then hurriedly dropped the rest of his clothing into his suitcase.

Gilbert settled into the back seat of a 1948 Mercury with bald tires. Twenty minutes into the trip the driver pulled to the shoulder of the roadway, stopped, and separated the two arguing children. Gilbert resettled himself in the middle of the backseat between the four and a five-year-old boy and girl. He faked a smile, leaned back his head and silently prayed he could sleep the whole trip. In Flagstaff, Arizona they replaced a fan belt and in Albuquerque, changed a flat tire.

At the bus station in uptown Atlanta, Gilbert lied and told the family he enjoyed the ride, then gave the children each a nickel. He took a deep breath, threw his jacket over his shoulder, walked across the street and bought a newspaper. "Delvine, if you're here, I'll find you," he said aloud. At Walgreens he ordered a corn dog and a Dr. Pepper for twenty-nine cents plus tax. When he'd finished eating, he opened the door to a phone booth and looked in the book for the name Delvine. None was listed so he turned to the yellow pages and looked under real estate. "Bingo," he said when he saw Arnold Delvine's quarter-page ad. "606 E. Oak Street, #205."

Towering oak trees shaded the square brick building. Gilbert opened the heavy double doors and walked tensely down the corridor to the stairway. Nervously gripping the railing, he climbed the stairs.

The stairwell smelled of cigarette smoke and various body odors. He topped the stairs, found room #205 and opened the door. The room was bare except for a waste can sitting in the corner near the window and a straight-backed chair. Gilbert looked around, out the window, into the tiny washroom. The room was empty; void of any sign of human occupancy. "Shit!" Gilbert cursed, charging out and nearly running over an old colored man with a push broom in his hand.

The Negro spoke. "Hep ya wit somthin'?" His eyes were like chunks of coal, but sparkled like shiny wet rocks in the sun.

Gilbert noted the man's long, lined face, placed his suitcase between his legs and pulled a piece of paper from his front pocket. "Maybe you can," he said. "I'm looking for a Mr. Arnold H. Delvine."

"Delvine long gone," the Negro offered. "Left nigh a year 'go."

Gilbert asked for the address of Mr. Delvine. The Negro shook his head. Gilbert sighed then asked the Negro if he knew why Delvine left. The Negro shook his head. Hope and patience were running short. Gilbert asked if Delvine still sold land. The colored janitor wasn't talking, but it was the way he shook his head and avoided eye contact that gave Gilbert the impression that the man knew more than he was saying. Gilbert felt himself getting angry. Anger burned his gut. "Look!" Gilbert said. "I didn't come two-thousand miles to find nothing! You know more than you're saying. Now I'll ask you again. Where's Delvine?"

The Negro started to back out. "I don' know nothin'," he said, holding his hands out.

Gilbert closed his hands into fists. "You do know something!"

"Please, Mister. I promised Arnie I wouldn't say nothin'."

Gilbert charged forward, anger building. He grabbed the front of the Negro's brown work shirt. "If you don't tell me where *Arnie* is I'm going to take that broom of yours and make a scarecrow out of you." Gilbert felt his face flushing as he twisted the handful of shirt fabric, nearly lifting the thin colored man off his feet. "Where is he?" Gilbert seethed. He clamped his jaw shut and spoke through his teeth. "Where?" He shook the Negro so hard the man's hat flew off backward.

"Arnie wouldn't like me tellin' on him. Please, mister, just go, now," the man pleaded.

"And my folks didn't like having fifty-some acres of prime woodland stolen from them either!" Gilbert yelled. He let go of the Negro's shirt and kicked the hat, and in one swift movement, picked up the straight-backed chair and threw it against the wall. "They're close to losing everything they've got! That man not only stole from *my* family, but from another mill owner near us. This Delvine character is bad news, can't you see that? I don't see that same evil in you. I can't believe you would condone his deceptive practices."

"Oh sir, he be killin' me if I tell." The man was moaning, sweating nervous perspiration and shaking his head.

Gilbert again gripped the man's shirt. "WHERE IS HE?" he asked between his teeth.

"Oh, please sir, don' make me tell."

Gilbert grimaced and put his face so close to the Negro that he could smell the sweat coming from the man's pores. "God help your soul if I get violent with you."

"Sir, I knowed he done wrong. I went home ever night knowin' he done wrong. I knowed that boy since he was scootin' 'round in diapers. Lordy, I knowed he done wrong."

Gilbert had lost all patience. "I'm going to ask one more time, then so help me God, I'm throwing you over that ledge." Gilbert shoved the Negro nearer to the window. "There's nothing but hard ground below."

Their eyes met in a long unsmiling look, and then the Negro whispered, "He's moved his business to Chattanooga. Please don't tell him I tolt ya."

Gilbert released the man's shirt. "Where in Chattanooga?"

The janitor reached into his hip pocket. "It's right here in my billfold," the Negro said, then offered unnecessarily, "He gave it to me so as I could send him some paperwork."

"Thank you," Gilbert said with calm politeness, taking a pen from his plastic pocket liner and writing the address on the back of a piece of paper.

The 140-mile bus ride to Chattanooga was miserable for Gilbert. Packed full of senior citizens on a field trip, Gilbert was cocooned in the back bench seat between two weighty women who kept looking at him and smiling. They ate Goo Goo Clusters, potato chips and homemade sandwiches all the way to Chattanooga. He leaned back his head and tried to rest, but his thoughts kept him awake and the more he thought of Delvine, the angrier he became. The women's hot bodies pressed up against him and made him feel like a wiener in a bun. He cursed under his breath.

At the depot in Chattanooga, Gilbert found a telephone and called home. Gus answered.

"I wanted to let you know where I am," Gil said, "and that I'm planning on confronting Delvine."

"Are you sure you want to do this, Gil? It could get dangerous. Ira tracked him down in Atlanta and Delvine threatened him," Gus said. "Delvine told him the contract was written in a legal manner and if Ira approached him again he'd kill him."

"The man's no longer in Atlanta," Gil said. "He's set up business in Chattanooga. That's where I am now. He cheated us, Gus. Your letter said it all and your words hang on my mind. I know how much Pa was depending on that Delvine property."

"Yeah, I know. Pa always said he was saving the best till last so we could all sit back and appreciate it. He held off cutting that stand because he said it was the best he ever had. Delvine has devastated the folks, Gil. There's agony in Pa's eyes, ache in Mom's heart."

"My leaving didn't help."

"You're darn tootin'." Gus cleared his throat. "When did you leave California?"

"I've lost track of time."

"Are you going back? Coming home?"

"I don't know yet, Gus. I'll know more after I find Delvine."

"Why are you doing this?"

"It's something I have to do. For the folks. For all of us," Gilbert said.

"I'm glad you're back."

"I'm not home, Gus. I'm only in Chattanooga. I still have a lot of thinking to do."

"Come home."

"I don't know if I can."

"The door was never locked."

"It's not that. I know nothing about milling. About the lumber business."

"We want you home. You can do something else. Go back to Fochs if you want. Come home, Gil."

Gilbert's shoulders slumped and he felt tears stinging his eyes. He blinked quickly to chase them away. "Maybe. But first, I have business here. This bastard hurt us, Gus. He's going to pay."

"What's your plan?"

"I haven't the slightest idea. I'll call you soon."

"Wait! Where are you?"

Gilbert glanced around, his eyes scanning the area. A block up the street he eyed a hotel. He craned his neck to read the name. "Westminster Hotel," he said. "I'll talk to you soon."

"Hey, Gil."

"What?"

"Love you."

"Me too, Gus."

"Wait!" Gus yelled.

"What now?"

"We've got a little brother."

"What's he look like?" Gilbert asked.

"He's a cute little bugger," Gus answered.

Gilbert grinned and replaced the receiver. He rubbed the last of the dampness from his eyes and walked toward the hotel.

The next morning Gilbert got up, shaved, put on a clean shirt and counted his money. On his bedside table was a half-drunk bottle of Coca-Cola. Gilbert tore the wrapping from a Moon Pie the lady on the bus had given him and washed a few bites down with the warm Coke. He tossed the remainder in the waste basket, walked to the window, pushed it open and lifted his face to breathe the fresh, river-water air. He turned, picked up his billfold, put it into his back pocket and walked out the door.

The bright sunshine made his eyes water. He blinked the moisture away. At the curb, he looked both ways then walked toward the farm co-op. The wooden floor planks creaked as Gilbert looked around the store. Red-faced farmers in overalls were buying feed and farm equipment. It didn't take long for Gilbert to make up his mind. He walked up to the man behind the counter and said, "I want to buy the gasoline-operated power chain saw you have in the window." Gilbert saw a display of sunglasses on the counter. "And these," he said, taking a pair and trying them on for comfort.

On his way out of the store Gilbert spotted a shiny red soap box with a small engine on the back. He stopped short. Memories flashed before him as he stared at the small go-cart sitting behind three bales of hay. It wasn't a regular thrown-together farm-kid scooter, the kind boys create with endless hours of imagination and whatever junk was accessible. No, this one was special. This soap box was just like the one Gus had wanted from Sears and Roebuck. Gilbert reached into his back pocket, tugged out his billfold and counted 23 one-dollar bills.

"I'll take this," Gilbert said, gesturing toward the motorized car he'd rolled beside him.

"She's a beauty," the clerk said, then, "It'll cost you seventeen dollars and fifty cents."

People raised their eyebrows as they watched Gilbert push the go-cart with the chainsaw on the seat down the hallway toward his room. He splashed cold water on his face and after glancing once again at the address on the paper in his front pocket, headed down the stairs and out the door.

Gilbert hitched a ride as far as the public square and was told he was within three blocks of Delvine's office. He walked past an ice house, a Baptist Church, the library and three little colored children playing ball. It wasn't hard to find Arnold Delvine. His name wasn't on the office door, but a white Cadillac with gold lettering on the car's door read, A.H. DELVINE'S PRIME PROPERTY and under that was a telephone number. Gilbert stopped briefly in front of the building, inhaled, walked up the steps and into the brightly-lit building. A painted black panther in a jungle setting stretched across the entire length of one side of the corridor. Gilbert glanced fleetingly at the mural.

There were only four offices in the small building. One was empty, one occupied by military personnel, the third was a newspaper office and the fourth had BY APPOINTMENT ONLY and DO NOT DISTURB signs on the door. "That's it," Gilbert said, his heart racing. "The bastard is sitting at a fancy desk behind this door." With one hand he clutched the yellow power saw he held tightly at his side. With his free hand Gilbert reached out and turned the brass door knob.

"What the. . . ."

"You Delvine?" Gilbert briefly studied the man's thick gray hair parted precisely in the center, the wide, heavy jowled face, a strong nose.

"Are you crazy or something? Can't you read?" Delvine glanced nervously toward the opened door. "I don't see clients before noon."

Not taking his eyes from Delvine, Gilbert reached back and closed the door behind him. He stood facing the desk and noted the A. H. Delvine nameplate. "A. H. Delvine," Gilbert read aloud. "Ass Hole Delvine," he said. "Is that what the A and H stands for? Ass Hole? 'Cause that's what you are, you know."

Delvine stiffened and sprang to his feet nearly knocking his chair over backwards. His dark eyes narrowed. "What the devil do you want with me?"

Gilbert suppressed a smile, then lifted the chainsaw and pulled the starter rope. The temperamental weapon sputtered and died. Gilbert's eyes quickly scanned the side of the saw. He noticed the choke, pulled it out, and pulled the starter cord again. This time it stayed running.

Delvine backed up. "What are you going to do?" his voice boomed out above the thunderous power saw. "Who are you?" He reached for the telephone, plucked the receiver off its cradle and held it limply in his right hand.

"My name is Wheeler. Gilbert Wheeler. You might recognize the name. You sold my father some timber several years ago. Sold the very same stand of timber to an Ira Irving. Hang up the phone."

Delvine shrugged. "Is that what this is all about? Those contracts were entirely legitimate." He placed the telephone receiver back into its place, pulled his chair back to the desk but didn't sit. "It was the buyer who failed to read, or maybe he couldn't read, but in any case, that's certainly not my problem."

Gilbert felt revulsion rise. "That's where you're wrong. It *is* your problem." The chainsaw sputtered and died but Gilbert held it as if it was still running. "You're a crooked, no-good-ass-hole-thief!" Gilbert yelled, his voice still at a level above the noise the now-still saw had made. "And I'm here to collect what is due my kin," he said. He waved the power saw in front of him. "Did you know this thing can cut down a tree in less than ten minutes?" Gilbert noted lines of strain on the man's face.

"Like hell," Delvine snorted, a smile curling half of his mouth. "Care for a cigar?" Delvine offered, reaching toward a wooden cigar box on his desk.

Gilbert reached down and pulled the rope. Delvine jerked his hand from the box. The saw's piercing sound permeated the room.

"Get out of here," Delvine yelled. "I won't allow some dinglefuss to come charging in here demanding . . . you ain't getting a thing from me."

Gilbert stepped forward and laid the chain lightly on the front edge of the desk. The sharp blade cut through the fine walnut wood. Gilbert lifted the saw, backing the blade out of the desk. "I want the money you stole from my folks, Ass Hole Delvine. That's why I'm here." Gilbert's attention was drawn to a small metal safe in the corner behind Delvine's desk. He gestured toward the box. "Open that up," he ordered.

"Over my dead body," Delvine said, a grin on his face.

"I can't hear you," Gilbert yelled above the racket of the saw.

Delvine leaned his head and upper body forward over his desk. "You ain't getting nothin' from me," he said pointing his index finger close to Gilbert's face. "Get out of here, now!"

Gilbert lifted the saw, leaned over and cut the two front legs off the desk. The desk slumped forward with a thud. Everything that was on the desktop slid to the floor. "Just like the trees on my Pa's stolen land," Gilbert said. "Wasn't nothin' left but stumps and lap." Gilbert almost laughed out loud at the look of horror on Delvine's face, his mouth gaping like in a soundless scream. "Where's your grin?" Gilbert asked as he bent over and picked the cigar box off the floor. "I think I will, thank you," he said, lifting the lid and helping himself. "Open the safe."

Delvine didn't move. Gilbert put the cigar into his pocket and stepped around the butchered desk. He slung the saw through the air, the blade coming so close to Delvine's forehead that his hair ruffled. Delvine ducked but still didn't move toward the safe. Gilbert placed the saw against one of Delvine's fine paintings on the wall. Within seconds, the picture was in two pieces, one on top of the other, on the floor. "That was worth two-hundred dollars," Delvine moaned.

"How much is this one worth," Gilbert asked, placing the chain against the second painting.

"No! Please, don't touch that one!" Delvine screamed.

"This one?" Gilbert asked as he drew the saw's blade vertically through the painting.

Delvine crumpled to his knees and scooted toward the door. Gilbert quickly swung the saw toward him. Delvine covered his head with his arms and hands.

"Open the safe," Gilbert said again. "My folks are due a refund." The blade of the saw was within inches of Delvine's thick mop of white hair.

"Okay," Delvine said, throwing his hands out in an I-give-up manner. "You win." Still on hands and knees, he inched toward the safe. His nervous hands fumbled and shook. After several tries, Delvine opened the door to the safe. "Take it," he said, pointing. "Just take it and get the hell out of here." He fell back onto his buttock and stretched his fat, short legs out in front of him. "Take it and go," he said, leaning his back against the wall.

Gilbert reached into the safe and pulled out four stacks of one-hundred dollar bills. "The Wheelers are honest people. Pa trusted you. I'll figure what you owe us, and what it'll take to settle with Irving, then send you the change. I'm a man of my word." Before Gilbert left the room, he placed the blade of the saw slightly above a framed 5 X 7 photograph. The old brown-toned photo was of a woman with a long dress, sitting stiffly in a high-backed chair. "Your mother?" Gilbert asked. He looked at Delvine slumped on the floor, his knees pulled up, face wincing. Gilbert's fingers flipped the kill switch on the power saw and he walked out.

When he quietly closed the door behind him, Gilbert saw several people poking their heads around their doorways. He took the dark sunglasses from his shirt pocket, put them on, smoothed back his hair with his hand and smiled at the faces staring at him. One man asked if A.H. was still alive. "I didn't touch him," Gilbert said in a steady voice, his ear close to the door listening and wondering if Delvine was making an attempt to come after him. Satisfied that he'd won this battle, Gilbert squared his shoulders, gave a quick look over his shoulder, stood tall, and trekked down the corridor toward the door. Before he'd left the building he thought he heard someone say, "Delvine must-a cheated that young man."

• CHAPTER 16 •

Gus walked to the pump to fill the men's water pail when he heard the phone ring then heard his mother's loud words.

"Norman!" she yelled. "Gus! He's comin' home! Gilbert's comin' home!"

Gus dropped the bucket and ran inside. "Is it true?" he asked.

Katherine's blue eyes were like shining crystals. "Let's go tell your father."

Gus hurried alongside his mother toward the mill. "He's comin' home," she hollered and Gus had to laugh at the little skip-hop she did when she said it.

Norman didn't look up, just kept prodding logs along the carriage and through the various saws. "About time," he grumbled, then glanced up at Gus. He lowered his glasses to peer over them. "What you grinning 'bout, boy? Your brother doesn't belong here. He doesn't know the first thing about blood loyalty!"

Gus parted his lips to speak then changed his mind. He threw out his arms in resignation.

Norman readjusted his glasses and continued his work. "The boy's roots got tangled up and fell off at birth. Been lettin' the wind blow him around like dandelion fluff."

"It's not fair to judge him that way, Pa," Gus said, causing Norman to jerk his head up and face his son. "He just don't have the same interests we do. That don't make him disloyal," Gus added.

Norman shook his head and continued to work.

Katherine bowed her head as she listened to the fussing, then looked up and said, "Gilbert is faithful to his kinfolk. It's in his heart." The saws were loud and no one was listening. She slowly turned to walk back to the house. "I know my boy," she said. Gus watched her walk to the chicken yard, open the gate and walk over to the chopping block. She glanced toward the mill, shook her head, then picked up the ax. The chickens scrambled, but Katherine was skilled at her farmwife duties. Gus knew that chicken and dumplings would soon be simmering in a large black kettle on the stove. It was Gilbert's favorite.

As the day came to an end, the Wheelers sat together at the supper table picking at their food and moving it about on their plates. "How far is Chattanooga?" Sara Jane asked.

"It's a good spell," Katherine answered.

"When did he say he was coming?" Gus asked, and Katherine told him for the third time that Gilbert would be here sometime tonight.

"Can I have a smidgen of honey for my biscuit?" Sara Jane asked, and Katherine passed the honey jar without looking at her daughter.

"He ain't coming," Norman muttered.

"He will, lessen he's sick," Sara Jane said, wiping honey off her chin.

"She's right," Gus said. "If Gil said it, it's so."

Sara Jane slammed down her fork. "For Pete's sake, Daddy. Why you lettin' on like you're mad about it?" she asked. "Don't you love Gil? Don't you want him home? Wasn't it 'cause he left that you got mad in the first place?" She shook her head. "Now you're mad 'cause he's comin' home! I plumb don't understand grownups."

Gus saw Norman's face muscles tensing and watched Katherine put her hand over her mouth. Sara Jane had a tendency to not listen to what was being said around her. Gus was surprised she'd been paying attention to this conversation. He was glad she had been.

Katherine remained motionless for a few moments, then with a large breath and a swift motion, was on her feet, her back to the family. Gus got up, pulled back the curtain and peeked outside. He saw nothing but darkness. When he turned, he saw that Katherine had a smile on her face. He walked up behind her and wrapped his arms around her narrow shoulders. She leaned back her head, resting it briefly on his chest.

Everyone jumped when Norman shoved his plate across the table. He snatched off his glasses and shoved them into his pocket. "The boy's useless to us. He's a shame and a scandal. What has he ever done that's been worthwhile?"

Gus pressed his lips together in anger and looked at Norman. His father's eyes were narrowed and he had a look of contempt on his face. Gus felt Norman's fury and it frightened him. Nervously he jangled change in his pocket and noticed his palms were sweaty. This would be a bad time for Gil to show up, Gus thought. Anger for his father swelled in his throat and chest. He's low-rating the person I love most in the whole world, Gus thought, and not being able to listen to another dissenting word, he opened the door and stomped outside.

Gus noticed the door to the root cellar was ajar and walked over to close it, but instead, raised it open and walked down the darkened steps. He flipped a switch and the cool musty-smelling room lightened dimly. Potatoes, turnips and cabbage lined the shelves. A wooden barrelful of dried apples scented the small room. He glanced around at the visibility of honest, hard work. Crocks of kraut, jars of pickled beans, a family's labor in the name of love, a family's belief and pride in a hard day's work.

He lifted a jar of pickled green tomatoes from the shelf and held it in his hands. To the touch, the jar was cool, but Gus could sense warmth, love, kinship inside the jar. Gus looked up and away, his gaze as far as possible from the jar he clutched in his hands, yet the sensation, the perception was still there, within his heart. He wrangled with his feelings of confusion. The jar was just a piece of molded glass, but it symbolized who they were, the same as the Wheeler name, and Timber Hills and this crazy little hollow in East Tennessee. His unsettled thoughts compounded and he knew that part of what his father said about Gil's leaving was right. With a quick gesture he returned the jar to the shelf, flicked off the light and walked up the narrow, darkened stairway.

Gus sat on the porch step in the cool misty air, thinking, wondering what he'd say to his father if he asked for an honest opinion. When the briskness of the night became uncomfortable and he rose to walk into the warm house, Gus had to admit to himself that he truly didn't know whose side he would lean toward.

Gus sighed and noticed through the windows that all the lights were off except for the low-watt bulb on the stove. Relieved that everyone was in bed, he slipped quietly into the house and closed the door behind him. On the stove top was a plate wrapped in tinfoil and Gus knew it was left there for Gil. Next to the plate was a sweet-potato pie, Gil's favorite. In front of the fireplace, embers still alive and warm, he sat alone and wide awake. In uneasy silence Gus lowered his head and cried.

It was a flash of light on the mop board that caught Gus's attention. He jerked his head up and rose from the chair. At the window he drew back the curtain and peeked out. A dark-colored 1952 Ford was rolling slowly down the lane toward the house. Gus turned the doorknob, opened the door and stepped out onto the porch. He stood there in the shadows, craning his neck, squinching his eyes trying to see who was there. Was it Gil? Gus tucked in his shirt, moved forward and took one step down, stopped, stepped down on the second step and focused his eyes on the passenger in the car. "Gil?" he said aloud, crossing his arms in front of him. His enthusiasm made him smile. He inched closer to the car. The driver's face was turned toward Gus. He lifted his hand from the steering wheel and gave a small wave. Gus nodded.

A man got out on the passenger side of the car. The dark figure moved from the car's front door to the back. It took several moments for Gus to adjust his eyes to the darkness. The rear door was opened and Gus saw the figure reach into the car. When the man pulled out a suitcase, Gus knew it was Gilbert.

Through the shadows of the yard, Gus scurried toward his brother then stopped within inches of Gilbert. They stood, staring at each other for several long seconds, then in unison, reached out and embraced each other.

"Boy, oh boy, have I ever missed you," Gus said, beating Gilbert on the back with a thud, thud, thud.

"I doubt that Pa missed me. Is he still mad?" Gilbert backed slightly away from Gus.

"Yeah, I reckon so," Gus admitted, then fingered Gilbert's half-inch-long beard.

Gilbert reached up, removed his cap and ran his fingers through his untrimmed hair. "I guess I need to clean up some," he said, then, "You sore at me?"

Gus smiled, looked down at the space between them, then back up into Gilbert's tired-looking face. "I won't be passin' no judgment," he said, then knew that would have been his answer had Norman asked him. He flicked a hand dismissively and added, "It ain't for me to judge."

They hugged each other again, this time refusing to let go of the other's grasp, and when they finally let their arms relax, Gilbert turned back to the driver of the Ford and thanked him for the ride.

"You stayin'?"

Gilbert frowned in thought. "Yeah, I think everything'll be okay. Thanks again."

"Weren't no trouble," the man said, and drove off.

But before the car rounded the curve, Gilbert was chasing down the lane after it. "Wait," he hollered. The car's break lights brightened through a cloud of exhaust and Gilbert ran up the driver's window. "I forgot something in the trunk."

The driver got out of the car and unlocked the trunk. "Some little kid in your family almost didn't get this. I'm leavin' for Arkansas in the mornin'."

Gilbert smiled. "It's not for a child. It's for my grown brother."

Gus watched Gilbert haul something big and bulky from the trunk of the car. "What'cha got there?" he asked, strolling toward the car.

"A bona fide store-boughten soap box. Just like you always wanted but better. This one's got an engine."

Gus wolf-whistled. The memory of the day he'd told Gilbert he wanted a soap box came flooding over him. "You remembered that after all these years?" Gus asked, laughing, eyeing the shiny wonder.

"I never forgot the look in your eyes that day you told me you wanted one."

Gus paced around the motorized go-cart, straddled it, then sat on the softly padded seat. The grin on his face got wider. He hunched over the steering wheel and imagined himself first place in a heat. "I feel like bawling!" he said. "How could you remember after all this time?"

"How could I forget?" Gilbert answered. "I love you."

Gus looked up mutely and stared into his brother's eyes. No words were needed. Gus got up, boxed Gilbert lightly on the shoulder, then reached down and took his suitcase. "I'll get this. It's the least I can do for my favorite twin," Gus said, lying the bag across the seat of the soap box and steering it diagonally across the yard toward the house. Gilbert followed Gus through the leaf-strewn yard, past a rusted wheel barrow, up the porch steps and into the warm, homey-scented house.

They walked past the tinfoiled plate and pie and into their room. Gus closed the door quietly behind them and set the suitcase in front of the closet door. He wanted to holler with excitement, but kept it locked inside. Gilbert took off his jacket, tossed it onto the chair then sat exhaustedly on the bed. Gus was shocked at Gilbert's tall bony frame. "Don't you ever eat?" he asked, and Gilbert said he missed their mama's cooking. Gus settled next to his brother.

"I'm staying home," Gilbert said. He reached into his pocket and pulled out a letter. "I got this before I left."

Gus immediately recognized what it was. His shoulders drooped and he sighed. "You got called up." Gus could feel his happiness fading. "I wondered when you'd get it. I always thought maybe we'd be able to serve our time together."

"Didn't work out that way, did it?" Gilbert answered as he rose from the bed and moved around the bedroom, picking up familiar things, putting them back down where they had been and probably would be until they were dead and buried. Gil's eyes moved over the wooden box full of marbles, their handmade knife, an erector set, comic books. "I want to *feel* this room, Gus. To ingest that little-boy's sense of belonging that I *must* have felt at one time." He turned to face Gus who was sitting tall, leaning slightly forward, trying to grasp his brother's sensitivities. He glanced at the knife Gilbert held in his hand and remembered the long hours it took to make it. The cork they'd wound tightly with fishing twine to form the haft, the metal saw they transformed into a blade after shaping and sharpening with a grinding stone. Gilbert laid down the knife. "Can you understand what I'm trying to say, Gus?"

"I'm trying as hard as I can, Gil. You're baffling at times."

Gilbert picked up several pieces of the erector set. "I need to feel a connection between existence and continuity. I've always felt like a misshaped puzzle piece."

Gus stood. "Gil . . . "

"Wait a minute," Gilbert said, holding up a hand to stop Gus. "The truth is, I've always deemed myself second-rate to you. I never held it against you. I couldn't feel the least animosity toward you, not even jealousy, so don't blame yourself. I'm not saying this to make you feel bad. It's just the opposite. I know you understand me, even if I don't understand myself." He placed the erector pieces back on the desk and sat next to Gus. "You always have."

Gus stared down at their knees not knowing what to say. His gaze rested on Gilbert's draft papers crumbled on the bed next to them and felt sadness wash over him.

"You were wrong to low-grade yourself, Gil. No one thought that way." *Had Norman?* Gus wondered.

"Pa did."

"Then I'm just as much to blame as Pa. I should have stopped it."

"You can't change feelings overnight, but I aim to work on it," Gilbert said, then picked up his draft papers. "I just got home and now I'm leaving again," he said.

Gus pulled up his overall pant leg to expose his knee wound. "I got this before I went in and they wouldn't let me stay," he said, holding his leg out. "Guess they thought I couldn't shoot straight with a bad knee."

Gilbert smiled. "I knew you wouldn't make a career of it." He looked down at his Orders to Report letter and jiggled it. "This is the best thing that could happen now."

Gus nodded. His eyes lifted to examine Gilbert's face, a face he loved and hadn't seen in more than a year. It was the same face, maybe quieter. Yeah, he thought, maybe it's best for now. Gus looked away, then back at Gil. "Want me to wake Ma? She'd want to know you were here."

"Let her sleep," Gilbert said, leaning back on his elbows.

Gus rose and hurried toward the doorway. "How about a piece of sweet-po-tato pie?"

"I'm too tired to chew it," Gilbert said in a worn down voice.

"Sure you don't want me to wake Ma," Gus coaxed, leaning against their closed door.

"I'd rather her see me shaved and cleaned up," Gilbert said. "The shit's gon-na hit the fan soon enough. I'd like to have a few hours sleep first."

Gus reached out and touched Gilbert on the knee. "Hey. No matter what's said, no matter what happens, I'll love you from hell to breakfast."

"No doubt about it," Gilbert replied sleepily, stifling a yawn with his hand. "No matter what kind of a tangled mess I have to face in the morning, together, you and I, we'll rope it into something manageable." Gilbert yawned again and his eyes watered. Gus watched Gilbert's eyelids close over the pale blue, tired eyes. Ever so slowly, Gilbert inched closer and closer to the feather mattress and Gus knew that even before Gil's back touched the bed, he was asleep. Gus leaned over, untied Gilbert's shoelaces and took off his shoes. His brother wore no socks and his feet were cold. At the foot of the bed, Gus opened the lid to the cedar chest and took out his favorite comforter. Like a mother tucking in a baby, Gus gently placed the blanket over his brother making sure his feet were covered. "I knew you'd come home," he whispered. "I just wish I knew that everything would be all right."

"What're you gonna do, bellyache all morning?" Katherine asked Norman the next day over breakfast. "I'm glad he's home, Norman, and I'm going to do everything possible to make him feel comfortable."

Norman humphed and took a gulp of his coffee. "He found out it wasn't all roses out there." He leaned back in his chair causing the front two legs to come off the floor. Norman frowned, looked toward the boys sitting on their bed, talk-ing, laughing, then turned away when Gus's gaze caught his.

"He said he was sorry," Katherine said, taking a pan of biscuits from the oven.

"It was a meaningless, guilt-edged apology, and long over due."

"I can't understand your disaffection for the boy," Katherine said. "Whatever made your heart so cold, Norman? You never used to be this way."

Norman set his cup down hard, splashing coffee over the rim. "He thought he could high-tail it to some exotic land and live a fool's paradise. Forget the family, forget responsibilities."

"And now he's home," Katherine said, slapping butter roughly onto the biscuits. "But he's got to leave again to serve his country." She laid down the knife and shook her head.

Norman sighed. "Well, maybe he has learned a lesson. After all, he did come home, didn't he? Maybe there's still hope for the boy. He *is* a Wheeler." Norman paused, then said, "Okay, Katy, I'll admit it. I'm happy he's here."

"Do you really mean it, Norm? Can there finally be peace in our home?"

Norman held out his plate and Katherine scooped a ladle full of grits onto it. "I'm going to recommend a cease-fire, Katy."

Katherine hugged Norman's neck. "I know how disappointed you are with him. How much you wanted the boys to take over and run the mill." She leaned forward and kissed his cheek then slid out her chair and sat at the table.

Gus couldn't believe what he had heard. Did Norman actually have a change of heart?

"I've got a surprise for you," Gus said to Sara Jane when she walked sleepily into the kitchen.

The little girl rubbed her eyes. "Gil!" Sara Jane screamed, running to his outstretched arms. "You're home!" she yelled.

"The three of us are headed down to the creek," Gus said. "We've got some catching up to do before I start work today. Okay with you, Pa?" Gus asked, snatching his jacket from the peg.

Norman flicked out his hand and nodded. "Go on. Take your time," he said.

Gus stood at the opened door and watched his grown brother and little sister run like cowboys chasing Indians down the path that led to the creek. He turned and saw his mother squeeze Norman's hand. Norman turned to her and she smiled warmly. "Thank you," she said.

"What on earth for?" Norman asked her. "I've been a callous old poop."

• CHAPTER 17 •

September 1953

Gus sat at the kitchen table listening to Norman and Gilbert talking in the next room. The door was ajar enough for him to see in. "Just tell him you love him, Pa," Gus mumbled quietly to himself. "Tell him you don't expect him to be a conquering hero."

"Maybe it's a good thing you were called up," Norman said as Gilbert packed his belongings. "It'll give us both time to think. Time to grow up some. *Both* of us."

Gilbert nodded, not commenting.

Norman leaned against the door frame, his back to Gus, just inside the boys' room. "I guess I have tendencies to take things for granted," he said. "When you boys were young I assumed you'd take over the mill. I wanted it that way, you know."

Gus rolled back his eyes and glared at the aqua-painted ceiling. Geez! Gus thought. How could Gilbert *not* know? You've told him often enough!

Gilbert looked up and spoke slowly. "I know I hurt you when I didn't take an interest in your dream. I used to feel guilty knowing I didn't fit into your mold." He picked up his cap and put it on, leaned toward the mirror and straightened the hat. Gilbert looked at his father's image in the mirror and said, "I have to find my own path in life."

"You should have found it already!" Norman huffed, then rephrased, "In all truth, Gilbert, you should never have had to look. It's right there under your big flyaway feet!" Norman threw out his good arm so hard that the pinned-under sleeve of his half-arm shook. "You didn't have to take off searching for something that was right in front of you! Christ, Gilbert, you're eighteen years old. How long are you going to stay lost?"

"Accept me for who I am, Dad," Gilbert said calmly, now facing Norman. "Maybe I didn't turn out the way you wanted, but corn seeds don't always come up in the perfect straight row you plant them in. Sometimes one stalk grows slightly forward or back from the one next to it. Does that mean you have to cut it down; that it won't produce a good ear? I have to be true to myself. Don't put me down or compare me to Gus or yourself. We all run on different tracks." Gilbert's shoulders slumped and he sighed. "I might take a different route. It might take me longer to get there."

"Now just you wait one minute. . . . "

"I'll never be Gus, Pa." Clutching his navy blue canvas bag, Gilbert moved toward the door, stopped in front of his father and said, "I almost forgot to give you this." He reached into his shirt pocket.

Norman turned his head away. "I don't want anything from you. What have you given to this family? Misery, that's what."

Gilbert stared down at the envelope he held in his hand. "I never meant to be a source of unhappiness for you." Gil held out the envelope. "I want to make it up to you. Here, take this."

"What is it?" Norman asked.

"It's something I got from Arnold Delv . . . "

"What would you know about that son-of-a-no-good?" Norman yelled. He shoved his hand into his pocket. "I won't allow that man's name in this house!"

Gilbert shook his head and stared at his father. "I wanted to iron out our bitterness, Pa. I love you."

That said, Gilbert walked out of his room, past Gus, through the kitchen and out the door. He inhaled the coolness of the air, then stuffed the envelope into his pocket.

Norman didn't move, just stared into the mirror Gilbert had spoken to him from. "You've got a strange way of showing it, son," he said.

Gus watched Gilbert hurry through the kitchen, listened to his fleeting footsteps move across the porch. He glanced back at Norman who was still staring into the small mirror. "You aren't even going to tell him good bye?"

Gus got up from the table, kicked open the screen door with the toe of his shoe and followed his brother. At the edge of the front yard, Gus caught up to Gilbert and grabbed him by the shoulder. Gilbert stopped, dropped his bag. "You gonna ride out of here without saying adios?" Gus asked, and watched his brother turn around and throw his hands out in bewilderment.

"I don't know what to say. He gets my stomach tied up in knots."

"Say you'll hurry home," Gus said. "I'll leave the walnuts for you to haul in," he joked, then said earnestly, "Let me take you to the station."

"No, I'd rather go alone. Pa needs you at the mill. I've already kept you . . . both of you from it long enough. Calvin said he needed to go to town later today for something. Someone can ride in with him and bring back your truck."

"I'm not worried about the friggin' truck! It's you I'm worried about."

Gilbert smiled. "I've been on my own for over a year, remember? You should know I can take care of myself." He looked up at the twin dogwood trees. "The leaves won't be pretty this fall. It's going from summer to winter. There's already a chill in the air."

"Take care, brother," Gus said, watching Gilbert scoot into the truck, roll down the window and mouth "I love you." Gus backed away from the truck. "I love you, too," he said, and watched the old, tired-looking pickup rumble away.

Gus forced himself to walk back into the house and into his room where Norman slouched against the door frame, peering into the mirror. Gus circled past him and stared through the window into the gray drizzly morning. He couldn't see the driveway or the truck, but he listened to the truck's creaks and clatters as it bounced down the lane toward the two-lane blacktop. His gaze wandered listlessly toward the unmade bed. Gilbert's coat lay on top of the quilt. "Gil, wait!" Gus yelled, snatching up the coat and running toward the door, but he was too late and Gilbert was gone. "His coat," Gus murmured, and Norman said, "He'll be cold. Winter's comin' on early this year."

Katherine sat in her rocking chair crying softly, Jon Wesley in one arm and Sara Jane in the other. Norman walked up next to her and touched her arm.

She looked up into his eyes. "Did you two talk?"

Norman nodded yes, then looked away. "I don't know."

"Is he okay?" she asked, wiping away a tear that had fallen on the baby's forehead.

Norman sank into his easychair. "I don't know that, either," he said, staring down into his lap. "He didn't seem to be." His hand fumbled nervously and he looked up slowly. "Have I been wrong, Katy?"

They looked at each other then each looked away. Katherine slowly rocked her babies and didn't bother wiping the tears from her face, but kept on rocking and staring straight ahead. The house was silent except for the clock ticking life away. Gus laid across his bed staring at the ceiling, a feeling of peril cutting through him. When the telephone rang they all jumped, but Thelma Jean had pushed the wrong button and it was a wrong number.

Gus strolled out to where his family sat and sank heavily into an upholstered chair next to the fireplace. The fire had burned low and there was a chill in the room. He fingered the frilly doilies on the arms of the chair then gazed up at Norman. "Shouldn't we get down to the mill, Pa?" Gus asked.

Norman flicked his hand, slowly shook his head no and continued staring at the frayed rug on the floor.

Katherine leaned back her head against the chair. Gus watched tears trail down her cheeks. He looked up at Norman and under his glasses, his eyes were also wet.

Gus jumped when Norman abruptly shoved himself from the chair and darted across the floor to the coat rack. "Get your coats!" Norman shouted. "We let him go off by himself the first time. I'll be damned if I'll let him go alone this time!" He hurried and put on his coat, then mumbled, "The boy is going off to fight for our country, for God's sake. What kind of family are we if we can't see him off properly?"

It took only a few moments for the family to pile into the old green Buick. With a cough of black smoke the car was rumbling down the rutted lane that led to the blacktop highway. "Hold on," Norman warned as he sped down the wet country road, knowing every dip and curve.

But as they neared the crossroads, they could see Vern's red bubble light and an ambulance approaching. Roadblocks barricaded the road.

"Oh God," Katherine said, "There's been a wreck."

Trepidation filled Gus's chest. Goosebumps rose on his arms and he felt an icy chill touch his body. Gus cringed and felt his blood run cold when he saw the flashing light of another emergency vehicle approaching. "No. It can't be Gilbert," Gus whimpered and Norman reached his hand over the seat and rested it firmly on Gus's arm.

"Pray it isn't," Norman said, but just as the words were out of his mouth, the wrecker truck moved forward and they had a partial view of the accident site. The vehicles involved in the accident were crushed beyond recognition. The air smelled of burnt rubber and caustic auto fluids.

Norman slowed the car, their eyes searching for signs of Gilbert.

"Do you think . . . ?" Katherine gasped, sitting erect now, the baby's rattle sliding from her lap. Her voice sounded thin with dread.

Gus laid his hand on her shoulder. "We don't know it was him," Mama. "We don't know."

A policeman Gus didn't know held out his hand and stopped them. "You can't go any further, sir. There's been an accident with a double fatality."

Gus opened the car door and got out. The rest of the family followed his lead. "Do you know who it is?" Gus asked, trying to keep his voice strong. His eyes scanned the emergency personnel gathering around the site.

"We don't know yet, for sure," the man in uniform said. "We'll know shortly."

Gus ran a few steps toward the crossroads but the officer stopped him. "You'll have to wait here."

"We need to find out," Gus told him. "There's a chance my brother's out there." Gus's legs felt like ropes and he thought he might crumble to the ground, but he knew he had to be strong, and suddenly wished he had the strength and bravery of Gilbert. Yes, it was stouthearted braveness that compelled Gil to leave home over a year ago. He wasn't happy here so his strength let him go.

"How did it happen?" Gus asked.

"The man in the pickup ran the stop sign. He hit that Chevy panel truck over there," the officer said, pointing. "The driver of the panel truck was delivering groceries for Piggly Wiggly. Both drivers were killed."

Gus stared toward the crossroads. "Gilbert's gone through that intersection hundreds of times. He knew the stop sign was there."

"If it was your brother," the officer said, "he must have had something heavy on his mind."

Gus felt himself turning deathly cold, colder and colder until he thought he'd freeze and his tears would freeze like his world was freezing all around him. "I've got to see for myself."

Norman reached out for Gus, but Gus edged away from his touch and moved toward the wreckage. One foot in front of the other he moved forward, his silent grief unheard. A silly child's verse came to mind as he inched toward the scene. *I had a little monkey, His name was Tiny Tim, I put him in the bathtub, To teach him how to swim.* Gus's eyes focused on the demolished vehicles. *In came the doctor, in came the nurse. . . .*

Norman hurried to grasp Gus's arm. "Here comes Vern. The sheriff can tell us what's happened, Gus."

Faintly, Norman asked Vern Peele, "Who was killed in the accident?"

"A terrible accident," the sheriff said, shaking his head. "It was Jess Jacobs and Crum Harper. Jess' brakes went out. He tried to stop."

Norman's hand shook as he held it out in front of him. "It . . . it wasn't . . . "

Gus completed the question. "It wasn't Gilbert?"

Vern raised his eyebrows. "Did you think . . . ?"

Gus looked over his shoulder. "I've got to tell mom! She thinks Gil's dead." He dashed toward the Buick and as he ran, Gus felt the sun come out and warm his body. "Gilbert's okay!" he shouted. "Come on, Pa! We've got to get to the bus station!"

Gilbert was the last one on the bus. He shuffled through and sat in the second to last seat next to a strong-built colored man close to his own age. It was the only available seat. "This spot taken?" Gilbert asked.

"Nope. No one seems to want it."

"I'll take it," Gilbert said, stuffing his bag under his seat. He settled in, leaned back his head and closed his eyes.

The Negro shifted in his seat. "You're one of the Wheeler twins ain't you? Your folks own and operate Timber Hills Logging and Sawmill."

"Yeah, that's right," Gilbert said, turning his head to the man. "I'm Gilbert Wheeler. And you shine shoes on the southside corner of Jackson and Broadway."

"Yep. That's me. My name's Willie Boy."

Gilbert nodded and saw the colored boy turn in his seat and wave to a large Negro family gathered tightly in a spot of sunshine. "Them your folks?" Gilbert asked.

"Uh huh. It was one big boo hoo party this morning," the colored boy said, smiling, and waving his hand side-to-side like a pendulum on a clock. "They didn't want me to leave."

Gilbert nodded slowly as the boy spoke. "Looks like a good family."

"That's Granny with the purple flowered hat. Lord, she's still snifflin'," he said, then, "Which ones are your folks?" the Negro asked, still waving.

Gilbert's moist eyes scanned the scanty crowd. "They had to work," he fibbed. When the bus driver started the engine, Gilbert's searching eyes glanced around the bus terminal, behind the bus and in front, then again at the colored folks bunched together in that circle of sunshine. He sighed, then leaned back and closed his eyes.

When a green Buick sped recklessly round the corner and jolted to a stop behind the bus, Willie Boy labeled them crazy people. "That car nearly plowed into the back of our bus!" he roared in a wheezy voice, his sinewy frame twisted to peer out the back window. "What the heck are they . . . ?"

Gilbert opened his eyes and looked at his new friend. "What're you whining about?"

Willie Boy was turned in his seat looking back. "Them folks back there," he said, gesturing. "They're pilin' out of the car an' tryin' to get on the bus! Look at 'em. They're beatin' on the door!"

Gilbert craned his neck and looked down the long, narrow isle toward the door. "I can't see them," he said as the apparently baffled driver opened the door and Gus jumped brazenly on board.

Dumbfounded, Gilbert's mouth gaped open but no words came as he watched the disapproving bus driver question his brother. "Back here," Gilbert finally said, half-standing, then watched speechlessly as Norman stepped onto the bus behind Gus.

"Get your bag, son," Norman said firmly. "Your family is taking you to Nashville."

Gilbert compliantly trailed Gus and Norman. Curious eyes peered down at them as they walked alongside the bus and toward the askew-parked green Buick behind the bus. Gilbert leaned into the car's opened front window while Gus got into the back seat next to Sara Jane. Katherine patted Gil's hand. "Get in, Gilbert," she told him, and when he did, she said, "We're going to Nashville."

Gus thought he saw a smile of fulfillment on Gilbert's lips. Maybe a purpose of life, a victory smile. He looked away and thanked God for his father's change of heart.

"You forgot your coat," Sara Jane said as Norman settled behind the steering wheel and started the car. "We thought you were dead," she added.

Gilbert laughed. "Huh? I ain't never gonna die, little sister. I've got too much to live for."

Norman looked over his shoulder. "We don't want you to go, Gilbert, but this time we know you have to. I'm proud that you'll be serving our country, but we'll miss you greatly while you're gone. I hope you know our door is never locked." He stretched his good arm back over the seat and held out his hand. Gilbert took hold. "And we all wanted to be here with you," Norman said.

"Those words mean a lot to me, Pa. More than you can imagine," Gilbert said, his voice quavering. He smiled awkwardly and squeezed his father's hand. Katherine, Sara Jane and Gus grasped it, too, family hands, warm, one on top the other.

It seemed to take longer to get back into the routine of things after Gilbert left the second time. Gus concluded the abundant energy they all had the first time Gilbert left was anger-fueled. This time there was a certain melancholy feeling throughout the household. Gus picked up the note that lay face down on the softly padded seat of the shiny red soap box, then sprawled out on the bed. He held up the half-sheet of paper and read again: *To my brother and best friend, Gus. You have a way of taking all the crazy bits and pieces, all the idiosyncratic things I say and do, and bunching them together into an understandable wholeness. Life has no guarantees, no assurances but at least I can carry on, knowing you understand me.*

"But I don't always understand you, Gil," he whispered. Gus lowered the note and recalled the panic the family had felt when they thought Gilbert had died in the wreck at the crossroads. He shook his head to release the sickening feeling. Gus got up, moped around the room touching the same items Gilbert had touched the night he got home, then straddled the soap box. The engine had never been started.

Gus prayed that Gilbert would be safe from harm. He worried more than ever, shook it off as silliness, but the disquieting presentiment lingered. For the next few weeks Gus feigned a chipper nature, but inside he ached with worry. He stayed busy, worked extra long days at the mill, but he couldn't shake the somber cloud of despair.

It was Arnold H. Delvine that rekindled Gus's mind. It was the malice he felt for this timber thief that activated his faculty, and when he saw the big white Cadillac with Delvine's name on the door roll into his front yard, Gus felt a bolt of raging energy.

He stared at the fancy car from his bedroom window and felt his face flush angry-red. Not taking his eyes from the Cadillac now stopping in front of their house, Gus stuffed his shirt into his pants and clinched his belt. He stooped and reached under his bed for his shoes, found them, stood up and stamped his feet. With his fingers he combed his hair, then walked out of his room.

"Gus?" Katherine said, turning from the stove to face him. Her curious eyes followed his gaze through the window glass. "Who is that?"

"It's the con man who stole our timber," Gus answered, opening the door and walking onto the porch. "What do you want?" Gus hollered, then turned his attention to Vern Peele's car parked a hundred feet or so behind the Cadillac. A deputy sat on the passenger side.

"I guess you remember me," Delvine said, looking at Gus. "You came to my office several weeks ago."

"That was my brother, not me," Gus said, glancing at Delvine, the sheriff's car, and back to Delvine.

Delvine shook his head. "Looked a hell of a lot like you."

"The minutes are passing and your time's running out," the sheriff said as he strolled up to Arnold Delvine. Do what you came here for."

"It's really your father I want to see, young man."

Gus stepped off the porch, walked down the steps and stood eye to eye with Delvine. "My father's down at the mill," Gus said. "You'll have to speak to me."

Sara Jane walked from the chicken yard with a basketful of eggs under her arm. "Who are you?" she asked the stranger. "You sure do have white hair," she said.

"Go into the house, Sara Jane," Gus told her.

Gus waited until she'd closed the kitchen door, then asked. "What is it you want to talk to us about?"

Delvine twitched his shoulders, glanced sidelong at Vern who was now leaning against his car's door, and said, "Your sheriff made me come to apologize to your family before he hauled me off to jail. Guess I deserve it," he said, then pulled an envelope from the folds of his overcoat.

"Read the note out loud, Delvine," the sheriff said. Delvine pulled out a sheet of paper from inside the envelope.

Gus recognized Gilbert's handwriting and listened as Delvine read: *Returning what you stole, Mr. Delvine, is the fitting thing to do. Enclosed is a carbon copy of a contract in my father's name for 60 acres of prime timberland. Sheriff Peele has the original contract and a copy of this note to you. I wanted to give the contract to my father before I left, and I tried to, but I guess the timing wasn't right. I think it would be proper for you to hand-deliver the contract to my father personally.*

With a shaky voice, Gus said quietly, "Thank you, Mr. Delvine, for delivering this, but you still ain't worth a plug nickel."

Delvine raised his lip into a smirk.

"Give him the envelope, Delvine," the sheriff called out.

Arnold Delvine lifted his arm and handed Gus the long white envelope with the signed timberland contract. "Take it . . . for your family's loss. The boy . . . your brother, was madder'n hell when he walked into my office, but I've never seen the likes of such character. He reminded me a lot of myself when I was his age." Delvine looked away and flicked his hand.

Movement caught Gus's eye and he glanced up and spotted Norman standing nearby listening, then he noticed Katherine standing on the porch, an autumn-colored shawl drawn tightly across her shoulders. Gus walked over to Norman and handed him the contract for the timberland Gilbert had purchased.

Vern ambled up to Delvine. "Okay, time to go," he said, then took Delvine's elbow and steered him in the direction of the sheriff's car. The deputy strode past them, offered a friendly smile and boldly got into the Cadillac. "I'll be behind you in Delvine's Cadillac," he said to Vern.

Gus watched Delvine put his hands behind his back and accept the handcuffs Vern clicked onto his wrists. Vern glanced up at the Wheelers, nodded, then guided Delvine into the back seat of the police car. The sheriff got into the driver's seat and Gus smiled when Vern turned the red bubble light on. Delvine leaned toward the half-opened window and said, "He reminded me of myself. The way I used to be."

Before the deputy got into Delvine's confiscated Cadillac, he said to Gus, "It's all over town what your brother did. He's a hero, you know." He leaned toward the dash, and started the car. "Not only did Gilbert buy the land for your folks, he located someone up in Campbell County that Delvine had swindled. This con man won't stand a chance in court." The deputy looked down and placed the shift lever into drive position. With his foot heavy on the brake, he said, "That's how we got him, you know. Delvine wasn't so careful with the wording on that contract." The deputy grinned and straightened his hat. "Messed himself up." Glancing back up at Gus, then at Norman and Katherine, the deputy asked, "Did ya'll know Gilbert had done this for you?"

Norman shook his head in wonder, "Not even a hint."

"Dang," the deputy said. "Gilbert Wheeler's a superstar."

"Yes, he is," Norman said quietly, gazing down at the timber contract he held in his hand. He looked up, faced Gus and Katherine and said, "All my young'ens are superstars." Norman pushed up his glasses, pivoted, and headed down the well-worn path to the mill.

October 1954

"This property is beautiful, nearly as good as the original 52 acres."

"You say that every time we come up here, Pa," Gus told his father.

"Yeah, I know," Norman said, grinning.

With his hands tucked into his pockets and face turned upward, Gus sniffed the crisp scent of evergreens and hardwood. He waited for Norman's next comment.

"Need to keep checking up on it to make sure it doesn't disappear!"

Gus laughed when he heard the expected words. "You say that each time, too. Okay, Pa, the timber's fine. Let's go home. I'm hungry."

The gingery scent of fresh-baked molasses cookies filled the air when they got out of the car. Gus smiled when he saw Katherine standing at the bottom of the porch steps. He gave her a hard hug. "I'm starved," he said, blending away a smudge of corn meal from under her eye.

"It's on the stove," she answered. "The cornbread's almost done."

Before Gus went into the house he gazed into the sky for a long moment, then said, "Looks like it could snow."

"It's too early to snow," Katherine said.

"Nupe. It's gonna snow. I can smell it in the air," Gus said.

And that night as the snow sheathed the hills and valleys like a huge down comforter, the Wheeler's relaxed, not in front of the new television, but circled in front of the fireplace sipping hot chocolate, telling stories and relishing old memories. It was a happy time, a family time.

Before bedtime Gus pulled back the curtain and gazed out the window. Silent, cottony snow was fluffed up on the windowpane. He noticed it had stopped snowing and the stars were bright. The barn's sloping roof, the hillside, the trees were covered with layers of brilliant, moon reflected whiteness. Gus moved his hand along the windowsill and felt cool air filtering in, bringing with it a hint of wood smoke. Yes, it might be briskly cold outside, but inside, with his family gathered around the fire, it was warm and comforting and the best place in the whole world to be.

Going to bed untroubled that night, Gus never expected to be awakened at midnight by loud pounding. Clad only in underwear, Gus blindly rushed to open the door. Norman and Katherine joined him, then Sara Jane stumbled out of her room. Vern Peele stood unsmiling in the doorway. He held a piece of paper in his hands.

"It's bad news."

Katherine wavered and Norman put his arm around her waist. Gus took the note from the sheriff's hand and read silently:

Military plane crashed . . . was killed while practicing maneuvers . . .
no survivors among the crew of. . . .

Gus's blue eyes glazed and his face turned ghostly white. He turned slowly to his family.

Norman leaned forward. "Son?"

Gus slowly looked from the note to his father. His voice was barely audible. "Gilbert's dead." The letter slid from Gus's trembling hand as he rushed past the sheriff and through the opened door. Swiftly he ran down the white, moon-shadowy path through the woods toward the creek. "Not Gil!" he shouted into the cold night. "Oh dear God, say it ain't so!" Tears flooded over his cheeks, down his neck, his chest.

On the creek's muddy bank, Gus cried and irrationally begged God to change his mind. He wanted to drown himself in the creek, the water they'd, together—always together, splashed in as toddlers, as young boys, as teenagers. "Gilbert," Gus said quietly, sinking to his knees. He swayed back and forth and envisioned the two of them barreling through the thick woods and into the refreshing water with a grand splash. He felt the cool spray wash over him and squeezed his eyes shut. Gus remembered Reverend Reed telling him that God would never give a person more than he or she could handle, that he'd never allow more grief than a person could stand. He wondered if the accident they'd come upon at the crossroads was God's way of allowing some temporary grief to vent itself so it wouldn't come all at once. Perhaps it was God's way.

A chilled north wind swept over the water, bending the tall brown grass around him. His teeth chattered when he got up and turned toward home. "Mama needs me," Gus said, regaining his senses, knowing he had no choice but to accept God's plan. Silent tears streamed down his face. He couldn't see the path through the tears, but it didn't matter, he knew the way. Halfway home one leg gave way, then the other and Gus crumbled face-down on the cold snowy ground and felt the wintry earth press against his cheek.

Gus laid shivering until Norman found him and helped him to his feet. "Come back to the house," Gus heard his father's hushed voice say. Slowly and awkwardly Gus drew his lean body up and allowed Norman to support him.

The wind was blowing the porch swing against the wall when they stumbled up the slippery stairs and opened the door. Katherine sat slumped in her rocking chair, her face white and still. She clutched the front of her gown with one hand and the arm of the rocker with the other. Gus pensively draped her shawl over her crestfallen shoulders, knelt before her and rested his head on her lap.

For the second time Norman constructed a casket for a son, and for the second time the Wheeler family gathered at the cemetery on a brisk, windy day to bury a family member too young to die. For Gus, there was nothing in his life that could compare to the anguish of losing half of himself. As he watched the casket lowered into the ground he felt part of himself perish, part of his body, his soul, his breath. Despondently he lifted his hands up before him. Both were there, yet he felt only one. Half of all his being was being swallowed by the cold black earth.

"Look," Katherine said, half weeping and half smiling. She pointed with her gloved hand. "A cardinal, just like the one at Garrett's funeral. There's two of them," she said, wiping her eyes.

Gus drew his mother into his arms and she pressed her tear-stained face into his shoulder. "One for each of my babies," she sobbed. Gus watched the bright male birds perched quietly on the white picket fence until the grieving family and friends began to leave the cemetery.

On Christmas morning the family bundled up and strolled to the cemetery to place wreaths on Gilbert and Garrett's grave. Tracking through the clean white snow, Sara Jane kissed her fingers then touched each marker. Katherine stood quietly, cradling Jon Wesley.

"You were my hero before you became a superstar," Gus said, staring down at Gilbert's grave. "Take care of our little brother," he said, gesturing easily toward Garrett's head stone.

Gus knew it would be a long time before he could feel himself living again. He walked around in numbness, a dull, aching feeling that smothered him like a heavy, wet blanket. It had taken a while to get over Garrett's death, but Gus knew it would take an eternity recovering from losing Gilbert. He looked heavenward and heard Christmas carolers close by. *Hark! The herald angels sing . . .*

"You go on," Norman said, as the family turned to leave. "I'll be there in a minute."

At the cemetery gate, Gus paused then turned and gazed toward the graves. In the sharp silence of winter's whiteness he stood quietly, peering at the fresh snow marked only by his family's footprints. His father was huddled at the foot of Gilbert's grave, his hat and gloves placed on the ground beside him. Gus followed the footprints back to where the family had gathered with their arms around each other. He stood quietly behind Norman. On Gilbert's grave, at the base of his marker, Norman had written in the snow I LOVE YOU.

"He knows that," Gus said, his voice low, reverent.

Norman straightened his back but didn't turn around. "I never told him."

"You told him that day in the car at the bus station."

When motion caught Gus's eye, he glanced up and saw, perched on the white picket fence, two bright red cardinals. Gus stood there watching the birds, their brilliant color aglow against the whiteness around them.

Norman picked up his hat, gloves and slowly stood. The birds took flight to a snow-covered branch in a nearby oak tree. "I love you, Gus," he said, looking up at the cardinals.

Gus reached out and patted his father's back. "Let's go home."